# THE GYPSY

# Books by Steven Brust

**The Dragaeran Novels**

*Brokedown Palace*

The Khaavren Romances

*The Phoenix Guards*

*Five Hundred Years After*

The Viscount of Adrilankha,

which comprises *The Paths of the Dead,*

*The Lord of Castle Black,* and *Sethra Lavode*

The Vlad Taltos Novels

*Jhereg*

*Yendi*

*Teckla*

*Taltos*

*Phoenix*

*Athyra*

*Orca*

*Dragon*

*Issola*

**Other Novels**

*To Reign in Hell*

*The Sun, the Moon, and the Stars*

*Cowboy Feng's Space Bar and Grille*

*Agyar*

*Freedom and Necessity* (with Emma Bull)

# THE GYPSY

STEVEN BRUST & MEGAN LINDHOLM

ORB
A TOM DOHERTY ASSOCIATES BOOK
NEW YORK

This is a work of fiction. All the characters and events portrayed in this novel are either fictitious or are used fictitiously.

THE GYPSY



An Orb Book
Published by Tom Doherty Associates, LLC
175 Fifth Avenue
New York, NY 10010

www.tor.com

Library of Congress Cataloging-in-Publication Data

Brust, Steven.
The gypsy / Steven Brust and Megan Lindholm.
p. cm.
"A Tom Doherty Associates book."
ISBN 0-765-31192-5
EAN 978-0765-31192-4
1. Lindholm, Megan. II. Title.

PS3552.R84G96 1992
813'.54—dc20

92-2761
CIP

First Hardcover Edition: June 1992
First Trade Paperback Edition: April 2005

Printed in the United States of America

0 9 8 7 6 5 4 3 2 1

This book is dedicated to Corwin and Katie, with our blessings.

# ACKNOWLEDGMENTS

The authors extend their individual and collective thanks to

Adam Stemple for help writing the songs.
Cats Laughing and Ravan's Tir, for playing the songs.
Tekla Dömötör for *Hungarian Folk Beliefs*.
Maria Pinkstaff for tarot consultations.
Beth Friedman for medical information.
The Interstate Writers Workshop (Scribblies) for helping to fix the manuscript.
Terri Windling for editing.
Victoria Fleming for copyediting.
Fred for taking care of the children.
The authors wish to express their gratitude to Lt. P. Jefferson, Public Relations, Lakota Police Department, for much assistance and knowing where the good coffee is.

Above all, the authors wish to thank each other.

# CONTENTS

Spin out a tale like a spider spins webs,
Lead me by voice and by feel.
Show me the places where beauty still walks
And I'll tell you why it's not real.

"TELLERS OF TALES"

He wore an old rag wrapped round his head
A shirt of yellow cloth woven fine
And scars on his face where once he had bled
And pants with a belt made of twine.

"THE GYPSY"

You have justice high and low,
A power over me;
Well you can rule your ship of fools
But no man rules the sea.

"CHANTY"

# Prologue

LATE AUTUMN, HALF MOON, WAXING

I hope you don't mind
If I rest inside your door
Please forgive the snowy footprints
I'm tracking on your floor.

"RED LIGHTS AND NEON"

*Doom teka teka teka doom teka tek.*
*Doom teka teka teka doom teka tek.*
*Doom teka teka teka doom teka tek.*
*Doom teka teka teka doom teka tek.*

There is something about the sound of the tambourine.

The zils rattle or ring in the same tones and pitches as the kettles in which you heat the water or stew the meat, and the calfskin head that is as old as Nagypapa will predict the rain by saying *dum* or the dryness by saying *doooooom.* When the tambourine is played well, the feet move on wings of their own, and the heart leaps with them, while the lips, distant observers above, cannot help but smile a little, no matter how somber the mood. This is why the dance and the laughter are one, and whoever says different is either deluded or in the service of You Know Who.

And You Know Who has many servants.

Some are weak, some are strong. Some need guidance day by day; others, well, others can work their evil on their own, and bring more souls into the sway. For example, there is the Fair Lady, Luci, who—

No. We will not dwell on that now, there is plenty of time later. Now, we are remembering the tambourine, which is as perfect a match for the fiddle as the onion is for the bacon, and the memory of the ear and the tongue is forever, which is as it should be. These things stay with a person, no matter how many years have passed, or what paths he has trod. Once those sounds are in his blood, he can never forget—

Never forget—

Umm. . . .

Somewhere, perhaps half a mile to his left, a siren divided the evening into sections. *Why do they call them sirens,* he wondered. *What sort of sailor would be attracted to them?* The question was rhetorical and ironic. He wasn't worried. He had no reason to think the siren was for him, so he continued to stroll down Saint Thomas, which seemed to be the street where appliance stores gathered, with a few grocers and liquor stores interleaved between them like the thick cloth that keeps the pottery from breaking against itself when—

Umm. . . .

He had been a sailor once—twice? Something like that. He remembered rope burns on his hands; endless buckets of fish soup; toothless, fair-haired men with food in their beards shouting to him in Dutch; salt water in his mouth; the sick-sweet smell of rum; earplugs so the batteries wouldn't deafen him; scraping sounds of a too-small tool against an ugly green metal hull; salt water in his mouth. He almost remembered meeting a small shark once, but this could have been a dream. He'd never met a siren, in any case.

It was coming closer. He almost ducked into a storefront from some urge to flee, but there was really no reason to think they were looking for him. He kept walking.

A wooden door opened almost in his face and a burly figure in a red plaid jacket walked away from him. He noticed the jacket and thought, *Is it cold, then?* He could see his breath, and there was a light coating of snow on the sidewalk, so it must be. He looked at his own clothing and saw only a very thinly woven cotton shirt, pale yellow with a few blue threads for embroidery. He wore baggy blue pants of the same material, and high doeskin boots. These should not be enough to keep him warm. Perhaps he ought to go inside. A sign above the door said ST. THOMAS BAR, which meant it was a public house. The door had opened before him, which could as easily be a Sign as it could be a Trap or nothing at all, and the siren, which ought not to have anything to do with him, *was* getting closer. He opened the door and stepped inside, entering another alien world, which is what any new place is, after all, isn't it?

Cigarette smoke, an anemic blue, hung over a pool table, entwined with a neon BUDWEISER sign, and crept over to a long bar where a fat man in an apron was talking with a smiling patron. The fat man's features were not unpleasant, and his nose had been broken at least twice; the patron hunched his shoulders as if the world had been too much for him for a long time, and he had a large scar down the side of his neck—a knife scar.

The fat man noticed him and said, "What'll it be?"

"I . . . that is, brandy."

"How d'you want it?"

"How—?"

"You all right, buddy?"

"I think so."

"Want me to call someone?"

"No. Just let me sit down."

"Sure. Sit down. Maybe you shouldn't have anything right now."

"Maybe you're right."

"You driving?"

"What?"

"You got car keys?"

"Car . . . keys? I don't think so."

"Good. Just sit there for a while and I'll call you a cab. You got any money?"

"Well, I—I don't know." He put his hands in his pockets and began removing things: An oddly formed lump of heavy grey metal, the key to room fourteen of some hotel somewhere, an empty bottle for sixty-five milligram pills of Darvon, a nickel and three pennies. He stared at this collection, wondering if it had any significance. The pillbottle; he remembered something about that—he had just been trying to get more pills, when—what happened? He shook his head, frustrated.

The fat man said, "Shit. Never mind, now. What's your name?"

"Ummm, Chuck—Charles, I think."

"Yeah, you look like a Charles. Okay, just sit tight. No one here will hurt you. You'll feel better in a while. I'm Tony, by the way."

"Thank you, Tony. Do not write the letter."

"What?"

"Do not write the letter. It will bounce three times and bite three times and leave you kissing dust."

"Is that a poem or something?"

"It is for you."

"What letter are you talking about?"

"I don't know."

The man with the scar looked up. "He some kind of nut, Tony?"

"Hell if I know."

"Did you write a letter?"

The bartender paused, glanced at Charles, then back at the patron. He cleared his throat. "I just told you about my daughter."

"The dyke?"

"Shut the fuck up."

"Hey, you said it first."

The bartender stared at a soapy glass in his hand. "I was gonna write and tell her not to bother coming home for winter break, but. . . ."

"This guy gives me the creeps, Tony."

"So go to the other end of the bar. He ain't bugging nobody."

"I guess not."

But Charles, after replacing his possessions in his pocket, decided he should be the one to move to the other end of the bar, as a result of which he spotted the policemen before they spotted him. His throat tightened. *They* can't *be looking for me. They can't be looking for* me. *Can they?* One was very young and made Charles think of the phrase, "One hand grabs for the reins while one foot runs for the ditch." Who had said that, and in what language? The other policeman was like an old wolf-leader, whose eyes miss nothing even if they appear closed.

Charles turned away, hoping to be missed in the blue fog, but he felt the old policeman's eyes seize the back of his neck. This was pursuit, and pursuit led to capture, and capture led to—

No, there was no time for that, now, either.

The room was heavy with tobacco smoke; it could become heavier, he knew that. He could hide himself in it, although there would be a price to pay.

He did what was necessary, vaguely aware that he was losing something as he did.

There was a back way, and he found it, and he was gone. His headache returned, bringing with it the memory that it had been an almost constant companion for a long time. He felt pursuit, and it frightened him, but at least now he knew it was not an irrational fear which had gripped him since—

—Since—

Blind man's night is music to the deaf, and everyone has *two* paths, not one, whence comes tragedy and comedy, forsooth and damn straight, son.

He stood just within the flap of the tent and the old woman saw him and he saw her and the statuette, and it would be hard to guess who was more surprised of these two strangers who somehow knew. And, oh, the things they said without speaking or moving; the anger, the pain, the justifications, all silent, perhaps all imagined, until he ran, once more, never stopping until he reached the river, which agreed to carry him, once more, away from one set of troubles into another. Out of pangs of the heart and into torments of the flesh.

Hell of a way to run a coach service.

—Since—

After all, they had entered the bar, and, more importantly, he *must* trust his instincts, which had gotten him out of as many fixes as they'd gotten him into. The same could be said of his knife, and perhaps there's a moral there.

Was this time going to be any different? Of course. They all are. He was breathing heavily but not painfully, his strides were long and even, though he was tired. He stopped and rested for a moment beside a high wrought-iron fence, with a lower chain-link fence outside it, then he walked on, looking back frequently.

There was a gate in the fence, and someone stood beside it. His first thought was, *It is Luci; I am caught.* But no. He could make out little of her form in the gloom, but her face had the stamp of beauty with suffering etched into the lines over her brows and next to her eyes. A squirrel at her feet chittered loudly as he approached, started to run, then relaxed. The woman turned at his footstep. He looked into her eyes and she into his. He felt a slight tingle at the base of his skull. Her eyes glittered. She said, "You are here to replace me, that I may rest?"

"I don't understand."

"Why are you here?"

"I am merely walking. Running, in fact. You?"

"I guard this place, so none may pass who should not. You should not, I think, unless you are to replace me."

He looked past her, through the high wrought-iron fence, and understood. "No, I still live. You must wait for the next to die to take your place."

"How then can you see me?"

"Because I am who I am."

"Who are you?"

"I'm not certain. Who are you, and how did you come to die, so young?"

"Leukemia," she said dreamily, as if it made no difference to her at all, and perhaps it didn't. "My name is Karen."

"How long have you stood vigil here?"

"I'm not certain. Only a few days, I think. I relieved a tired old man who had been here four days."

The squirrel jumped closer to him, then back again.

"You will not have to wait long, I think. Then you may rest."

"Yes," she said. "Will you see to my man? We lived together for three years, and he was very kind when I was dying, but it was hard for him. Harder than for me, I think."

"What is his name?"

"Brian MacWurthier. We lived at three twenty-seven Roosevelt, upstairs."

He repeated the name and address to himself, so he wouldn't forget it. "Very well," he said. "I will—" A light fell upon him. He turned and his heart jumped as he saw the police car. He began to run, knowing already that it was too late.

"I'm sorry," he heard her say. The squirrel bolted between the bars of the cemetery as if escaping from a cage.

"It is nothing," said Charles softly as the two policemen took his arms and threw him against the chain-link fence. Their hands were rough and thorough as they searched him. What are their feelings at such times, he wondered. Boredom? Professional pride?

"My head hurts," he said softly. They didn't seem to hear him.

The older one found his knife and let it fall with a gesture half careless and half deliberate. Charles winced as he heard it strike the sidewalk. The younger one held his upper arms in a grip like steel. It was painful. He thought about resisting then and there, but he couldn't decide, and soon it was too late, for they wrenched his arms behind him and put handcuffs on him.

This felt familiar. Why? A piece of the Sight, or the shards of real memory? The policemen pushed him into the back of the car. He had to sit sideways because of the cuffs. He tested them, and found that they were connected by a rigid bar, rather than a mere chain. They knew him then. He frowned, his shoulder pressed uncomfortably against the seat back. There was a time when it would have pleased him that they showed such fear. There was a time. . . .

*He walks aimlessly upon the Old Manor Way, his feet twisting in the coach tracks. He sees her before him—the one whom he had loved, and who betrayed him to marry a rich man.*

*"You have destroyed me," he cries. "You have broken my heart." He reaches into his chest, then, and pulls his heart from his body to show her, but she, filled with shame or pride, won't look, so he flings it down onto the road.*

*Soon, an old dry-nurse comes along and sees it. "Well," she says. "We can't have this." And she calls three times like a raven and screams three times like an owl, and a shape appears beside her. The apparition, a woman who is younger than the nurse and older than the lover, takes the heart from the roadside, and brushes the dirt from it and holds it to her bosom. He looks closely, and sees that it is the ghost of his mother, still watching out for him from beyond the grave.*

*Lover, dry-nurse, and mother all vanish into the mist, into the dust. He takes back his heart and replaces it in his chest and continues on his way.*

The holding tank was seven paces by nine. The walls were of tile, to chest height. The floor was of cement, with a large drain in the middle so the place could be hosed down. A tiled bench, perhaps eight inches off the floor and eighteen deep, was built into two of the walls. Across from it was an aluminum toilet, all of one piece. Charles realized, after a moment's thought, that this was to ensure no one could use the toilet seat as a weapon. The sink was also aluminum. There were neither soap nor towels. The cold water worked, the hot didn't. A chest-high wall next to the toilet provided a token measure of privacy from the thick, wired-glass window next to the door.

Two pair of fluorescent light fixtures, two bulbs in each, made the tank very bright. The fixtures were covered in heavy plastic shielding. To protect them when the place was hosed down, perhaps, since the ceiling was far too high for anyone to reach.

There were two others in the tank with him. For just a moment, Charles thought of his brothers, but, though he no longer remembered what they looked like, he knew these were not they. One prisoner was in his later thirties, perhaps. He had already been there when Charles was brought in. He was tall, stringy, with dark hair that was graying just a bit at the temples. He was sitting on the bench and he wore a black tee shirt. The other looked to be in his middle fifties. He'd been let in just a few minutes before, and Charles had the impression that this wasn't his first time in this place. His grey hair was slicked back, he had a bit of a potbelly. He wore a faded red shirt with fake pearl buttons, very old jeans, and cowboy boots. He paced in a lazy oval near the door. He was short and he stank very badly when Charles got too close. Charles wondered if he'd been fished out of a sewer. All three of them avoided proximity with each other, so staying away wasn't difficult.

He tried to reconstruct the events since he'd been picked up, but they blurred and faded and slipped through his fingers. He had been thoroughly searched by two bored guards with a camera watching, and there had been an old, sour-faced woman who took his picture and fingerprints while a fresh-scrubbed clerk with a weak attempt at a blond mustache had asked him questions he mostly couldn't answer, and then his possessions and even his boots had been taken and he'd been put into the tank by a guard who looked like a Nazi and carried the largest key Charles had seen since—

—Since—

He'd been a child, and his mother carried a huge ornate key on a chain around her neck. "What is that for, Anya?" he had asked.

"It is the key to our palace," she said.

"Palace?"

"We are royalty, you know. And someday we will take our place, and you will be a great king." She smiled and winked as she said it.

"Will I like being a king?" he had asked, all somber and earnest.

She had smiled, like the rippling laugh the fiddle made when Sandi led the *csardas.* She said, "Ah, my little man, sometimes I think you will never like anything you do, because you must suffer to be happy." She hugged him, and his face pressed against the ornate iron key she wore, and he wondered.

—Since—

He sat down on what could perhaps be called a bench, and looked at his companions. He wondered what their crimes were. It came to him then that not everyone put in this place was innocent. A shiver began somewhere low down on his spine and shot up it like a rocket. To be innocent of a crime and to be in this place, stripped of identification, dignity, and shoes, with people who smelled like pigs, behind wired glass, yes, that would truly be damnation. A man could panic in here—think that he'd been forgotten, that no one would ever come for him. There was no way to see the sky, nor was there a clock.

Suddenly desperate to take his mind from these thoughts, he addressed his companions. He said carefully, "Do either of you know how long they're likely to keep us here before something else happens?"

Echoes echoes echoes, banging around inside his head, which now hurt so badly he wanted to scream. If the police, for some reason, wanted to listen in to conversations in this place, they would be unable to hear anything but echoes. Charles wasn't sure if his companions had understood his question, but he had no wish to repeat it. The one who stank glowered at him, and Charles was startled by the deep blue of his eyes. The younger, taller one shook his head and went back to contemplating the floor between his arms.

Charles closed his eyes and took two deep breaths. He assessed his options as best he could. From the way he was treated by the policemen, and the diligence of their search, he was considered dangerous, and was wanted for a serious crime. Had he, perhaps, killed someone? His feelings gave him no answer, except that the idea of having taken a life filled his heart with no sense of denial.

If he left himself in their hands, could he expect justice? Did he *want* justice? The answer to that was: Yes, but it was doubtful that they would see justice in the same way he did. The bench was hard, but the floor not as cold as he would have expected. He waited, his eyes fixed on the door, hardly blinking, hardly breathing. The younger of his companions spared him one curious glance, almost a grimace. The older continued to pace.

Charles could not say how long it was before the door opened once more. A policeman with a straight back and a grey mustache stood with the huge key in his hand and called out, "Jeffrey Simmons." The taller one stood and moved toward the door. The policeman said, "Vincent Petersen," and the smelly one looked up and shuffled to the door. The policeman's eyes locked with Charles' for just a moment, but he couldn't see anything in them.

The cell door shut, sending off echoes like a stone thrown into a pool. The echoes, hard and metallic, set off a ringing in his ears. The ringing continued, too high to sing comfortably, like the long screeching note of the violin at the end of a wild *csardas*. In his mind, he filled in the tambourine. *Doom teka teak teak doom teka tek. Doom teka teka teka doom teka tek.* His throat burned and he tasted his tears. He reached out, as if to touch his home, and then squeezed, as if to tear apart anything that would keep him from it.

*Doom teka teka teka doom teka tek.*

The ringing became louder still, until it filled all of the world that was or ever could be, and he breathed with the imaginary tambourine.

*Doom teka teka teka doom teka tek.*

He wrapped himself in his arms, and, as he did, the rhythm became buzzing of bees and the ringing became church-bells. He let it take him, fill him, expand him, and move him in a way that was more physical then he would have thought.

Movement?

Music.

His headache was gone.

The fiddle came to accompany the tambourine once more, and, just for an instant, he remembered his brothers. But then, the instant was enough, that time.

*Doom teka teka teka doom teka tek.*
*Doom teka teka teka doom teka tek.*
*Doom teka teka teka doom teka tek.*
*Doom teka teka teka doom teka tek.*

# One

## A WOLF, A MAN, AND AN OLD GYPSY WOMAN

### 05 NOV 17:30

**My partner is an asshole, my ex-wife is a bitch.**
**My daughter is a hooker, the suspect is a witch.**

"STEPDOWN"

"Will you guys pipe down?"

No one noticed. The background buzz and rattle in the squad room, loud for a Sunday, didn't even falter. Bad enough that his desk was out in the middle of the room, with other guys always walking behind him, spooking the hell out of him on bad days. Did it also have to be butted up against Dumbshit's desk? He lifted his eyes from the smudged keys of the Smith-Corona-matic and the multilayered sheaf of paper that he'd just crammed in its maw and found himself looking at Durand's butt. Dumbshit was sitting on his own desk, his back to Stepovich, his feet on his chair, for all the world like a high school punk bullshitting his way through study hall. The kid had about twenty extra pounds of gear packed into all the shiny leather pouches on his Sam Browne belt. Including the nonregulation and probably illegal sap Stepovich had had to take away from him earlier, when he'd wanted to use it on the gypsy. Dumbshit Durand hadn't been content with throwing him up against the fence, he'd wanted to sap him, too. Asshole.

Stepovich spoke to Durand's butt. "What's the name of the street that goes past the cemetery?"

Durand interrupted his monologue to say, "Quince." And

resumed it again, saying to Colette, who was hanging on his every word, "so I just catch a glimpse of him going into the St. Thomas, and I say to Step, here, 'There's the bastard now,' and I hit the brakes and I'm out of the car and after him before Step's even got his seatbelt unbuckled, and . . ."

Stepovich let Durand's words dwindle in his mind. Step. Where'd that dumbshit rookie get off anyway, shortening his name? Mike, that's what he could call him if he wanted to be informal. Mike. That's what Ed had always called him before he retired eight months ago. But Dumbshit had to take his last name and cut the end off it. Yesterday one of the office temps had called him Step. Pissed him off. The kid had been his partner for three months now, and Stepovich still couldn't get used to him. If anything, he just grated on his nerves more each day.

He glued his attention to the form, used the release lever to recenter it in the machine, and tapped in "South on Quince." He paused, his fingers on the keys, thinking how to recount the arrest. He'd already left out losing the gypsy inside the bar, simply because he couldn't think of any way to explain it. Nor any way to explain how he had picked up the man's trail again. "Instinct," he'd growled at Durand when he'd had the brass to ask him. Stepovich typed in a couple more bland but informative sentences, in which the gypsy became "the suspect" and he and Durand "the arresting officers." Like that traditional Japanese theater, where the actors held up the masks and struck the poses, the expected faces that hid the real faces behind them. Get the arrest report about two steps away from reality. No one wanted to hear how the chain-link had sproinged when Durand threw the gypsy up against it. There hadn't been a struggle, not really. So leave out the sudden chill that had run over him when he'd touched the gypsy, don't mention how Durand had bared his teeth and swore and pulled out his sap in a response that was totally out of proportion to the gypsy's preoccupied glance and passive resistance.

He typed a few more sentences and read them over swiftly. He'd leave out that Durand had wanted to give the gypsy a "screen test" in the car. "You know, Step, build up some speed and hit the brakes? He's got nothing holding him down back there. So when he hits the screen between the seats, we can see if it holds like it's supposed to. Screen test, get it?" And Durand had giggled, like a kid. Stepovich wondered if there were any cop jokes he hadn't already heard.

He realized he'd forgotten the knife. An unexpected tightness coiled briefly around Stepovich's spine, a clenching of almost guilt. How had Durand not noticed the knife clattering to the sidewalk at the scene of the arrest? He'd certainly said nothing when Stepovich had failed to turn it over when they were booking the gypsy. And that was wrong. If Stepovich leaned back right now and pressed against the support of the creaking chair, he'd be able to feel the knife in its sheath against his spine inside the lining of his jacket. The knife had slithered quickly through the hole in his pocket and into the lining of his jacket like a small animal seeking shelter.

Stepovich's fingers went on typing. He glanced briefly at a scribbled note and filled in the name as "Chuck?—John Doe." But he wasn't thinking of the paper before him, nor the other work to be completed before his shift was over; he was feeling the weight of the sheath knife pulling at his jacket like someone touching his shoulder; he was thinking of the unusual hilt, bone or antler, not plastic; and the sensible leather sheath. He should put the knife in the report, should have turned it in when they booked the guy. Hell, it was another offense, carrying a concealed weapon, and maybe it tied into the killing they'd collared the gypsy on. If anyone found out, they'd nail Stepovich for concealing evidence or some such shit, and for what?

For what?

Stepovich didn't have any answer to that. And when you start doing things that you don't have reasons for, and they're things that could get your ass chewed off, it's time to back off from the job and take a break. But get yourself clear. He should do something like lean back and then jerk forward, saying, "Oh, shit, I forgot the knife, it musta fell through the hole in my pocket." Then fish it out and hand it to Durand, and have him go explain to booking while Stepovich used the whiteout to fix the arrest report. Then everything would be all square. Easy.

His desk phone rang, and without even looking, Durand reached back and snagged the receiver off the cradle. "Hello," he answered it, irking Stepovich even more. Damn kid couldn't even answer a phone properly, didn't identify himself, didn't even say the caller had reached Stepovich's line. "Just a sec," he said, and handed the receiver to Stepovich.

"Who is it?" he asked as he took it.

Durand shrugged. "Dunno. They wanted to talk to you."

Stepovich swallowed an irritated response, took the phone. "Officer Stepovich here, can I help you?"

"Daddy?"

"Laurie! How's my girl?"

"Fine, Daddy, except that I'm in the school square-dance program this Friday, and I have a skirt that's okay for it, but I need a blouse, a white frilly blouse."

There had been a time when Laurie would have beaten around the bush, would have told him all about the program and who her dance partner was and if he was yucky or nice, and then hinted, ever so slyly, that she'd be able to dance better in a frilly white blouse. Not anymore. And Stepovich didn't know if it was because she was getting older and more direct, or because now she only called him when she really wanted something, and didn't want to bother with him anymore than was necessary.

"Daddy?" came her voice, and he realized he hadn't answered her yet. "I know you sent the support check, and Mom got it and all, but this is the month she has to pay property taxes she says, so she says we can't afford it. But I thought, since you're in an apartment and don't have property taxes, maybe you. . . ."

"Sure thing, pussycat. You want me to come by this evening and take you out to one of the malls to get it?"

"Um, well, actually, I know the one I want, it's twenty-two dollars at Carson's, and uh, if you said okay, Mom said I could go get it on her card right now, with Chrissy and Sue. They're like, you know, waiting right now."

"I see." Stepovich tried to think of some other words to say, something that would reach down the phone and touch her, pull her closer to him. He leaned back in his chair, shifting his weight, and the chair squeaked as the gypsy's knife pressed up against his spine. He straightened quickly. "Well, honey, you tell your mom I'll put an extra check in the mail, and you go get your shirt. When is this dance thing, anyway?"

"Friday at seven. We're doing it for the PTA meeting. Uh, Daddy, don't forget tax. I mean, it will probably cost more with tax and everything."

"Right. I won't forget." Stepovich scratched $30 on the corner of his blotter, drew a lazy circle around it. "So, what else is new around there? Got a boyfriend yet?"

"No." The irritation in her voice was not feigned. He guessed that the old tease really wasn't funny anymore. Which meant that maybe, yes, she did have a boyfriend. She was what, almost fifteen? Already fifteen? He sampled foot in mouth, swallowed it.

"Just teasing, sweetheart. So, what is going on with you lately?"

"Nothing, really, Dad, just this dance thing. Look, Chrissy's waiting, and Sue has to phone home to make sure it's okay if she goes with us, so I've got to hang up now, okay? Oh, and if you make the check to me, I can cash it while Mom's at work, and she doesn't have to stop at the bank. Less hassle, you know. Thanks a bunch. I'll tell Jeffrey you said 'hi.' "

"Yeah, okay, Laurie. Listen, I'll try to make it Friday, okay, but if . . ."

"Okay, Daddy, that's great, I'll see you then. Bye."

And she was gone and he was holding the phone too tightly, listening to its emptiness. He wanted to reach out and punch her number in again, call her back, say something to her to make her understand how much he missed her, how afraid he was that she was growing up and leaving him behind like a worn-out stuffed toy.

Instead he rolled the report pages out of the machine, scanned them quickly and inked in a couple of corrections and signed it. Then shoved it at Durand's butt.

"Here. You take care of the rest."

And before Durand could turn around and say anything, Stepovich got up and stalked out of the room. He had to move, had to be doing something, not sitting still.

He got a drink at the water fountain, then walked past the elevator, down the hall between walls the color of old sour cream to the door marked EXIT–STAIRWELL. He went up two flights, listening to his footsteps echo, not using the handrail, forcing his body to do this extra little bit just to prove it still could. The knife rubbed against him as he walked. The gypsy was up here, locked into one of the holding cells.

Stepovich slowed his progress up the stairs. The man had shown no understanding of why he was being arrested. It hadn't felt good to Stepovich, not like a righteous collar. This wasn't the guy. He already knew it when they stopped him, and he hadn't really wanted to haul him in. But that damn Durand was like a pit bull, all jaw and no brain. The gypsy matched the description of the killer who had shot the liquor store clerk, right down to the clothes, and Durand was always dreaming those hot glory dreams, about commendations and the five o'clock news and grateful feminine hands groping his crotch. It had been an ugly killing, one of those things where the thief already had the money in his hands when he shot the guy. There'd been no reason to shoot the clerk at all. Ugly. The press would play with this one, and everyone would want blood.

Maybe that was why he'd held back on the knife. He was sure the gypsy was going to be shaken loose, eventually. But they would let him go reluctantly, and it was going to be damn tough on him until then. And maybe he felt the guy didn't deserve a concealed weapons charge that would stick, simply because he looked like someone else, someone who'd blown away a liquor store clerk for a hundred and seventy-nine dollars plus loose change.

They waved him through the checkthrough, not casual, but respectful. He was the guy who'd made the big collar for the day. No one was going to stop him from inspecting his catch. He replied to their congratulatory words without thinking, a few nods, a couple of sure, sure's. Holding cell three.

He walked down the hallway, and remembered for an instant the first time he'd walked through here. It had reminded him of visiting the zoo, of looking at animals made unreal by their unnatural enclosures. Now it seemed normal. Now when he went to the zoo, it reminded him of this place, and he'd stare at the animals and imagine what they'd been booked for and which ones would be found guilty. The zoo. Hell, it had been two years since he'd taken Jeffrey to the zoo. It only seemed more recent than that because of all the empty spaces between then and now. All the afternoon matinees of movies neither he nor Jeffrey really wanted to see. That was the trouble with this kind of fathering. Too much of doing stuff with the kids, and not enough of just being around. Too many organized outings and carefully planned days. Not enough watching the tube and knowing they were in their rooms doing homework or messing around with their friends. Too much acting like a father, and not enough being one.

Shit.

And here was holding cell three, and someone had screwed

up, because the gypsy wasn't in it. He checked two and four, and then one, quickly and professionally. The gypsy wasn't in any of them, either. Funny. If this were the zoo and those had been animals, the gypsy wouldn't have been so out of place. He'd seemed feral to Stepovich, naturally dangerous the way some men pretended to be. The gypsy would have been right at home caged between the tigers and the wolves. But he didn't belong here. And that he wasn't here seemed to prove that.

Stepovich leaned against the door, staring into the tank. He wasn't there. And he should be hurrying to report that to someone, to ask if he'd been kicked loose by mistake, if he'd been taken somewhere for questioning. But instead all he could feel was the hanging weight of the knife in the back of his jacket lining.

## SOMETIME

The Lady smiles when she looks into your face
She open up her arms for you, awaiting your embrace.

"THE FAIR LADY"

*The Fair Lady is hard at work, knitting a scarf. It must be pretty, or no one will wish to pick it up, and it must be strong, to snare a soul. When it is done, she might cook a broth in which to boil the purity of a maiden, or craft a bellows with which to create a storm to wreck ships. She has done these things for a thousand thousand years, and she takes no less care then she ever has. At her side sits a bald-headed* nora. *In front of her stands a mother who has killed her own child in order to become a* midwife. *The Fair Lady rocks before her hearth, in which burn the bones of those she has caused to die before their time, and she is content.*

*"Well?" she says.*

*The* midwife, *all a-tremble, says, "Here it is, mistress." The* midwife *hands the Fair Lady a lock of grey hair.*

*The Lady inspects it carefully, and grants the* midwife *an approving smile. "It will do," she says. "Did the old woman suspect?"*

*"No, mistress. She never saw me."*

*"Then how did you get this?"*

*"I bribed the bellboy to let me into the room, and I took it while she slept."*

*"Very well. You are resourceful, my dear. Go back to your knitting, now."*

*"What must I knit, mistress?"*

*"A veil to confuse the sight of an old woman. With this lock of her hair, it should not be difficult."*

*"Very well, mistress. It will be done—" she pauses, confused. She cannot say when it will be done, because she no longer understands the passing of time. The Fair Lady grants her another smile, however, and she is content.*

## NOVEMBER ELEVENTH, AFTERNOON

Old woman, your hands are thin,
And I think as scarred as mine.
Old woman, is this all a lark,
Or is it how you spend your time?
Old woman, they tell me here
What you do is called a crime.
Old woman, your predictions
Aren't worth a copper dime.

"BLACKENED PAGE"

She woke with her hands in her hair as if she'd lost a comb, not realizing what had wakened her. A glance at the old wind-up alarm clock told her that it was too early to be leaving to see her sister, and what could it be?

The Sight was a rare gift, and one that could come or go at its own whim, so she should not have been surprised that at first she didn't recognize it. There had been so many years, so many roads, so much living. Yet, after all of that, here it was. Hardly surprising that she didn't know, at first, what had caused her to wake from her afternoon nap, or why she felt that vague, undefined, yet familiar disquiet that was located somewhere below her heart.

She sat up in the narrow motel bed and looked once more at the clock. Sitting up was often the most difficult thing she did all day. Once she had been frightened by the way her heart sped up, but now she accepted it, as she had accepted each day since—

Ah, there it was.

She knew it for a Seeing because it brought to her the memory of those dark, haunted, condemning eyes. Shirt open to the middle, baggy pants tied around the ankles, dark curly hair, strong hands, yes, she remembered that one, and it was something about him that had awakened her. The Sight then. She accepted it without amazement, and with only a little pleasure, for she had lived enough to know that knowledge is a burden exactly as often as it is a blessing.

She got out of bed, stepped over her pile of knitting, and put on her torn quilted blue robe. The suitcase, small, brown, handle missing and one snap broken, was under the bed. Inside it was a cedar box, inlaid with knotwork similar to Celtic, though perhaps not as finely detailed and with a bit more baroque filigree work. Inside the box, folded in red satin, was a two-inch length of quartz crystal. It was about half an inch thick, with a small chip out of one side, and felt very slightly cool as she held it between thumb and forefinger. The quartz had been given her at a fair somewhere in New England, by a customer who had liked the reading she'd given him. Tarot, she thought, or perhaps the leaves. But he'd been a nice young man, with eyes that were unusually innocent for this time and place, and the crystal always carried a certain part of the nice young man, which was why she used it. If she had realized then that she'd come to like it so much, she'd have asked him of its history, but most likely he'd bought it at a museum or something, so it was just as well she didn't.

*My mind is wandering again. Must stop that.*

She worked herself into the stuffed chair the hotel provided, and stared idly at the crystal. She turned it with her fingers, and wondered about the man in baggy pants with a scarf around his head, the man who had stumbled into her life and out again, so quickly, so long ago. Who had he been, she wondered once more. There had been that mark on him, even then, that said he would become part of her life in some way. If anything, she was surprised it had taken so long. What sort of difficulty was he in? The police? Did it have anything to do with an old policeman with grey eyes and a wide jaw, holding a knife? The knife was probably important, although not in any obvious way, perhaps only in that the policeman thought it was. Who was the policeman, and why was he so confused about which side he was on? Should she look for him, or for *him?* And how should she begin to look, if she chose to do so? Perhaps she ought to begin with Little Philly, and check hotels there, especially one facing the sunrise, with a narrow street where the curbs were broken and there was a motorcycle shop with a long crack in its window, and several young men sitting protectively in front. And perhaps she should do so soon—before the brothers failed to come together, or coming together, found themselves paralyzed by ignorance.

Yes.

She rolled the crystal between her palms. It was rather like a bullet, in shape. Interesting that this should occur to her. Her mouth became dry, and there was a moment of fear, of a palpitating heart. She had become more and more aware of her heart over the last few years, more conscious of its strength and weakness. She would probably know before it gave out, which might be good or bad. It wasn't about to give out now.

She got dressed slowly, her mind racing, her thoughts unfocused. In her left earlobe she put two thin silver hoops, in her right she put three smaller ones. A skull ring went over her little finger because she had worn it the first time she'd seen him. About her neck she fastened a lapis lazuli on a gold chain. Her dress was conservative and pale yellow, with a light blue shawl. She studied herself in the mirror, looking for traces of the future and finding none. At last she called for a cab.

## SATURDAY AFTERNOON

What is your desire? Fame, or love, or gold?
It's there in your hand, my friend.
But answer if you can, my friend
What are you reaching out to hold?

"THE FAIR LADY"

"So what? So at least I did it, didn't I?" Laurie tossed the check her dad had sent her on the dresser. Thirty dollars! More money than she'd ever asked for at once in her whole life. And her dad had sent it, right away, but now they said it wasn't enough. She walked past that stuck-up Sue girl and flopped down on her pink bedspread. Strawberry Shortcake. She'd had it since she was nine, but now she hated it, especially because of the way Chrissy's older friend was looking at it. She was beginning to wish this Sue would just leave. Where did Chrissy get off, anyway, just bringing some stranger over to her house? Anymore, all Chrissy talked about were her "older" friends, and how mass cool they were. She made Laurie feel like a baby. And her mom would be home soon. She wouldn't be cool about Laurie having a guest that she hadn't met yet. Especially someone like Sue. She must have been at least sixteen, maybe eighteen. And she acted so rad, it was like she was even older. Like now, lighting a cigarette, like it was no big deal.

Sue exhaled smoke at Laurie. "So, really, you blew it. Getting twenty or thirty bucks, that's easy. I told you, we need fifty. And you coulda got it if you'd done it like I told you."

"But I don't really need shoes." Laurie protested.

"Shit!" Sue blew smoke out her nose in long thin streams. "I know that. You don't need a blouse either. All you had to say was, like, 'My old shoes pinch my feet a little when I dance, but Mom says they'll do until the next paycheck.' He'd a been in such a hurry to show up your mom, he'd probably express the money to you."

"No, he'd probably have called my mom and asked about it," Laurie said. She was getting tired of this older girl pushing on her, acting like she knew everything. Look at her now, blowing smoke out her mouth and inhaling it up her nose. Gross. Laurie was beginning to think she didn't like Chrissy's new friend at all.

"I betcha he wouldn't have called your mom. Hell, your dad hardly ever calls you, let alone your mom." Chrissy jumped in.

Great! Now her best friend was siding against her. Laurie wished they'd both leave. The cigarette was stinking up her whole room. Sue saw her looking at it. She flicked it, sending ashes all over the rug.

"Hey!" Laurie objected, but Chrissy just giggled. "Use this for an ashtray, okay?" Laurie added, taking the saucer out from under one of her African violets. Sue took it from her like it was a big favor. No one said anything for a while. Sue just sat there smoking and looking around her room and smirking.

"Look!" Laurie began fiercely. "You might think you know it all, but you don't know my folks. They might be divorced, but when it comes to us kids, they're still together. He'd phone her. Besides, a cop doesn't make that much. My dad probably couldn't send me fifty bucks if he wanted to."

"Shit!" Sue said again, and Chrissy giggled. "Cops make all the money they want. Half of them are on the take. I oughta know, I seen enough of them. There's this one old fart, down in juvie, said if I'd come across, he wouldn't write up my probation violation. Don't talk to me about cops."

"They're not all like that!" Laurie's heart was beating really fast. She knew her face was getting red, like it always did when she was mad.

"Bullshit!" Sue drawled, and looked sideways at Chrissy, cracking her up. It suddenly dawned on Laurie that she was being baited, that Sue was getting her worked up and sharing the joke with Chrissy. Her eyes hurt like she was going to cry, but she didn't let the tears out. Her old bear was still on the bed, and she picked him up and squeezed him tight. Chrissy seemed to see how upset she really was, because she sat up suddenly and changed the subject.

"So. What now?" she asked brightly, sending Laurie a brief look that said sorry. But she didn't say it out loud, Laurie thought bitterly. Not in front of her new friend.

"What now?" Sue echoed. She leaned over and deliberately stubbed her cigarette out against the soft furry leaves of the violet instead of on the saucer. Laurie gritted her teeth, trying not to show her anger, but the little smile on Sue's mouth showed she knew she had scored. "Now nothing, Chrissy. Your little friend blew it. If I take you to meet the Lady and Her friends with less than fifty bucks, they'll laugh in my face. The Lady expects presents from Her friends. You wanta be Her friend and be in with Her, you gotta bring Her presents. Money and jewelry and stuff."

"Well, maybe I don't wanna be Her friend!" Laurie broke in.

"Fine with me, Miss Piggy," Sue said, and Chrissy cracked up. It took a few seconds for Laurie to catch the joke. Then, "Get the hell out of my house!" she cried out.

"Fine with me," Sue said slowly. She got up lazily, looked around the room in disdain. "I'm a little tired of sitting around in the nursery, anyway. You coming, Chrissy, or you want to stay here and play Barbies?"

Chrissy looked trapped. "I'll be along, I guess," she said lamely. "In a little while. I gotta get my stuff."

"Yeah. Sure. Well, better hurry, kid, cause I ain't waiting. I got other things to do. See ya around, Miss Piggy." Sue drifted out of the room, and a few seconds later Laurie heard the front door slam.

"Great, Laurie, you really blew it for us!" Chrissy huffed as she grabbed up her bookbag and coat.

"I blew it? What do you want to go around with someone like that for? She's awful!"

"Not usually. She was just pissed because you didn't get the money. Usually she's really cool, and you should see her boyfriend's car! Talk about rad! On the freeway, night before last, he got it up to a hundred and twenty! And then he turned off the headlights! It was like flying in the dark. Oh, Laurie, you got to get that money, so you can come with us. You should see the stuff that Lady gives her. Jewelry like you wouldn't believe, and this scarf, it looks black, but when you shake it, it's silver! And. . . . Look! I gotta go, because she won't wait for me. But I'll tell her you were sorry, that you were feeling sick or something. And I'll try to get the rest of the money, cause we've just got to meet this Lady. Usually, you got to be at least a senior to be invited, so we're really lucky."

Motormouth Chrissy was still talking as she wrapped her scarf around her neck and left the bedroom. Laurie didn't bother walking her to the door; Chrissy didn't notice. Some best friend. Ever since she met that Sue, she'd been acting like a jerk. As soon as Laurie heard the door shut, she got up and took the cigarette butt out of her plant. It was the new one, too, the one that was supposed to have double blossoms. A burnt hole gaped angrily in the soft green leaf. Laurie carefully pinched it off, and carried both cigarette butt and leaf into the bathroom, where she flushed them down the toilet.

## NOVEMBER ELEVENTH, LATE AFTERNOON

Old woman, it's only
A false joy you bring.
Old woman upon your hand
I see a death's-head ring.
Old woman, it's our winter,
We'll never see a spring.
Old woman, it's time to cry,
Why must you still sing?

"BLACKENED PAGE"

The cab driver was a fat man who reminded her of Jackie Gleason, which made his deep, gravelly voice quite startling. When she told him where she wanted to be taken he didn't say anything, but gave her a quick, speculative look in the rearview mirror as he pulled away from the curb. During the ride, which, because of the Veterans' Day traffic, took half an hour, she paid little attention to the area they were passing through. She let her mind drift, free associating, finding melodies in the whine of passing cars and patterns in the cracks along the streets.

He let her off at a corner where an old black man sold newspapers and shoeshines in front of a grocer whose green and yellow produce lay in bushel baskets below the barred storefront. The thought of trying to connive her way out of paying the fare popped up unbidden from her childhood, and she tipped the driver lavishly by way of putting the thought back where it belonged. She wondered at it, though. Was it a sign of age, or was there significance to this unexpected recurrence of the old ways?

The cab roared off; she sniffed, as if hoping to catch a scent, and began walking east down the block, because it seemed to be slightly downhill. She knew that what she sought was around here somewhere, and she would find it more quickly and easily on her feet, slow as they were. They hadn't always been slow. Once she had danced. Once she had danced well enough to earn—

Stop now, she told herself firmly. Fools live in the past, as saints live in the future. It was her lot to feel the waves from the one—she couldn't afford to let her mind remain in the other.

Children played in the street, and didn't see her, because she had nothing to do with their world. She passed men and women her own age, all of whom were so wrapped up in their dreams that they never looked outside of themselves. She came to the place she had Seen, and the excitement of a true Seeing was far back in her mind. The scene before her held a promise and a threat, and she could almost taste them both on her tongue, sour and juicy as lemon, fear and pleasure.

She identified the hotel by its neon sign, which was mostly burned out, then looked around briefly. It was on a hill, and the side she could see was done in peeling red paint. It had a single door, also red, that was no bigger than the door to a house and had no window. She felt almost young again as she pushed it open and entered the lobby.

# Two

## THE WOLF AND THE GYPSY

11 NOV 13:22

**The city is a cesspool, my apartment is a mess.**
**You say you got a problem, just give me your address.**

"STEPDOWN"

"Hell of a thing," said the hotel manager. He wiped his shining forehead with a dirty hanky, dragging it roughly across two ripely swollen pimples. He shifted around, glancing at the body, and away, shying like a nervous horse. Guy was too young to be managing a flop house. Stepovich could tell the kid felt ill, but that being here made him feel so important he couldn't stand to leave. This poor old woman leaking blood onto the hotel's cheap carpeting was probably the most exciting thing that had ever happened to him.

"Think they raped her?" The kid scrubbed at his forehead

again, scratched at one of the zits, then absently squeezed it. Stepovich looked away. He'd rather look at the body.

"Sure," Durand said, heavily sarcastic. "What man wouldn't get it up for her? I mean, the streets are crawling with granny bangers, aren't they?"

"Shut up." They made him tired, both of them. Someday, when Durand had seen what elderly women looked like after they'd been raped, he wouldn't joke about it anymore. "Leave the kid, uh, witness alone. Homicide will want him first."

"Yeah. They'll have a lot of questions for you. And they like their meat fresh. Hope you don't have any plans for the next twelve hours or so," Durand said cruelly.

The kid stared at him, not sure if Durand was serious or not. Durand cop-stared at him. "I, uh, I should be down where I can answer the phone, shit like that," the kid muttered uneasily. "If I'm not right at that desk, you'd be surprised how many people try to sneak out without paying."

"Probably not," Durand said.

"No, really, they do," the kid insisted righteously. "They . . ."

"No. I mean I wouldn't be surprised. Go ahead, get back to your phone, kid. We want you, we'll call you." Then, "Try not to touch the door as you leave, okay?"

Stepovich wondered why Durand bothered. The kid had already smeared it up once, coming in here, and then again when he led them up here. Besides, it wasn't like homicide was going to get all worked up and dust the whole place. The department's funds were limited; right now all of them were going toward that child mutilation case and the Exxon Basher. Media loved those. Some old gypsy woman getting herself killed wasn't exactly the Manson murders. What was it Durand had said as they came in? "Mighta known. A gypsy. They're always killing each other."

He'd already phoned it in. Now there wasn't much to do except wait until homicide arrived to take over. He and Durand had taken the call as a domestic violence. Well, maybe it had been. But the kid manager hadn't seen anything, and wasn't even sure who the room had been let to. Stepovich glanced back to the body. It pissed him off. Dying bloody in a cheap hotel room, that was something to happen to a pimp or a pusher, not to an old woman. Anybody who'd lived that long deserved a better death.

She'd fought it. He had to say that for her. There would be

skin under her fingernails, he'd bet, and it was obvious it had taken more than one blow from the knife to take her down. The last one had been as she lay there, a driving jab into her back and out, to make sure of her. Her legs were flung wide, one shoe half off. An intricately patterned blue shawl led from her body to the door. Had it snagged on her killer's watch? No one would ever know. Her face was turned away from him but her hair, thick as a young girl's, though grey, had come half undone. A pink edge of ear and a silver hoop earring peeked out of it.

Durand was crouched over her, staring at her face. His head was cocked, like a puppy staring into a stereo speaker at a recording of wolves howling. Puzzled.

"What?" Stepovich demanded.

"Gypsy told my fortune, once. I was wondering if it might have been her."

Stepovich frowned. "You saying we should call bunko, that she's been working scams lately?"

"No. Naw," Durand seemed embarrassed. "It was a long time ago, at a fair when I was a kid. In a little white trailer covered with dust, hooked to a battered old Caddy. She said that thirty-two was my number, and that foxgloves would be important to me."

"Foxgloves?"

"You know, kind of a pinkish flower, grows by the roads some places."

Stepovich stared at his partner, waiting.

Durand stood. "So." He cleared his throat, folded his arms. "Maybe we should call bunko, maybe they'd recognize her."

"Maybe. And maybe we should let homicide do it, so we don't have to repeat everything bunko says to us to them." Most homicide cops Stepovich knew got bent out of shape if they thought a regular cop was trying to muscle in on their work. No, it was better to just take it easy and wait here, protect the scene until the homicide dicks got here and took over. Then it would be time for their afternoon break, and then there'd be another couple of hours of riding around, and then he could go home. He walked to the room's single window and stared down at the street, wondering how long it would take for homicide to arrive. And how many questions they'd ask, and how long they'd keep him and Durand here. It seemed to Stepovich that time had stopped, and wouldn't start again until they got here. It would never start again for the old woman. But when the detectives got here, it would be the end of the "waiting by a body" time and the beginning of the "waiting for the shift to be over" time. He wanted to go home.

And then he could get rid of that knife.

The thing was sticking in his brain, bugging him.

He wished he'd never seen the damn thing. Just touching it made him feel crawly. He should have left it on the sidewalk, he should have gone ahead and booked the gypsy for concealed weapon. He thought of all the times he'd leaned switchblades up against the curb and stomped them so he wouldn't have to book a kid for concealed weapon. Well, the gypsy's knife wouldn't have yielded to that sort of treatment. Thick blade, at least two inches across at the hilt. And a weird hilt. On the surface of the hilt, toward the blade, there were these three little pins or pegs, shaped like stars. All three stars were enclosed in an engraving of a crescent moon. He'd never seen anything like it. He had it at home, in the bottom drawer, with his socks. It had been there since that night he'd gone to the tank and the gypsy hadn't been there. No one had sorted that out yet; all the paperwork said he should still have been there. What the hell. Stepovich was betting he wouldn't see the gypsy again.

So maybe the best thing to do was to take the knife back to the cemetery gates where they'd rattled the gypsy. Dump it there, kick it under the bushes. He sure as hell didn't want to keep it. He'd thought about tossing it into a dumpster or slipping it down a sewer. But those solutions didn't feel right either. No, he'd take it to the cemetery, and toss it in the bushes, where it would have ended up if they'd overlooked it when they shook the gypsy down.

"Step?"

"Yeah?" He didn't look away from the street. He was kind of watching their car, and kind of watching the loungers in front of the motorcycle shop down the street. Were they lounging, or were they watching? Looking out for what? Protecting what? And was it worth his while to make an effort to find out?

"Step, you think maybe this dead gypsy's got anything to do with the one we booked last week?"

He shrugged. "City's full of gypsies this time of year. Come in from God knows where, renting old storefronts, selling cheap tapestries from Japan in rundown bars, making up futures for people who don't have any. A week or a month from now, whoosh, they're all gone to God knows where. Makes you wonder if they were really here in the first place. And that's why we'll never know who killed this one, or where the other one went."

"Step?"

"No, I doubt if they're connected." He sighed and turned away from the window.

"Wish we knew what happened to that one we dragged in. I got a gut feeling he was the one blew away the liquor store clerk."

"Yeah? Well, I got a gut feeling he wasn't."

"How come?"

"Just because." He turned back to the window. An unmarked car pulled in behind theirs. A man in a, for God's sake, trench coat got out. He didn't know him, but the other detective was Scullion. Good. Scullion was fast and thorough. They'd be out of there in no time. A meat wagon was turning the corner.

"You know," said Durand softly. "I really think she was the same gypsy. The one that told my fortune."

## TWENTIETH CENTURY

Walkin' down an empty street
  In a city I don't know,
Whistlin' something catchy
  As I make my way through snow.
Ain't got no gloves so I keep my hands
  Balled up in fists;
I'm trying not to think
  How it all came down to this.

"NO PASSENGER"

The Coachman awoke, realizing that he'd been drunk again. This made him laugh, until it came to him that he was no longer drunk, and yet he was awake. This puzzled him. Next to him was a bottle labeled Mr. Boston Five-Star Brandy. There was about a third of the bottle left. He started to unscrew the cap, then closed it again. He blinked.

He remembered that he had dreamed that he'd had a passenger.

And now he was suddenly, inexplicably sober.

He stood up, looked around the shabby room he could afford from money he begged and what he didn't drink, and suddenly laughed. Something was happening, somewhere.

He unscrewed the cap, smelled it, and decided it wasn't good enough. If it had been, he'd have poured a shot into a glass and drunk it that way, to celebrate, but it wasn't so he didn't. He checked his pockets and found almost three dollars in change, which would be enough to get him coffee and a Danish. Good. He whistled as he showered, no longer minding the low water pressure, and he wondered how and where he would find his coach.

## LATE FALL, EARLY EVENING

I haven't seen or heard from them
In far too many years,
But banging from the copper pans
Still echoes in my ears.

"RAVEN, OWL, AND I"

The Gypsy went walking, as he had so often before, not so much looking for anything as just looking, only he was walking where there was nothing to see and nowhere to go. He wore yellow, but it was brighter than he thought it should be, and his boots felt softer, although it was too much effort to look at them.

A hand halted him, and he, oddly, recognized the ring on it; he couldn't remember from where. A pair of familiar dark eyes locked with his, but then the light in them went out. The thought came to him that he'd just been saved from something.

He walked further, and there was a wolf, growling and bristling. He paused, and looked closer; the wolf's foot was trapped. He thought that he would release the foot, but the wolf snapped at him. He stopped then, puzzled. "Why snap at me?" he said. "Am I your enemy? No. I'm the one who is trying to help you."

The wolf stared at him with old, intelligent eyes. He continued, "I will let you go, but you must not attack me; you must find your proper prey. Will you do that?"

The wolf studied him carefully, suspiciously, and it occurred to him that the wolf wondered, not if he could be trusted, but if he were *capable* of releasing him. The Wolf is no fool, he thought to himself, staring into its eyes.

The eyes contracted and became one, against a field of darkness, then they resolved until they became a single pinpoint of light, which became the universe, and it pulsed a very pale blue. His concentration was total, his questions, none. A moment ago, it had seemed, he could hear that pinpoint, that blue, that pulsing. A moment ago it had been the beat of the tambourine, zils laughing merrily, head thrumming. It had been that way forever, a moment ago, and now it was a pinpoint of light, and had been that, too, forever.

There was the smell that came from cars, and it was stifling. The pinpoint grew into a flower as sound returned, and he opened his eyes to the dryness of his mouth and gravel against his cheek, and a beam of evening sunlight striking his face, as he tried to remember what he had just escaped. He squeezed his eyes tightly shut. Visions came at his bidding, and then wouldn't leave: something scary chased him, then became his brother with a knife, then became his other brother, crying, yet he knew it was not from his brothers that he had fled.

One vision was of an old woman, who pointed her finger at him and said, "Do not squander my gift," to which he had replied, "It was not just to me you gave it, Mother, yet I'll make the best use of it I can." Another was of a small girl, who seemed to be the old woman with brown eyes at the same time, only she laughed as if she knew it were only a game. Another was of a man in an apron asking his name, and he being unable to remember. That was strange; he knew who he was. He was . . . Charles? No, that wasn't right. What did they call him? Umm . . . "Cigány," he said aloud, and began coughing from the dust. He swallowed several times, but was still very thirsty.

Overhead, a cement bridge held up a freeway; next to him a street passed below it, and around him was a retaining wall, which had kept him hidden, in the open, in the middle of a large city. He smiled at this, in spite of his discomfort. The day seemed to be ending. He realized that he had lain there for more than a day, perhaps several. Could he have died from exposure? Why not? He needed water, a toilet, and food, in that order.

He almost relieved his bladder in his protected cement

grove, but this felt wrong, as if by doing this he would be sacrificing something he couldn't afford to lose, now that he lived in the wilds of the city. He pulled himself to his feet, braced himself against the wall, and began walking. He saw a filling station just across the street and knew that he would live.

11 NOV 19:00

I look for troubles all over town,
My nerves are shot but it don't get me down.

"STEPDOWN"

He wanted chicken and biscuits for dinner. Like they used to have, the chicken braised and then cooked in a gravy, and Jennie's white biscuits with the crispy brown points on top, and Jennie laughing as she told Jeffrey and Laurie that by God she never wanted to see them sopping up gravy with biscuits like their dad did. And then he'd laugh and tell her his manners were her fault, for making the gravy so good he didn't want to waste a smear of it.

Maybe that's what he wanted, more than the food. The laughing around a table.

He dumped the can of Dinty Moore stew into a pan and put it over a burner. It smelled like dogfood, cold. Hell, it looked like dogfood, but heated up it was okay. A little too peppery, but okay. And the peas came out the color of an old fatigue jacket, but it was okay. It was okay. It was all okay, just take it easy, don't get worked up.

He took his beer to the couch, turned on the television. News. He clicked through the channels, not wanting to hear about an old gypsy woman found stabbed to death in a cheap hotel. He found the Jetsons, a quiz show, "Sesame Street," more news, and a Jesus for sale program. He went back to the quiz show. A woman was jumping up and down and screaming while holding onto the host's arm. She'd just won a refrigerator. It was frost-free, with a no-fingerprint surface, a drink dispenser, and an ice maker.

The Gypsy said, "Too bad there wasn't a no-fingerprint surface on the knife."

"Yeah," Stepovich agreed. He took another pull off his beer.

"You bring me the message from the old woman?"

"Yeah. I got it here somewhere." Stepovich slapped his pockets for the letter, but he couldn't find it. He found a rock crystal and pulled it out instead. "Scullion found it in her scarf. Inside her bag. It was addressed to you." Stepovich held it out, but the Gypsy wouldn't take it from him.

"That's your name on there, not mine," said the Gypsy. He was carving on a stick with his knife, and the shavings were going all over the floor. Jennie would be mad. Stepovich held the crystal close to his eyes, trying to see whose name was really on it. "Don't bother," said the Gypsy, making long curling shavings. "All it says is, 'Find out who killed me.' " A raven hopped up and pecked at the shavings. The Gypsy shooed him away with a wave of his knife.

"Not my job," said Stepovich, taking another pull off his beer.

"No one's job," agreed the Gypsy. "No one gives a shit anymore." He got up and took the blackened coffee pot from the fire. It was made of that old blue enameled ware, the kind that has black speckles on it. Stepovich wondered why it didn't burn him. The Gypsy poured himself coffee into a heavy china mug. He stirred it with his finger. He sipped at it, and the rising steam from the mug floated up toward the crescent moon. He pointed at the coach, where a dark figure waited, holding reins that drifted off into fog. Or was it a knitted scarf? "You just want to leave?"

Stepovich frowned, wondering. Did he want to leave? "What about the old woman?" he asked.

"Not your job. Remember?" The Gypsy smiled kindly. "We can leave any time you want. How about now?" He scratched his chest through his yellow shirt. Stepovich could see that a few threads of the blue embroidery were coming undone. Jennie could fix that in a minute. He knew she could, but she wouldn't. She didn't fix things anymore.

Something else was cooking on the fire, something that boiled over the lip of the old kettle and fell in slow drips into the fire. The flames leaped up to catch the drips, eager to devour, and a terrible stench and smoke arose. The smoke stung Stepovich's eyes. "Where does the coach go?" he gasped, rubbing his eyes and trying to see the Gypsy through the smoke.

"The one place you can't get to from here," the Gypsy said. He stood up and put his knife away. "Do you want to go?"

"It's the only place I want to go," Stepovich said, and stood up.

The corner of the coffee table hit him on the cheekbone, and the sharp pain almost stunned him. He got slowly to his hands and knees, staggered to the kitchen, dragged the pot off the stove and turned the burner off. He clicked on the fan in the range hood. It squealed annoyingly, but he let it run. The stew that was left in the pot looked disgusting, thick and stringy. He scraped it into a bowl and got some bread to go with it. And another beer. He set it all out on the coffee table, turned off the fan and went to look in the bathroom mirror.

Well, it was going to swell, but at least it wasn't going to be a black eye. He looked at himself. Square jaw. Blue eyes. The kind of hair they called sandy, just starting to slip back at his temples. He'd lost weight in the last two years. Steadily. At his last cop physical, the doctor had complimented him on it. "Looking fine, Stepovich," the man had said, prodding his belly muscles. "You'd put a lot of younger men to shame. Work out regularly?" Yeah, he'd told the doctor. Sure. Real regular. For a while, it had been the only way he could stop thinking. Now even that didn't work.

He went back to the couch. The quiz show was gone. Three people were in a living room, and the studio audience was laughing uproariously while one of the characters struck an offended pose and the other two simpered. Stepovich opened his beer, drank, had two spoonfuls of the burnt stew. He reached to the other end of the coffee table, dragged the phone toward him. He punched in the number, then hung up before it could ring.

He wondered what she'd do if he ever really did it. Just called her up and said, "I'm sorry, it was a big mistake, I love you, can I please come home?"

He ate more stew. Probably get another restraining order. Probably send the kids to her mother.

He drank some beer. It hadn't been a mistake. They both

knew that. The divorce had been right. And he didn't love her. He loved something else, the idea of being married and having the kids and all. That's what he loved. If he went home right now, they'd probably have a fight before two hours were up. No. He'd screwed it up too badly. Screwed it up once by walking out when she dared him to. Screwed it up again by following her everywhere, always trying to talk to her, phoning her up at midnight, being outside the building when she got off work, by following her as she drove home each day. She'd thought he was going to hurt her, had gotten the restraining order, had filed harassment charges, had nearly made him lose his job.

So now it was this. Send her a check, talk to the kids on the phone. Eat alone, sleep alone, because you're too damn tired to go through all that dating shit. So zone out on the tube, after exercising for three hours so you can sleep, then fall asleep and dream about goddamn gypsies.

He set down the empty bowl. Well, he was through with the last part. He was going to take the knife back to the cemetery, tonight. Somehow he was sure that would get the Gypsy out of his mind.

# Three

## THE GYPSY AND THE WOLF

### LATE FALL, AFTER SUNSET

**Beasts and demons laugh and yell,**
**The lonely midwife sings;**
**They dance around like puppets,**
**But the Lady works the strings.**

"THE FAIR LADY"

Cigány left the diner without paying; simply got up and walked out before they noticed him, turned the corner around a building and was gone. He was cleaner, though he wished he could jump into a river, and there were two pieces of tasteless chicken in his stomach along with a great deal of city water.

As he walked, scenes from his most recent past began to return to him. The holding tank, for one; where they put you before they knew where to put you. That, he had figured out. He wasn't certain how he had escaped it, or what the cost had been. Moreover, he wasn't certain why they had arrested him. He didn't think he'd done anything, but, then, it was always like that. A pal from Ireland once sang him a song about being born in the wrong place. He smiled at the memory. But he, Cigány, had been born in the *right* place, and then had left. Why?

His head began to hurt, and he reached for, for something he couldn't remember. Pills of some sort? He had had this sort of headache before, he knew; in fact, now that he thought of it, he almost remembered getting it every time he ate—that strange pulsing in his head, and then his vision would waver, and then the pain.

He shook his head. Ignore the pain. There was something he had to do, he knew that. He'd been trying to do it for so many years that he could not longer estimate the decades that had passed. But what was it? Had it been so long that he'd forgotten his mission? He had promised to do something, he knew that. He took a deep breath, brushed his mustaches, and—

—And realized that his knife was missing.

He began to tremble.

Of course it was missing, the police had taken it. Why was he so upset? What was it about the knife? He knew that it could protect him, but—

It had killed. While out of his possession, someone, who didn't know what he had, had allowed it to kill. That meant that there was an enemy who knew that he, Cigány, didn't have it, and that he was vulnerable, and the enemy had killed a friend.

He leaned against the wall, and he wondered who his enemy was. He almost knew. Was it his brother in the vision? No, his brothers were scattered, lost. The enemy was the one who had been preventing him from completing his mission for so long.

What mission? What enemy? He ducked behind a building squatted there, and tried to think. His head throbbed, like his skull was being split with an ax.

It had snowed, not too long before, and then melted, although he hadn't noticed it at the time. But there was water dripping from the gutter, and it formed a puddle on the paved ground, perhaps a foot wide.

Cigány felt his mouth become dry again. Here he was going off to find his knife, and, because he didn't have it, he hardly dared to go. He stood up and waited for several minutes until the moon was in the proper place over his shoulder. It wasn't quite full, but he thought it might be close enough. He stepped forward once with his left foot, once with his right, and again with his left, the last landing him squarely in the puddle.

*The Fair Lady looks up, suddenly, seeing before Her a figure all of fire, with one leg that of a goose and the opposite arm that of a horse. She puts down Her knitting and smiles sweetly. "Yes, what is it?" Her voice is the tinkling of fine crystal, with a very faint echo if you listen closely. Her face is young. Her eyes are old, and they reflect the firelight; Her hair and skin are fair. There is a crown of candles on Her head, making folds in the skin of Her forehead. There are nine candles, but three of them have gone out.*

*"Fair Lady," says the* liderc. *"Someone is coming."*

*"Coming? Here? A visitor?"*

*"Indeed, yes, mistress."*

*"Well, who can it be?"*

*"A mortal, fair mistress. A Gypsy."*

*"But his name," She says gently. "Don't you know his name?"*

*"I do not, for he knows it not."*

*"Ah, well he may attend me then."*

*"It shall be as you wish, most precious one," says the* liderc, *and rushes to admit the visitor.*

*He stands before Her, and his black eyes reflect the firelight too, so that for a moment they seem to be kin, and She says, "Well, little boy, what is it you want of me?"*

*He says, "You have my memories, Luci, and I will have them back."*

*"Your memories? What would I do with them?"*

*"Keep me from completing my task," he says.*

*"But what is your task, little boy?"*

*"I don't know, for you have taken my memories. And my knife, Luci, return me my knife."*

*"How is it you know to come here without your memories? And how is it you dare without your knife?" The* nora *thinks this very funny and begins to laugh. The Fair Lady cuffs him without rancor, and he scampers away on his arms and legs, like an ape.*

*"If I do have these things, little boy," says the Fair Lady, "why should I return them?"*

*"Because if you don't, I shall find the calk from a Coachman's whip and send you back to your home below the earth."*

*The Fair Lady laughs, "Well, little boy, you have found your task. But I fear it is too late to find your knife, for it has killed the only one who could have set you on the path. And it is far, far too late for a calk to help you. And since you have come here unguarded, there is no reason to let you leave at all." With that, she lifts the bellows and begins to work them, and he suddenly finds that he cannot breathe. He struggles, but to no avail, until, at last, he pulls from his pocket an oddly formed lump of grey metal, which was made by pouring molten lead into holy water, and he throws this at Her, and She cries out, and—*

—Cigány fell backward against the building, taking many deep breaths. For several minutes he stood there, wondering if the dream had been real. He checked his pocket, but the lead was gone, although he still had his key, and a scrap of paper which he now remembered had something to do with his headaches, although he couldn't remember the spell nor understand the symbols. But, hadn't the police taken these things before? He couldn't remember. He shrugged. He hoped he could do without it. His headache seemed to be receding.

Whatever had happened, it had taken a long time; it was now fully dark. When he felt strong enough, he pushed away from the wall, not sure where he was going, but needing to walk. Somewhere, not too far off, a siren wailed. He winced and continued through the back streets. The night brought with it a slight chill, but he scarcely noticed.

After a while he realized that he had been here before. Yes. The cemetery. *Why have my feet brought me this way?* he wondered. He remembered the ghost, and wondered if someone else had died yet, allowing her to rest. Poor child. So young. But she had died of the wasting disease, and that was the work of a *liderc* if anything was, and the *liderc* was a creature of Luci, the Fair Lady, who dwelt below the world, with the dark sun and the dark moon to light Her dark ways.

What had allowed Her to reach the middle world, with the half sun and the half moon? And how had it become his, Cigány's, job to return Her to where She belonged?

He stopped in his tracks. Suddenly there was a Wolf before him, blocking his path, bristling. He shook his head to clear it, and saw that it was only a man. The man was staring at him, shocked. Cigány wondered if he were the last to die, who had released the girl.

But another step closer and he recognized him, even without his uniform, and his mouth became dry and his heart beat very fast within his breast.

11 NOV 23:40

Someone knifed a granny, someone shot a clerk.
I'm sick of seeing bodies, but it's just a day at work.

"STEPDOWN"

Three beers. No, maybe four. Hell, even if it had been six, that was still no excuse for this. Stepovich swayed slightly, in rhythm with the big oak that rustled softly from its side of the high wrought-iron fence. Hell, maybe it had been six. He was almost hoping it was six, and that as the man came closer, his features would resolve into the face of someone Stepovich had never seen before.

The Gypsy halted, no more than a step and a lunge away. His dusky face seemed pale in the gloom, and Stepovich wondered how that could be. His eyes were dark in his face, darker than the night around them, and that, too, made him wonder. They stood facing each other on the quiet street. Neither spoke. Neither wanted to offer the other an opening.

The knife in his jacket pocket dragged, seemed to weigh twice what it should. He could feel the pull on the fabric at his shoulder, could feel the shape resting against his hip. His hand reached into his pocket, gripped the sensible leather sheath. The Gypsy did not move as Stepovich reached for the knife, but he sensed the change in the Gypsy, the activated stillness that was really a readiness to move in any direction, to attack or flee or defend. Stepovich's eyes didn't leave him as he drew the knife from his pocket.

He'd expected some reaction. But the Gypsy's dark eyes only flicked once to the knife, and then back up to Stepovich's face. Like a cornered animal, he waited. Stepovich shifted the knife through his fingers, felt his fingers brush the raised stars on the hilt before he got it turned so that the hilt extended toward the Gypsy. Stepovich held it out, waiting. Got nothing. The Gypsy offered him only stillness and carefully empty eyes. Not even the phony innocence that most suspects tried for. Not a blank face, either. This was more like a mask to trick authority.

A red-hot wire of anger speared down his backbone, raced along his nerves. The Gypsy's impassive face was like a challenge. No. Like an insult. The careful mask was classifying Stepovich as not human, as a blue uniform with shiny buttons, filled with rules and laws and legal technicalities. During the day, he would have expected it. But somehow, by night, out of uniform, on this deserted street, for the reason he had come here, it was the worst kind of insult.

Anger won, or perhaps humiliation. He flipped the knife, a hard practiced movement, so that it struck the Gypsy's breast hilt first and then clattered to the pavement. And still the Gypsy moved not at all, though Stepovich would have sworn that he could have caught the knife in midair and returned it blade first if he had chosen to do so. So Stepovich spoke, broke the silence with hard cutting words, as cold and callous as he could make them. "We found a dead gypsy granny today. Stabbed to death in a cheap hotel. Don't suppose you'd know anything about something like that."

For a long time the Gypsy didn't speak. Stepovich listened to his own words hang in the air between them, the vocalization of the law-thing the Gypsy's mask had invoked.

"With this knife," the Gypsy said at last.

Music in the voice, accent of a homeland whose existence was lost in the shadows of time. And accusation, it seemed to Stepovich.

"You asking if I offed her," said Stepovich, "the answer is no. But I suspect you'd have a line on whoever did. Not that you'd tell me anything. But maybe you won't have to. Whoever did it left behind plenty of sign. Before noon tomorrow, we'll know the size and shape of the weapon, and a hell of a lot about the man who used it, right down to his blood type." Bluff, you're bluffing, Stepovich, and that Gypsy knows it. Look into his black, black eyes and see how he despises you.

"You find the one who held the knife," and again the accent

left Stepovich wondering if the words were a request, a command, or merely a question, a comment.

"Damn right we will," he growled, and felt himself grow smaller with the lie. "With or without any help from you," and he tried not to let the last sound like a plea.

The Gypsy moved, very slightly, looking down at his own hands which opened and clenched, and opened again, as if he were making sure they were empty. "I have nothing to give you." He stooped in an unconcerned way, picked up the knife carefully, as if it were dirty with unspeakable filth. "I wish you had been more careful with this. But you didn't know what you had. The fault rests between us." His eyes moved in his face, and it was as if his whole body had shifted, as if he looked at Stepovich from another place and time. "It isn't a comfortable harness to share, is it?" There might have been kindness in those black eyes, or pity, or maybe just a stray glint from a street lamp. The Gypsy moved his hands, and the sheathed knife was gone, secreted somewhere on his person.

"You knew she'd been murdered?" Stepovich asked, groping after professional suspicion. "You knew the old woman?"

"I guessed only that a friend had been killed. Nothing more."

"You didn't know her?"

The Gypsy looked disoriented. "What was her name?"

"Which one? She had ID for four different ones, and two social security cards. Rosa Stanilaus? Cynthia Kacmarcik? Molly Kelly?" He uttered the last name with heavy sarcasm, but the Gypsy appeared not to notice any change in his voice. He tipped his head to one side, as if he were listening to some other voice.

"No," he said, and it did not seem to be in answer to any of Stepovich's queries. "She left no message for me." Statement? Question?

Stepovich felt an insane desire to laugh. "Only the crystal. And all it said was, 'Find out who killed me.' " The words were out before he could curb them. Shit. That had been stupid. The crystal was just the kind of detail Homicide might hold back, might reserve to test who knew it was in her purse and who didn't. And he must have sounded like an idiot, voicing the words from his dream.

But this Gypsy was nodding, as if it was something he had

expected, but was not glad to hear. Nodding and turning and walking away from him. Stepovich watched him go, his dark shape fading into the night and his footsteps were lost in the sound of the wind blowing trash down the street.

And then it was suddenly late, very late at night, and Stepovich shivered. His jacket was too thin for this cutting wind. He wondered how long he'd been standing there. As he walked back to the corner where he'd parked his Dodge, he was thinking that tomorrow was a day off, and that Ed had asked him to meet him. If he had the time. As if time wasn't the only the thing he had.

As he walked back to the car, he felt strangely light. Not lighthearted, but unburdened. He was opening the car door before he realized what it was. The weight of the knife was no longer dragging at his pocket.

## NEAR MIDNIGHT

I only want to stop and rest,
Don't want to start no fight;
I'll just stay here for a while
'Til the police car's out of sight.

"RED LIGHTS AND NEON"

The Wolf stood bristling and growling, as surprised to find Cigány in its path as Cigány was to find it. *That is what I must remember,* he told himself. *It is frightened of me, and will not attack unless I show fear or threaten it.* The unbidden voice of his grandmother from long ago added, *Or it is desperately hungry.* The Wolf growled again, daring Cigány to show fear. Cigány held himself still and met the Wolf's gaze until the growling subsided a little.

He became aware that his knife had appeared between his feet, and realized that the Wolf must have brought it. Why? How? The Wolf growled some more and Cigány spoke softly, soothingly. It seemed that the Wolf was questioning him, asking him for help, for guidance.

Cigány said, "Yes, this is my knife, you are right to bring it to me."

The Wolf growled again, puzzled. Cigány struggled to explain as much as he could. "The Fair Lady held the knife. You find Her servant and the old woman will have peace. I cannot help you. Or perhaps I can. I don't know." The Wolf growled again, angry or frustrated, and Cigány said, "I would give you what I have, but I have nothing. Should there come a time, I will feed your pack, with my body if need be. What more can I offer?"

The Wolf seemed to consider this. Cigány picked up the knife and shuddered as he did so. He could feel the cold touch of Luci's fingers on it, and he knew that this knife had killed the old woman. He stared at the Wolf, wondering, but wolves do not kill with knives. Although he could have wished the Wolf would have found it sooner or kept it safer. The Wolf's head twisted, as if it could sense Cigány's discomfort. "No," he said. "You have not known how to keep it from Her hand. It is a knife made from the iron at the heart of the world, iron that never saw the light of day before it was forged; how are you, wolf-brother, to know the care one must take of it? You have done what you could and I do not blame you."

There was a blurring and a sundering and a tearing, and the Wolf was gone; in his place was, once more, the policeman Cigány had known he was from the beginning. "Did you know she was slain?" the policeman demanded.

Cold shivers raced down Cigány's spine. Yes, he almost answered. *In my dreams, I knew.* Instead he said, "I knew someone died—someone who was bound to me, though I don't know how."

"You didn't know her?"

Know? What does "know" mean? "What was her name?" he said, stumbling to answer.

The policeman snorted and listed several, none of which meant anything to Cigány. He shook his head, wondering desperately how to escape. Why was this man asking about his dreams? How was he to parry questions that the policeman could not have known enough to ask? And it is one thing to set tasks to a dream wolf one meets on a city street; it is quite another to do so for a policeman. Dreams are real to one, not to the other. All Cigány could think of was, this man can confine me again. I'll not let him. I will kill him if I have to. No. I will not. I cannot. By my lost brothers, what am I to do?

The policeman was demanding help, but what help could he give? Was he supposed to lay the burden of his life on this man?

But he thought about the dreams, and the old woman who had spoken to him. *Had she said anything I could pass on to the old Wolf to satisfy him? No, she left no message for me. What can I—*

But the policeman was speaking again. "Only the crystal," he said, as if answering a question Cigány hadn't asked. Or had he? "And all it said was, 'Find out who killed me.' "

A crystal? The woman told fortunes with them, perhaps, but how could that . . . still. The bargain was plain. He had been given his life and freedom by the policeman on the condition that he discover who had killed the old woman. It was fair, he decided, since she'd been killed with his knife, and, moreover, since she'd as much as told him her death had prevented his, and allowed him to continue his quest.

He nodded, looking the policeman in the eye to secure the bargain, and walked away. He was well around the corner before it came to him that a policeman, not a Wolf, had returned him the knife, and that policemen *can* use knives to kill old women. He shuddered there, in the dark next to the cemetery, and he hurried on.

## LATE TWENTIETH CENTURY, AFTERNOON

Been looking for a sparrow
In a city full of wrens,
Been asking for the cost
So I can make amends,
Been waiting for the questions
So my answers will make sense,
Been looking for the way home
But the snow is much too dense.

"NO PASSENGER"

Maybe it was a mistake to stay sober, for this was certainly not the coach.

Ten years ago their language would have been giggles; now it was full of strange words and hints of things these two couldn't know enough to hint about. But it was really no different. Fourteen? Fifteen? Sixteen? Wishing they were eighteen, which was the age at which they would be trying to be twenty-two. And they were dressed—how? What did it mean here and now? What had it ever meant? Maybe it was a mistake to stay sober, for this was certainly not the coach.

He climbed into the driver's seat, pretending that he was climbing up high on top, above the count and his current mistress, who sat inside, below, with the curtains pulled against the wind from the mountains and—

But never mind. The horses knew him by now, and Bunny's ears flicked back as he spoke to them. Bunny liked his voice, had liked it the first time they'd met. Stallone was slower, but her neck came up high, like a feeble old grandmother who pretends, for a moment, to her former pride and health. Heh.

There were only the five of them, Bunny, Stallone, and two children as he set off; and, of the five, the two passengers were in their own world, one of cars and boys and stolen cigarettes. He picked up their names from their conversation, but said nothing because they didn't speak to him, and habit is habit, and a job is a job, even if a ride through the park isn't a race against a mountain storm.

"Hey, driver," said the one called Sue. "Can't you make this thing go any faster?"

"Yes," he said, "I can." But he didn't. The question made him realize how much he enjoyed these occasional chances at the seat; he wouldn't risk them for the likes of these.

"Oh come on," said the other one. "Let's really move."

For a moment, something almost snapped, but he held it back. Every time the young "driver" (he couldn't be called a coachman) let him use his "rig" (it couldn't be called a coach) two or three customers would try to make him race the horses, or attempt to bribe him to take them off the regular path. He was always tempted, but he held it back.

The one called Sue began to abuse him, but he stopped listening. The wife of one of his old masters used to do that, two or three times a week, when he refused to take the Bobolos Trail (which his master had forbidden). He was good at ignoring abuse.

But he heard the other one say, "Oh, cut it, Sue. It's his job."

There was a sound like Bunny made when she got food in her nose. "Some job. Shit. Driving snotty assholes around the park all day."

The Coachman remained impassive.

"It's probably all he can get. Right, mister?"

That called for an answer. "It is what I do," he said.

"What," said Sue. "You can't get a taxi gig, so you do this?"

"I am the Coachman," he said.

"So?"

"I am the Coachman."

"Is that s'posed to mean something?"

"My horses are called Vision, Experience, Wisdom, and Love. By the skills of my hands I hold the reins of Will and Desire. I will take you by roads that climb and fall, twist and go straight."

He was no longer speaking to them, didn't care if they listened, or even if they could hear him. "Sometimes the horses try to run wild, and I fight them, or let them run, as may be. Sometimes they go where I guide them, and I can bring you to places of which you have never dreamed, or perhaps you have. Sometimes you, in the coach, may direct me, and then I will bring you where you wish. Perhaps you will be glad to arrive.

"But, always and ever, I drive the coach.

"I am the Coachman. You are here. Ten dollars, please."

He watched sadly as they walked away after paying him and even tipping him a quarter. Across the path, a man who was far too old for them watched them leave with an intensity that, in another place and time, would have gotten him hanged. But this was here and now. The Coachman reached down into the seat for his bottle, thought better of it, shook his head and went around to scratch Bunny between her ears.

"I am the Coachman," he told her.

She nodded.

# Four

THE WOLF AND THE BADGER

12 NOV 13:31

**Can't take the aggravation; I'm tired to the bone.**
**I'm sick of watching cable and sleeping here alone.**

"STEPDOWN"

The park was a pleasant place, still. The neighborhood around it was declining, and the people walking the paths and the mothers pushing babies in strollers reflected the change, but the park itself—the plantings, the grass, the pond—seemed immune to the changing fortunes of the economy. More swings were vandalized, perhaps, and the ducks more wary of stone throwers, but the park itself was still nice. Cold. Quiet, this time of the morning.

Stepovich found a bench and sat, facing the play equipment. A small boy dug determinedly in the sandbox, despite the cold and the snow. A couple walked by the pond. The swings hung slack and empty. He could remember sitting on one of those swings, holding Jeffrey and swinging. And singing. Old songs, the same old songs his dad had sung to him. And Jennie and Laurie feeding the ducks, pretending they didn't know the strange man who was belting out "Barnacle Bill The Sailor" to the little kid on his lap, swinging high and pumping his legs to carry them even higher.

For one aching instant, he wondered if Jeffrey could remember any of that. Jeffrey had been so small. Stepovich reached back into himself, trying to see where his own memories of his father began. But he couldn't put a date to it. Big hands. That's what he thought of when he remembered his father. Big hands, with the thick nails rounded off short. Big hands that could swing him up to touch his head against the ceiling, but could also tie his shoelaces in double knots that wouldn't come undone. He looked at his own hands, and wondered if Jeffrey would ever remember them.

He glanced from his hands to the ground. Two small sneakers faced him. He looked up to find the sandbox kid regarding him steadily with confident brown eyes. "Push me," he said, and then turned and ran toward the swings. Stepovich didn't move. The boy grabbed the chain of one swing, rattled it impatiently. Stepovich pulled himself to his feet, wondering why, and obediently came to help the boy get into the swing. He pushed him, small pushes at first, and then as he laughed aloud and kicked out his short legs, harder. Then, "Down, down," he was saying, and Stepovich caught at him, slowing the swing's momentum, catching boy and swing and easing them to a stop. The kid jumped from the swing, his shirt pulling out of his jeans.

"Merry-go-round," he announced, and reached up for Stepovich's hand.

"A moment, little man," he said, and knelt to tug the boy's shirt straight and pull his jeans back up over his shirt tail. The boy wriggled in his hands, giggling as if tickled.

"Get up, you son of a bitch!"

Stepovich came up from his knee in a controlled spin that put him face to face with the male half of the duck-feeding couple. He had muscular arms and a punk's spoiled face and he was still trying to look tough as he stepped back from Stepovich. "Touch my kid's pants again, I'll kill you, asshole," he snarled. Stepovich glanced past him, habit of a career, keep the eyes moving, and spotted the woman, still clutching her bag of bread. She was watching the scene with neither fear nor anxiety, but absorption, as if it were her two o'clock soap. Stepovich's eyes went back to punk dad, locked there. He kept his face impassive as he said, "The kid's shirt was untucked."

"Yeah, I'll bet it was," Dad sneered, rocking away as if he knew how deep and still the other's anger was. He sidestepped Stepovich at a distance he probably believed was out of fist range and glared at the kid. "You, Jamie. Didn't I tell ya never to let no one touch you?" You let that old faggot shove his hands down your pants?"

Jamie's eyes went from bright to confounded. Much like Stepovich, the boy could think of nothing to say.

"You get your ass over to your mother. Right now." And as the boy scrambled away, Dad put his fists on his hips and swelled his chest. "I oughta kick your ass for touching my kid.

I catch you hanging out around here again, I just might, old man."

"I wasn't molesting your child," Stepovich spoke softly. "But if you want to try kicking my ass, feel free." Little bits of anger, floating loose for days, at Durand for answering the phone wrong and always being such a dumbshit pup, at the old gypsy woman for dying so ugly, at the Gypsy for not knowing or giving him the answers to who had killed her, all the little bits of anger were coalescing in him, not hot, but cold and uncaring. He'd rip him a new asshole. He'd make him bleed, not the easy blood from nose and cheekbones, but the deep blood that comes out over the tongue and chokes a man with his own salt.

Punk Dad took a step back. "There's laws in this town about people like you. We don't like your kind."

"It's mutual," Stepovich said softly. His hand went slowly to his jacket pocket, groping after the knife as he set his balance and waited. A smile he didn't feel gripped his face and twisted his mouth.

Something in punk Dad's face changed when Stepovich smiled at him. His own sneer faded, to be replaced with an uncertain fear. A fear that blustered. "You touch me, I'm calling a cop."

Stepovich had started to lift his foot for the step towards him when the horn sounded. No little import car toot, but the deep throated bellow of the all-American Cadillac. The punk glanced toward it as he was backing away and Stepovich's eyes instinctively followed.

Ed. In his goddamn baby blue land-yacht. The window glided down and Ed leaned out. Even across the distance, his dark brown eyes locked with Stepovich's and drew his anger out like a poultice draws poison from a wound. The couple and the kid were gone, the father hurrying them down the pond walkway and Stepovich was halfway to the car before he had his next thought. He felt just wakened from a dream. He took his hand from his pocket, half-surprised to find it empty.

As he got in the passenger side, Ed demanded, "What was that all about?"

"Damned if I know," Stepovich replied, settling back in the seat and stretching his legs out. One thing this car had was room. Lousy gas mileage, and a dinosaur in a parking garage, but roomy. Ed toed the gas pedal and they glided away from the curb.

"I didn't even recognize you for a minute, back there, you know," Ed pushed.

"Yeah. Me neither." The car interior was warm after the morning's brisk air. It smelled of car wax and spice from the little tree-shaped car deodorizer and Ed's pipe tobacco. Stepovich leaned back into it as if it were a summer hammock. "Sometimes," he said conversationally, "I feel like an old bull elephant. One the young males have driven out of the herd. And any time I get close at all to the females or the young, they turn on me. Instinctively. You ever feel anything like that?"

"You need a few days off, Mike," Ed told him.

"I need a few days off like you need a few days of work."

"Well, maybe that's true, too. So why don't we combine them. You take a week off and help me do a little work on this baby, and then go fishing on the lake. Or maybe get out of Ohio all together. I know a kid in Michigan, in the U.P., who said he could get me a special rate on cabins on Black Lake."

"What you doing to this car now?" Stepovich asked idly. Not that he was actually considering Ed's plans. But it was easier to distract him into talking about the Caddy than it was to argue with him.

"Automatic dimmer switch. See, it's a two person thing. I'm supposed to be able to set it on automatic, and then it dims when it senses oncoming headlights, and goes back to bright after they're past."

Ed was lighting his pipe, a nerve-wracking juggling of steering wheel, pipe, tobacco and lighter. Stepovich looked out the window and reminded himself of all the times their squad car had survived the pipe-lighting ritual, and observed, "You had the Caddy dealer adjust that a month ago."

"Yeah, well, they didn't get it right," Ed replied testily.

"Oh." The dealership never got anything right according to Ed. He was always redoing adjustments he'd just had them make.

"No. It dims way too late. So, what I need is someone outside the car, to set off the dimmer switch with a light, while I'm inside doing the adjustment. Won't take long, I promise. And then we can go fishing."

It would take four hours, if it didn't take all day. The Caddy was an older model, a pre-gas-crisis dinosaur among cars and Ed's pride and joy. He insisted that everything in it had to work perfectly, not just the power windows and the clock, but the automatic dimmers and the adjustable steering column and the hydraulic load levelers and the button in the glove compartment that opened the trunk from inside the car. Sometimes Stepovich got tired just thinking about all the gadgets in the damn car. And there wasn't a one that Ed hadn't taken apart and put back together. He was always saying that when he got it running perfectly, he was going to take off, crisscross the U.S., see the whole country.

"Well," said Ed. "What about the fishing?"

Stepovich half turned in his seat. "There's this gypsy," he said, not even knowing that he was going to to say it. But once he had started he told him, not just what had happened, but all of it: The knife and the dream and the creepy feeling and the crystal in the old gypsy woman's bag. By the time he had finished, they were pulling into the parking lot of the Shamrock Bar and Grille. Ed stopped the car and turned the key and the gentle vibration of the engine ceased. He looked across at Stepovich.

"Well?" asked Stepovich after a long pause.

"I think you need to go fishing," Ed replied.

They got roast beef on rye and potato salad and dark Becks to go with it and the sweet hot mustard-horseradish spread that was the Shamrock's only claim to fame. They sat in a high-backed booth with red leather on the seats and ate as they had eaten when they were partners, companionably, without speech, giving their attention to the food and trusting some other parts of themselves to pay attention to whatever problem was currently besieging them. Occasionally Stepovich stole a glance at Ed. He hadn't changed that much. A little thicker, his chest merging into his belly. Less hair, and what there was getting grayer. Same snapping dark eyes. Eyes that could ask one question while Ed was asking a suspect another, and half the time the guy would end up answering both questions before he'd thought about it. A good cop and a better friend.

Stepovich went for two more Becks, and when he sat down, Ed asked, "You want I should look into it a little?"

"How?"

"Turn over a few rocks, shake out a few people who used to know things for me. Ask some tactless questions in ways you aren't allowed to ask them. You know."

Stepovich did know. "I don't want you getting your ass in a crack over this," he said.

Ed snorted. "Give me a little credit. But here's the deal. I shake out what you want, then you take a week off and we go fishing. Right?"

"Okay," Stepovich conceded. Some part of him felt relieved, and another part of him felt ashamed to have dragged Ed into this. Over what. Over a bad dream and a peculiar feeling.

"Feeling guilty?" Ed read him, and Stepovich nodded sheepishly.

"Good." Ed grinned wickedly. "We can spend the rest of the day adjusting my automatically adjusting dimmers."

## AFTERNOON

I got no home I can go back to,
I got no one to call a friend.
I can't find the place I started.
I can only guess how it will end.

"HIDE MY TRACK"

*They almost caught you*, said the Voice. *They almost caught you, and now they're closing in.*

Timothy moaned and rolled over, pushed damp sheets away from him, and pounded his fist into the pillow. The Voice didn't go away, though; it never did. *They almost caught you*, it repeated. He sobbed.

*Tim*, it said. *Timothy. Little Timmy.*

"No!" he cried. He hated being called Little Timmy. He'd always hated that. Little Timmy got pushed around, Little Timmy got beat up, and, most of all, Little Timmy got laughed at.

*Little Timmy*, said the Voice.

He sat up and cried to the air, not caring by this time if the whole building heard him. "If they catch me it's your fault. You said you'd protect me, damn you."

There was a pause, but then the voice inside his skull answered him. *Damn me?* it said. *How redundant.* Timmy felt a shudder go through him, and, more than anything else, he wanted to be away. But it wouldn't let him go. *I disguised you, Timothy. I made you look like someone else, and the police caught him, but he escaped. You were almost found three days ago, Timothy, but I protected you. So you see—*

"You did that?" he spoke to the walls, and there was hysteria in his voice. "I did that. You made me kill an old woman who had never—"

*Shush, Timothy. You tire me. Yes, you killed her, but what took you so long? Was she too strong for you? If you had killed her quickly, they wouldn't be after you. But I acted to protect you. Now I will act again. It is time for you to get up and go out. It is no longer enough to count on your police, Timothy. You must act yourself.*

He sat on the bed and looked at his hands. There was a power there, as there was a power in the Voice. His stomach churned once more as he thought of the old woman, her eyes bright with anger and pride and hate, and he felt the fear in his bowels as she had struck the gun from his hand, and then he'd been holding a knife, and where had it come from? And where did it go?

"What must I do?" he said.

*The knife has fallen from our hands, and we could not use it against him in any case. You must get your gun. I will tell you what to do with it.*

He still sat at the edge of the bed and stared at his hands. "Why are you doing this to me?" he asked.

To his surprise, she answered.

*Because I can, Little Timmy.*

## MID-AUTUMN, AFTER SUNRISE

I keep finding hands to help me with the load
So I'll keep walking further up this road.

"UP THE ROAD"

Early morning: Cigány sat cross-legged in his hidey-hole beneath the overpass and stared at the knife. It would need to be cleaned, he knew, before he could fully trust it again. Until it was, it could draw the Fair Lady to him, and who knew what form the attack would take? He was not invulnerable, he knew that. He had lived a long time because of his wits, and skill, and luck, but now the Fair Lady had seen him, and he Her, and the battle was joined in earnest, and he knew that She had the power to destroy him if he wasn't careful.

Death didn't frighten him, but the idea that he could die after all of those forgotten years, and all of that heartache and pain; this was not to be borne.

As he stood up, the sun's rays struck him across the face, and he shuddered, knowing that today someone would try to kill him. He made the sign of the cross in the air and looked around for a piece of wood to touch. There were none, so he picked up some gravel and threw it in front of him saying, "May my road be higher than the river and lower than the sun, and may my feet find a safe way home."

He brushed his hands on his shirt and set off, keeping to alleys as much as possible, always staying alert for the police. As he walked he found a clothing store and stole a snakeskin belt (the only snakeskin he could find), pulled a twig from a hazel tree, and begged a small quantity of holy water from a confused priest. He drank a bowl of tasteless soup and a cup of weak coffee at a Howard Johnson's, then continued to forage. As he walked, his vision began to blur, and he felt his headache coming back. He took the piece of paper out of his pocket and tried to remember how the scribbling on it could cure the headache, but it was no good. He laughed grimly to himself. "When my head doesn't hurt," he thought, "I don't think of it, and when it does, I can't read it." He took wheat flour from a grocery store and a white candle from a pharmacy. He took a piece of bark from an oak, and, with the knife, scratched designs of the moon and the stars on the bark.

Armed with these things, he made his way back to his place beneath the overpass and waited for the rising of the full moon of autumn.

## 1980S

They said, "Why are you here?"
I said, "I'm doing time,
'Cause I'm willing to break laws
But I won't commit no crime."

"NO PASSENGER"

It was humiliating to be a coachman and to be forced to ride in a cab; a humiliation only partly alleviated by riding up front, with the driver. Sometimes they wouldn't let you do that, but this man, big and burly like an innkeeper and gnarled like a peasant woman, didn't seem to mind. His nod was an implied shrug, and as the Coachman settled into place he said, "Where to?"

"The bus station," he said. More humiliations in store.

The cab pulled away. "Meeting someone?"

"No, going somewhere."

The driver's frowned for a moment then shrugged. The lack of luggage probably puzzled him. He said, "Where ya going?"

"I'm looking for birds," he said, only coming to realize it as the words were spoken.

"Birds?"

"I have to find a Raven and an Owl before the Dove kills himself."

The driver cleared his throat and twitched nervously, obviously having second thoughts about having this wacko in the front seat. "Whatever you say, buddy," he finally said. They spoke no more during the journey.

13 NOV 09:47

My partner doesn't even know my name.
If he did I think I'd hate him just the same.

"STEPDOWN"

Stepovich wished he were driving. Durand always talked while he drove, and flapped his right hand at Stepovich, as if that were an essential part of talking.

"So the lab guy says, 'Yeah, that bastard drove that knife into her like he was trying to shove it clear to China, but that wasn't the weirdest part of it, though,' so I says, 'Oh, yeah,' kind of casual, and he says, 'No, the weirdest part was the wound configuration. I didn't know what the hell it was, I thought maybe the killer had a defective knife or something, but one of the older guys, he looks at it and says, hey, will you look at the hilt impressions on this wound?' "

The taxicab at the corner barely curtsied to the stop sign before it swung out in front of them. Durand crammed on the brakes and Stepovich's palm slapped the dash as he braced himself.

"Shit," hissed Stepovich, and spent a few futile moments groping for the ends of the seat belt, but as always it was stuffed somewhere in the crevice of the seat back.

"Yeah!" Durand agreed enthusiastically, hardly pausing in his story. "You know, a hilt impression. It's a mark around the knife wound when a blade gets really driven in. This one was really weird. The lab guy tells me the old guy said the knife must be a custom job. It left these three little bruises around the wound, like there were little studs sticking out from the guard. That knife—"

"Durand." Stepovich spoke without looking at him, but his cold tone stopped the story in midsentence. "It's a homicide, isn't it?"

"Well, yeah," Durand sounded sulky.

"Then leave it to the homicide guys. They hate it when guys like us sniff around in their shit. You won't get any thanks for it. No one's going to think you're Sherlock Holmes. Even if you come up with something, you won't get the credit. The only thing you'll get is a reputation as a hotshot boy scout who can't mind his own business. Worse, they're gonna figure you're out to make them look bad, so they're going to devote a little time to making you look bad. Only they're going to be better at it. You're suddenly going to find that you've screwed up any crime scene you're called to, that you've mishandled evidence and handled witnesses all wrong. And that's going to go in your file. You get what I'm saying?" Dumbshit.

"Fuck."

"Yeah," Stepovich agreed, and leaned back, scanning the street and listening to the gabble and hiss of the radio.

"But don't it count for nothing that we were there first, that we found her? And that we probably even had brought them the guy, cause the description from the tenant next door matched our bust. Hell, we had that gypsy, all locked up, and it never woulda happened if some fuckup hadn't cut him loose before . . ."

A sick, cold little animal had gotten into Stepovich's belly, and now it was stretching. He hadn't been listening that closely to Dumbshit's story, and he should have. "You talking about that old gypsy woman? And the guy we'd hauled in from in front of the cemetery, on suspicion of the liquor store killing?"

"Shit, yes! I wouldn't a been pumping the lab guy if I didn't think we had a stake in it, and . . ."

"Say the thing about the knife again," Stepovich cut in, but he didn't really need to hear it again. He could feel it, cold under his thumb as he pressed down on the little stars and wondered what they signified. He hadn't really thought about what kind of marks they would leave when he was sitting on his bed looking at the piece of evidence he hadn't turned in. Hadn't thought of anything at all but getting rid of it. Of returning the damning evidence to the murderer. . . .

"Couldn't have been," he said, suddenly remembering that he'd had the knife when the gypsy woman was killed, that it had been tucked away in the drawer of his night stand. But whoever had one custom blade was likely to have two, or would at least know where the other one had come from, hell, it could be some kind of cult, all of them using the same weapons, and maybe Durand had been right, they'd had the thread that could unravel it the day they'd had that John Doe Gypsy.

"You okay?"

Durand's question was very careful, and Stepovich suddenly realized it had been very quiet in the car for some time. He looked at his hands braced against the dashboard as if to hold off some sudden collision. He forced them to drop down, felt his elbows rubbery with tension. "Just stretching. And thinking. That lab guy, he say anything else?" He stared out at the passing panorama of Cushman Street. Transition blocks. Old hotels that were more like cheap rooming houses now, lobbies full of snoozing winos and the smell of dirty carpets, interspersed with cheap bars and sex show places. LIVE NUDES ON STAGE flashed the sign. Well, hell, at least it didn't say DEAD NUDES ON STAGE. Maybe that would be next week's show. "I mean, was there anything else weird about the killing?" he nudged Durand. Shoulda been listening before, he chided himself.

"Thought you said it wasn't smart to get mixed up in a homicide investigation?" Durand asked coyly.

Stepovich flicked his eyes at his partner, and away. Like Joey Petmann, he suddenly thought. Ted Petmann's little brother, and when Stepovich and Ted were kids and best friends, Joey had followed them everywhere, bugging the shit out of them. But his favorite thing to do had been to get something they wanted, and then hold out on them. Bubble gum or the latest *Blackhawk* comic or a Polaroid picture of Stevie Caldwell's big sister in the bathtub. That's how Durand's face looked right now, just like Joey Petmann's face had looked as he leaned over the edge of the tree fort with the rope pulled up and waved the Polaroid out of reach.

Stepovich turned and looked out the window and said, "Well, those lab guys are taught to be pretty tight-lipped. Probably wouldn't part with anything important anyway. Not to some patrol cop in a bar, anyway. Hey!" Stepovich interrupted as Durand's mouth opened in an "oh, yeah!" face. "Hey! How in hell did Willy get back on the street so soon? I thought Rich and Trope busted him hard for beating one of his girls."

"Where?" Durand demanded, and nearly sideswiped a parked car craning his neck to look back.

"You missed him. Or maybe it wasn't him." Durand hated Willy. The wiry little pimp was meaner than hell, and completely unafraid of cops. No one liked to bust him because Willy had ways of making it unpleasant for the arresting officers. Cut up the upholstery in one squad car. Smeared the chili burger he was eating down another cop's uniform. Rumor had it he'd taken a dump in the back seat of Kelly's patrol car. And the first time Durand had collared him, Willy stuck his finger down his throat and threw up all down the front of him. The guy was crazy.

"Where was he?" Durand demanded again. His bottom teeth clamped against his upper lip. Looked like a bulldog. Tenacious as one, too.

"Hell, he's gone now. You want to take a coffee break pretty soon?" Stepovich smiled at him.

"I guess." Durand kept glancing in the rearview mirror, and then over at Stepovich, as if unable to decide which to pursue. "There was one other weird thing about the dead gypsy woman," he offered.

"Yeah? Well, turn left at the next light and go about six blocks, get us out of this hole. I don't wanta get served by some waitress that probably gives hand jobs on the side. Let's go to Norm's, okay? It's clean and cheap."

"I mean, the knife was weird enough, you know, but it gets weirder," Durand offered desperately.

Hey, Joey, we don't wanta see your stupid Polaroid. We got a whole *Playboy* at our fort, and it's fulla pictures of *real* girls, not somebody's sister. Stepovich flicked a glance at Durand. "Yeah?" he offered, then, "Or we could go to that new place, the one the Korean guy opened on Fifteenth. I hear it's clean. You been there yet?"

"No. Uh, Norm's let's go to Norm's. But there was something weird about that killing. I mean, besides the knife with the little studs. Four separate stab wounds, I tell you that? Every one right to the hilt. Lab guy says the first one was the fatal one. She musta known she was already dead, but she kept on fighting. Can you beat that?"

"Mean old ladies are like that. Harder to kill than cats." Stepovich knew he just had to wait now and he'd get all that Durand had.

"Maybe. Yeah, maybe. But stuff had been done to the body."

Stepovich was silent, a little sick. What could she have done to make someone want to kill her? And what kind of a person could push a knife into another human being, not just once, to kill her, but over and over as she was struggling and dying? He thought of the Gypsy with his black unreadable eyes and empty face. Could you do it, he asked the image in his mind, and the Gypsy in his mind shrugged his wide shoulders and told him nothing.

"Not rape. It wasn't anything like that. Someone had cut a lock of hair from the back of her head, down underneath at the nape of her neck."

"Souvenir?"

"Maybe. Or maybe proof that a job had been done."

Stepovich shook his head wearily. "Lock of grey hair is too generic. They'd have taken something more personal, a piece of jewelry, something like that. Sounds like a souvenir to me."

Or a cult killing of some kind, some kind of a crazy with a special knife who kills her and takes a lock of her hair, some kind of a wacko. Or a very personal revenge of some kind. Or a total crazy, with no reasons at all, only impulses. The Gypsy in his mind was smiling secretively now. That day they busted him, he hadn't even seemed sure of his name. Chuck maybe, but he wasn't sure, so they'd made him John Doe. Man like that, couldn't remember his own name, maybe he wouldn't remember what he'd done the day before. Maybe he'd look in Stepovich's face and seem baffled and innocent.

"Here's Norm's."

And he'd sent Ed after him, to look at things a little. Great, Stepovich. Don't just fuck your career up by withholding evidence, and then turning over what might be a murder weapon to some whacked-out gypsy by a cemetery. Go ahead and drag Ed into it, send him out to look for someone who was probably psycho, who'd probably cut up your old buddy and take a hair sample when he was through. Great. Some cop you are.

"We going in, or what?"

"What?"

"You want to get a cup of coffee here?"

They were parked outside Norm's, Stepovich noticed belatedly. He wondered if Tiffany Marie was working, hoped she wasn't. She always looked so damn glad to see him. He didn't want to deal with any kid grinning and chattering at him right now. He shouldered the door open, nearly banging it into the parking meter, and stumbled out. He felt as if he'd been asleep and had suddenly wakened. Durand was looking at him funny. He restrained the impulse to glare back, and followed him into Norm's. They claimed a couple of stools at the counter and ordered coffee. "Back in a second," Stepovich told Durand, and headed for the phone. Time to start cleaning up the mess he'd made.

Ed's phone rang. Four. Five. Six. "Hello." Pissed voice.

"Ed, it's me. Listen. About that little thing I asked you to look into. Don't bother. It's fizzled out into nothing, no big deal. No sense you messing with it."

"For this I come in all the way from the garage? To hear you tell me to forget it, it's nothing. Shit. Just when I thought I had a hot tip for you, too. Hey. Guess what? This is gonna make you laugh but it ain't really funny. I opened the trunk of the Caddy this morning, and you know what I find? A big hole in the carpeting. I look around a little more, and I find this wad of paper and fiber in the spare tire well. A mouse nest. I got a mouse living in my car. Chewed the hell out of the carpeting in the trunk and I think part of the nest is made from my upholstery stuffing, so God knows how much damage it's done. Pretty weird, huh?"

Weird? Weird is cutting a lock of hair off the nape of a dead granny's neck. Weird is killing someone with a knife with little stars on the hilt that leave telltale bruises. "That's pretty strange, all right. Set a trap for him, Ed. What was this hot tip, anyway?"

"Hell, nothing probably. Guy I got it from's been doing coke so long that he's only got three brain cells left and none of them connect to the others. Told me something about a guy driving a horsedrawn cab in the parks on Sundays when the regular guy's off. According to him, this guy probably knows every gypsy in the city. But he also says he's usually drunk. People been complaining about him because he don't always keep the cab on the right path, you know. Guess they caught him on the bike trail one day. Regular guy's called Spider. Has a rig with two horses, a grey and a brown. Anyway. You coming over Saturday night? Game's on at six. You bring the beer, we'll have spaghetti."

"Yeah. I guess so. Hey, thanks, Ed. Sorry this came to nothing like this."

"Yeah. Me, too. That info cost me ten bucks, pal. But I'll

forget it if you bring some munchies to go with the beer. Hey, why not bring your kid? Jeff's old enough to watch a game now."

And Jennie had warned him that she'd have his visitation rights reviewed the first time he started taking the kids around any of his "cop buddies." "Not this time, Ed. He asks too many questions. Maybe another time. We'll see you."

"Okay. And if I get any more back on the feelers I sent out, I'll let you know."

"Forget it, Ed. It's dead, come to nothing, I told you."

"Sure. Go ahead, treat me like an old man. I can still kick your ass, if it comes down to cases. Tell Durand I said hi. And lighten up on the kid. He's not that bad. Not too different from someone else I knew as a rookie."

"Bullshit," Stepovich told him, and hung up. Damn Ed and his instincts.

He went back to the counter, sat down heavily on the stool. Durand held up his coffee cup and a passing waitress gave him a refill. "Tiffany's not working today?" he asked her. She shook her head, went on without speaking. Stepovich sipped at his own still-brimming cup. It was lukewarm and on the bitter side.

"Know what?" Durand said.

"What?" He tore open two sugar packets and stirred them in.

"I think we should go back to that bar where we picked up the gypsy. He might be a regular there, they might be able to tell us where to find him."

"Waste of time." He tasted the coffee.

"Maybe not. I really think he was our man. And if not, I suspect he's a lead. I'd like another look at that knife."

Stepovich's cup rattled as he set it back in the saucer. He centered the cup carefully, mopped up the few spilled drops and motioned the waitress for more. The cold little beast in his belly was sharpening his claws now. He didn't dare ask, couldn't stop himself. "What knife?"

"Gypsy had a knife when we shook him down. You don't remember it?"

"Whoa, that's plenty. Thanks," and he motioned the waitress off. Added another packet of sugar, hoping that keeping his hands busy would cover the slight trembling. "No," he lied carefully, and lifted his cup. It tapped against his teeth twice before he had it steady and could sip at it. Hot.

"Sure you do. Knife in a leather sheath, we took it off him by the cemetery . . ."

Stepovich borrowed the Gypsy's eyes to look at Durand. Empty eyes. No expression in them, no clues, no betrayal. "I don't even remember him having a wallet." That much of the truth for Durand.

"No. No, he didn't that I remember, either. But I woulda sworn that when we shook him down, he had a knife."

"We didn't turn one in when we booked him." Another little bit of the truth.

"No. Hey, that's right, we sure as hell didn't. Crap. I wonder if we just went off and left it laying there on the sidewalk."

"I doubt it. I really think we would have noticed a knife lying on the sidewalk." Funny. The lies and half truths weren't getting any easier. Sure, this was Dumbshit, and Stepovich didn't owe Dumbshit anything. But he was also his partner. And the one thing any cop owed his partner was the truth. Not bits of it, but the whole truth. Especially when what he was lying about was something that could get his partner written up, too. The one thing that had to be true between cops was that your partner would put it on the line for you. If you didn't believe that, it didn't work.

And it doesn't work, Stepovich realized as he took another long sip of bitter coffee. Not because I don't think Durand wouldn't put it on the line for me. But because I'm not sure if I'd do it for him. I'd face down a gun barrel for Ed, kid. But maybe not for you. Not cause you're such a Dumbshit either. But just because I don't want to give a damn about you.

That was a dirty little thought, one that made him feel slimy and selfish.

Durand had been chewing on the cuticle beside his thumbnail all this time. Evidently this had helped him reach some sort of decision, because he now announced, "You're probably right. Probably there wasn't a knife. Maybe I got him mixed up with that other guy. Hey. I told Dispatch we were only taking ten or so. Gotta be getting back to the car, Step."

"Sure." He paid for their coffees and left the tip. Feeling guilty as hell, he walked out behind Durand. There were already too many people that he cared about, and he wasn't doing any of them any damn good. Why add Durand to the list?

He had a sense of crossing another line. The first had been not turning the knife in. The second had been giving it back to the Gypsy. And now he was holding out on his partner. Last month he'd have punched anyone who'd insinuated he could do such things. But now he was doing them, getting farther and farther out, and he couldn't really see how to get back to where he should be. It was like when Jennie had divorced him, when he'd had to go out and find his own place and start taking care of only himself. Come home to an empty place, just the sound of the toilet running because there'd been no one there all day to rattle the handle. "This is all wrong" he'd thought to himself every evening, eating alone, going to bed between cold sheets. This is wrong, this isn't what I signed up for. But he'd kept going, just the same way he kept going if he got off on the wrong freeway exit. Keep going and don't even slow down, because if you do the jerk behind you is going to smash into you and you're going to crash and burn. So just keep going. Look out the window and watch yourself get farther and farther away from where you're supposed to be.

"My turn to drive," he told Durand as they walked around the car. Driving was a hell of a lot easier than thinking.

# Five

## HOW THE RAVEN LOOKED FOR THE DOVE

### MONDAY AFTERNOON

**We left the fires behind us**
**We followed a carriage track,**
**And I'll never see my brothers,**
**But perhaps they made it back.**

"RAVEN, OWL, AND I"

When Daniel had first started working around University and Dale in St. Paul, many years ago, children had thought he was an ice-cream man because of the bell on his truck. They were disappointed when they found out he only sharpened knives, but he won them over. He told them jokes and made coins vanish and by now he was part of the neighborhood. They waved as he came by and he waved back, ringing his bell.

Dumpy Mrs. Holgrim came out of her lower duplex, wearing a dirty white apron like a uniform and holding out today's worthless pieces of cutlery along with one good French chef's knife that she'd been given as a present and didn't know the value of. He pulled the little truck up to the curb and put the parking brake on. He didn't turn off the engine because it had trouble warm-starting. By the time she had reached him, he had picked out the appropriate grade of stone and put some oil on it. She smiled her yellow teeth at him and handed up the knives. He put the first one, a cheap little vegetable knife, on the stone and began to work before he'd even greeted her. Then he said, "How are you today, Mrs. Holgrim?"

"I'm fine, Daniel. Robert's home with a cold, and I'm sure he'll give it to the girls, but there you are."

"Indeed, Mrs. Holgrim."

"How are you, Daniel?"

"Oh, I'm always fine." Mrs. Holgrim nodded, believing it because that was how she thought he always must be. Daniel said, "A poultice of garlic on his feet will cure the cold, Mrs. Holgrim."

"Really?" She looked skeptical. Daniel didn't press the issue. He returned the vegetable knife and started on an equally worthless paring knife. They made small talk for a while, then, as he began to work the steel of the chef's knife, her one good cutting utensil, he said, "You know, Mrs. Holgrim, if I may say so, if you were to learn to use a butcher's steel, you could keep this in fine shape without having it sharpened nearly so often."

Mrs. Holgrim's blue eyes, which were still very pretty, opened wide. "Really, Daniel?"

"Yes, ma'am."

"Why haven't you told me this before?"

He returned the knife to her and accepted two dollars per knife plus a one-dollar tip. He wiped his hands on his shirt, the oil blending into the moss green. "Because, Mrs. Holgrim, then you wouldn't have needed me to sharpen your knives for you."

Her mouth dropped open, closed again. She seemed to think about getting angry, but finally said, "Then why are you telling me now?"

"Because I won't be here."

"Won't—where are you going?"

"I'm not sure. I won't know until the driver comes, but I think it's somewhere in the midwest. Ohio, I believe. Or Indiana."

"You don't know?"

"No, I only know that it is time to pick up my fiddle and find my brothers. Good afternoon, Mrs. Holgrim."

Daniel continued down the street, ringing his bell.

## AUTUMN EVENING, FULL MOON

Scarf wound tight around my head
To keep hair from my eyes;
My knife would cut deeper
Then I could realize.

"RAVEN, OWL, AND I"

". . . And the captain told me, 'My whole crew's a bunch of yo-yos.' Well, I didn't give it another thought until we were halfway back to the States and we hit an iceberg. The ship sank." Pause. "Sixty-five times." There was some scattered laughter as the large comedian shook his head sadly, and crossed the stage.

He stopped in front of a small, attractive woman at a front table. He puckered his lips obscenely for a moment, then said, "Hey, cutie, wanna go halfsies on a baby?" This got more laughs than the ship joke had.

The gypsy, who had forgotten his name, sat in back, wondering how he'd gotten there. He found little humor in the comic, J. J. McNair, yet he appreciated the skill of the storyteller. He admired the comedian's timing and ability to read the audience. How? Why did he know these things when he couldn't remember his name? He remembered being called "Little One," but that wasn't right. And how had he gotten here? The last thing he could remember clearly was performing a ritual over his knife, to purify it. He knew it had worked, but why had it been necessary?

The comic was saying, "I'm a great lover, honey. I am. Really. I taught myself." A bit more laughter. "I bought a complete sex manual and I've been following it. I'm up to page eighty-three. It says, 'Get a partner.' " He raised his eyebrows lewdly while the audience laughed, more at the woman's obvious embarrassment than at the jokes.

McNair wasn't bad. It was not a sort of storytelling the observer was used to, yet it made him unaccountably homesick. Homesick for—

For—

A voice, that's all it was. A melodious, half-drunken voice that told stories with an ironic bite to them, for all their seriousness. Tales of fairies and heroes, and he, the "Little One," had listened eagerly and believed them. He remembered the champing of horses, the ringing of the bridle loops like the tinkling of the zils of the tambourine. He remembered the black horses, and a black coach.

Yes.

And he had learned from that voice. He had learned that if you make a promise, you must *always* carry it out, or else you might have to behead the cow with one horn who had always given you food when you were starving. Yes, you must always keep your promise.

What promise had he given, then? And who *was* he? Gypsy, that's what they called him. The name came back with a certain sense of relief. That wasn't his name, but it was one of them. There were other gypsies, he knew that, but he was the Gypsy. Yes. Now, if he could only remember the promise, and to whom it was made, and if he could only find his brothers. He needed them for—

For—

The comedian was now in front of a group of middle-aged women off to the side of the tiny stage. "I understand one of you ladies is going to have a baby." When they looked confused, McNair added, "I haven't decided which one yet." More laughter. More, decided the Gypsy, than it deserved, but that was because he had the crowd now. All of them, he thought, except me. And that isn't his fault, it's because I don't fit in. I don't belong here. I'm not one of them. I'm—

I'm—

He stood up and made his way to the door. The comedian said, "Hey, buddy, I didn't leave when you showed up." The Gypsy didn't begrudge him the laughter.

The street did not look familiar. It was crowded, and it was evening, and there were lights everywhere racing up and down the buildings, and it came to him as a revelation that these lights were to attract his notice, that they were intended to draw attention to themselves and away from the other lights. As he stood there, a black-and-white police car crossed by in the traffic opposite, and he pulled himself into the shadow of the building from which he'd issued. Memories returned of entering it for just that reason. He had gone this way, aimless, after the purification, because it was empty and deserted. And then, as the sun fell, people emerged from everywhere, as if they sprouted from the sidewalk, and he'd felt the trapped animal fear, and then he'd seen the police car and ducked into this place. What was it called? "Tiny's," that was it. But what reason had he to fear policemen?

Yet, he *did* have a reason. He knew that and believed it. He felt for his knife, hilt tucked into his waistband beneath his shirt, and the cold feel of the grip brought a freshness, and a certain clarity. *Here, take this, little one. I don't need it.* That voice! The same as from the stories. Tears welled up in his eyes, though he could not say why.

The police car was gone, now, and he began walking. A few people stared at him, but only for a moment. He tried to ignore them. He aimed toward places where there were few people, through alleys and side streets. After half an hour, in a more deserted area, he stopped, staring at a street sign. Why? What was it? Something about that street. He stood there until he was afraid he would attract attention to himself, then began walking along it.

The night grew older, and he realized he could see his breath. Was it cold, then? That thought, those actions triggered a vague sense of familiarity. As he walked he noted that the lights were gone now, leaving small brick buildings with plate-glass windows. An hour or so later, these gave way to old houses, most with open porches and heavy doors, collapsing steps and two or three mailboxes.

It came to him that he had stopped; that he hadn't moved for some time. He stared at the house and kept blinking. It had once, perhaps, been yellow or green; it was difficult to be certain in this light. A big porch, two mailboxes, two doors. One door led upstairs. He tried it and it was open. The stairway was very narrow and curved for the last three steps at the top. The hallway here was narrow, too.

He hesitated for what felt like a long time, then, he knocked. He heard a chair shuffling, and heavy, slow footsteps. From the other side: "Yeah, what is it?"

He took a deep breath and said, "Please, let me in. Karen sent me."

The door flew open as if it were being ripped off its hinges, and the Gypsy stared into a pair of cold blue eyes, wide with shock and anger. Around them was a round, clean-shaven face more suited to grins than rage. The hair was well-groomed, and he wore a checked sports shirt unbuttoned over a white tee shirt. He said, "What the fuck do you mean, Karen sent you?"

"Are you Brian MacWurthier?"

"Yeah."

The Gypsy read confusion behind the anger. "Karen sent me. She told me that you had cared well for her, and that I was to see that you were all right, and—"

"When did she say all this?"

"I . . . I'm not certain. Several days ago, I think."

MacWurthier blinked. "Karen is dead." He choked a little as he said it.

"Yes, I know."

"But—"

"I see that you are well, so that is all I was to do. Goodbye."

"Wait a minute!"

The Gypsy turned back, waited. "Yes?"

"I don't get—who are you, anyway?"

"Gypsy."

MacWurthier glanced at his clothing and nodded. "You look it." He blinked. "You must be freezing out there. It can't be much above zero. What's your name?"

"Gypsy," he said. "I think that is my name."

"You don't know your name? You got amnesia or something?"

"Yes. That must be it. But it doesn't matter."

"Well, why did you say I'm all right?"

The Gypsy considered this, then said slowly, "You have been keeping yourself shaved and cleaned, and there is no liquor on your breath. The redness in your eyes is nearly gone. You have passed the worst of your grief, and it won't destroy you."

MacWurthier stared at him. "Man," he said. "This is weird. Well, can you come in for a minute?"

The Gypsy hesitated, then nodded. MacWurthier stepped aside and the Gypsy entered a short hall, with a small kitchen to his left and a small living room on his right. Karen, the ghost, stared at him from a picture on the far wall of the living room, above a matte black stereo system. The place was small and neat, save for a few magazines scattered here and there. The Gypsy read the titles: *Time, Computer World, Datamation.*

"Sit down," said MacWurthier. The Gypsy did so, sitting stiffly at one end of a brown Naugahyde sofa. "Can I get you a beer? Coffee? Coke? Tea?"

"Tea would be nice."

"Sugar?"

"No, thank you."

"All right. Just a sec."

He went into the kitchen. The Gypsy felt Karen's presence in the room, and felt hints and traces, as of a remembered fragrance, of what the two of them had been for each other. There had been anger as well as love here, but the anger had never been violent, and the love had still been strong when Karen had died.

MacWurthier returned with two cups of tea. The Gypsy tasted it. It was black and bitter, but of a good kind. He felt a warmth as it went down his throat that made him wonder if he had, in fact, been cold.

"So, did you meet Karen while she was ill?"

*No, I met her while she was dead.* "Yes."

"She asked you to look after me?"

"She said you cared for her very much, and she was worried."

He swallowed, and there was pain on his face. He would have new lines in a year; he would become older. It was sad. It was inevitable. "Well, thanks."

The Gypsy nodded.

"It was leukemia," MacWurthier continued. "Hell of a thing."

"Yes."

"I think I'll move out of here."

"Perhaps that would be best." As he spoke, his vision began to blur, which meant that soon his headache would return.

MacWurthier continued, "It's hard, you know? All the things we used to do together. Every time I go by the park, I see those horse-drawn cabs we used to ride in, and I almost cry. There was this one guy we used to get on Sundays who'd take us off the main paths. Once we went all the way around Circle Lake."

He was staring off into the distance, but the Gypsy almost dropped his teacup. The vision came to him of the Coachman, thin and dark, cynical and drunken. He must find him. He must.

He dimly heard MacWurthier ask if he had a place to stay the night, but his concentration was elsewhere. He must find the Coachman, and his brothers. Soon.

If only he could remember why.

14 NOV 08:47

They say the weapon vanished, they say the suspect split.
Point your finger somewhere else; I couldn't give a shit.

"STEPDOWN"

"Please," said Stepovich. He felt the word grate up his throat.

Marilyn swung back to look at him reproachfully. "Stepovich, you bastard, that isn't fair!"

"I know," he said. "But it's the only thing I have left, so I'm saying it. Please."

She said nothing as a secretary tip-tapped past them in high heels, but as soon as she was safely out of hearing range, she leaned closer to Stepovich and hissed, "Listen, I know I owe you. And I've said any number of times that I'd make it up to you in any way I could. But I didn't mean something like this! This is bending a lot of rules, Mike. And people like us don't do that. It's one of the reasons we get along so well. So don't ask me."

He clenched his teeth a moment, standing with his head lowered. He knew it wasn't fair. He knew this wasn't the kind of thing she'd meant when she'd promised to pay the favor back. She'd meant dinner at her house, or an evening out at her expense or something else that might have led to places he wasn't ready to go. Not a favor that could lead to her losing her job. So she was upset, not just because he'd asked her for this, but because he'd never asked her for the other. She put her hand on the door of the ladies' room again. He'd deliberately caught Marilyn out in the hall, away from her computer and coworkers. She probably had to go to the john pretty bad, and she'd already told him "no" twice. But he needed help. And he'd been the one to go in and find her nephew in that rat-ridden flophouse, and drag him out and help Marilyn drive him across to Pennsylvania and check him into a drug rehab center. Marilyn wasn't even the kid's legal guardian. They'd bent a rule or two then, and she knew it. He'd sweated day and night for six weeks that the kid was going to have his parents press some kind of kidnapping charges. But Stepovich had done it, because even if it was against the rules, it was still right. And maybe what he was asking of Marilyn was the right thing to do also. Maybe.

"Please."

She spun on him, a transcription clerk with doggie brown eyes, suddenly transformed into a hellcat. She took a step toward him and he involuntarily stepped back, expecting to feel the rake of her nails. But she snatched at his sleeve and pulled him closer.

"Listen!" she hissed, sharp as broken glass. "Give me the damn description, and I'll do a search. Nationwide, if that's what you want, and to hell with my job if someone wonders why I'm using unauthorized link time. But listen, pal, you gotta do something for me, too. And then we're going to call it square and no more favors between us, right?"

Stepovich hated the way this was going. Marilyn wasn't his friend, exactly, but they'd been good at working together, more than acquaintances. She'd thought that he would never ask her to put it on the line for him, not on something like this, anyway. But, damnit, it was the only thing he could think of to do. Bend a few more rules to get himself back on the right track. Bend them so he could clean up the mess he'd made of things with the Gypsy thing. He didn't hesitate to grant her favor, but only asked, "What is it?"

"You put a muzzle on that horny little shit you call a partner, that's what! He's hitting on Tiffany Marie two and three times a week. You tell him she's no whore, not anymore, and he'd damn well better quit treating her like one."

"Okay, okay," Stepovich muttered. He felt like he'd just stepped in dog manure. Durand and Tiffany Marie? Next Dumbshit would be going after the jump–rope and jacks set. Marilyn snatched the carefully wrought description from his hand, and spun away to the rest room. "I'll call you tonight, okay?" he said after her. She gave no sign of hearing him, but he was sure she had. She pushed the door open so hard it bounced off the stopper. He turned away. The day had turned rancid, all its good intentions gone to slickness and deceit.

He knew he'd lost whatever it was they'd shared, mutual respect, whatever it was. She'd never trust him after this, and he'd miss that. But she was the only one he knew who could take his carefully remembered description of the Gypsy and turn it into possible names and criminal histories, without his having to fill out a bunch of forms and official requests.

He stuck his head into the coffee room. The walls were lined with vending machines, and folding tables with singularly uncomfortable attached stools filled the center of the room. Durand was there. He'd solved the stool problem by sitting on the table. He had a cup of coffee steaming next to him and was trying to coax a Twinkle out of its wrapper. "Durand! Let's go!" was all Stepovich said, and then continued down the hall. He heard his partner's protesting cry of, "Hey, just a second . . . ," but he didn't pause. He picked up their shotgun and radio and went outside into a sulking grey morning and down the back steps.

He found their assigned car for the day and did his standard walkaround, looking for unreported scratches and dents that the previous shift might have left on the car. It was okay. The bright blue shield on the door said, LAKOTA POLICE DEPARTMENT, and under it, TO PROTECT AND TO SERVE. He grimaced. Once, he and Ed had painted over the shield on Richart's unit the motto, OVER 4 MILLION BUSTED. It didn't seem so funny anymore.

He unlocked the back door and jerked out the seat, checking under it for any little goodies the last passengers might have left behind. Once he'd found half a gram of coke under the seat, and another time there'd been a zip gun. Stepovich didn't believe in leaving anything to chance. Never assume the night shift had checked under the seats.

He'd finished his inspection and put the back seat in and was behind the wheel before Durand came outside. Durand got in, shaking hot coffee from his fingers. Stepovich glanced at him briefly before turning the key. "Wipe the Twinkie cum off your chin," he told him in disgust as he slammed the car into gear.

Durand scrubbed guiltily at a smear of white frosting before demanding, "What the hell's eating you?" He slurped coffee from a paper cup.

Stepovich gunned the engine to see if he could make Dumbshit spill coffee on himself. No luck. "Nothing. You got to talk all the time? Can't we ever just shut up in here?"

"Sure, boss," said Durand ironically. "You want quiet, you got quiet."

The quiet lasted perhaps forty-five seconds before the first calls sparked out of the radio. The Exxon Basher had struck again late last night and Little Philly precinct got stuck with the follow-up, and there was a cold burglary, which Durand jumped on. Stepovich hated them. There were too damn many of them, and he couldn't feel anything about them anymore. East Lee, this time, in an apartment building that was trying to pretend it wasn't in Little Philly. Someone had just painted the lobby, but the graffiti was already bleeding through the white paint. Second floor, apartment E. The girl who let them in looked like she'd been crying. She couldn't have been more than twenty.

"I was just gone overnight," she said. She was trying to keep her voice from quivering. "And when I got back this morning. . . ."

Stepovich let Durand do it. It was all just routine these days. They were supposed to remember that no matter how many burglaries they saw every day, for each victim this was the one that mattered. He knew she felt violated, outraged, and scared. He knew she was wondering, if they got in here while I was gone, will they come back when I'm here, when I'm asleep and alone? But there'd just been too many of them lately.

Durand took down all the routine stuff. When did she leave, when did she come back, how'd they get in, what was missing, who knew she was gone, had she suspicions about anyone, and all the rest of it. By the time he was finished, it sounded like the ex-boyfriend, and that too was becoming routine. Durand took his name and number and address and description, more to make the girl feel better than to act on it. Chances were they'd never get enough evidence to bust him. Durand went through the spiel—suggesting dowels in the tracks of the sliding windows and a new dead bolt on the door. Stepovich only listened with half an ear. He knew, even if the girl didn't, that it wasn't that bad. Whoever had done it had known what he was after and had simply taken those items. The place hadn't been tossed or trashed. He knew from what she'd said, though, that this was the very first place she'd lived all on her own, and that what had happened had taken some of the shiny off it. He looked around, at the stuffed yarn cat doorstop and the doilies on the end table and the half-finished afghan in a basket by the coffee table. It reminded him of a little girl's playhouse, each thing just so, as if the idea of living there was more important than the reality of it. Her canisters in the kitchenette were labeled, and he'd bet there really was tea in the one that said tea, and that the spices on her spice rack were alphabetical. The towels in the bathroom all matched, and the three potted plants on the windowsill were in color-coordinated pots. Barbie's first apartment, the doll set might say, and he knew with a sudden ache that someday Laurie would want a place like this, with a ceramic spoon-rest on the little range top and copper pots hung in order by size.

The girl looked at him with sudden surprise when he said, "It's a shame that someone can steal your peace of mind from you, not to mention your radio. Listen. Durand's right about putting dowels in your window frames. I know it won't bring back what you've lost, but it might keep it from happening again. Don't you give up. You got a right to feel safe in your own place."

"Okay," she said, and her eyes suddenly misted up and her chin shook just like Laurie's had when the neighbor's dog had torn off Raggedy Ann's leg, but he'd assured her that Jennie could fix her good as new. It must have been his tone more than his words that catapulted her into his arms, and she was crying on his shirt front, and Durand, damn him, was smirking like a puckered asshole. Stepovich patted her awkwardly, remembering briefly how fragile women felt to him, as hollow-boned as birds, how he'd always been afraid that if he really hugged Jennie her ribs would crumple beneath the strength of his love. Then she was pushing away from him, muttering apologies, her long hair sticking to her tear-wet face, and he was saying it was all right, she'd had a tough morning, but things had to get better.

"They couldn't get worse," the girl agreed with a sniff and a smile so carefully fragile that Stepovich had to turn aside from it. Damnit, he had to find time to phone Laurie tonight, and he had to make time to do something with Jeffie this weekend, he had to. Then they were leaving, and Durand called in that they were available again, and almost immediately they got their next call, this one for a vandalized car.

And so the morning went. In between calls, they drove, Durand not talking at all; but that little tension stretched between them because they weren't getting along. The only talk was the stupid business of asking the routine questions at their stops. Nothing hot or interesting this morning, three cold burglaries and two stolen bicycles and one drunk and disorderly and one patron leaving without paying his tab. The closest they got to a heartbeat was a domestic abuse in progress that turned out to be a cat in heat shut in the bathroom. Stepovich had to admit the cat's passionate yowling did sound like a tortured baby. Durand assured the woman who called it in that they'd rather be called out for nothing than not called when they were needed, while Stepovich persuaded the cat's owner that her "goddamn nosy neighbor" had meant well. Then they left.

In the car Stepovich thought about asking for a new partner. They'd give him one. All he'd have to do is go in and say, hey, this isn't working out. Guys did it all the time. But the guys who changed more than once or twice were the ones the brass watched. Man couldn't get along with his partner, there had to be a reason. Better watch him. And the last thing Stepovich needed right now was to be watched. By anyone.

# Six

## HOW THE DEVIL FOUND THE GYPSY AND THE WOLF FOUND THE SPIDER

SOMETIME

Through doors that lead to a fire blazing red,
Where she makes no distinction 'tween
The living and the dead

"THE FAIR LADY"

*The Fair Lady sits with Her feet in the fire, watching Her toes heat up. She wriggles them with pleasure. They are very long, and the nails gleam like mother-of-pearl. There is a scampering from outside, then scratching of goose-feet at the black iron door. She frowns and causes it to open and the* liderc *enters. One leg is that of a goose, one arm that of a horse, and where he walks he leaves little puddles of fire, but the fire has no smoke. He bows many times to the Fair Lady.*

*"Speak," she says, in Her voice that is like steel bound in silk.*

*"Fair Lady," says the* liderc. *"The Wolf is still on our track."*

*She frowns at this, for She knows that, while wolves have served Her before, in the end they serve only themselves. "We shall have Little Timmy slay the Wolf," She says.*

*But the* liderc *shakes its head. "I don't think he will, Fair Lady. He is more afraid of wolves than of you."*

*She almost cuffs him for this, but then reconsiders. Perhaps he is right, for to Timmy She is only a dream, but he has lived among the wolves all his life, and they are real to him.*

*"I am not unprepared," She says. "One of his cubs will come to me when I will it, and he will follow his cub."*

*"You are ever wise, mistress. Will you call her to you now?"*

*She shrugs. "Soon. If Little Timmy can slay the Dove, there will be no need to do more. We will see if he succeeds first. If he fails, we can perhaps throw him to the Wolf, thus distracting the Wolf and punishing Little Timmy at the same time. And perhaps we will even allow Little Timmy to see us. Yes, that might be best. But for now, we will wait. Go and do my bidding."*

*"Yes, Fair Lady." The* liderc *scampers away. The door behind him closes with the clang of iron. The Fair Lady sees that Her feet are about to turn black from the fire, and regretfully removes them from the flames.*

## AUTUMN MORNING

He came into town on a hot summer's night,
The flies was giving us fits.
Drove an old Ford that had about lost the fight,
His eyes was as black as the pits.

"THE GYPSY"

He awoke in the chair, and there was a blanket around him. MacWurthier was reading a newspaper and drinking coffee; he looked up when the Gypsy stirred.

"You must have been tired," he said. "You've slept more than twelve hours."

"I . . . thank you."

"You're welcome. Would you like some tea? Maybe some breakfast."

"No, thank you. I must leave now. You need not forget her, but you will please her most by trying to be happy."

MacWurthier stared at him. "I know that," he said, as if to himself. "I've been trying. But it's not easy." He seemed lost in reflection. The Gypsy rose and let himself out, not saying anything more, because nothing more was necessary. He returned to the street and made his way toward the park.

## 13 NOV 12:00

I'll lower me another beer, have another dream;
Everything is all confused, nothing's what it seems.

"STEPDOWN"

Stepovich glanced away from the traffic at Durand. He was sulking in his corner of the patrol car like a spoiled brat. Something childish in Stepovich didn't want to break the silence, but need overturned it. "Lunch?" he said.

"Yeah." Durand kept his eyes focused on the street. "Norm's."

"Okay," Stepovich agreed sullenly. That was where Tiffany Marie worked. "But to go."

"Bullshit! I'm not eating in this stinking car."

"I wanna take it over to the park. Guy there I got to talk to."

"Well, do it later. It's too drizzly for picnics in the park. And there's someone at Norm's I want to talk to."

"Tiffany Marie."

"So what's it to you?"

Stepovich glanced at him. The kid's cheeks were pink. Durand plainly knew he was in the wrong, so Stepovich let him have it.

"I busted her twice for whoring before she was fifteen," Stepovich spoke deliberately, slowly, coldly. "She was a runaway, working the streets, too stubborn to work for a pimp. So she was taking it from both sides, getting the real dirt-bag tricks, and the pimps' girls threatening her all the time. Both times Ed and I busted her, the court sent her home. Both times her dad beat the living shit out of her. Not for spreading her legs, but because she was doing it for money instead of for dear old dad. Which was why she kept running away. Third time we picked her up it was because her john had left her unconscious in the motel room, and the manager of the motel wanted an extra two hours' rent from her when she didn't leave on time. She didn't have it, or any money. The john had taken that, too. What she did have was cracked ribs, a broken collarbone and the clap. Crabs, too, from what I hear."

Durand's hands were fists on his knees. Stepovich loosened his grip on the steering wheel. If that damn kid came across the seat at him, he was going to nail the fucker good. He pulled up in front of Norm's and coolly called in their lunch break. He half turned toward Durand when he was done. Right in the mouth was where he was going to hit him if the kid came at him. Smash his big mouth, and to hell with the bloody knuckles.

"You think you're telling me something I don't know?" Durand's voice was thick with an emotion Stepovich couldn't identify.

"No. I think that's all you know. I think you don't know that the last time, Ed and I dumped her on Marilyn's doorstep at two in the morning after they let her out of Emergency. I don't think you know that Marilyn took her in. Tiffany Marie is no whore, Durand. Not anymore. She's going to school at night and she's paying Marilyn a bit of rent and she's going to make something out of herself. All she needed was a chance. What she don't need is you hitting on her and treating her like a whore."

Durand made a move that might have been something that started out to be a punch and ended up a slap on the dashboard instead. "I don't treat her like a whore." Durand's words were as individual as single shots. "Not that it's any of your business."

"You saying you aren't banging her?" Stepovich deliberately baited him.

"I'm saying it's none of your fucking business," Durand roared, and in the roar was an edge that let Stepovich know one thing and suspect another.

He poked at the idea. "So you ain't screwing her. I suppose you're in love with her skinny ass."

"Fuck you," Durand replied with controlled fury. And he got out of the squad car and walked away, into Norm's. Stepovich slowly followed him in. Long habit made his eyes scan the diner before coming to rest on Durand. He was bellied up to the counter, and Tiffany Marie was already taking his order. Stepovich looked at her, remembering how he and Ed had shook their heads over her name. Tiffany Marie, a diamonds and velvet name for a cracker-butt kid with carroty hair and pink lipstick on a pouty little mouth and eyes made up like a Technicolor raccoon. Tiffany Marie, with hickeys up the side of her neck and chipped fingernail polish and runs in her sexy black mesh nylons.

Shit.

He added up the years. Yeah, she probably was eighteen now, maybe even nineteen. The soft swells under the clean white blouse were probably all hers, and when she turned to pass Durand's order to the cook, her hips weren't exactly the skinny little ass he remembered wrapping a blanket around when he carried her out of that cheap motel. The carroty hair was more like burnished copper now, and was probably long, but he couldn't tell with the way she had it pinned up. Had it been that long since he'd really looked at her? He took the stool next to Durand's, and Tiffany Marie turned to him with a smile. Her lips needed no lipstick and for the first time he realized how blue her eyes were. "Hey, Mike, having the usual?" she asked, and her voice was so casual and warm that he knew Durand hadn't said a word to her about what he'd said in the car.

Stepovich felt slimy.

He glanced at Durand, but the kid wouldn't look at him. The kid. Hell, yes, just a big kid, what was he, twenty-two, twenty-four? Not exactly cradle-snatching for him to be looking at Tiffany Marie. And she was looking back. As she set silverware and napkins before them, it was her hand that brushed against Durand's. He studied Durand in small glances between spoonfuls of chili. What was the kid, six-two, six-three? A little puppy fat on him, maybe, not much. Dark hair, grey eyes. He had a job, he made money regular. He was clean, mostly. He was a dumbshit, but at least he wasn't a drunk or a junkie or a sponge. Probably didn't hit his women. Maybe Tiffany Marie didn't think he was an dumbshit.

Maybe he wasn't a dumbshit around her. Would she keep a dumbshit's coffee mug filled all the time like she was doing? Would she keep turning around and smiling at a dumbshit?

Stepovich crumbled crackers into his chili, mashed them in. Boy, Marilyn was going to be pissed; she had called this one wrong.

And there had been more than one dumbshit in the car this morning.

He was thinking about that so hard that he was more than halfway through his Chili and Cheeseburger Special before he realized they hadn't ordered to go like he'd meant to. Damn. He'd wanted to go to the park, and talk to the driver of the horse hack that Ed had tracked down for him. Ed hadn't known the guy's real name, only the handle of Spider, and that his horses were mismatched, one grey and one brown. Stepovich had been counting on catching him near the espresso stands where a lot of the yuppies went to eat lunch and be picturesque. Horse-drawn cabs picked up fares there, the same yuppies being dashing and romantic before going back to their offices after lunch.

And now Durand had screwed him up.

After a moment's reflection, he decided to call it square. He'd acted like a jerk in the car, grilling Durand about Tiffany Marie. So let Durand get away with this. Besides, it was just as well. Durand would have wanted to know what he was talking about to the cabby, and that wouldn't have done at all. It had been hard enough to get the rest of the tip from Ed without him getting suspicious. Well, actually Ed probably *was* suspicious.

He let Durand pick up the tab and leave a tip, and even followed him out to the car. He was still trying to think of some way to let Durand know he knew he'd been out of line. He called in on the radio to let it be known he and Durand were back on the streets. He'd about decided he'd have to apologize, and was thinking of the right words when the dispatcher saved him. She acknowledged their call, then added in an almost human voice, "Three messages for Stepovich to phone Jennie Edwards at his earliest convenience."

Edwards. Jennie Edwards. Somehow it had really hurt him that she'd gone back to using her maiden name. And made a big point of notifying all their friends. Like she didn't want to keep the least little scrap of their life together. "Be a second or two," he grunted at Durand as he got back out of the car.

There was a pay phone at the rear of the diner, outside the restroom doors. He dialed her work number, dumped in a quarter when she answered. "You wanted me to call you," he told her without preamble. No hello, how are you, what's up, just get right to the message. This was how they did it now.

"Yeah. It's about Laurie . . ."

"She okay?" He cut in, visualizing hospitals, kidnappers, car wrecks, rapists.

"She's fine." Impatience at his fear in Jennie's voice. "And that's just the trouble, really. Since school started this year, she's been running with the wrong crowd. Faster kids, kids older than her. Some of them are driving, for Christ's sake. She's come in past midnight the last two nights, and I'm sure I smelt liquor on her breath. And the clothes she's wearing . . ."

"Hold on. Wait a sec." Something wasn't adding here. His Laurie was what, thirteen, no, fifteen? And into frilly blouses for square-dancing for the PTA, for God's sake, not staying out until midnight with older kids with cars. "What the hell are you letting her run around like that for, Jennie? And how is she dressing weird? Where the hell is she getting the money for all this?"

"From you, and don't think I don't know about it! Sneaking around, sending her extra checks behind my back! How do you think it makes Jeffie feel, when he finds out daddy sends big sister thirty extra bucks to blow and nothing for him? Not to mention what it does for my authority when she goes out and buys spandex leopard-spot pants without even asking me."

Spandex. What the hell was spandex? Whatever it was, it didn't sound like something Laurie should be wearing. "Jennie. Wait a minute. She phoned me up and told me she needed money for a blouse for a square-dancing program. . . ."

"And you believe that? Without even checking with me? And you just sit down and write the check, because mean old mommy won't buy her a blouse? Michael, get real!"

The phone was getting slippery in his grip. Durand had come in and was leaning on the counter, talking to Tiffany Marie. They were both watching him, he knew it, taking quick little glances like he was a pimp under surveillance or something. He turned his back on them so they couldn't see his face, and tuned back into Jennie's ranting.

". . . maybe shoplifting. She was wearing these earrings, very pretty and very expensive-looking, and when I asked her about it, she said she just found them. And she gets this look on her face, I swear, it just makes me want to slap it off there. And that cheap little snot Chrissy that she's always running around with, she smirks and says, 'Just consider it a gift from the Lady, Ms. Edwards.' "

"What the hell is that supposed to mean?" Stepovich demanded.

"You tell me! Unless she's some drug pusher or into child pornography or something. Chrissy drops that name all the time, like it's some secret club or something and—"

"Look," Mike cut in. "It's obvious we have to talk. All of us. I'll come over tonight as soon as I'm off shift, and—"

"Oh, no. No way. I talked to her counselor at school, and Ms. Simmons said the worst possible thing would be for a male authority figure to suddenly descend and try to take control of Laurie's life. This "Lady" thing may be a sort of reaching toward womanhood—"

"For Christ's sake," Stepovich butted in, annoyed at her parroting the counselorese at him, but Jennie talked right over him, her voice just getting more insistent.

"—that the girls are doing, a redefining of themselves as women rather than children. And Ms. Simmons says that while it does need to be talked about, it needs to be talked about in a nonthreatening atmosphere."

"Well, if Ms. Simmons has all the fucking answers, what the fuck are you calling me for?" He was mindful of where he was and that Durand might overhear him. So each furious word came out in a stiff separate whisper, though they wanted to burst from his chest in a scream. Every six months or so, Jennie seemed to find a new way to do this to him. He was Laurie's father, damnit, he had a right to know, he had a right to help, to be there for her. And now she was telling him that he'd hurt Laurie if he "interfered" by talking to her. His throat squeezed shut and he couldn't get anymore words out.

"I should have known you'd react that way. Listen, Michael, I don't buy everything this counselor says either. And we both know, real well, that you have big problems with believing that any woman can know more about something than you do. But I'm willing to listen to Ms. Simmons if it will help Laurie. So anyway. I'll tell you why I called you. Because Ms. Simmons knows of a women and girls encounter therapy group that she feels could help Laurie. But it's expensive, and my health plan doesn't cover it. All I want to know is if yours will. If the police insurance doesn't have some clause for family counseling, it should, all the families that your police work breaks up and destroys."

"I don't know." Little lead words. "Call Bevvie at the services number. You've got my policy number. Ask her. Even though she's a woman, she knows more about the cop insurance stuff than I do."

"And that's all? Call Bevvie. Don't you give a damn at all about your daughter?"

"You've already told me you don't want me to come over and talk to her. So what the hell can I do?" He couldn't contain his voice.

"Oh, forget it! I'm sorry I asked. I'll check with Bevvie. I'm sorry you called at all."

"Yeah. Me, too." He slammed the receiver down on its hook. He looked over his shoulder and both Durand and Tiffany Marie looked hastily away. Durand said something to her, and she shook her head slightly, not a denial but a commiseration. Stepovich took a deep breath and turned and strode out past them. "Durand. Let's go," he said, and ignored Tiffany's timorous, "You take care now, Mike."

The afternoon passed. That was all he could say for it. Passed the same way time passes for a ball in a pinball machine. Hit the bumpers, light the lights, make the buzzers, but at the end of the play it falls through the flapper gates, and not a damn thing is really changed, not the ball nor the buzzers or lights. It's just time for a different ball to set them off. Neither he nor Durand spoke much, but the tension was different now, it was Durand keeping quiet because he didn't want to set Stepovich off, not keeping quiet to spite him. In an odd way Stepovich was grateful for that.

So when he had finished typing the nineteenth report up, he looked up at Durand and said, "I was out of line, earlier today."

"Yeah. You were. Well, let's forget it," said Durand, and in that moment they were as close to being real partners as they'd ever come.

Stepovich thought about that, driving home. Durand was doing better, no doubt about that. Sometimes, anyway. But a real partner would have noticed that Stepovich hadn't changed out of his uniform after shift, and wondered why. And a real partner would have told the kid that he was going to do a little after-hours rousting, and invited him along. Shut up, he told himself, and agreed with himself.

## LATE 1980S

Raven had his fiddle,
  And Owl a tambourine,
And I'd love to hear them play again
    And tell them all I've seen.

"RAVEN, OWL, AND I"

"I think I know you, my friend."

"Know me? Well, yes and no, Daniel. We've met, in another time and place, but your youngest brother knows me better."

"Yes. You're the Coachman, aren't you?"

"I am. Do you know where your older brother is?"

"No, where?"

"Hmm. I don't know either. I was hoping you did. Well, never mind. You must come with me."

"I know. I've been expecting you since yesterday."

"Of course."

"Where are we going?"

"Lakota, Ohio. Does it matter? Your youngest brother needs your help."

"I am ready to help him. I've been trying to find him since—"

"I know. We've all been waiting. The time of waiting is ended. You have your fiddle?"

"I have it."

"Then come. The coach awaits. It's a Greyhound."

# Seven

## THE WOLF AND THE SPIDER, THE OWL AND THE CHIPMUNKS

Little Timmy feeling blue
Doesn't know what he should do.
Little Timmy feeling bad
Doesn't know what makes him mad.
Little Timmy pushed around
Doesn't know who makes the sound.
Little Timmy hears the voice
Knows he doesn't have a choice.
Little Timmy on the run
Goes to buy a little gun.
Little Timmy waits for dark
Goes to sneak around the park.
Little Timmy feeling mean
Goes to where he can't be seen.
Little Timmy off his head
Gonna shoot somebody dead.

## AUTUMN, DUSK

I was dressed in yellow,
My brothers in green and red.
I don't know what we heard,
I only know we fled.

"RAVEN, OWL, AND I"

There was an itch in the back of the Gypsy's neck when he got to the park. He didn't know why, but he wanted his knife in his hand. He did not take it out; there was still some daylight left, and he knew the knife would make him conspicuous. For reasons he didn't understand, he kept to the edge of the park, then moved over to the fountain, keeping it between himself and the grove of oaks.

There were a pair of coaches on the street across from him, but something kept him from moving toward them. In the growing darkness and the snow, he couldn't see what either of the coachmen looked like. He strained his eyes, and the scene shifted and blurred, and there was suddenly a Wolf loping toward the coaches. He took a step backward as one of the coaches drove off, while the Wolf approached the other.

The Gypsy shuddered and hurried away.

14 NOV 19:23

This ain't the job I thought I signed up for,
But show me a way back out the door.

"STEPDOWN"

It was already getting dark in the park when he climbed out of the car. Chances were that the horse-drawn carriages were all turned in for the night. The evening was turning cool and grey and snow was falling, not at all the atmosphere for a carriage ride through the park. But no, there were two of them drawn up side by side beneath a street lamp that blossomed into light even as he looked at it. It had the eerie feel of a stage set, coming to life for his benefit. The horses were blanketed against the chill, and their drivers wore great coats buttoned to their chins and scarves swathed around their necks and faces. It could have been an engraving, a scene from a hundred years ago. Stepovich's stride faltered. If he climbed aboard one of those carriages and the driver whipped up the horses, would he be carried back to an older, simpler time? Then one of the drivers took out a pack of cigarettes and tamped one out and lit it with a disposable lighter. The illusion burned in that brief flaming, and Stepovich lifted his voice and called out, "Spider."

One of the men lifted an uncertain hand in greeting. Even gloved, the hand was thin and long-fingered, and the arm that stuck out of the coat sleeve was skinny. Like a spider he was, sitting in a dark blob up on the seat of his carriage, his long legs and arms dangling. Stepovich walked up to him slowly, giving him full time to assess his uniform. The other cabby tipped his hat, lifted his reins and clucked his team into motion. Good. The spoked wheels of his carriage grated on the pavement as his team drew him away, leaving Stepovich alone with Spider.

"Whatsamatter?" Spider demanded suspiciously as Stepovich drew near.

"Nothing. Nothing yet, anyway. I just want to ask you a few questions about the man who drove for you last Sunday."

"Oh, shit," Spider breathed fervently. "Not again, man. I tole you guys, none of it was my fault. Man's good with horses, I wanted to take a day off, have a little free time with my old lady. So I let the guy drive sometimes, we split the fares. How was I to know he'd get weird?"

"We just want to get clear what happened." Stepovich drew out his notebook and pen, tried to look as if he already knew it all. "So, one more time, if you don't mind. When did it start?"

Spider looked pissed. "How do I know? I wasn't here, remember, I took a day off. Ask the guy whose car got kicked. Ask the joggers who say he nearly ran them over. Ask those guys that was riding in the carriage when it happened. Hell, it was half their fault, anyway, offering him extra money to go off the carriage trails, and then daring him to make the team gallop. They were all drunk; they probably gave Coachman the booze."

"Okay. I see your point. Maybe the thing for me to do is to talk to the relief driver himself. Give me his name and number again."

"Hunh? I tole you I don't know it. This some kind of cop trick, or what? Coachman don't have no name. Coachman don't have no address. All he's got is booze. How come you're—?"

"I just—"

"What is this, anyway? Who are you?"

Stepovich thought quickly. "Sorry. No, the idiots at precinct screwed up again and I got the wrong info." He stopped and gave Spider a sizing-up look. "All right, I'll be straight with you. Can you keep something under your hat?"

"Hunh? Yeah, sure. What is it?"

"There may be more involved in this."

"Like what?"

Stepovich shook his head. "Did you ever see Coachman with a knife?"

Spider stared at him, and Stepovich recognized the look of the witness who wants to be part of something interesting. "A knife? Well, he had a hoof pick. That's how we met. Bunny was throwing her leg a little funny, not limping, really, and this guy walks right in front of the team and reaches up and grabs their heads and stops them. Before I can say more than Shit, he picks up her foot and pops a nasty little piece of gravel out of the frog."

"Frog?"

"Her foot. That was what was making her walk funny. So, a hoof pick, yeah."

"No, I mean a sheath knife with a bone handle."

Spider looked disappointed. "Naw. Once, maybe, I saw him cutting his nails with an old clasp knife that might've had a bone handle. I don't know. Maybe. Hell, maybe it was someone else. You want me to, uh, keep my eye out or anything?"

"The department would appreciate it," said Stepovich. "And if you should happen to find his address, let us know."

"Hey, you bet. What did he do?"

"Nothing directly. It's part of something else. When everything's settled, I'll see if I can let you know."

"Hey, thanks."

"The least I can do," said Stepovich, and returned to his car.

Well, that had turned out for shit. Except that there might be more information on this Coachman on one of the witnesses' statements, if he cared to try and dig through them. If only he'd turned in the knife as evidence in the first place, put the extra charge of concealed weapon, none of this would have happened.

As he was getting into his car, a Chevy very much like Durand's heap drove past. Stepovich stared after the blue car until it faded into the fog. He was sure he was mistaken. Damn, he was getting paranoid.

## AUTUMN, NIGHT

He found the table where Timmy D. sat
And settled in like he wanted to stay,
Put his money out on the board
And said, "Hey, boy, teach me to play."

"THE GYPSY"

And around it went, like the steps of the csardas, always back to the same place, only different, with a new tension. He was in front of Tiny's, almost exactly twenty-four hours later. What had he done? He tried to remember, and a headache came on. Where were his pills? A walk to an apartment, a conversation, a debt fulfilled, sleep, a meal, a walk in the park, a wolf, and now back here. What had he gained? What had he lost?

Two girls came came out of a bar down the street and walked past him, complaining about the "prick" who had thrown them out. Too young, he thought.

They stopped and turned back. "What was that?" He hadn't realized he'd spoken aloud. The one who queried him had blonde hair with dark roots and wore a very short leather skirt and stockings. The other, dark of hair and taller, with a fuller body though a younger face, was dressed in tight-fitting jeans with grey splotches on them. They both wore very short jackets that didn't look like they would keep snow or cold out.

"I said, too young," repeated the Gypsy.

"Who asked you?" said the blonde.

"There is a time to be in the adult world, and a time to be in the child's world, and you will cheat yourself if you leave the one too soon."

They looked at each other and giggled. "What a weirdo," said the dark one. As she spoke, the Gypsy shivered. Something about her voice resonated within him, seemed familiar.

He shrugged and said, "The road will be there, whenever you set foot on it. But you won't be the same after. You can't go back."

"Ooooo," said the blonde. "Heavy stuff, huh?" She looked at her friend and giggled again. Then she said, "Wanna get lucky, big guy?" and laughed some more.

The dark one said, "Chrissy!" in a tone that mixed shock and humor.

"Oh, he won't do anything. If he does, we'll scream. Right, big guy?"

The Gypsy looked away, and said, "If you give all you have to the Fair Lady, what will be left when She's finished?" When he turned back, they were staring at him, wide-eyed.

"How do you know about the Fair Lady?" whispered the one called Chrissy. Groups of people walked by, ignoring them. The police could go by any minute, but he couldn't leave these two unwarned.

"There are three worlds," he said. "Each held in place by a

tree, each with its sun and moon, each with its own sky full of stars. The top branches of the tree of our world reach to the roots of the next, the roots of our tree reach to the branches of the world below. The Fair Lady comes from the world below, which She has covered in darkness, for She wishes to be the only brightness in the world. She has climbed the tree of Her world and come to ours, and now wishes to cover ours in darkness. To some, She brings gifts, hoping they will serve Her. Others She directs by fear, or by casting their minds in darkness so She is all they see clearly. I am the one sworn to return light to Her world, but first She must be cast out of ours. She is Luci, the seductress, who brings the diseases that waste. Do not listen to Her. She will draw the light from your youth and cast you into the darkness that will ravage your soul."

He stopped at last. They stared at him, then, without a word or a look between them, turned and ran up the street and were soon lost in the crowds. The Gypsy stood alone, his own words coming back to him.

"So," he said to himself, very slowly and quietly, not noticing those who took wide detours around the oddly dressed man who stood talking to himself. "So, now I know what I am to do. But I cannot do it alone."

14 NOV 20:18

I can see the ravens gather
From the places where they feast on last night's news
I am guessing they'd really rather
Find out exactly who they should accuse
They can't get me 'til I've collected
what I'm owed.
So I'll keep searching further up this road.

"UP THE ROAD"

He drove home slowly through the snowy streets, his windshield wipers on the low setting to keep the wet flakes cleared from the glass. He hoped it wouldn't stick. Least bit of snow on the streets, traffic got all screwed up. He didn't want to spend all day tomorrow calling for wreckers and investigating people sliding into guardrails. Shit.

Home, he shucked off his uniform and got into his sweats. He added his uniform shirt and pants to the rest of his laundry to make a load and took it down the hall to the laundry room. Set it sloshing.

Back to the apartment. Part of a package of fish sticks, part of a bag of frozen French fries. Dump them on a cookie tray, stick them in the oven. Get out the ketchup. Frost had formed inside the packages from being open in the freezer compartment. The French fries came out wet and hot and steamy. Flavorless. He ate them anyway. Go down the hallway, take the wet stuff out of the washer and stuff it in the dryer. Go back to the apartment and open a beer.

Stepovich began the nightly ritual of flicking through the channels. Apartment came with cable. Cable TV and roaches, free with the rent. At least having the cable gave him plenty of channels to flip through. He watched about three hours of television a night, and as Ed had once observed, that was a lot, at only three minutes per channel.

The steamy romance potboiler on four put him in mind of Durand and Tiffany Marie, and he watched the couple on the tube make fish mouths at each other while he thought about what a jerk he'd been today, climbing on Durand about Tiffany Marie. When he got to feeling too abashed, he switched to seventeen. Quiz show time, stupid questions and dumber answers, because the contestants were movie stars and they were more concerned with being witty than with getting the answer right. That was him in the park with the horse-hack, and he'd learned about as much from him as he was learning from the show. Click the channels some more, to a rock video of young girls writhing and moaning. He could call Laurie. Hell, he should call Laurie, except that Jennie probably wouldn't put him through. She'd as much as told him to butt out. Not that she would really make him butt out, but she could make it uncomfortable. But he could call and promise he wouldn't say anything to her about what her mom had talked about today. But, hell, that wouldn't fool anybody. Laurie would know why he was calling. She was one smart kid, Laurie was. Growing up so fast. Too fast, and he was missing it. Click the channel selector.

Thirteen had on a horror flick, with unavenged ghosts and a battered old gypsy woman telling the hero to beware, but also telling him that he was the one destined to free them all. Find out who killed me, that sort of line. Click.

A cop show. Two partners had gone bad, were dispensing vigilante justice, and the good cop was hunting them down.

Click.

Rocky and Bullwinkle. He watched Boris and Natasha once more temporarily vanquished, watched the little fairy sweep up the fractured fairy tale, and was just getting into Shermie and Mr. Peabody when the phone rang.

Eleven o'clock. No one but Ed ever called him this time of night. He picked up the phone and said, "Yeah?"

"I thought you said you'd call me," Marilyn snapped. He sat up straight on the couch, zapped the TV set into oblivion.

"Jeez, I'm sorry," he said, "I meant to, but . . . ."

"I thought this was so all-be-damned important to you, and so I go ahead and . . ."

"It is, it is," Stepovich assured her hastily. Where was his notebook? End of the coffee table. He reached for it, knocked the ketchup bottle rolling onto the floor, but let it go. It was a squeeze bottle, it wouldn't leak much anyway. Grab the pen, and "Go ahead, what did you find for me?"

"Too damn much, that's what, and not much at all. You want stuff done by gypsies, I got a ton of it. You want stuff done by John Does, possible first name Chuck, I got a ton of that, too. I mean, good lord, Stepovich, half the gypsies in the world have facial scars. Doesn't this man have a tattoo, or a lisp, or a birthmark or anything?"

"Not that I know of. There was no overlap, no gypsy of that description, possible first name Chuck?"

Marilyn sounded miffed when she replied. "I knew you'd ask that. I knew it. So I dug, and I dug like hell. How about a vagrancy, possible involvement in an arson, six years ago? In Kansas City?"

"That's not really what I was looking for," Stepovich muttered, not sure if he felt frustrated or relieved. No serial killings in some obscure part of the U. S. at least. No string of crimes attached to that description and name. "Is that all there was?"

"I swear to God, I been working with you too long. If you aren't too fussy about the gypsy description, I can give you about thirty-two shoplifting cases. Three grand theft auto, two of those from auto dealers in Sacramento, looks like a regular scam. A porno ring in Fort Lauderdale, but the ones they caught weren't really gypsies. Still, there was a Chuck involved. Airplane hijacking. In Oklahoma. Almost funny, that one's so stupid. Cropduster hijacked from one field to another."

"That's not what I meant," Stepovich cut in frustratedly. "I was looking for a felony, or a string of felonies, something serious. The arson and vagrancy were the only ones where there was a good overlap between the name Chuck and the description of the Gypsy?"

Marilyn sighed. "Almost. I had a feeling you were going to be stubborn on this. I pulled up stuff I didn't even know I could access. Stuff I would have sworn was too dead or too cold. How's this. New Orleans. A stabbing. In a bar room. Victim Timothy DeCruz, also known as Timmy Dee, sometimes Tim del Monico. Not much on the killer, but the victim had a file of past convictions as long as your arm. Mostly little scams, but the kind that hint he was involved in bigger, nastier stuff but didn't get caught. Cause of the fight was possibly cheating at cards, it was never clearly established. Ugly crime. The medical report comments on the strength required to drive a knife that size through a leather vest and completely into a man's body. The hilt left a bruise, it impacted so hard. Talk about your crime of passion. The guy was either horribly strong, or totally enraged. Witnesses described the killer, and it fits your guy to a tee. But for all that, they didn't seem too hot to help the investigation. The perp was never found."

A little prickle of certainty ran up Stepovich's spine, that little tickle of instinct that never betrayed him. "It's him. When was it, and who handled it?"

Nasty satisfaction as she said, "August 12, 1935. But the description does match your man."

"Shit, Marilyn, my guy probably wasn't even born then."

"Maybe it was his father then. Maybe it's a gypsy crime family, and you're tracking the youngest member."

He was beginning to get an inkling of just how bad he'd

pissed her off. "Jeez. I'm sorry. I guess I wasted a lot of your time today." Cautiously. "You sure that's all there was?"

He heard her breathe out through her nose in disgust. "You talk to Durand today?" she demanded, ignoring his question.

"Yeah. Marilyn, I don't think it's quite how you're seeing it. I think he really likes her."

"That's why he stood her up tonight, right? She turns down a date with a nice college boy to wait for a sleazy-ass cop who doesn't even show."

"I don't know nothing about that," Stepovich objected.

"No. Of course you don't. You didn't drag him off on this wild goose chase of yours, did you?"

"Swear to God, I didn't, Marilyn," Stepovich said fervently. "And Jesus Christ," he said, becoming annoyed in turn, "I lit into my partner like I was going to tear his throat out, just on your say-so, and it turns out the damn fool's in love with her. How do you suppose that makes me feel?"

"What makes you think—?"

"I see them together. You don't. All right?"

"Hmmph. I'd have seen them together if he'd shown up tonight."

"Marilyn, he's my partner, not my goddamn kid. I did what you told me to, and you were wrong about him."

"Well," she said, relenting a little. "Well. Maybe I was. Sorry. But you have a talk with him anyway. He's not right for Tiffany Marie, he isn't going to bring any good to her life. You reason with him."

"Sure," Stepovich said. "Sure, I'll do that. And you talk to her. Okay?"

"Okay."

The click as she hung up was a relief. For a moment he stared at the blank television screen. Then he heaved himself up with a sigh to go get his laundry out of the dryer. It was all stuck together with static, and as he sat on the couch and peeled it apart, he remembered the shiver up his back, and wondered how a patrol cop was going to get hold of the notes on a 1935 murder in New Orleans.

## NOVEMBER FIFTEENTH, MORNING

Raven, the hunter,
Was content to stay and poach,
Owl wished to go back home,
And I, to find the coach.

"RAVEN, OWL, AND I"

Raymond had seen three airplanes this morning, and nineteen birds. It was now four thousand, six hundred and twelve days since he had seen his brother, the Raven, and as for his other brother, he had lost count some time ago, much to his regret. Another bird went by overhead. Twenty. He unwrapped his tambourine from the old towels that protected it from the elements, and idly tapped it a few times.

Raymond looked nothing like an Indian. His face was swarthy, but not in the same way. His cheekbones were high, but his forehead was all wrong. His eyes had just a hint of slant. But still, tourists thought he was an Indian, and so paid him well to guide them through the Rockies, near Boulder. It was just as well. He knew the land. He spent most nights huddled in the ruins of the old "castle" on Mount Falcon, overlooking Red Rocks. He could find the best hiking, rock climbing, and sight seeing. The authorities for the most part ignored him.

It was full dark, and the stars were out in all their glory, the Pleiades as clear as spring water, looking like he could touch them. Four chipmunks gathered near his small fire. He held out nine pieces of bread for them to nibble from his hand. He couldn't always tell them apart, but two of these he recognized. One was a small, old female he called Brandy, and the other a very dark, large male whom he had named Fleetwood, after a Cadillac he had owned many years before. Fleetwood took the bread and said, "The Raven is flying. It is time for the Owl to do the same."

Raymond studied the chipmunk, surprised at how calm he felt to be addressed by the animal; it was almost as if he'd been waiting for something like this, and perhaps he had been. He said, "It is years since I've seen the Raven, or the Dove for that matter."

"It is time to see them both," said Fleetwood.

"Where?" said Raymond.

"That I cannot tell you."

Brandy spoke in a high, clear tenor. "The road will tell you. It is only for you to set foot upon it."

Raymond nodded. "If it is time for me to find my brothers, then find them I will. But what is our task to be?"

"I cannot tell you that, either."

"Will there be a way home again?"

"That will depend," said Fleetwood, "on whether the Coachman is loyal."

"You mean sober."

"Well, yes."

"And on whether your brothers are loyal, as well," said Brandy.

"That's clear enough," said Raymond. "I'll set out in the morning."

The chipmunks nodded, and accepted more bread, and spoke no more to the gypsy guide who looked nothing like an Indian.

## WEDNESDAY, AFTER SCHOOL

She can find your secret madness,
She knows your secret name.
What demons do you hide, my friend?
What creatures lurk inside, my friend?
To her, you know, it's really all the same.

"THE FAIR LADY"

"I stole it," Laurie said boastfully. Or tried to. The words didn't come out quite right, and she wondered if Chrissy could hear they weren't quite true. Laurie had gone to the stupid rummage sale at the youth center yesterday evening after Chrissy had stood her up to go downtown with that Sue and her friends. Now she wanted to make Chrissy feel as if she'd really missed out on something; not just Laurie finding the black sort-of-tapestry cloth that now covered her bed, but the adventure of Laurie stealing it.

And Laurie really had intended to steal it. She'd wrapped it up in the two dollar silky bathrobe she was going to pay for and stuffed it in her shopping bag with the old books Jeffrey wanted and the sweater she thought her Mom would like. The tapestry with the weird old square-footed animals on it was marked twelve dollars, and she wanted it but couldn't afford it. So she decided to steal it. All the way up to the cashier she'd justified it, thinking this rummage sale was supposed to raise money for the youth center, and all the stuff was donated anyway, so it wasn't like they were really losing money when she took it. But then the lady at the counter had just said, "It's all three dollars a bag after five o'clock," and had taken her money. Six months ago, she would have told Chrissy the whole story, and they'd have laughed about it. Now she just wanted Chrissy to believe that she had stolen it.

But Chrissy only stared at it for a minute. She didn't even seem to notice that all Laurie's dolls and stuffed animals had been packed away, or that there were candles and incense set out on her dresser or the way she'd hung towels over her curtains to make the room dimmer. Chrissy's eyes got that apprehensive look they sometimes got lately as she stared at the tapestry spread. "Looks like something of Hers," Chrissy said in a whispery voice, and then giggled in a funny way. Like she'd meant to whimper and giggled instead.

"What?" Laurie demanded, feeling stupid. Again. Lately she always felt stupid, or left out when she was around Chrissy. It was the same way she and Chrissy had felt when they were in the bathroom at school and some of the popular girls came in and started talking about boys and makeup. Only this was worse, because it was Chrissy making her feel like there was something big and important going on, and she was too much of a kid to understand it. If Chrissy grew up and left her behind, then she'd really be alone.

"Those things, there. Like lions only sort of square. She's got a thing like that. Except it talks. And it looks even weirder than those things do." Chrissy's voice trailed off and she continued to stare at the bedspread.

"Who has an animal like that?"

For a long time, Chrissy didn't answer. And when she did, it was in an odd, breathy voice, and she didn't close her mouth between the sentences. "The Fair Lady. Sue finally took me to see Her. She lives, well, in a place like an elevator stuck between floors, only it's a whole world. So the floor is blue, like a sky under your feet, only cold and hard. But sometimes it seems like you're standing in it, instead of on it. And the ceiling is like rocks and dirt and roots hanging down. Only not natural, not uneven like in a cave, but all polished, like someone made it that way. It's like columns in some old temple or something. And the walls are like—I don't know, banks of stone, with these fossils in them, only the walls aren't always in the same places. There was this window, only Sue said maybe it was only a painting, because it looked out but only into the sky, and all you could see from it was half a sun and half a moon. Sue said it was only a painting, but when Sue wasn't watching, I saw Her throw the skinned kitten out of it. It looked so much littler without fur." Her eyes grew even more unfocused. "It was like that man said, that gypsy guy: There wasn't much left when She was through with it." Chrissy's face went a shade paler, and she talked faster. "It's always warm there, even hot, but She has all these fireplaces, and some of the fireplaces have chimneys that go down instead of up. And She has these . . . things. Like people made of animal parts . . . or something."

"Chrissy," Laurie objected tentatively. This wasn't like her. She'd never been into imaginary games or stories of any kind. "Are you—are you doing drugs with Sue?"

She gave that giggle again. For a moment she didn't answer. Then she looked directly at Laurie and blinked her eyes a few times. "Drugs? Naw. No one needs drugs around the Fair Lady. She can make you feel so good. Sooo good." Chrissy stood vacant-eyed, idly rubbing her wrists together. It was an odd movement. "No one can make you feel so good as She can," Chrissy said softly. "Or so bad," she added in a fearful whisper. "But what's going to be left when She's through?" She cowered suddenly, like a small animal swept by the silent shadow of an owl's wings.

Laurie reached to put an arm around her, like they had used to do when they were best friends and one of them was crying. But at her touch, Chrissy gave a sudden start and backed out from under Laurie's embrace with a contemptuous hoot. "Hands off, Laurie! You turning into a lezzy on me?"

It was like a punch in the stomach. Laurie turned aside, fixed her eyes on the tapestry animals as if suddenly fascinated by them. Get it under control, she told herself, wishing her eyes could suck back the tears that welled in them. She and Chrissy had never said things like that to each other, not even jokingly. She stared steadily at the tapestry animals but they wavered before her. She didn't lift a hand to wipe at her eyes; that would have given her away. Instead, she said, "I got a bitch of an algebra test tomorrow. I'd better start studying now if I'm going to pass it."

Still without looking at Chrissy, she crossed to where she'd dumped her bookbag on the floor when they came in and began digging into it. With her head bent forward, her hair came forward too, hanging like curtains on either side of her face. She blinked quickly, hoping it would disperse the hanging tears.

"Like, you want to go with us some time? Sue and me, I mean?" The voice was almost like Chrissy's old voice, almost apologetic. But the old Chrissy would have been over beside her, saying she was sorry for saying such a rotten thing. Still.

"My mom would never let me go," she said. Laurie found the algebra book, dragged it out of the bag. She opened it and pretended to be looking for a certain page.

"Well?" Chrissy demanded suddenly. "So what? Do you want to go with us to the Fair Lady's place, or not?"

"I'm not supposed to go to houses of people she doesn't know unless she has a phone number and has talked to them first." The words came up out of her throat like rough-edged rocks, but she forced them out. It was the rule and she was stuck with it. She couldn't break it without hard consequences; not like Chrissy's mom, who hardly noticed anything she did anymore.

"Well." Chrissy paused. "So Mommy won't let you. Well, the Fair Lady probably wouldn't let me bring you anyway. You're not at all what She's looking for."

"I guess not," Laurie said in a disinterested voice.

"See, the Fair Lady, She's going to change the world. But She has to have faithful followers to help Her do it. People who can do what She says, right now, without asking questions. Later, they'll be rewarded."

"Sounds like a comic book," Laurie said in a low voice. She was dragging out her binder, scuffling in the bottom of the book bag for a pencil. She'd show Chrissy. She'd actually go ahead and start doing her algebra homework right in front of her. Chrissy was only in pre-algebra.

"Go ahead, make fun of it. But don't blame me when you miss out later because you were afraid to take a few chances." Chrissy paused, to allow Laurie a chance to plead for more information. Instead, Laurie picked up her binder and book and took them over to her desk.

"See, it's like a war, right now," Laurie suddenly resumed. "And, we're like Her spies and stuff. And some of us do even harder stuff, like being ninjas for Her, or something. See, there are people out there who know about Her and would do anything to keep Her from carrying out her plans. Because once She comes to power, well, everything's going to change. People who used to push us around are going to be real sorry, because we'll belong to Her and they'll have to do what we tell them. She's going to make them crawl for us."

There was great satisfaction in Chrissy's voice. Laurie glanced sideways at her through the curtain of her hanging hair. She was staring off through the wall, a look of petulant gloating on her face. Just the way she used to look when she'd talked about running away, and how her Mom and Dad would be really sorry they'd been so mean to her once she was gone. Only then she did run away and hid out at the shelter for two days, and her parents never even called the police. She glanced at Chrissy again. It suddenly struck her how dumb she looked, with her bangs starched up stiff over her forehead, almost like a rooster's comb, and one shaved spot over her ear. It was a tough punk hairdo, but she still had that fat, round little face she'd always had. Laurie's dad had always said Chrissy looked like a Cabbage Patch Kid with too much stuffing in her. She still did. Cabbage Punk, Laurie thought to herself, and giggled.

"So what's funny?" Chrissy demanded, instantly suspicious.

"Nothing," Laurie muttered. "I was thinking about something else."

"Listen, Laurie. You want in on this or not? Because if you do, you're gonna have to take some chances, and not worry so much about what Mommy and Daddy say." Chrissy thrust one hip out and put her fists at her waist. Like that one rock poster. Laurie wondered if she'd been practicing in front of the mirror.

"I don't know," she muttered. She didn't. The way she was acting, she didn't even know if she wanted to be friends with Chrissy anymore. Except, if she wasn't best friends with Chrissy, then she wasn't best friends with anyone. Heck, she was hardly any kind of friend with anyone. "I gotta think about it, okay?" she amended. She finally let her eyes meet Chrissy's. But there was no understanding there. Chrissy only shrugged.

"Well, don't take too long," she said flatly. "There's stuff going on. Big stuff. You wait too long, you won't be in on it. You'll be one of them."

Laurie just stared at her. Waiting for her to say something else, to add something that wouldn't make it sound so flat, so final. But she didn't. Finally, she turned away from Chrissy's unsmiling face.

"I got an algebra test tomorrow. You know?"

"Yeah. I know. Hope you get a hundred percent and Mommy sticks a gold star on your forehead."

Laurie didn't look up again until after the door slammed. Then she stared at the space where Chrissy had stood, trying not to let the tears loose, and vaguely wondered where Chrissy had gone. And how long it would be before she gave in and followed her.

### NOV. FIFTEENTH, AFTER WORK

Watch the trail, now, it's coming to an end;
The river speaks the terms of my fate.
I can hear the laughter of the falcon and the wren;
I fear my repentance comes too late.

"LANNAN SIDHE"

Not even the stupid waitress uniform could make her look bad. She still had her hair pinned up out of the way, but that couldn't stop the streetlamps from snapping copper highlights off it. Durand looked at her, and felt angry at Step all over again. How the hell could that idiot look at a woman like Tiffany and still remember some stupid mess she'd gotten into as a kid?

She spotted him and came over to the car, opened the door and slid in, just as if she'd been expecting him. She leaned over and hugged him and gave him a quick hard kiss before she said, without malice, "You stood me up last night, you asshole."

"Couldn't be helped," he told her. "Cop stuff doesn't stop at five o'clock."

She sat looking at him with those huge eyes of hers. If any other woman had called him an asshole, he'd have told her to take off, find someone else to abuse. But coming from Tiffany, it didn't even bother him. Sometimes, when he wasn't around her, he wondered why. He knew all the stuff Step had told him was true, and always before he'd had a rule against dating women who had any kind of trouble in their past, divorce or illegitimate kids or smoking pot, or anything. Sometimes he tried to tell himself she'd been a whore and he shouldn't like her so much. But when he was with her it didn't matter. So he'd broken his own rule, to date her, and she kept right on breaking all his rules of how he thought a woman should be. Like now.

After two seconds of thought, she shrugged and forgave him. "Next time, try to call," she said, and settled in beside him.

"Buckle your seat belt," he told her, as he always had to.

Reluctantly, she slid back to her side of the car. As she dragged down the shoulder harness, she observed, "You ought to install a seat belt in the middle, so I could sit next to you instead of clear over here."

"In my spare time," he promised her, in the joke they shared about him never having any spare time. "What would you like to do? Dinner and a movie?"

"Okay. But I got to go home and change first. You mind?"

"Nope." He pulled away from the curb, the old Chevy's clutch slipping. That was another thing he was going to have to fix in his spare time.

Durand was content to drive in silence, just smelling the faint trace of perfume that Tiffany brought with her, feeling her left hand rest on his shoulder as he drove. But Tiffany asked, "Aren't you even going to tell me about it?"

"About what?"

"About what kept you last night?"

"Oh. Cop stuff." He always hated to talk to her about anything to do with Step. He was the one thing they could never agree on. It was ironic, because if it hadn't been for Step, they never would have met. He was the one who had introduced them, on Durand's first day on the job. Of course, it had been Tiffany who'd followed up on the introduction, and called him at work to say she'd like to see more of him. No woman had ever done that before.

"It's Mike again, isn't it? What did he do to you this time?"

He drove two more blocks before answering, and she let him have his silence. Then he said, "I'm starting to think he's mixed up in something dirty."

"Oh," she said. That was all. Waiting to hear the rest before she said anything more. Probably only he knew her well enough to hear the tiny chill in her voice.

Durand sighed. "It's like this. You know, I told you about that gypsy guy we busted, and how he got turned loose somehow. And the murder at the hotel and everything. Well, Step's been talking to me like it's over, homicide gets to handle it now, forget it. But yesterday I noticed he didn't change out of his uniform after work. So I kind of followed him, and saw him go to the park and talk to this guy with a carriage. And after he'd left, I go talk to the guy, and it turns out Step's been asking him all kinds of questions about a gypsy and a knife."

"I don't see how that means Mike is doing something wrong. I mean, don't cops do that all the time, follow up on cases?"

"Yeah," Durand admitted uneasily. "Only usually they let their partners in on it. And this bit about the knife; I think I remember that the gypsy had a knife when we busted him, but I don't ever remember Step turning it in. And the hotel murder was done with a knife. See?"

"Not really." Her tone flatly denied that Mike could be mixed up in anything he shouldn't be.

"Look," Durand amended. "I'm not saying he's done anything wrong. But I think he's bending the rules, a lot. And no cop can afford to do that, even a little. My dad taught me that, when I was real small. A cop always has to play by the rules, whether he likes it or not. A cop without rules is nothing."

"Rules without common sense are stupid," Tiffany said flatly.

Durand was silent for three blocks. This was as close to a fight as they'd ever come, and he didn't want to get any closer.

"So," he finally said as the Chevy idled roughly at a stoplight. "What would you do? Ignore it?"

"Of course not! For crying out loud, you're partners! Come right out and ask him about it."

"And of course Step will tell me the whole story," Durand observed with heavy sarcasm.

"He will, if you ask him right," she said quietly. He glanced over at her. She was staring straight ahead, and he knew that, in some odd way, he'd hurt her. It bothered him a lot more than he'd have thought it would. Especially since her left hand had never left his shoulder. He tried to find words to apologize, but it didn't seem like apologizing was the thing to do either.

The Chevy crept out into the intersection, clutch complaining all the way. "Okay," Durand said quietly. "I'll do my best to ask him right."

"Thank you," Tiffany said, just as quietly. Durand was left reflecting on why it was that the times when he understood her least were also the times when he loved her most.

## FALL, 1989

If there's more to making choices
Than luck and happenstance,
I hope I do it right
Next time I get the chance.

"NO PASSENGER"

The bus hissed like a tired snake as the door opened. The Coachman was the first man off. He leapt to the ground and pirouetted, smiling. "Welcome to Lakota," he said.

Daniel climbed out, buttoning his heavy green coat. He followed the Coachman out to the street, and looked up at the glass skyscrapers. "A city," he said. "Is a city."

"Not so," said the Coachman. "Each has its own rhythms. You'll see."

Daniel snorted. "If you like. In any case, we're here. What now?"

"Now? Well, it is Wednesday. Tomorrow, we will begin looking around. If we haven't found anything, I'll try to borrow a coach on Friday. I'm sure to get it on Sunday, if we haven't had any luck before then."

"What will we do with a coach?"

"Ride around the city. If your older brother has arrived, and your younger brother hasn't let himself be killed, I will find them, and pick them up, and then we will see what happens. Or maybe not. I don't know as much about this as you may think I do."

"Well, I know even less. As I said, what now?"

"Have you any money?"

"Some."

"Good. Let us find a place to sleep. It would be good to stay out of sight, if we can."

"Whose sight are we staying out of, Coachman?"

"The Wolf's, of course," said the Coachman, smirking, and hailed a taxi.

# Chapter Eight

THE WOLF, THE BADGER, AND THE OLD WOMAN

15 NOV 22:00

**Old woman, I hate too much, I must give it vent.**
**Old woman you are hiding here inside your tent.**
**Old woman, how much more will I have to repent?**
**Old woman will I have left a mark**
**When my days are spent?**

"BLACKENED PAGE"

"Mike!"

At the shout, Stepovich jerked awake. Reflexes rolled him off the couch and onto his feet as he scrabbled for a gun that wasn't there; shoelaces tied together brought him down just as swiftly. He caught himself painfully on one elbow, managed to avoid hitting the coffee table more than a glancing blow.

"You son of a bitch," he said with great feeling.

Ed laughed. "Works every time," he observed cheerfully,

even though it was at least four years since he had pulled the same stunt. He turned his back on Stepovich and headed for the apartment's tiny kitchen. "You want coffee?" he called back over his shoulder.

"That dead bolt cost me fifteen dollars. If you've screwed it up, I'm gonna feed it to you."

"Me?" Ed stuck his head back around the corner. "Thing wasn't even shot, Stepovich. Door wasn't locked. I just waltzed right in."

"Liar," Stepovich muttered, working at his knotted laces. He'd never been able to figure out how Ed did it. The man was overweight and clumsy as an ox, but there wasn't a lock he couldn't slip, and Stepovich couldn't count how many times in the years of their partnership that Ed had taken him unawares. When he was a rookie, Ed had almost convinced him that he, Stepovich, just wasn't alert enough to be a good cop. It had taken him a long time to realize that the big man could walk softer than a cat, and could take damn near anyone by surprise. Grabbing cat burglars from behind had been one of his favorite tricks, once upon a time.

Stepovich retied his shoes and got up to make his way into the kitchen. Ed had half the stuff out of his cupboard stacked on the floor. "Where in hell are the coffee beans?" he demanded as Stepovich came around the corner. Sneaky bastard didn't even bother to turn and look at him. Just knew he was there.

"Don't have any." Stepovich reached up to the shelf over the stove, took down a jar of instant. "Coffee's right here."

"That shit?" Ed stepped casually away from the mess he'd made. "Let's skip it, then. We can grab some on the way." He glanced back once at the packages and cans he'd rummaged through. "Pretty sorry haul, Mike. Nothing there I'd feed the neighbor's cat. When's the last time you went shopping, anyway?"

"Don't go shopping, I just pick up what I need for the day on my way home from work. Where we going? And what the hell time is it?"

"Just about midnight. Witching hour. Best time for witches, vampires and gypsy fortune tellers. But, hey, Mike, this is no way to live. Coffee is not something to take casually. You've seen how

I do it, little hand grinder, drip pot, and keep those beans in the frig until you're ready."

"Where we going?" Stepovich repeated wearily. Midnight. Shit. He had to work tomorrow. Maybe Ed had been retired long enough that he'd forgotten what it was like to drag his ass out of bed at six in the morning. Look at him. Eyes bright, hair combed, black bomber jacket that could no way meet over his gut anymore. Looked like a teenager going out cruising. Same stupid shitty grin when he finally met Stepovich's eyes and answered.

"Where we going? We're going to get our fortunes told, sweet baby mine. Madam Moria sees all, and I've got her primed to tell all. Let's go."

He tossed Stepovich's jacket at him and the flying sleeve stung his face. Ed was humming "Captain of the Pinafore" as Stepovich followed him out the door. Despite himself, Stepovich felt a small quickening of pulse. Gilbert and Sullivan had always been Ed's hunting tunes. Quick, Watson, the game's afoot and all that.

They were into the Cadillac before Stepovich remembered to say, "But Ed, I told you the thing with the Gypsy was all done and it turned out to be nothing after all."

"Bullshit," Ed said kindly, and slammed his door so hard that Stepovich's ears popped. The engine started with a roar, then Ed eased it back to a purr like a big cat's. It slipped into gear with a barely perceptible whump! and prowled off down the street.

Stepovich heaved a sigh, and then sniffed curiously. Sniffed again. "Smells like a delicatessen in here. You got a pizza in back or something?"

"Naw." Ed cleared his throat. "It's the cheese." A little further down the street he added, "In the mousetraps, you know. I mean, I hate to kill the little buggers that way, but I tried everything else. I even stole my neighbor's tomcat and locked him up in the garage with the car one night. I left the trunk and all the doors open. Even the hood. I figured he'd get hungry and nail that mouse for me."

"Didn't work, huh?" Stepovich asked idly.

"No. Bastard got in the trunk all right. Sprayed all over the place!" Ed sounded righteously outraged.

"Ah." Stepovich tried to sound commiserating and

couldn't. He couldn't hold back his snickering either. "That's what I'm smelling then. Cheese and cat cum. Thought it might be some wow new aftershave you were using. Well, guess the cat knew a pimpmobile when he saw one."

"Shithead," Ed growled. "Work my ass off for you, and you make fun of my car. Nice guy."

"What are friends for? Now, truthfully, what's with the Gypsy thing? I mean, for real, that's all done and closed. I should be at home, resting up for another day of protecting and serving the public."

They drove in silence. Traffic was down this time of night, and the store fronts were dark. North of Roosevelt. He hadn't patrolled in this area at night in years; it looked the same as it did then. He tried to avoid Little Philly when he wasn't working; he got enough of it during his shifts.

Traces of snow in the less trafficked areas. Only the garish lights of neon tavern signs and stoplights flickered over them in bars and splashes amidst the pale wash of the street lamps. West on Carradine, now. The streets were black with a layer of white from the earlier snowfall.

"You think I'm getting old," Ed said suddenly, softly.

Stepovich was startled. "What? No, man, nothing like that, it's just that this thing is done, and . . ."

"You're a sorry liar, Mike. Always have been, always will be. Your voice gets too sincere; it's a dead giveaway." A quick stab from Ed's dark eyes sank into Stepovich, gave him a tight pain somewhere in his sternum.

"Yeah." He admitted two stoplights later. "I'm lying. I'm still digging at it. But I wanted you clear, not because you're old, but because this could get real messy." He looked over at Ed, demanding he meet his eyes. "Messy enough to screw up your pension."

"Oh, yeah?" Ed turned a corner, slowed as he chose a parking spot for the Cadillac. He cut the engine, turned to Mike an indecipherable smile. "Well, fuck 'em if they can't take a joke." He stretched in his seat, rolled his big shoulders to crackle them loose. "Now," he said, his voice changing entirely, becoming businesslike and instructive. "Here's the setup, and it's taken me two days and seventy-eight dollars, so keep that in mind and don't blow it. I'll go up with you, but you gotta act like you been in on this all along. Here's how it goes. I got Madam Moria's name from my little friend."

"Little friend," Stepovich snorted to himself. "Your little friend must be getting old by now." He'd never been able to discover the identity of that particular snitch.

"Never mind that. He turned me on to this fortune-teller. Honest to god gypsy from what my little friend says, and one with a lot of ties to the community, or whatever you want to call the gypsies that pass through here. Anyway. Madam Moria's got an upstairs apartment over that sleazy music store we kept busting for selling hot instruments. Apartment C. I went there to get my fortune told. Gave her ten bucks, and she sat me down in a little back room. Candles, scarves, incense, crystal ball, the whole bit. She gave me a standard spiel, and then started feeling me out for more. So I gave her another ten for a more complete reading, and told her confidentially that I was considering investing my savings in a friend's business, but didn't know it if was a good move. Said that several of my little ventures lately hadn't gone as well as I'd hoped."

Stepovich groaned. He knew what came next. "Turned out your money was cursed, right?"

Ed grinned white. "Righto! How ever did you guess? So she told me to bring her all my life savings, and she'd lift the curse."

Stepovich knew the old con. It was familiar enough to any bunko squad. The crone would take his money, wrap it in a scarf and do some mumbo jumbo, and give him back the scarf packet, warning him to put it in a safe place and not disturb it for two weeks, nineteen days, two months or whatever. Had to give the curse-lifting magic time to work. And by the time the gull opened his little package, and found the neatly cut strips of newspapers, Madam Moria would be three states away. He'd even heard of one sap who opened the packet early, and went back to confront the gypsy. That fortune teller must have been one smooth talker, because she convinced her gull that it was still the curse at work, and now he would have to bring her more money to add to the packet before the curse-lifting charm could work. Damn fool had, too. Bunko squad had a laugh riot over that one.

"Then what happened?"

"Then at her suggestion, I gave her all the cash I had on me right then, and she wrapped it and told me she'd hold it for me."

"And?"

"I went back earlier tonight, and let her give me her whole spiel again. Then I ripped open my shirt and showed her a wire taped to my chest and told her she was busted. Then I told her that maybe I could see my way to go easy on her if she could give us a little help with something else, something gypsy related. I left her alone to think for awhile."

Stepovich glanced up at the dark windows. "And you really think she's still there?"

"She'll be there."

"What makes you think so?"

"Her face when I dropped the name Cynthia Kacmarcik. I'd say she has a personal stake in this one, Mike. Even more personal than getting herself off the hook."

The slams of the Cadillac doors were very loud on the quiet street. This was a poorer section of town, one that was the edge of the encroaching industrial district. Many of the storefront windows were blind and empty, soaped shut to the night. The surviving businesses had an air of desperation to them, the signs in the windows curling, their merchandise dusty. Litter whispered in the snowy gutters.

Ed pushed open the glass door that opened onto a narrow stairway. Stepovich followed him in past three dilapidated mailboxes dangling on the pockmarked wall. A single yellow bulb lit the stairway. The carpeting was worn through to the wood in places, and someone had left an empty pint bottle on one of the steps. Ed moved stealthy as an old ginger cat and Stepovich followed, trying not to let the stairs creak under his lesser weight. Ed scanned the narrow hall at the top of the stairs, then nodded to himself as much as to Stepovich. He knocked at the third door, and it opened almost immediately.

The young woman inside had chestnut hair and piercing grey eyes. She wore something Jenny would have referred to as a power suit. Like it hadn't been chosen because she liked it or because it suited her, but because it made her look like an executive. She was just a little too young to pull it off; it made her look a bit like Al Capone's little sister. Ed looked at her for a few seconds before shutting his mouth.

"Come right in," she said briskly, bitterly. "Do come right in. Ignore the fact that Ms. Sarinsky is an old woman and her health is poor and this isn't exactly business hours. Just come right in. And talk to me. I'm Ms. Peabody, from the Neighborhood Legal Coalition. And just for starters, I'd like to see your credentials."

Stepovich could feel his guts sliding down his legs. Ed didn't look like he was doing much better. He bobbed his head several times, and Stepovich had the feeling he would have whipped off his hat if he'd been wearing one. Ed crabbed into the room past her, and Stepovich followed him reluctantly, feeling as if he were walking into a lion's den.

Blankets and tapestries and woven stuff draped the ceilings and walls, giving the small room the feeling of a tent. Every color in the world seemed represented, with reds taking dominance. The stuffed chairs had feet carved like paws, and overflowed with cushions just as the several small tables in the room looked as if they were tottering under their burdens of bric-a-brac. Patterned carpets of various shapes and piles were layered underfoot, contributing to Stepovich's feeling of uncertain footing. Of Madam Moria there was no sign at all.

"Now, Mizz Peabody, I can see you're upset, and I think that really if we just talk, you'll find there's no basis for it." Ed began placatingly. Too placatingly. Stepovich watched Ms. Peabody's hackles rise.

"I believe I asked for your credentials," she observed icily. She looked from Ed to Stepovich sternly. Ed made a show of reaching inside his jacket. In for a dime, in for a dollar, Stepovich told himself, and flashed out his badge.

"Officer Stepovich, ma'am. I'm in charge of this investigation. Ed here is just my man. If you've got any quibbles with the way it's been conducted, I'm the one you need to talk to." He flipped the case shut, hoping she hadn't had time to get his badge number.

"Quibbles!" She puffed up like a blow fish. "Quibbles are not what I have, Officer Steppopick. What I have are grievances. Have you ever heard of entrapment? Of harrassment?" She paused. "But those are just small potatoes compared to the fact that I called the police department today, and they had no record of any ongoing investigation, or any officer in charge."

Stepovich was suddenly sure that the mild indigestion he'd been experiencing was now a full-fledged ulcer. He made the tiny hand motion he'd always made when he wanted Ed to go first around a corner or check out an entryway. But this time he made it toward the door. Let Ed get the hell out, they'd have nothing to connect a retired cop to this. Ed took a step, but not toward the door. Closer to Stepovich. Leaning toward him, shaking his big stupid face like a mournful jackass and saying softly, "No way, buddy."

"Yes way, buddy."

Stepovich looked at Ms. Peabody, who was glaring triumphantly, like a vulture who'd found a dying mule in the desert. "Wait a minute," he said. "We have to talk."

"You can talk to me," she snapped. "I'm going to—"

"Wait," he repeated, putting as much force into it as he could. Before she had the chance to speak, he grabbed Ed's arm and walked him into a corner by a hanging tapestry of a green owl and a red raven standing over a wounded knight. "Listen, idiot," he said. "You got a pension to think about. I can—"

"You can get your ass fired, buddy. I'm not going to let you play lone wolf and pay for my screw up."

"Wolf?" The voice was high and querulous, a granny wakened from her nap by noisy children. For a moment, it seemed sourceless. Then the tapestry twitched, pushed aside by the tip of a questing metal rod. Both he and Ed instinctively stepped away, going into defensive postures, before recognizing it as the end of a cane. A woman slowly shouldered her way past the heavy hanging, revealing a doorway behind it. She was old, but vitally alive, her alertness independent of her failing senses or stiff body. Her dual canes, one black and twisted wood banded with iron, the other burnished aluminum, thumped her slowly into the center of the room.

"Ms. Sarinsky, as your volunteer advocate, I have to insist you let me handle this," Ms. Peabody advised her sternly. "Actually, it's better if you say nothing at all to these persons," she added in a condescending undertone.

"Madam Sarinsky," the old woman shrilled imperiously. "I am Madam Moria Sarinsky, seer of the unknown. And I know what is best here. I."

Stepovich thought Ms. Peabody looked as ruffled as a church soloist who'd lit into the wrong selection. "For the sake of preserving your legal rights, I advise—" she began again, but

Madam Moria Sarinsky lifted her black cane and made a shooing motion as if the legal advocate were an annoying chicken.

"It's different now," she said, not explaining, but dismissing. "I did not see the Wolf before. I thought it was only this old grey Badger, trying to dig me out. Go on, go on, girl, you can do nothing here. You. Young man." She waved a cane at Ed. "Clear a chair for me. No, not that one, stupid. Any fool could see it has a wobbly leg. That one. Hurry up."

Stepovich was torn between watching the vanquished Ms. Peabody gather her briefcase and leave, and watching Ed meekly obeying the old crone.

". . . she obviously doesn't understand what you're doing. Which means she hasn't been properly Mirandized, and nothing she says can be legally used. And when the time comes, I'll be a witness to that. So if you think—"

"Yes, yes, yes," Madam Moria intoned testily. She pointed the twisted black cane at Stepovich. "You. Shut the door."

And he did, giving Ms. Peabody just time enough to get through it. He turned back to find Madam Moria settling in the chair with various small hisses and groans. She thumped a cane on the floor until Ed got the message and placed one cushion where her slippered feet could reach it. Then she breathed noisily through her nose for several more moments while she settled the folds of her gown around her. Dressing gown was too poor a description for that brocaded and embroidered marvel. Her slippers matched it, for god's sake. When it was arranged to her satisfaction, the old woman lifted her head and fixed her gaze on Stepovich. "So, Wolf. What have you come to ask?"

Maybe next year's power suits would be lavish brocade bathrobes. Stepovich started to pull up a chair, but she pointed imperiously to a cushion near her blue-veined feet. He sat. Better to go with it than to lose it.

He looked up into her eyes. They were dark and old, the browns sort of leaking into the whites and staining them. And if she wasn't at least half blind, he'd eat his badge. Blind. But seeing him, too, in a way that put the creeps up his back. He cleared his throat and heard himself say, "I want to know who killed Cynthia Kacmarcik."

He heard Ed shift his weight in a chair at this novel mode of interrogation. So did Madam Moria, for she lifted her aluminum cane and pointed it at Ed commandingly. "You. Go to the kitchen. Make tea. You keep an old woman up late, you have to care for her throat. Go."

Ed stood reluctantly. "How do I know where the tea is?" he demanded.

"Dig for it, Badger. Dig. Hurry up. And mind you steal nothing, or I shall know!" she called after him as he blundered off through the tapestry she'd emerged from. Ed dismissed, she leaned closer to Stepovich. Her blind eyes swam over his face. She reached out a bony hand, and startled him by gripping his hair. It was all he could do to keep from jerking free.

"Someone has her," she whispered. "Just like this. She'd like to be dead, poor Cynthia would, but someone won't let her go. Am I right, hum?"

Stepovich's throat went dry. Her pale old tongue emerged, wet her withered lips, and the fingertips of her free hand. She rubbed the spittle together on her fingers as if listening to it. "A little boy is in it. A nasty little boy, who hides behind Her skirts after he's done his dirtiness. But it would be a mistake to go after just him. He's only a puppet, you know. But he's a puppet with a knife, so don't turn your back until you've cut his strings. Hum?"

He could hear Ed clattering cups, heard water run into a kettle, but the sounds seemed distant: Not muffled by the hangings and the apartment walls, but distant, miles away, like dogs barking outside a village or the creak of cart wheels over a bridge. She wasn't seeing him with those rheumy eyes, but she was seeing something and he couldn't break away from her gaze.

She flicked a handkerchief in his face, and he never even flinched. "Here's a scent for you, Wolf," she told him, and there was a scent to it, like cheap macho cologne, all musk and sharp with no sweetness. He breathed it in and it seemed to vanish from the air around him even as a part of him vowed not to forget it. The handkerchief, too, vanished, as if it had never been.

"You could hunt with the Raven on your shoulder. But this Wolf always wants to hunt alone, doesn't he? The Owl could give you eyes in the night, but you think you've eyes enough, don't you? And the little one, the Dove who could coo secrets to you? Him you'd close your jaws on with one great snap. Stupids. Four great stupids, the lot of you. The world cries out for heroes, and what are we given? Three scatterbrained birds and a mangy dog."

She released his hair with a final shake and leaned back in her chair, breathing heavily. She half-lidded her eyes. Stepovich felt as if a great pressure had lifted from him. Someone made a peculiar scratching sound right outside the door, but before he could react to it, Madam Moria lifted her head. "I don't care!" she cried out defiantly, and he wasn't sure if she addressed him or not. "I'm too old to fear you, you patchwork demon! Run and carry tales! You're not the only one who can tattle little secrets!" Her voice seemed to catch on the final words, and she leaned back suddenly in her chair with a wheezing sigh. Her shriveled lips sank in on themselves, her eyes faded deeper into blindness.

"Madam Moria?" he ventured.

She took in a deeper breath, blinked several times. She reached for her black cane, thumped it weakly on the layered rugs. "Where is that tea?" she demanded, but her demanding now seemed more piteous than imperious.

"I'll check on it," Stepovich told her, and started to stand up, but Ed was pushing the tapestry aside with his back and ushering in a small tray. It was silver, the etched pattern old and lovely under the patina of years. A fat ceramic pot sat on it, and beside it an elegant cup of fluted bone china. None of the items matched, yet they obviously belonged together just as old friends do.

"Pull up . . . that table. Any table." She seemed suddenly a very old woman in a way she had not before. Stepovich didn't even smile as Ed carefully poured her tea and offered her the cup. She took it, and though her hands trembled, not a drop escaped as she raised it to her mouth and noisily sucked at it.

"She tell you anything?" Ed asked in an undertone.

Stepovich shrugged. "Not really," he answered, and wondered why it felt like a lie.

Ed went into a heavy crouch beside her chair. "How about it, Madam Moria? Can you tell us anything about Cynthia Kacmarcik?"

"I can tell you she made better tea than this! Who taught you to put water only warm on the leaves? Better the steam stands out a foot above the kettle before you pour it! Tea like this, Cynthia would pour on the floor!"

"But can you tell us . . ."

"Young man, I am tired. You think an old woman like me, she can stay up all night and talk and not be tired? Stupid. You want to know more, you come back another time."

"Maybe you could just—" Ed began, but Stepovich shook his head at him silently. Ed got the message and rose.

As they turned to the door, Madam Moria thumped a cane on the floor. "Fifty dollars!" she said, when Stepovich turned back. "You think I do a seeing for free? No! Fifty dollars, Wolf."

Ignoring Ed's incredulous look, Stepovich gave her the twenty-three he had in his wallet. She took it disdainfully. "Next time you come, you bring the rest. Or I will tell you nothing at all. Nothing at all."

They were in the Cadillac and headed back to Stepovich's before Ed spoke. "Not healthy," he observed, shaking his head.

"Well, she's pretty old," he conceded.

"Not her." Ed snorted in disgust. "She's a healthy as a horse, behind the phony wheeze of hers. Hell, that cast-iron teakettle of hers must weigh twenty pounds. If she's hefting that every day, it's probably as good as a Jane Fonda workout. Her hair hasn't even gone grey. No, I wasn't talking about her. I mean you."

"Me? I'm not sick. A little indigestion now and then, but you show me a cop who doesn't get an acid stomach, and I'll show you a cop who's too dumb to be scared."

"Naw, Mike." Ed gave a sigh. "It's the way you're living. It's starting to bug the shit out of me. At first, I thought, well, it's just going to take him a while to get used to things. But it's been more than a while, and you just aren't adapting."

"What the hell do you mean?" The sudden anger he felt was unreasonable in its intensity.

"I mean like that kitchen of yours. It doesn't look like you live there. I mean, it's more like you're camping out for the weekend, and expect to go back to Jennie and the kids next Tuesday or something."

"I don't like clutter."

"The hell you say. I'm not talking about clutter. I'm talking about having something besides ketchup in the cupboard, or more than three forks in the drawer. When's the last time you bought a carton of ice cream, or ate some meat that didn't come out of a can? You don't even have a real salt shaker, only those cardboard things from the store. And I'm talking about having books. You used to read all the time, in the break room. And I'm talking about the way you fall asleep on the couch most nights rather than go to bed and admit you're sleeping alone. And why you're sleeping alone, I don't know. And—"

"Ed. Give it a rest, okay?"

"I've given it a rest too damn long. You can't just put your life on hold. You got to—"

"Look." Stepovich was having trouble keeping his voice level. "You've made your point. Let it go. I know you're my partner, and—"

"No, Mike. I'm not your partner. And that's another thing. Who's your partner is that big green kid who isn't learning a damn thing because you aren't bothering to teach him. 'Cause you think maybe he isn't permanent. Well, you ignore him long enough, he damn sure won't be permanent, because he'll be dead."

"Let me off here." Stepovich's words were cold and hard.

"Oh, fuck you," Ed replied unhappily, and drove the rest of the way to his apartment in silence.

# Chapter Nine

## THE OLD WOMAN AND THE DEVIL

### AUTUMN, LATE MORNING

It seems like I been on this road
Ever since I was a kid;
I could tell if I was sorry
If I remembered what I did.

"RED LIGHTS AND NEON"

The Gypsy spent the night below the freeway bridge, waking up to morning fog and a promise of more snow. He stared straight up, unmoving, and tested his memory. Yes, he was the Gypsy, a name that would do for now. And, yes, he had sworn, long ago, to bring light to the world below—Her world, if you will, because all worlds that don't have the warmth of the sun, the promise of the moon, or the beauty of the stars are Her domain. He had sworn to bring the light to a dark place, in spite of Luci; that much he remembered.

But what had She done that made the memories come and go? And what had happened so that She was now in his world? Had he ever known? Would it come back, the way his recent past was beginning to? Most of it was there: The capture by the cemetery, the knife, the Wolf Who Waited Before Striking. All that was missing were his brothers.

He pulled himself up, and breathed city air, faintly cloying with traces of exhaust and humanity. Cars and trucks roared by overhead, and he marveled that man could build bridges that would stand up to such traffic. Harsh fog from the sewers swirled before him. He called to it, "Stay, brother mist. Stay and speak to me. You who travel beneath our feet through the length and breath of the city, you who hear all we say, stay and tell me where to find the old woman." On a sudden impulse, for no reason he knew, he threw a piece of garlic and the cord from his trousers into the mist, and was not surprised when he failed to hear them strike the ground.

The warm air swirled before him.

It was no voice that spoke out of the mists, but the Gypsy heard words saying, "You must do this no more."

"Do what?"

"Use the skills of another world in this one. This time, I can protect you, but—"

"Protect me from what?"

"Those skills have no place in this world, and your memories of this world have no place in the other. You cannot have both."

"I think I understand, but—"

"Do not forget again."

"But—"

"And you must neither eat, nor drink, nor must you sleep."

"Not eat or drink? Not sleep? That is impossible."

"Not for you."

"Why?"

"Fool! Do what I say!"

"Who are you, and how can I help you?"

"Who am I? You know who I am, you have asked the Wolf to set me free. And to help me, here, you must make a spinning wheel from the mist, and send it to me. It will keep the Fair Lady from tormenting me while I do what I must."

The Gypsy began to make his hands spin, and soon the mist was spinning with them. As he did so, he said, "Is there anything you can tell me, that will help me drive the Fair Lady back to Her own realm?"

"You must find the Coachman."

"But where?"

"Where? You'll find him driving a coach, fool." The voice was very faint now. "And you must find your brothers. And you can do nothing if the Wolf eats you, and eat you he will unless you place yourself within his jaws. But only at the right time. Too early and he will devour you, too late and he won't protect you."

"How will I know the right time?" he asked.

But there was no answer. A soft breeze blew the mist away, and he was staring at a foggy street and the beginnings of the morning traffic.

## SOMETIME

I don't know why
You don't cry
For freedom.

"IF I HAD THE VOICE"

*The Fair Lady puts down Her knitting and frowns. The* midwife *glances up and says, "What is it, mistress?"*

*"I don't know," says the Fair Lady. "Something is wrong."*

*The* midwife, *who has also been knitting, sticks her tongue out and wags it around. Perhaps she tastes the thickness of the air, perhaps the flavor of the woodsmoke. "Perhaps it is the prisoner, mistress. I will check on her."*

*But before she can move, the* nora *comes scampering into the room on his hands and feet. "Mistress, mistress," he cries.*

*"Well, what is it?"*

*"The woman has gotten a piece of garlic from somewhere, and she rubs it on her breast so I can't go near her!"*

*The Fair Lady smiles and pats the* nora*'s head. "Is that all?*

*Well, that must be what I noticed. Come, I will attend to that nasty young woman."*

*But when she gets there, She finds that She cannot enter, for the room in which the prisoner sits has been tied shut with a piece of trouser cord.*

*"What do you think you're doing in there?" She cries, but there is no answer. She calls to the* midwife, *who sings a gentle song to the trouser cord, and at last it unties itself. When the Fair Lady enters the room, Her prisoner is still there, but she is smiling now, and with her hands she works a spinning wheel, and she is spinning, though nothing appears upon the wheel.*

*"Now, though I am a prisoner, you can't touch me," says the old woman.*

*The Fair Lady gnashes Her teeth with anger, and stamps Her feet until the* nora *is afraid She will stomp them right through to Hell, but at last She is calm again. "I know who did this," She says. "And he will pay for it. And though I can't touch you, here you will remain until you fall asleep at your work, and then you will be mine again." And the Fair Lady slams the door.*

*After a while, She goes back to her knitting.*

## AUTUMN, 1989

The Coachman smiled down at me
When he saw I was behind him.
He said, "Your brother Raven lives,
But I think you'll never find him. . . ."

"RAVEN, OWL, AND I"

"Is that what I think it is?" said Daniel.

The Coachman looked up at the green-clad gypsy, who had just come back from walking around the city, and smiled.

The brothers looked somewhat alike, the Coachman decided, and some would say he looked similar, although he knew of no gypsy blood in himself. Daniel was thinner and his mustaches longer and his hair shorter, yet they could have been brothers. The Coachman strained his memory to when he had last seen the three brothers together. They had been young, then, but still the one now called Daniel had been thinner, frailer. The youngest brother was as pale as his yellow shirt, and the other brother, who wore red, was the largest. They had all the same pointed chin, though, and the same deep, dark eyes, and brows that met over the nose. The same hooked nose, for that matter, even as young men.

The Coachman nodded. "It is, indeed. Help yourself. I'm not drinking just at the moment." He passed the brandy over and Daniel took a healthy swallow, grimaced.

"You didn't pay too much for it, I hope."

The Coachman shrugged. "Didn't have much to pay. Is that a fiddle case?"

"Yes."

"Ah. The same fiddle as when we first met?"

Daniel nodded. "I've had work done on it. A new bridge, mechanical pegs, and I had a chin rest added. But it was good work. Sandi would have approved."

"Sandi?"

"He taught me to play. Back before—" Daniel's voice caught, then he turned away.

"Play something for me," said the Coachman.

Daniel hesitated. "The neighbors—"

"Can go hang." He looked around at the cheap plaster walls, the single, narrow bed, and the plywood chest of drawers. "In a place like this, one doesn't have neighbors."

Daniel shrugged, took the fiddle from its wooden case and set it to his chin. He drew forth a low, tentative, hollow sound, with just a hint of vibrato, then began one of the simplest dance tunes. The Coachman smiled and wished for a tambourine player. These gypsies, whatever else one thought of them, could play.

Daniel began another pass through the melody, this time more boldly, with surprising grace notes, and sometimes holding back the melody for a beat longer than expected. The Coachman sat back and nodded, and Daniel played through it once more, this time accenting the high, piercing notes, sometimes nearly leaving the melody behind altogether, in the improvisations of gypsy dance steps, of gypsy life, of travels through lands foreign and mundane, meeting people dangerous and friendly, harmless and cold. The Coachman wasn't aware of when the original melody had been entirely left behind, save for faint hints and echoes of phrasing; by this time he was seeing colors swirl before his eyes: Hard blue in the rumbling low notes, yellows and greens in the slow, mournful passages, vibrant reds and violets in staccato high notes.

Then it was no longer colors, but scenes and faces he saw: The roads in the Old Country he had traveled a thousand times before he had met the three gypsy boys, the passage from There to Here, the old man in the gutter asking for coins, the walls and ceiling of the hotels he had stayed in, drunk, night after night.

Then he saw that which he knew had not happened, yet might happen soon, and he sat transfixed, watching it unfold with horror and fascination, until he became aware at last that Daniel had returned, somehow, to the original, simple dance melody; the music trailed off into silence.

"Did you show me that on purpose?" he asked.

Daniel seemed startled. "I showed you something? No, I wasn't aware of it. Perhaps it was your—"

The Coachman stood. "I must go."

"Huh?"

"That you have no notion of what you said makes it no less true, my friend. If I don't return—" He shrugged. "Learn to drive a coach."

Daniel started to speak, but the Coachman was already gone, his feet fairly flying down the stairs. He took the stairs three at a time, then out the door, into the street, and through the early morning mist.

## THURSDAY MORNING

. . . And Owl still watches all around
And listens more than speaks,
But he'll never understand
That it isn't you he seeks."

"RAVEN, OWL, AND I"

A lonely, middle-aged salesman had driven Raymond all the way through Ohio, and had left him off in Ashtabula County, just an hour after sunrise, less than fifty miles from his destination. They had gone through twenty-eight small towns along the lake on I-90, and seen three Highway Patrol cars.

He hadn't expected to get this far this quickly. He set down his pack, and his tambourine wrapped in an old towel, and waited for another ride. After half an hour, sixty-one trucks, and more cars than he felt like counting, a big, new Peterbilt stopped and give him a lift into Lakota.

He studied the city disinterestedly as the truck driver, an old wiry man with a few strands of grey hair sticking out from beneath his baseball cap, made conversation.

Raymond rather liked the ships he saw as they passed near the docks. The driver turned south on I-79 toward Youngstown. Raymond was pleased with the number of parks (nine), though he wished there were more trees in them.

As they passed one, near what the truck driver said was downtown, Raymond noticed a horse-drawn carriage making its way around it. He asked the driver to let him off there, and they exchanged polite goodbyes.

He walked over to one of the concrete benches and sat. In spite of his first impression, he found he wasn't comfortable in the park. It was exactly two city blocks square, with concrete walks and trees arranged just so, and it seemed as if the soil under the grass was hardly a foot deep, carefully built up for the lawn. He closed his eyes and thought of the mountain above Boulder, hard and rocky, yet thick with pines. He listened to conversations of the few birds (six) that remained this late in the season. It was growing cold. He pulled his heavy wool coat of red and black squares closer around him and wondered what to do next.

16 NOV 07:18

Mr. DeCruz, won't you shake my hand?
Do I look too much better then what you had planned?
I been back since late last fall,
Now who you gonna call?

"BACK IN TOWN"

Nothing was going right today. He hadn't been able to fall asleep, and when he finally had, he tossed through fragmented dreams like clips from cheap horror movies. Giant chickens were scratching on his door. There was a dead dove on his coffee table and he was trying to resuscitate it. Cynthia Kacmarcik dropped in for tea, and his kettle wasn't big enough. When he finally sank deeper into a dreamless sleep, he'd overslept and still awakened with a headache worse than a hangover. Traffic had been awful, and he'd gotten to work before he remembered that he'd given Madam Moria all his cash the night before, so he didn't have a dime on him and no time to go to the bank. And now he was hurrying down the hall, trying to catch the last ten minutes of the morning's roll call, when someone behind him called out, "Oh, Step!"

He turned, feeling at once weary and impatient. Seemed like the whole precinct was calling him Step now. Fuck you very much, Durand. He tried to summon up a smile for the woman pushing a brown envelope into his hands. He couldn't even remember her name. He took the envelope numbly.

"What's this?"

"Oh, just that old case file from New Orleans. I promised Durand I'd have it by this morning, and then I missed him, but he said it was really for you anyway, so I guess I caught the right man after all, right?"

"Huh?" She'd lost him after her first few words, her voice dissolving into a chirpy cheerfulness. New Orleans. Durand. "Sure. Uh, thanks. Thanks."

"No problem, always glad to help a friend. Tell Durand I said hi. He's such a good kid, isn't he?"

"What? Uh, sure."

"Well, you're welcome. I hope it's what you're hoping for.

And Step, no offense, but next time you need something, why don't you come yourself? Durand's a good kid, but he wasn't sure of the date, and he could hardly read your handwriting. Said it looked like you wrote it in the middle of the night. It would be easier for me if I got it straight from you. Speeds things up for all of us, right?"

"Aah, right. Yeah. Thanks again. Thanks." He went off down the hallway, muttering to himself. Forget the briefing, he was late anyway and he was sick of hearing about what new indignities the Basher had perpetrated on Exxon stations. He was trying to remember where he had left the scribbled notes from his conversation with Marilyn. Probably folded it up and stuffed it under the clay pencil pot Laurie had made for him when she was in kindergarten. That had always been his private, hands-off spot when he and Ed were partners. But somehow Durand had gotten the notes and gone asking for the files.

Another thing occurred to him: Ed had dropped Cynthia Kacmarcik's name last night, before he had mentioned it, and he was sure he hadn't told Ed the name of the murdered woman. Or had he?

He sat down at his desk and dropped the brown envelope in front of him. Then he slowly reached over and lifted the pencil pot. Nothing there. But maybe he hadn't left it there. Maybe he'd left it right out in the middle of the blotter, and the puppy had decided to be industrious. But forget that for now.

There wasn't much in the envelope. Fresh clean paper with long-dead facts on them. Teletype print, only it wasn't a Teletype anymore, was it? He scanned it hungrily. An August night, a card game that might have been rigged, and a dead man named Timothy DeCruz. And a great description of the killer, and two eyewitnesses, and they'd never managed to catch him. The knife even sounded familiar. There was a coroner's note about the unusual wound it left. But the killer himself had just vanished. Stepovich shuffled through redundant reports, found the eyewitness descriptions and read them slowly. The witnesses hadn't missed much. A knife scar that ran from under the left eye to just in front of the left ear. Discolored patch at left jaw hinge. Broken nose. Slight squint in left eye.

"It's him, isn't it," Durand asked from behind.

Stepovich spun to glare at him. Durand ignored it, reached past him to finger the description clear of the other papers. He picked it up. "It's our gypsy, Step. And the bastard hasn't aged a day since 1935."

"He's not a bastard," Stepovich corrected automatically. "He's a Dove."

## AUTUMN MORNING

A wanted man in New Orleans
Matches my description,
Mister druggist please be kind enough
To refill my prescription.

"RED LIGHTS AND NEON"

The Gypsy sat, for a time, in the eye of the storm. He could feel the tension around him—the Wolf beginning another day's hunt, a murderer who trembled with fear and tried not to touch the weapon with which he had killed before, another who rushed, desperate to save a life that had been unknown to him moments before, another who wrestled with temptation without understanding the stakes, another who tried to bring growth out of the pain of loss.

All of these, he knew, were connected to him. And he knew that he could help some of them, if he could only find them, but to find them might mean forgetting why he had sought them. He clung to his memories as a miser to a gold coin, and sat in the eye of the storm, waiting.

Two and a half miles away, a bartender woke up much earlier than he had to, since he wasn't on until the afternoon. He glowered at the clock and lay back thinking for a while. After a time, he decided that he'd procrastinated long enough; he had to either write the letter or not. A few minutes later he got up, showered, dressed, then sat down and wrote a short note to his daughter in which he said nothing about her revelation, but that he hoped to see her over Christmas break, and they could talk then. He put his coat on and walked out to the mailbox with it, before he changed his mind.

The Gypsy sat in the eye of the storm and smiled, though he didn't know why.

## NOVEMBER, 1989

This city seems so cold,
And it isn't just the wind.
It would be easy to say
I'm here because I sinned;
Well I'm here because someday
Someone will need a ride,
And I'll throw away my drink and say
"The coach awaits outside."

"NO PASSENGER"

The Coachman paused, at the threshold, and listened. The old woman's voice was high-pitched and sharp as needles, and, as near as he could tell from just outside the door, held no trace of fear. He was in time, then. He waited for her to finish bilking this customer. It would be soon enough afterward, to go in and warn her that—

"So, it's you," she was saying. "I must say I'm surprised. I had expected some other of Her slaves."

There was another voice, but he couldn't make out the words. The old woman's voice came again. "Slave I said, and slave I meant. Or would worm be better? Madam Moria isn't afraid of worms. Now that I see you, I'm less afraid. How does She control you, worm? Does She promise you riches? Does She come to you in your dreams? In Voices out of the night? As a fire—oh, Voices, is it? Well, that shouldn't surprise me." More muttering that he couldn't make out, then, "Oh, and you have a nice shiny toy to play with? Well, get on with it. Madam Moria has friends on the other side she hasn't seen in years, and she'll have a good laugh with them about this. But don't think your mistress will be able to hold me like She's holding Cynthia. No. I've been ready for you since yesterday, and it's too late for that. Well, what are you waiting for? Shoot if you're going to."

The Coachman stepped into the room, as the skinny, short-haired man turned, holding a gun that looked as if it were too large for him. They stared at each other for a moment, then the man with the gun stepped back so he could watch both of them.

"Who are you?" snapped the old gypsy woman.

The gun began to tremble. The Coachman ignored the gunman. "Your servant, madam. Is this fellow troubling you?"

Something like amusement came into the old eyes, and she said, "Yes. See him out, will you?"

The gun trembled more. "I'll kill you both," stammered the gunman. "I have a gun."

"So I see," said the Coachman. He reached into his back pocket, slowly, smoothly, as if it was the most natural action in the world. "I have a knife."

He opened the Nevaja with a harsh, ratcheting sound. "I have learned something from all these gypsies, you know," he said. The blade was seven inches long, the handle of glittering steel with parts of the antler of the red deer worked into the grip. Blade and handle curved into a thin and wicked shape. The Coachman held it to the side, blade in and slightly up, and he waited. The gunman pressed his lips together and raised his pistol.

# Chapter Ten

## HOW THE WOLF TOOK TO TRAVELING

16 NOV 08:32

Did it cross your mind to wonder
Who put in the call?
Did you take the time to ask
What I'm doing here at all
I don't know why
I even try
To talk to you

"IF I HAD THE VOICE"

"What?" Durand asked distractedly.

"I said," Stepovich began, and then recalled his own words and couldn't make sense of them. Dove? The word had come to him as a picture in his mind, and he'd vocalized it. The tattered

Gypsy reminded him of a small snowy dove. He pushed the image out of his thoughts. "I said some bastard's been pawing through my private papers," he extemporized. He pointed accusingly at the clay pencil pot. "If it's under there, it's private," he instructed Durand.

The puppy seemed unmoved. "Didn't know a murder file could be private," he said coolly. "Unless you're personally involved in it somehow."

There was a little moment of silence in which all the implications of that statement settled.

"Are you asking if I'm dirty?" All sorts of minor variables were flipping through his mind. Whether to stand up first, or to take him right from the chair. Where to hit him first. Brain just humming along like a computer, while he watched Durand know what he was thinking and not back off. One of two things; Durand was either braver than Stepovich had thought, or stupider. Maybe both. He just stood there, blinking those big eyes like a calf. Tiffany Marie probably thought he was cute when he did that. Somehow the thought ballooned the anger inside him. Who the hell did this kid think he was, to imply Stepovich was dirty? He'd been copping since Dumbshit was in grade school.

"Are you telling me there wasn't a knife?" Durand asked softly, and Stepovich felt his anger turn cold and leak away. Durand had known it all along. Stepovich felt old, and sick, and weary. I want to go home, a little voice inside him wailed, and he suddenly felt the truth of that cry, and the despair of not knowing where home was anymore, or how to get there. He turned his chair away from Durand and tried to slide the papers back into the envelope that was suddenly too small for them. He felt again the sick weight of that knife in his pocket. Are you asking me if I'm dirty, he demanded of himself, and all of the answers were hedging and hesitant.

"You want to talk about this in the car, Step? Or here and now?"

Stepovich didn't want to talk about it at all, but Durand was taking the papers and envelope from him and sliding the ones into the other as if it were easy. Taking charge. In another minute he'd be taking Stepovich by the elbow in a firm grip and walking him out the door. That thought was enough to get Stepovich to his feet. He walked ahead of Durand down the hallway. Part of him suggested that if he'd bothered to get to know Durand, if he'd bothered to really make him his partner, that now he'd have some idea of what the kid would do. But he hadn't, and he didn't.

His mouth was dry, the grey day seemed too bright, everything was too sharp. The pavement of the parking lot gritted under his feet; he saw brown crumbs of broken beer bottle, cigarette butts, noticed the lettering on the tires of the patrol car. The weatherman had lied—the heavy fog of the day was not dispersing, he felt it damp on his face, and the door handle was cold with it. Frayed spot on the upholstery of the seat. A dead leaf was caught under the windshield wiper. He smelled Jade East cologne from whoever had driven the car last shift, and Camel cigarettes. Once, in his third year on the force, he'd been shot. A kid had done it, with a stolen twenty-two, in a panic when they'd caught him up on the roof of a school with a bag of petty cash. The bullet had gone through his shoulder, clipping one bone, tearing muscle and meat on its way through. At the time the pain had been numbing and he'd thought he was dying and every little thing had suddenly been like this, sharp and concise and realer than real life. He wondered if he thought he was dying now. Maybe. Maybe the last piece of his life that he had any control over was about to be snatched out of his grip. Maybe that was the same as dying.

Durand started the car. "Step," he said firmly, and Durand couldn't meet his eyes. It made him sick to know the power Durand had over him right now. "I want to know what's going on. All of it," he said, and Stepovich found himself nodding shakily, already editing Ed out of it, already shaving the corners off the truth, he who used to take such pride in telling the whole truth and nothing but. From the moment that damn knife came into his hands, it had cut his life to ribbons.

Sidewalks and parking meters were sliding past the window. Somehow they'd gotten out of the parking lot and onto Cushman without Stepovich noticing. He took a deep breath. "When we first saw the Gypsy, I knew it wasn't him. I mean, I know he matched the description and all, but I knew he wasn't the guy who did the liquor store clerk. Just the way you know stuff sometimes, you know what I mean." Durand wouldn't, couldn't know what he meant, the kid just hadn't been a cop that long.

Sure enough, at the next red light, Durand turned onto Eucalyptus and gave him another shot of calf eyes.

Stepovich shut his eyes for a second, tried to find some logic to hang his reasoning on. "Number one," he said, trying to sound orderly, except his voice was too shaky. "There's the weapon of choice thing. Perp uses a gun in one holdup, generally that's what he'll use in all of them. The liquor store killer used a gun. But when we stop the Gypsy, all he has is a knife."

"So now you remember the knife?" Durand asked softly.

Stepovich was suddenly too tired to even flinch. "Expired plates," he said, pointing at a battered red Chevette. Durand put on the lights, hit the sirens for one pulse. The Chevette pulled over obediently. Stepovich sat in the car, feeling heavy, while Durand went forward to talk to the driver. It was an effort to pick up the mike and call in the plate and driver's license number. But there was nothing outstanding. Stepovich would have let him off with a warning to get it taken care of, but Durand ticketed him. That was like Durand. By the book, no matter what. No matter who.

Durand got back in the car. They watched the Chevette pull back into traffic, followed it a few moments later. "So," Durand said after a few blocks. "There was a knife when we busted the gypsy."

"The liquor store was done with a gun," Stepovich pointed out stubbornly.

"And he used the knife later."

Stepovich took a breath to try a different beginning when the radio spit at them. "Shots fired, thirty-four sixteen Oak Street upper, all available units in the area please respond."

Durand looked at him, eyes wide. Asking, does she mean us?

"Left on St. Thomas," he barked at Durand, and was suddenly in control again as Durand hit the sirens and lights and whipped around the startled drivers in front of them. Stepovich picked up the mike, said, "Four dash eight responding," replaced it, and gripped the seat at exactly where the upholstery was frayed, and he wondered briefly how many other cops had grabbed this car here. "Two more lights, then go right and we should be there, or pretty damn close." Durand's jaw was jutting out like he'd been chiseled out of rock, and Stepovich realized this was the first time he'd been on a "shots fired" call. The kid's eyes were darting and bright. Stepovich's own guts were clenching already, hot damn, this was it, real-time, but it was a better, cleaner kind of fear than what he'd been feeling earlier. Guess he'd rather face a wacko with a gun than answer Durand's questions.

The merciless daylight exposed the street's dreariness. Trash mixed with snow in the gutters, and fog lurked sulkily between the buildings with the sodden winos. It took Stepovich a moment to connect where he was to where he'd been last night. When he did, he felt cornered. This gypsy thing was going to have him, there was no avoiding it, and he didn't need to see Madam Moria stepping up into a park carriage drawn by a mismatched team of horses to know just how bad it had gotten.

Durand drove right past the team and carriage as Stepovich snapped, "Stop here." The man helping Madam Moria into the carriage was dark; no gypsy, but there was something odd about him anyway. He wore contemporary clothes, but they no more fit him than Groucho glasses and a plastic nose would have. It was in the way he tucked the carriage robe around the old woman, covering her against the damp mists and the lake wind, the way he handed up her canes to her, in the forgotten courtesy of a time long past.

Had to be the Coachman. Stepovich's eyes took in details with practiced speed. The Coachman wore a flat leather cap pulled down hard over black hair that curled at the turned-up collar of his worn jacket. His eyes were dark and black mustaches framed lips full and soft as a whore's, but even sadder. His skin was olive, and wind-leathered and lined with good nature despite his mouth. His jacket just grazed the top of his narrow hips, and his jeans were tucked into boots that never came from a store. He looked at the blue-and-white as if it were a pack of wolves. He lifted an arm in a strangely defensive motion, and for an instant Stepovich thought he was reaching for a weapon. But the Coachman only clutched the front of his own shirt, and then clambered up onto the driver's seat of the carriage.

The Coachman was picking up the reins as Durand crammed on the brakes and nosed the patrol car in right in front the carriage. He and Stepovich were out of the car in an instant,

Durand already pulling his gun out. Stepovich tried to calm him. "I'll take those two and fasten them down. You . . ."

"I'll check upstairs," Durand cut in, and he was off, either ignoring or not hearing Stepovich's, "Damnit, not alone, wait a second . . ."

And there he was, torn, his partner going off in the one direction he shouldn't go alone, and the carriage driver picking up the reins and the wheels were starting to turn, grating against the asphalt. "Damnit, Durand, get your ass back here," he yelled, and then spun to the carriage, shouting, "Hold it!"

He had his hand on his gun, letting them know how serious he was. Madam Moria looked at him with disapproval, as if she were a dowager looking down at him from the back seat of her limousine, and he were a street urchin waving a dead rat at her. She was unimpressed. The driver, in contrast, was sitting very still and straight. Stepovich moved up on them quickly. The Coachman sat so stiffly, Stepovich wondered what was wrong with him. Hiding something? The fingers that held the reins were strong and somehow elegant, a magician's hands. The horses, grey and brown, were stolid, waiting. The Coachman looked straight ahead, between his two horses, as if he were totally uninvolved in what was happening here.

"All right. Get down from there, both of you. Move slowly." He intended to shake them down quick, get them into the back of the patrol car and then go after Durand before he got his stupid ass blown off.

They weren't moving slowly; they weren't moving at all. "Did you hear me?" he demanded, wanting to grab the driver and shake him right out of his coat. The Coachman swayed slightly as if getting ready to move, then was still again. Sweat was making Stepovich's uniform stick to him, and his ears were straining against hearing that single gunshot that might come at any moment. There were more sirens approaching, thank god.

"Get in." Madam Moria spoke softly, but testily, a grandma directing an ill-mannered child. "And be quick. The thread grows brittle in my fingers. If we are to follow it back and see where it leads, we must go now, before She sees it and cuts it short."

She pushed her canes to one side and gripped the edge of the carriage and leaned back as if to make room for him to climb in past her, and that was when he saw the brightness on her fingers, shining red, wet and fresh and vital. He caught movement from the corner of his eye, the driver turning and lifting something, something black, and Stepovich dove for the man, launched himself across the side of the carriage and over the seat. He hit the point of his pelvic bone going over, and landed sprawled awkwardly in the carriage, gripping the driver's wrist and shaking the handle and curled lash of a whip out of it.

The driver released it easily, and did not struggle at all. Stepovich dragged his feet up under him and knelt on the seat, gripping the man by one wrist and the front of his jacket. Christ, his hip hurt, and he tasted blood in his mouth where he'd bitten his own lip, but this guy was sitting there as straight as he could with Stepovich hanging off him, and his face impassive, only his mouth pinched tight and hard. Stepovich stared into black eyes deeper than the pits of hell.

Stepovich tightened his grip. "Now, asshole, we are going to get down quietly and slowly, you hear me?" The man nodded slowly, and Stepovich thought he saw a glint in his eyes, but it might only have been the reflection of Madam Moria's wooden cane as she brought it down smartly on the back of Stepovich's skull.

## AUTUMN DAY, AROUND NOON

Most of his money was gone before ten
When he smiled, and took out his knife.
"All right," he said, "we'll just try once again,
But this time, we'll play for your life."

"THE GYPSY"

The fog still rested on the city like a coachman's blanket, and the Gypsy decided that there was something at work beyond the capricious ways of the weather. Yet he smelled nothing of evil in it, nor of good for that matter.

So then. What could lead him to the Wolf, and at the right time? What could lead him to his brothers? His hands twitched, and he thought he could remember a time when he would have been able to learn such a thing easily, and perhaps another time when he would simply have known. He felt a slight desire to escape, to run away, to walk by paths that only he knew. The desire wasn't strong, but it was familiar. He knew, then, that he had not only felt it before, but had acted upon it. He had turned away and run, and—

His head hurt. He took out the piece of paper, which he understood at last, and crumbled it up and threw it away. To clear his head, he breathed deeply of the fog. Even as he did so, he heard the siren—the siren that had followed him for all this time, and seemed to warn of danger impending rather than to call him toward it.

He turned in the opposite direction and began walking. The fog swirled before him, making patterns that amused him although he knew—*knew* they were meaningless. *What an odd thing to know,* he thought. *Are there patterns in the fog that* do *have meaning?*

Then he nodded to himself. *Yes. This is the magic of the day, and this is a day of magic.* He reached out his hands, to take hold of the power that floated in the air around him, and— *"You must do this no more . . . use the skills of another world in this one."*

Very well, then. But this world must have its own power and skills. He could find and use them, and he would, because he was—

He was—

*No!*

He gathered his memories as a child gathers spilled marbles. No distractions, not now, when he had, perhaps, the chance to do something.

He was here, in the city, in the forest of walls, the ocean of lights, the wilderness of sounds, meadows of currents and tides of forces beyond the imaginings of the old gods. Light? Moving, twin beams stabbing through the streets, eyes to peer and a voice to warn. Walls? Endless, one leading to another, all of them high and eternal and shimmering. Sound? The siren was gone now, but something rumbled under his feet, and music came from nowhere and everywhere, and it was the voice of the Beast. And the streets which linked them, forming a mosaic as intricate as the veins on an oak leaf, each different, each the same.

Pick one.

Light, then, to guide him through the eternal day.

This one, the glow of a storefront office that advertised daily employment, led to that one, the eyes of a panel truck, which pointed to that one, the neon of a barbecue lunch counter.

And on and on, and faster and faster, as beautiful and terrible as the Fair Lady's kiss, which he had known once, as well.

## SOMETIME

All your hungers there to sate
All your thirsts to slake
Look what you've been given,
You can't see what she'll take.

"THE FAIR LADY"

*The sound of the spinning wheel in the next room is constant, and has been for a timeless time when the Fair Lady puts down Her knitting and removes Her feet from the fire. The* liderc, *which has been chewing on its goose leg, looks up. The* midwife *stops her song, which she sings to her own newborn babe that she killed, and she also looks up. The* nora, *which has been been playing with its genitals in the corner, hobbles over as well.*

*"The Wolf is on the scent," She announces. "And the Dove is taking to the air."*

*"What shall we do, Mistress?" says the* liderc, *in a voice that sounds like the hiss and pop of the fire in which the Fair Lady has been roasting Her feet.*

*"Well, you must get onto the track of the Wolf and sour the trail. You may let him follow you back here if you wish, but don't let him catch you or you'll be eaten."*

*"Yes, Mistress," and it leaves through the door.*

*"You," She continues to the* nora, *"must see to it that the Wolf is kept busy with other things. Go fetch me its cub."*

*"Yes, Mistress," and the* nora *leaves through the window.*

*"What about me, Mistress?" says the* midwife.

*"You must sing a song to catch a Dove by the wing."*

*"Yes, Mistress. Of what shall I sing?"*

*"Sing of cages that look like feather beds, and blood that smells like apple blossoms.*

*"Yes, Mistress. How loud shall I sing?"*

*"Sing so loud the nests shake in their trees, but not so loud the wolves howl in the hills."*

*"Yes, Mistress. How long shall I sing?"*

*"Sing until the snow falls up from the ground, but stop before the first note reaches your ear."*

*"Yes, Mistress," says the* midwife, *and she puts her face near the fireplace flue and begins to sing.*

16 NOV 12:09

Keep them hounds off my trail,
And them jailers off my back.
Get these bracelets off of me,
A little rain to hide my track.

"HIDE MY TRACK"

He was very comfortable, except that something was jabbing him in the back of the head. He was warm, cuddled up in a blanket tucked all the way up to his chin, but a cool breeze was blowing against his face. He shifted, trying to move his head away from whatever was poking him, and remembered that he'd been hit; then he sat up, struggling to get his gun out of the holster he was half sitting on.

"Sit still!" hissed Madam Moria. "Do you think this is easy?"

Stepovich ignored her, twisting to stare wildly around him. He shook his head, trying to clear it of fogs, but the mist swirling and eddying around the coach and in through the open windows was real. So was the good calfskin upholstery under him, and the bright brass catches and handles and trims of the coach, and the brocaded lining of the coach's ceiling. A heavy red coach blanket was tucked around him, with a large M embroidered in one corner. Nothing remained of the small park carriage he had jumped into. Nothing.

There was a small window facing forward, with a leather cover flap undone, and through it he could get a glimpse of the

Coachman up on his box. Stepovich swayed with a sudden wooziness that was only part pain. He gripped the sill of the open window beside him, thrust his head out. Forward, he could see the dim shapes of dark horses, four perhaps, shrouded in fog. Around the coach, nothing. He could see no buildings, no lampposts, no parking meters, nothing. Stepovich had a sensation of movement, but it was a nasty, queasy sort of movement, as if the coach wobbled forward on wheels of Jell-O. There was no sound of hooves hitting pavement, no sound of wheels on asphalt. No normal sound at all, only the wind and Madam Moria's muttering, and other voices, giggling and gibbering at the very limits of Stepovich's hearing. "Stop the coach!" Stepovich roared, but the fog gulped his voice down whole, reducing his command to a pitiful plea.

"We're nearly there," Madam Moria said comfortingly.

"Nearly where?" Stepovich demanded. She ignored him, and went on with her muttering as she fingered something he could not see, for all the world like an old woman telling her rosary beads. He reached up to feel the lump on the back of his head. Wet, sticky lump. It made him feel sick. Serve her right if he puked all over both of them. He knew he should be taking control of the situation; a good cop would have this situation completely under control. He unsnapped the strap on his holster, but Madam Moria shot him a fierce glare.

"Cold iron and steel, oh, yes, fool, that would be a great help to us! Do you want to fall through completely? No? Then sit still!" The wind had fingered some of her hair free of her shawl and the black strands whipped across her face, veiling her brown eyes and high cheeks. Stepovich stared at the snap of command in her voice. He had heard it before. It was the obey-me-or-die voice of a commander in a life or death situation. Something in him bowed to it instinctively.

"Where are we going?" he whispered.

"I don't know. Back. Following the threads, back to before She was hiding him."

"Who?" he asked helplessly.

"The worm. Hush. If She hears us, She'll cut the thread, and there'll be no following it forward nor back. There'll only be the mist and the Coachman."

"Trust me," said the Coachman, the first words he'd spoken, and folktales and violins shimmered in his voice, and Stepovich did. But Madam Moria laughed, the laugh of a skeptical old woman. "Trust you? Trust you right down the neck of a bottle!" Stepovich glanced at her blind but focused eyes and then away, clenching his fists. Good Christ, what the hell was happening to him?

He leaned forward to the window again. Mist and fog and clammy air, no more than that. Or was that glimpsed bit of façade, bared by the mist for only an instant, the decorated cornice of the old Masonic temple? If so, he knew where he was; but just as suddenly as it had come, his brief sense of orientation was swept away. They'd torn down the old Masonic temple six years back. The gooseneck street lamps that he could glimpse now had been gone since he was twenty-three. He remembered coming home from one of his attempts at a college education to find them gone.

Understanding broke over him like a cold wave and he refused it, clinging instead to his own reality. "Almost there, mistress," said the Coachman, and he leaned stiffly down and peered in to speak to them. He wore a top hat now, and a black wool greatcoat, but his face had not changed, not one line or hair of difference, except that now he smiled at Stepovich and his teeth were very white. Somehow that was the worst of all, and Stepovich felt his reasoning throw back its head and howl at the moon. Instead he turned back to his window and gripped the edge of it like a drowning man clutches at flotsam.

The mist was thinning around them, tattering away like cobwebs. Warmth suddenly filled the air and the sun broke through like a woman's smile; trees lined the suburban street of turn-of-the-century Victorian-style houses, children played and laughed, but Stepovich felt as if he saw it all through a dirty plate-glass window. There was an echo of distance to the bark of the terrier chasing the ball a small boy threw, and neither child nor dog turned their heads to watch the horse-drawn coach pass. Big elms lined the street. The city hadn't seen elms that size since the Dutch elm epidemic of '63 had left the suburbs near treeless. The Coachman wasn't bothering with the street, either, hell, he wasn't even on the sidewalk; he was taking it across the lawns, through sprinklers that didn't wet them, down to an empty lot, overgrown with deep grass, littered with pop cans that weren't aluminum, and presided over by a live oak.

A ramshackle treehouse perched in its branches, a genuine kid's treehouse, all impossible angles and salvaged scrap, and a lively battle was going on for possession of it. Two boys in jeans and plain white tee shirts were in the upper level, energetically shaking a knotted rope that a smaller boy clung to. The smaller boy was dressed in clean pale blue corduroys and a button-up-the-front short-sleeved cotton shirt that matched the color of his pants exactly. His belt was white and his sneakers were black and low, like girl's sneakers, and new looking, not like the battered black hi-tops that Stepovich could glimpse on the other two boys. Everything about him screamed Mama's Little Precious, and Stepovich wasn't surprised to hear one of the older boys tease, "Go home to Mommy, little Timmy. She's calling you. She wants to wipe your nosey."

Timmy? Timothy Decruz? No, they hadn't gone *that* far back.

"Naw, Josh, she wants to wipe his little baby butt!" jeered the other, and together they gave the rope one final shake that ripped it out of Timmy's hands. He fell awkwardly, not like a kid, but like a frightened old man, and landed badly, on his back in the dirt. The other boys snaked the ladder up quickly while little Timmy lay on his back, trying to wheeze back the air that had been knocked out of him.

"Lookit, little baby Timmy's gonna cry now!" one boy sneered, the same one who had made the remark about his butt. Stepovich thought the other boy looked mildly worried. He himself, powerless to intervene, stared at Timmy, feeling a sick sort of sympathy for him, one that was tempered with an innate understanding of how the older boys felt. Spray a sparrow with paint, and the other sparrows will peck him to death.

Timmy got up, his narrow shoulders still shaking with tears. No. Not tears. An unchildlike rage convulsed his round little face. "I'll get you sonsabitches," he vowed, his voice breaking on the words.

"Oh, he's gonna get us, oh, Josh, hold my hand, I'm so scared," mocked one of the treehouse boys, and he was laughing wildly, mouth open, when the rock hit him.

It was well aimed and flung with fury and it struck right

between the boy's eyes. Stepovich saw his eyes roll up a fraction of a second before he fell from the treehouse. The boy landed with a force that made him bounce, his arms and legs flopping like a straw man. "You killed him!" wailed Josh, and came snaking down the ladder to kneel by his friend. For an instant Stepovich feared it might be true, but then the boy on the ground stirred, and then began crying, the terrible sound of a child who thinks he is too old to cry but is hurt too badly not to. Little Timmy seemed to devour the sound, staring with his pale eyes round, his hateful little mouth drawn up in a bow of pleasure. "I gotcha, I gotcha!" he screeched gleefully, but the two older boys were too deep in shock to heed him. Josh tottered his friend off toward home, and the instant they were clear of the treehouse, Timmy was at the rope, doggedly and clumsily shinnying his way up the knotted length. Once up in the tree house, he pulled up the rope. He leaned out of it, his small face bright with hate and triumph. "I gotcha, and the treehouse is all mine now!" he shrieked after them.

Stepovich was willing to bet he was right. There was something in that boy's face that no sane kid would cross twice.

There was a thing then, a creature of flames and animal parts—goose leg, horse arm—coming at them, burning over the ground like a range fire. The Coachman cracked his whip at it, but it made Stepovich suddenly realize that none of this was real—that something very bad had been done to his head and he was probably even now in an ambulance, if Durand had it together at all. He wondered if the bullet was in his skull this time, and if the dream would stop when the doctors pulled it out. Madam Moria was shaking her fist at the creature and yelling what were probably curses, but the Coachman was shaking the reins and leaning forward, and suddenly he split the whole world, wide and black, with a piercing whistle.

# Chapter Eleven

HOW THE OWL AND THE RAVEN SANG

THURSDAY AFTERNOON

He said, "You can go back home
  And never face the dangers,
Or continue toward a life
  You will live among strangers. . . ."

"RAVEN, OWL, AND I"

Daniel waited for the Coachman until he couldn't wait any longer—almost ten minutes. The Coachman's words about each city having its own rhythms had stayed with him, and now he wanted to taste this city's. He took his fiddle and went out to meet the fog in the air and the snow on the ground. He hardly noticed the cold; he'd been living in a place where winter was colder and lasted longer.

He wished the Coachman would find his little brother; both of his brothers, in fact. His big brother could sit and do nothing for hours on end and not seem to mind; he'd just smile with his little supercilious smile and nod from time to time. And his little brother, well, he never had to wait, because wherever he was, things were exciting. But he, Daniel, always seemed drawn to the excitement, but he never quite knew what to do when he got there.

But no, that wasn't right; he'd never really been tested. All of these years of wandering and waiting, and, except for the first mistake of leaving his little brother, a mistake he shared with Owl, he'd never had the chance to learn what he was made of; never the test, never the hard choice, never the need to put everything into one, horrible, wonderful moment. He knew it, and he missed it, and he waited for it.

He sat down on a wrought-iron bench and waited for something flashy to catch his eye, but nothing came; there were few passersby. There was one tall young man who seemed very dangerous, and wore animal skins that had been dyed black. There was a woman who hurried by who had painted her face so heavily it was impossible to guess at the texture of her skin, except that her hands showed signs of age.

Daniel took out his fiddle, stood, and played waiting music. As he played, he thought of his little brother, and worried about him. "If my fiddle were a shield," he thought, "I'd play music to protect you, wherever you are." So he played to ward off the evil eye, and to baffle Luci's creatures, and he smiled from the pleasure the music gave him. After a while he drifted off to other airs, then, with an odd feeling of having accomplished something, he sighed and went back to the hotel. He finished what little brandy was in the bottle and tried to wait patiently for the Coachman.

## NOVEMBER SIXTEENTH, AFTERNOON

. . . His eyes softened for a time,
I could barely hear his voice:
"It isn't easy to decide,
But few get the choice."

"RAVEN, OWL, AND I"

Raymond sat in the fog, a bit troubled by the chill, but not too much; where he came from winters were colder and lasted longer. He studied the vague shapes that passed in the fog, twenty-eight of them, noticing the way this one huddled into his coat, or that one clutched her purse tightly as she walked. And, more, he listened to the way they walked, and to the odd rhythms created by the tap-tap of high heels or the slap of shoe leather against the endless murmur of the city: A door slams, and another, closer; hisses; a small car with a standard transmission shifts from first to second; a larger car dopplers away, leaving a faint buzz which blends into the sound of a train that is so far away it is only a low moan.

He became aware of the Dove's presence; not near him, but that his brother had been in this city long enough to have an effect. There were lives the Dove had changed, somewhere, flowing and breathing. A tremendous longing to find both of his brothers filled him, but there was nothing he could do. He knew that, had he the powers of his youngest brother, he would be able to bring them together; he did not begrudge him those powers; with powers come burdens, and Raymond could not lighten them. His other brother—what had he been calling himself? Daniel, that was it. Daniel would have wanted to redraw the paths to suit himself, but Daniel was a doer, not a watcher; he could lighten the Dove's burden. Daniel, too, might be nearby; Raymond couldn't tell. They had each their paths, and perhaps their paths would cross.

He sat up straight, suddenly. *Something has just happened*, he thought. He frowned. It was like the trembling of a web, when the spider, far away on the other side, jiggles a strand. Raymond had a guess who the spider was, and wondered what strands She was jiggling. For a moment, he felt the frustration that Daniel must live with all the time—wanting to act, but being unable—but then old habits came back, and he relaxed, watching, listening, waiting.

At last, just to have something to do, he took out his tambourine, wrapped carefully in old towels. He tapped the head and winced at how lifeless it sounded in the damp weather: It must be proximity to the lake; cold weather was usually very kind to the calfskin. Nevertheless, he sat in the park and tapped at it, playing with rhythms of the city, and finding counterpoints to a strange singing he almost fancied he heard, coming from the wind around him.

He sat for hours, playing his tambourine, neither noticing nor caring whether some passerby stopped for a while to listen before continuing on his way. Two girls, one dark and one fair, watched him for some time with that oddly bemused expression people get when they realize for the first time that the tambourine is a musical instrument. He felt a certain pride in getting this reaction, and then he noticed that they seemed frightened somehow. They spoke to each other of only the most inconsequential things; shoes that were too tight, hair that wouldn't behave, yet underneath it all they shared a common terror, which neither would admit to. He thought he saw an animal scurry past, but when he looked he saw nothing. Presently they went on their way after giggling and putting a dollar in the pocket of his coat. They seemed not as frightened as they'd been a few minutes before.

He played until dark and the chill began to penetrate his fingers, then he put his instrument away, got up, and began to walk around the city, looking for nothing in particular.

16 NOV 13:13

You got your pen and paper,
You got your book of rules,
You got your little list,
Of kings and crooks and fools. . . .

"IF I HAD THE VOICE"

Stepovich fell. His stomach told him so. Fell fast and hard and boneless, just like that boy coming out of the tree. He wondered if it would hurt when he landed, and then he wondered if this blackness had a bottom. Maybe the blackness was the surgeons taking the bullet out of his head. Or maybe the blackness was what came when they couldn't get it out. He could feel someone gripping his hand; maybe Jennie had come to be by his deathbed, maybe this blackness was the dying part. He'd heard there was supposed to be a light when you died, and that you'd want to go toward it. He strained his eyes, looking for it, but all he could see was blackness. He could feel the hand in his and smell cheap brandy and garlic mixed with horse sweat.

The carriage landed with a tremendous sproing, like a body thrown against a chain-link fence. He opened his eyes, half expecting to see Marilyn by his deathbed, but he saw fog and buildings and his blue-and-white by the curb. Someone gripped the front of his uniform. The damn Coachman couldn't have been that strong, but maybe he was that scared. He lifted Stepovich half up and gave him a push that sent him sprawling. Stepovich skinned his palms as he landed mostly on his hands and arms in the street. Madam Moria evidently wasn't pleased about this, because she was still screaming in gypsy, but the Coachman seemed to have some plan of his own. Stepovich fell the rest of the way out of the carriage as the black whip cracked. The hooves of the mismatched team skidded and slipped on the damp pavement as the carriage careened off down the street and into an alley. Madam Moria was looking back and shaking her aluminum cane at him as if it were all his fault.

He got his knees under him, was almost up when Durand trotted up to stand over him. "You okay, Step?" he asked anxiously. It was the only thing that could possibly have made it worse: The puppy helping him up like he was some dazed citizen, gripping the front of his shirt to steady him. "You hurt?"

"No!" Stepovich pushed him roughly away, then had to lean against the building. Shit, his head hurt. He reached up to touch it. Lump. No bullet hole. What the hell.

"Well, if you're not hurt, how did they get away?"

"In a carriage," Stepovich said viciously. He took his fingers away from the back of his head, looked at the blood.

"Wanta chase them?"

"Fuck, no!" Stepovich took a shuddering breath, realized that Durand was only trying to get the senior officer to take charge of the situation. "What did you find upstairs?" He tried to sound hard and professional. Sounded dazed to himself.

"Nothing."

"Nothing?"

"No one in the apartment. No weapon. No sign of a struggle. But I did smell powder. Someone let off a gun in there."

"Blood?"

Durand looked nonplused. "Well . . . I didn't really notice . . . I mean, every rug up there is red, and I didn't think to . . ."

"Right," Stepovich said. He walked ponderously to the squad car, leaned in to reach the mike. He told the dispatcher it was all under control, no sign of any gun or quarrel, cancel the call. The dispatcher came back, her annoyance sounding clearly through the static. "Heard you the first time, Stepovich. Canceled it ten minutes ago."

He turned to Durand. "Did you cancel the call?"

"Huh? No." Durand looked puzzled too, which made Stepovich feel better.

There was a feather on the seat of the car, and the interior stank like a barnyard, or a kennel.

His head was buzzing as he straightened up. He scanned the street, not certain what he was looking for, then he stopped and frowned. "What do you make of that?" he said.

Durand looked back. "What?"

"On the door of the building."

Durand walked over and stared at the smear on the glass. "Blood," he said.

"That's what I thought."

Durand said, "What do we do about it?"

Stepovich sighed and shook his head. "Nothing."

Durand came back to him, and stood a little too close; his voice was a little too demanding as he began, "Enough shit, Step, I want to know—"

"It's Stepovich, God damn you!" he roared, and swung with the weight of the world in his fist.

## SOMETIME

Look into a deep dark pool, tell me what you see,
Stars overhead.
Echo of a midnight sky, branches of a dream
Turnings of a maze.

"STARS OVERHEAD"

*The Fair Lady nods to the* liderc, *who has suddenly appeared before her. His face is bleeding, and he holds a hand over one eye. "What is it?" She says, not unkindly.*

*"It's the crawling one," he says. "He is hurt and asking for you."*

*"Hurt?" The sound of the spinning wheel is constant now, and neither of them notice it.*

*"He says he's been cut up," says the* liderc. *"I think it was the Coachman who did it."*

*"Indeed? How could that be, when he was with an old woman following spools of thread down lanes of curses?"*

*"I don't know, Mistress. Perhaps before they left?"*

*"Perhaps. And did you cut the thread, little one?"*

*"No, Mistress. Not in time. The Coachman saw me and he struck out my eye with a calk on the end of his whip, and then he took them back."*

*"I see. Well, here is another eye for you." She draws a cinder*

from the fire and places it in his head. Then She thinks for a moment, and finally nods. "Very well, then we will cut a different thread. Let the Worm bleed. And, for that matter, let the Wolf have him. For now, prepare another guest room. We shall need it soon, I think."

"Yes, Mistress."

"And as for the Coachman, we will send him a bottle of brandy, so that when he drinks it he will be crushed by a horse with five legs and gored by a bull with three horns."

"Yes, Mistress," and the liderc runs off to do Her bidding.

At that moment, there is a scampering of feet and hands across the floor as the nora enters the room. It grovels at the Fair Lady's feet. Its bald, leathery head seems to absorb the firelight.

"Well?" She says, beginning to become impatient. "Have you failed, as well?"

"Yes, Mistress," it says. "She was protected."

"Protected? How?"

The nora wiggles its rat-ears back and forth, agitated. "There was a sound like the chiming of bells and the thundering of cannon, so I could not come near."

"So? It's his damnable brother. Well, we shall see what we can do about that. Send him a good meal, so that when he eats it, the ground will open and swallow him up."

"Very well, Mistress," and it rushes off to prepare the meal.

Near the fire, the midwife continues to sing.

"Are you having any luck?" asks the Fair Lady.

"None, Mistress," says the midwife.

"How is that?" cries the Fair Lady, gnashing Her teeth with rage.

"There were screams, Mistress, like the screams of impaled men, so he can't hear me sing."

"That will be his other brother. Well, we will fix that. We will send him the wench, so that when he kisses her, he will fall down dead on the spot."

"Very well, Mistress," and the midwife goes to find the wench.

16 NOV 16:27

If I had the voice, I'd shout it from the rooftops,
If I had the strength, I would bend it in my hand;
All I've got's a notion, all I need's a plan,
To bring it back to where it all began.

"IF I HAD THE VOICE"

The rest of the shift was horrible. Durand wasn't talking, either because he didn't want to, or because his face hurt too bad. He'd stepped into the punch, taking it on the side of the head instead of the jaw. Stepovich glanced over at him guiltily. Purple. And swollen as hell. Probably hurt almost as bad as the back of Stepovich's head.

Lunch had been Seven-Eleven burritos and coffee inside the car. They hadn't gone to Norm's for lunch. Neither one had had to suggest that change of plans. Nobody wanted to explain any of this to Tiffany Marie. Stepovich didn't want to explain plugging her sweetie, and Durand probably didn't want to admit that an old man like Stepovich could drop him with one punch. Stepovich rubbed his bruised knuckles unobtrusively on the side of his thigh. Ten more minutes of driving around. Then reports to write. Then go home, eat something out of a can, and lay around and stare at the boob tube or the ceiling. Wonder what the hell had ever happened to his life. He sighed.

"S'matter?" From Durand, grudgingly.

"I feel like shit. I feel fucking stupid." And too damn tired to be anything but honest.

"Y'should."

Poor kid couldn't even get his jaw open. Stepovich was willing to bet the inside of his mouth was cut to ribbons on his own teeth. "I know."

Silence felt a little easier. Streetlamp light ebbed and swelled through the car. Getting dark earlier all the time. And colder. "You put a hot washcloth on it when you get home. Hot as you can stand. And drink something cold, milk shake or something like that."

Stepovich paused, remembering. Ed had loosened two of his teeth. For what? So long ago. It came to him. For the stupid habit of taking his gun out in the car and checking to see if it was loaded. About six times a day. Until the day Ed slammed on the brakes, punched him one, and screamed, "Play with your dick instead, asshole! At least you can't blow me away with that!"

"S'not funny." Durand sounded hurt.

Stepovich realized he was grinning. He wiped the smile off his face. "I was thinking about something else. That blood, on the door. Whose do you think it was?"

"That's funny?"

"No. That isn't what I was thinking about either, but I am now. Whose do you think it was?"

Durand shrugged carefully. "Don't know. You?"

"No. The Coachman guy and Madam Moria seemed pretty chummy. I don't think they were shooting at each other. If there was someone else, he was gone when we got there." Stepovich took a breath, sniffed, forced himself to open up. "I did see some blood in the carriage. On her fingers. But I'm not sure if it was hers. She didn't act hurt."

"Driver?"

"He didn't act hurt either." Stepovich frowned to himself. "Or maybe he did. Acted kind of stiff, like maybe he was holding himself careful. Didn't seem to bother him when he threw me out of the carriage, though." Stepovich glanced at Durand and the kid jerked his hand down from cradling his jaw. He remembered something else from the day Ed had busted his chops.

"Kid. After work, you wanna go for a beer?"

Durand looked at him long through the dimness of the car. He nodded slowly.

"Good," said Stepovich with a heartiness he didn't feel. What the hell had he done that for? The last thing he wanted was company tonight.

Maybe it was the first thing he wanted, too.

## THURSDAY, AFTERNOON RUSH HOUR

Ripples on the surface, currents underneath.
Ripples on the surface,
Stars overhead.

"STARS OVERHEAD"

Brian MacWurthier drove slowly home from work through the fog during the last hour of the day. On impulse, he stopped at a liquor store to pick up a small bottle of creme de menthe. He had two reasons for doing so. In the first place, he was beginning to want to live again, and that meant treating himself to fancy desserts once in a while, like he'd made for Karen. And, two, she had never liked creme de menthe, and he knew that if he made something she had liked, he'd just get melancholy again. It was time to let go.

While he was there, he picked up a paper and glanced at the headlines. "Damn shame," he muttered.

The man behind the counter handed him a bill and some change and said, "What?"

Brian indicated the headline. "The accident. Six dead. Bet they all had families."

"Don't I know it," said the clerk.

Brian studied him. Late thirties, maybe. Big, with a small mustache. Maybe wore a stupid hat and laughed too loud, but he was probably kind to his dog. What the hell. Brian nodded. "You lose someone recently?"

"No." Then he said, "Well, not really."

Brian waited, holding the little paper bag with the creme de menthe in it.

The clerk looked at him and shrugged. "A friend of mine."

"A good friend?"

"Naw."

Brian kept waiting, he wasn't sure why. The clerk said, "It was just nasty 'cause I was here when it happened."

"Oh."

"We weren't real close, though." After another pause he continued. "But it was violent. I still don't sleep too good." Then he said, "What about you?"

Brian hesitated. "My girlfriend. She died of leukemia not long ago." There were still tears inside, but he could say it without choking now.

"Yeah, that's a shame, buddy."

Brian nodded. "I'm getting over it. I finally talked about it, and that helped."

"Yeah. I know. Some shit, you can't keep inside, you know?"

Brian nodded. "This gypsy said—"

"Who?" His voice was surprisingly sharp.

"Her friend. The guy I talked to."

The clerk scowled.

"What?" said Brian.

"Don't talk to me about gypsies. It was a gypsy who blew my friend away. Right here. I was in back, too fucking scared to move, and this gyp— now that's odd."

"What?"

The clerk stared off into space for a while. "Why did I say he was a gypsy?"

Brian shrugged. "Did the police mention it?"

The clerk shook his head. "No. That's weird. He looks different now."

"Huh?"

The clerk blinked a few times. "I dunno. Man, this is strange. It's like my memory's changing. The description I gave the cops, it's all wrong. But I could have sworn—I hope I'm not flipping out or—"

"You all right?"

"Yeah, I think so. But I better call the cops back right away. This is too fucking strange."

Brian waited while the clerk made the phone call, then waited some more just to make sure the man was going to be all right. When the blue-and-white pulled up, he shrugged and headed out the door, still vaguely curious.

## A WEEKDAY EVENING

Mr. DeCruz, hope you're feeling well.
Mind if I sit here just for a spell?
Sorry I couldn't be gone for good
Like you thought I would.

"BACK IN TOWN"

Timothy lay on his bed, bleeding from cuts in his side and on his upper chest just below the collar bone, for most of an hour before it occurred to him that something was wrong. He spent most of the next hour denying it, until he couldn't anymore. I could die, he thought, and the other side of that thought conjured up childhood memories; he feared hell for the first time in twenty years.

The next hour lasted forever. The words, "She has forsaken me" never quite took shape in his mind, but they lay beneath the surface, like walking through a swamp knowing there is a snake in there, somewhere. He opened his eyes and tried to sit up, failed. It came to him that now there were bloodstains on his nice, clean, white sheets, and he'd never, ever, ever get them out. He wanted to yowl, but had no strength. The thought that he could die kept returning, until in an agony of fear he peeled off his shirt, and pressed his pillow tightly against his side, resigned to getting that soiled, too.

*Damn them, damn them, damn them all to hell forever. Why won't She help me? I did everything She said. I tried to kill the old lady, but the man with the knife. . . .* The man with the knife. Why hadn't he gone down when he'd been shot? Right in the middle, just like the liquor-store man. This guy jumped, once, then struck with the knife, and Timothy had run from the room, not even realizing he'd been cut until he was halfway down the stairs and saw blood soaking through his shirt.

*I won't die*, he thought. *I won't die. I'll live, and I'll show Her that I'm worth something. I still have the gun. I'll go back, and find that man, and shoot him in the head this time, and the old lady, too. No, better. The Gypsy man. That's who She really wants. I'll get him for Her, and She'll come back to me.*

*I need Her. I need Her. I need Her.*

He lay there awake for hours, pressing the pillow against him. Finally, as it grew dark outside, he fell asleep, thinking thoughts of vengeance, still holding the pillow pressed against his side. As he slept, with no magic other than his body's own, the bleeding stopped.

## AUTUMN LATE AFTERNOON, BEFORE MOONRISE

If I had it to do over,
This ain't the life I'd choose,
But the road still runs and so do I
And at least I made the news.

"RED LIGHTS AND NEON"

It was mere moments before sunset, and the end of the day's magic, although the fog held the day's light as leaves hold the dew. It didn't yet look like sunset, but the Gypsy knew. And as twilight sank through the layers of fog, consciousness of it sank through minds, and more and more lights came on. It became harder and harder to find the light that was his next signpost, amid all those that were on by chance.

He frowned. Why should it be so hard to tell? He followed his feet, his instincts, and if they were true, they should lead him well. So it was, so it had always been. He had been confused for a while, not understanding the ways of the city, but now he did, and the rules should be the same. If not, he was helpless.

He stood, pondering. He closed his eyes, and thought he heard faint singing, as far away as the sea and as soft as the wind across the plains. He shuddered, and his hand went to the knife beneath his shirt, though he didn't know why.

He stood on a street corner. Four paths, the crossroads. But here there were so many crossroads, so many. If a shirt were left at each to bribe the *csuma,* there would be no shirts left to wear. Not to mention that any shirt left on the crossroads in the city would be taken by whoever first saw it whether he needed a shirt or not, for such were the ways of this place. The crossroads ought to be a place of power for him, but he felt none. It ought to be a place of danger too, but he felt the danger everywhere.

He stood for a moment more, looking around, hoping for a sign that he was to take one direction, or avoid another. Even as he looked, however, the fog began to clear, the night fell, and the day of miracles had ended. He sighed, defeated.

And as the fog cleared, he saw, directly before him, a circle with a dot in the middle. It was on a narrow door with a sign above it. The sign, in baroque lettering, read, MADAM MORIA, PSYCHIC AND SEER, APARTMENT C.

Almost, the Gypsy smiled. There was no hesitation in his steps as he opened the door, which led up a long flight of stairs. He climbed with easy confidence and knocked at the door with an upside-down C hanging by a single nail. He opened it at the same time the high, thin voice called, inviting him in.

She sat behind a narrow table, and a deck of tarot cards, bright roses on the back, sat in front of her. There was a small stool opposite her.

"You took long enough getting here," she snapped. "Sit down and cut the cards."

# Chapter Twelve

## HOW THE DEVIL SET HER TRAPS

MID-NOVEMBER, 1989

I got to wonder who it was
Gave the key to you;
I got to wonder what they pay
For the things you do. . . .

"IF I HAD THE VOICE"

The Coachman walked slowly. At the best of times, he hadn't liked walking. On the ground he felt shortened, vulnerable; give him the high box of a coach any time, with sixteen legs before him and four wheels under him. Two legs are not the same, especially not when a Worm has eaten a quick hot hole right through the middle of you.

He thought briefly of Madam Moria's upstairs apartment. He had gone back there, once the Wolf had gone away. He went up to her door, thinking she would take him in, would at least let him sit and breathe if not bandage his wound. But she hadn't. She was been angry and hard as only old women can be. "Away," she told him, waving at both him and a grey cat sitting on her door mat. "Be gone. I had my Wolf and you threw him away. Do you think I will let you chase away the guest who comes to me tonight? Go on, go read your future in the bottom of a bottle."

And then she shut the door on him and the cat. The cat looked up at him with cold yellow eyes, obviously sharing Madam Moria's opinion of him. "You don't understand," he explained. "The Wolf was hungry. It wouldn't have gone away unfed." The cat was unimpressed. Useless to argue with yellow-eyed cats or old women, he told himself. And made his way gingerly down the stairs.

And Spider had been very angry as well, when the Coachman returned the carriage and team with no fares at all to show for the day. "You won't drive for me anymore, you drunk son of a bitch!" he yelled. "You're nothing but trouble, bringing cops and every other damn thing down on me. Get the hell out of here!" And he shook his whip at the Coachman, as if he knew how to use it. The Coachman thought about cutting him up with his own, to show him. But he'd done enough cutting for one day, and he was cold and tired and in pain, and one drink too sober to stand up to any of it. He started the long walk home, wondering if anyone would be there when he arrived.

His feet had taken him down an alley, behind the warehouses, past the loading docks where the streetlights were yellowing the night and two cursing men were trying to get a crate up on a forklift. He stopped to watch, one hand pressing gently against the warm wet bandanna inside his shirt. *She could at least have bandaged me properly.* The workmen stopped briefly. One wiped his forehead, sweating despite the cold, while another brought out a pint bottle and unscrewed its cap. They passed it between them and the sweet note of brandy rang clear in the air. The Coachman snuffed after it longingly. That hot kiss, that comforting warmth could ease his pain now.

They went on with their work, and he leaned against the end

of the loading dock, shivering and watching them. A semi was backed up to the dock, its open van gaping black. There were six large crates labeled LAKOTA MUSEUM OF SCIENCE AND INDUSTRY waiting on the dock. The men were cursing someone who hadn't shown up to help with the work, and the way they moved told the Coachman they weren't experienced at what they were doing. One mounted an idling forklift on the dock, and maneuvered it awkwardly up to one of the crates. But the crate edged away from the machine, and the man throttled the engine, making it snort white plumes of exhaust like an angry bull. "Put it in reverse," yelled the other, and the forklift driver yelled something back, but the machine surged forward instead, and the huge crate buckled before its roaring advance.

"Reverse, damnit!" shouted the other man again, and the driver pulled a lever and backed the huffing machine away. A piece of the crate tore away with it, pine planks ripping yellow, and the Coachman felt a cold shiver run down his spine as flashing silver eyes and a tossing white mane were revealed. Blue roses were braided in the mane, and the stallion champed a silver bit in his white teeth. Veins stood out in his proud muzzle and in the forelegs lifted high to paw at the sky. Whoever had carved the carousel horse had known what a horse was about. The Coachman would almost swear that it was held motionless only by the vertical pole through its body, that but for the pole the stallion would leap forth from the remnants of the shipping crate. In spite of himself, he stepped closer.

There was a great deal of swearing and yelling from the two men, with the one throwing his hat down in disgust. They changed positions, with the other man climbing up on the snorting forklift while the former driver pushed vainly at the crated horse, trying to get the crate into a position for the forklift tines to go under it. It was too heavy.

The Coachman moved a step closer. "Your pardon," he said.

They noticed him for the first time. The driver looked impatient and annoyed, the other annoyed and curious. "For some of your brandy, I'll help."

The crate man stopped his useless shoving. He wiped his forehead on his sleeve, looked at the Coachman, nodded, and dragged the flask from his pocket, handed it over. The Coachman took it, feeling the liquid weight welcome in his hand. He tipped it back once, and it kissed his mouth deep, promising to take the chill away. A second time, and it curled itself warm around the pain in his gut, quieting it like sleep quiets a colicky child.

"That's enough," said the crate man, snatching it back. "You can have the rest when we're done." He set the bottle down on the dock behind them, and gestured toward the crate.

The Coachman nodded. He took his place, and together they tipped the crate up and toward them. The forklift came closer, its tines lowered, snorting and reaching for the crate.

It came too fast, and the crate man yelled and jumped aside. For one moment the Coachman had the full weight of the crate, taking it, standing eye to eye with the rearing white stallion, and he thought he could hold it. But then his heel bumped the brandy bottle, and even through the snorting of the forklift and the driver shouting, "Where's reverse?" he heard the bottle break. His boots grated on broken glass and then he was slipping, falling backwards off the dock. The white stallion came after him, hooves pawing the sky, and then he felt the hot breath of the forklift sear him as it careened off the loading dock as well. A gleaming metal tine tore his hip, letting his blood out in a rush of warmth and red. He was tangled with the stallion, the front legs straddling him and the angry silver eyes staring down into his. Somewhere nearby the workmen were yelling, and a woman was laughing, a throaty sweet laugh as the horses of the Coachman's mind broke their traces and ran away into the engulfing blackness.

## THURSDAY NIGHT

Let the moonlight show the path
To a standing cypress tree.
I'll tell you tales along the way
Of what you've done to me.

"GYPSY DANCE"

When the Coachman didn't come back, Daniel put on his green overcoat and went out. The grimy walls of the room had become oppressive. The cold night air was preferable to the moldy exhalations of the ratty little hotel room. His fiddle went with him, as naturally as his feet and hands and heart. The street before the hotel was lit with red and blue neon, flashing names of beers and GIRLS GIRLS GIRLS. On one corner, three girls tiredly smiled. They weren't as young as they wished they were, and the sequins on their dresses dangled loose from too many casual caresses, the seams strained from having too often been hiked up in the back seats of cars. They reminded Daniel of dancing bears, ruffs on their necks and rings in their noses, fur gone patchy with bad food. He moved a little down the street from them, opened his case on the sidewalk, and played them a tune, innocence and dreams. He saw them listening and becoming uneasy, so he changed it to an old ballad with laughter beneath the tears, with sorrow amid the joy. Their lives were the words and they knew the song well. They stood quietly in the wash of the music, watching the cars stop and go again at the light, waiting more passively than they had before.

He wondered where the Coachman was. He thought of his brothers, but it made the music grow unbearably sad, so he played for the whores once more.

A fourth one came out of a nearby bar, riding a wake of crude laughter. "No hair on her pussy yet!" someone shouted after her, and she hurried away from the bar and toward him. Her heel caught in a crack on the pavement and she teetered briefly before getting her balance again. As she hurried past Daniel, he caught a reek of animal musk in a cloying perfume. Her eyelids were painted purple and silver, and her cheekbones had been rouged so heavily they looked bruised. She hesitated, then edged toward the other whores on the corner.

They turned on her swiftly, mercilessly. "This ain't amateur night, sweetie!" one snarled at her, while another advised her, "Get home to your mama, girl."

"I'm . . . I'm looking for my friend," she said, and her voice trembled like a fiddle string.

"You ain't got no friend here, jail bait. Get your skinny ass outta here, 'fore it gets kicked."

She moved away quickly, wobbling on her high heels, and the way she glanced up and down and across the street convinced Daniel that she was telling the truth, she was looking for her friend. She fled past him once more, the perfume again assailing him. Five or six steps, then she paused, then backed closer to the building to let two men pass. They glanced at her, one shaking his head and the other making a laughing comment before they entered the bar. She did not move away from the wall after they had passed, but pressed against it, like an animal trying to conceal itself. Daniel played on, the songs that seemed comfortable in a city, and after a moment he sensed her venturing closer. He looked at her from the corners of his eyes.

"Hello?" she said tentatively.

He went on playing. So young, this one. She should be home with her mother. Perhaps the old ways were better, when a girl like this would have a man chosen for her, would know that she had a future planned. She was old enough, this one, that in some *kumpanias* she would already have a babe at her breast, and perhaps another on the way. But those were the old ways, the very old ways. Now these people liked to torment their young, to keep them between, neither children nor women, but creatures of both worlds, and vulnerable to the hurts of both.

"Remember me?" she asked softly, venturing a little closer. He wished she were downwind of him; the reek of her perfume overpowered even the dirty air of the city. He shook his head slowly and he continued to play.

"Don't you remember me?" and the plea in her voice was very real. "We saw you earlier today. Chrissy and I stopped to listen to you play and I put dollar in your coat and then Chrissy and I went to her house and changed because she said we were going to a party. Only when we got to the bar, her friends weren't there. So she told me to go fix up my face, because I forgot I was wearing makeup and rubbed my eyes, but when I came out, she was gone, and they chased me out of the bar. Please, have you seen her? Remember her? She has curly blonde hair, she's real pretty, she had on silver Spandex and a black Guns'n'Roses tee shirt and red high heels."

Her voice was running down and his fiddle followed it, going softer as she spoke, so that when she paused, his fiddle was a whisper in the night. He shook his head again slowly, studying her. He looked at her. The shiny blue pants bagged at the knee, the high heels were a size too big for her; her feet kept sliding down in them. Chrissy's clothes, he thought to himself, like the low-cut shirt that exposed the tops of her breasts. "Your perfume is awful," he muttered, the first words he'd spoken to her.

"Chrissy said it was real expensive, and she got it from a

woman with really good taste," she said, and then her face crumpled slightly. "I know. It's awful. It's giving me a headache. I tried to wash it off in the bathroom, but it wouldn't go away. Please, didn't you see my friend?"

He shook his head slowly, his fiddle moving with it.

How could he know where her friend was? Perhaps her friend was playing a child's trick, and thus leaving her stranded with an adult's problem. Or maybe she had just left; children playing at being adults were never patient.

"I don't know what to do," she said softly, fear snaking through her voice.

It isn't my problem, he thought, and then wondered what his brothers would say to that. But where do you draw the line? Where do you decide when to step in and when to stay back? The Dove simply knew, while the Owl could point to a hundred little signs that would have told him all he needed. But he, Daniel, was forever stumbling through such decisions and then torturing himself afterwards. He cursed silently, and the curse translated itself into a wail the leapt from the fiddle into the night.

The girl took a step back, and somehow that hurt. To mend the hurt, he said quickly, "Stay here with me."

"Here?" she said, puzzled.

What did I say that for? he wondered. Because I wanted to, came the answer. "Maybe your friend will come back. Maybe she's looking for you." He knew it would be useless to tell her to go home.

"I don't have any more money for you," she said in a small voice.

He shook his head. "That was not me you saw."

She seemed offended. "Yes, it was. You were on the other side of the park, wearing a red coat and playing your tambourine. I put the dollar right in your pocket."

"No, I don't have a—" he stopped, then her words suddenly made sense to him. A tambourine? Raymond! A sudden joy lilted from his fiddle, and she stepped back, startled by its strength. Then it made her smile, and she was pretty, he could see her prettiness through the cracks in her thick makeup.

She moved closer, standing almost in his shadow, the smell of her perfume thick in the night. He took his fiddle through a sweet little waltz and saw her comforted by it.

"Tell me of this tambourine player," he said.

She frowned, as if wondering if he were teasing her.

Then she said, "You were playing a tambourine, sitting on a bench, a bus-stop bench. Near Pine, I think."

"It wasn't me," he repeated. "But perhaps it was my brother. Please tell me about him."

She blinked. "Well, he played for us, and I gave him a dollar. He was just," she struggled for words. "Really nice." She paused, looking up and down the decayed street. "Like you're nice," she said suddenly, honestly. But the next words came after too long a pause, and he knew they were not new with her. Probably, like the clothes, something borrowed from Chrissy. "I've always liked men older than me. They seem so much more sure of themselves."

He looked at her, letting all his years ride in his eyes. He expected her to falter, but she edged closer, as if drawn to him. She wrapped her arms around herself and huddled deeper into her thin shirt. He turned away and tried to ignore her standing at his back, found that he couldn't. He could feel her sheltering behind him. He glanced back and she looked directly into his eyes. All her fears looked out at him for an instant, and then she looked aside, a modest casting down of eyes that he had not seen in many years. Daniel sighed. Despite all her silly pretenses and false boldness, she was afraid. He'd have to help her.

He felt her edge closer. This time he turned slightly as he kept on playing, so he could watch her and still see the street. She'd got her courage up again, for this time she met his gaze squarely. Deliberately, she dropped her arms, set her hands on her hips. Thrust one hip out a little, and cocked her head. It reminded him of the pose of a store mannequin; nothing natural about it, no reason to stand that way except to display clothes or body. Especially not on a chill night like this. He deliberately dropped his eyes to her body, then met her gaze again. She almost stepped back, but when he made no other advance, her face grew puzzled. He suspected none of this was going the way her friend had told her it would. She was supposed to taunt, he was supposed to react, then she got to repulse him. A dangerous sort of game for young girls to play.

It was cold tonight. He could feel her shiver. Not just from the cold, but from this game of dares she played against herself. She challenged herself, to see if she dared face the danger after she'd created it. He didn't see any way she could win.

"My name's Lorelei," she told him coquettishly, and he heard part of the truth in the name. When he made no response, she twitched her young hips kittenishly and moved closer, so close that he nearly brushed against her each time he drew the bow across the strings.

"I'm Daniel," he told her, putting no more into the words than a polite exchange of names. A man in a passing car called to the whores on the corner. Lorelei flinched, clutched at his elbow for a second, and then snatched her fingers back.

Her cheeks, already reddened with cold, darkened further with embarrassment. She had lost face before him; he sensed a sudden hardening of her determination. She'd show him. He tried not to sigh. She took a deep breath, steeling herself, and chose a new line. "I really like your hair," she said. "The blackness, the way it curls. And I like your mustache. I wish more men grew them. I like men that are really, you know, masculine."

He knew what really masculine was. He was willing to bet she didn't.

She giggled, nervous and high, pushed herself deeper into her game. "I always wonder, though, how you kiss through a mustache like that. Know what I mean?" Teasing invitation.

Again, he did and she didn't. He glanced at her. She was so close now that when his arm moved with the bow, it brushed her upper arm. He breathed out heavily, trying to clear her perfume from his head. So young, this one. He watched her body moving gracefully, unconsciously, to his music. She reminded him of something, of someone so long ago it seemed like another life. Maybe it had been. Had he ever really been that young boy, sneaking away from the fire to follow the girl to the edge of the woods and then into them, or were they just the memories of the music? So long ago. The sweet stirring in his loins was like an old ache, and the music went warm with longing, not for this painted little girl, but for a young girl and boy who had kissed and touched, how may lifetimes ago?

The music touched her and the night filled up her eyes, edging her one step closer to womanhood, reminding her of something that as yet she had no memories of. The next man who passed sensed it. Daniel had paid him no heed when he'd slowed down and looked at the whores on the corner, but then he noticed the girl. The man watched her for a moment, a smile quirking the corners of his mouth, then he walked over, threw a twenty dollar bill down into the fiddle case and jerked his head at her. Daniel heard her breath catch as she edged behind him.

"Your mistake, friend," Daniel said mildly, and nodded at the money, hoping the man would just pick it up and leave.

Instead his smile changed to a scowl. He stared at the girl, started to walk on, then stopped and stared again. Daniel wished she wouldn't look at the man so. It was the fear in her eyes that was drawing him, that made him lick his mouth wet and ask, "How much, then, damnit?"

Daniel looked at him: husky, but not too husky; short, reddish hair beneath his cap; wearing a brown vest of some synthetic material that must be warmer than it looked. Daniel shook his head slowly. He didn't want this. His fiddle might get hurt. He stopped playing and lowered it slowly, hoping he'd be able to set it down gently if he had to. "It's a mistake, friend. She isn't for sale, this one. They are," he said, and gestured toward the whores on the corner, feeling diminished but not knowing what else to do.

The man didn't move. His eyes went colder. Daniel could almost feel the man's toes curling in his cowboy boots as he tried to decide whether this gypsy was pushing him around, and whether this girl was worth fighting for. The girl moved, gripping the back of Daniel's coat. He felt both her fear and the man's lust growing. Carefully he set the fiddle down in its case, put the bow in its holder, and closed the case. He held out the twenty toward the man, but he slapped it aside. "Damnit, don't fuck with me. Give you fifty for her."

Daniel tucked the money into the man's shirt pocket. "We are leaving now," he said softly, and stooped to pick up his fiddle case. The man swung at him as he did, and Daniel rose, his knee coming up into the man's crotch as he pushed him backwards. He hit a parking meter and stumbled into the street. A passing car blared its horn and splashed oily water over him.

"You sumbitch, I'll kill you, I swear I'll kill you," the man yelled, but Daniel had his fiddle under one arm and the girl on the other and was walking swiftly away.

The girl was trembling and clutching his arm; he could feel the soft warmth of her through his sleeve. He put his arm around her and walked faster. Three blocks later her trembling was getting worse. She kept tripping on her shoes. Poor little thing. He stopped at the mouth of an alley, set down his fiddle and removed his coat. He wrapped it around her, turning the collar up around her bare neck. But as he did so in all innocence, she stepped into his arms, turned her face up to his and kissed him.

Despite himself, his arms closed around her. She was so young, so much innocence, so much wonder, everything was new to her, a child, a woman, and for an instant he believed he could just take her and go somewhere, start again, a life that was not filled with omens and destinies, a life of babies and meadow grass and traveling the land, always as young as she was. A life that belonged to him alone, that was not owed to his brother. Her mouth was very soft in its inexperience, and the cloying perfume seemed suddenly, dizzying sweet. The kiss she had started became something he taught her. And, when that should have been all, she began to respond—to hold him closer than she should have, to feel desires he had no business bringing out in her, or she in him, and yet he knew her passion was as real as his, which should have frightened him more than it did. And it should have frightened her much more than it seemed to.

Her hand went to her mouth when he stepped back from her, touching her lips as if still feeling the brush of his mustache.

"So. Now you see. That's how you do it," he told her, and heard the pleased silliness in his own voice. She looked up at him, asking for more, her eyes very bright and shining; shining for him. He felt intoxicated with the girl, the night, and even the perfume. His thoughts reeled through her scent. She fit under his arm as snugly as his fiddle fit under his chin. Something suspiciously like romance swelled his soul. He laughed aloud, and when he did, her arm came around his waist. They walked together, he didn't care where, and then they were outside a cafe.

"I didn't get any dinner," she said, so tentatively that his heart broke over her hunger.

"I'll feed you," he promised, and opened the door, not caring that he hadn't a cent in his pockets. This was not a night to worry about practical things, it was a time to be young again.

They sat down in a booth together, side by side, Lorelei near the window, and he thought he had never seen anything as lovely as this girl wrapped in his weathered green coat. He took a napkin from the dispenser, and gently wiped some of the paint from her face. Her skin beneath it was beautiful, and she sat still beneath his touch.

Someone set glasses of water on the table. "Ready to order?" asked a redheaded waitress, and he suddenly realized she had been standing there for some time. He looked at his Lorelei, smiling encouragement.

"Burger, fries, and a Coke," she said without hesitation.

"Coffee," he added, and didn't care about the waitress's grim disapproval as she turned away.

"Are you warmer now, little sparrow?" he asked her. She nodded shyly, and looked down at the table top. He had to put his fingers under her chin and lift her face so he could see those eyes again, and when he did, he had to brush his lips across her forehead, because he couldn't stand not to.

## NOVEMBER SIXTEENTH, EVENING

The city lights, they hurt my eyes
And the noises make me wince.
The Coachman left me here
Which I've regretted ever since.

"RAVEN, OWL, AND I"

There was a raw edge in the wind, threatening as a knife. Raymond walked a little faster, reached up with his hand and held his collar a little closer around his neck. Another twenty steps, and he couldn't deny it anymore. The coldness and the wind weren't all he was feeling. The chill was in his soul, as if a strong wall were falling away, leaving him exposed.

He put his hand to his chest, felt his wrapped tambourine snug there. He thumped it lightly, felt rather than heard the muted jingle of the zils. As if in counterpoint, his stomach growled. Food and shelter, that's what he needed this night. Something was keeping him from the Coachman and his brothers. But what? He shrugged. Perhaps the best way to fight it was to ignore it. Some food and a night's sleep would leave him better prepared. He had not eaten in sixteen hours, nor slept in twenty-nine.

On Mount Falcon, when the sun went down, and Denver was no more than a greasy glow on the horizon, the darkness of the night had been a clean and comforting thing. Even when it was blackest and the stars pressed down on the hillside, he had not felt threatened by the night. He could lie in his bedroll and listen to the life in the scrubby brushlands around him, scale on gravely soil as a snake went by, the wicket, wicket, wicket of owl wings, the tiny pattering as the hunted mouse sought shelter.

Here it was never night, and the colored lights were like bulbous tumors on the outsides of the buildings. Raymond felt blinded as any owl would be, felt battered by their insistent flickerings. EAT EAT EAT one nagged him, and he felt his mouth stretch in a hard smile. That was exactly what he hoped to do. Soon. This icy blowing wind was cutting through him. Warmth, and a little food would be good; he couldn't be oblivious to such things, as his youngest brother was. He wondered, and not for the first time, what it would be like to trade places, to have the power, and the burden that went with it. No matter. His younger brother had it, and it was up to Raymond to find him. If his brothers were anywhere in this city, they'd forgotten everything they'd ever known about leaving signs; he'd found no symbols scratched in the dirt near a crossroads, no broken twigs or bits of string to guide him.

Well, not precisely true, he supposed. There were other kinds of signs. Sometimes he thought he could feel his brothers, that he would step around the next corner and there they'd be, waiting for him, laughing to see him. But at times like this there was just emptiness around him, as he walked through the not-light, not-dark of the city.

Hungry. Time to eat.

He was turning toward a bar door, wondering if it were the sort of bar that kept dishes of nuts and crackers on the tables when a car pulled up to the curb behind him.

"Hey you!" called a girl's excited voice. "Hey, gypsy-man!" Then louder, "Hey, gypsy-man! Wanta party with me?"

He stepped closer to the big car with a grill like silver teeth. He tried to make out the girl's face in the night's deceptive grey wash. Yes, he knew her. Earlier, she and her friend had stopped to hear him play. But she had been younger then; the night lights had aged her. Her breasts swung free under a black tee shirt with a garish picture on it as she leaned out the window to him. Earlier today, the wind had blown her curly hair into appealing disarray. Now it stood up stiffly around her face, reminding him of the way a horse's coat looked after lather had dried on it. Makeup enlarged all her features, distorting her face into mouth and eyes and lashes, everything wide and wet. He took another step, trying to see where she had gone behind the paint. Which was real and which the lie? His brother, the Raven, would have known at once; he could always tell semblance from actuality. He, too, might have known, he thought, if it were real night: prey or not prey. But he didn't, so it was far better to be safe. And yet, he remembered what the Dove had always said about chance meetings. He would be careful, but he wouldn't walk away just yet.

She opened the door of the car, slid over and patted the seat invitingly. "C'mon, gypsy-man, come join the party."

There were two in back and three in front. There was a young man with a tattoo of a cross on his cheek in the back seat with her. His head was thrown back, lolling on the neckrest. His eyes were closed, his mouth loose, but Raymond did not think he slept. Two more boys were in the front seat, with another girl wedged between them. The driver had a cigarette dangling low from his mouth, and the good leather of his coat was draped with chain. The other boy was occupied by the girl between them. Her shirt was open, and as the boy nuzzled her breasts she stared out the window over his oddly cut hair. There was no expression at all on her face.

"Come on, man," the girl in the back seat urged him. "Remember me? We gave you a dollar earlier today. My name's Chrissy. We been looking all over town for you. We got something for you from a friend.

Could this be a Sign? Yes. Or a Trap. The Raven or the Dove would have known at once. "Who?" Raymond asked.

Chrissy smiled. "Get in, and I'll tell you, gypsy-man. But here's a hint. They told me to watch for an Owl."

A moment more he hesitated. His brothers were not the only ones who knew him by that name. But the night was cold and the car was warm, and whatever he learned, whether of his brothers or of Her, must be useful. And that, after all, was what he did: watch, wait, and learn. He edged into the car as the girl giggled delightedly. She pushed the boy further into the corner, as if he were just so much bedding. She reached past Raymond and pulled the door shut, then continued to lean against him. The car pulled away from the curb.

"What do you have for me?" he asked, pushing the girl's hands gently away from his chest. But she only laughed and reached over to tap his tambourine through his jacket.

"Man's got music in his heart," she told the driver, and laughed again, in a way that struck Raymond as witless. The driver was watching Raymond in the rearview mirror. Raymond met his eyes squarely, asking no questions and telling him nothing. After a moment the boy nodded, as if confirming something.

Paper rustled as he passed a bagged bottle over his shoulder. "Warm up first, man," the boy said. "Then we'll give you the message."

"No, thank you," said Raymond.

"Suit yourself," he said, and drank from it.

"I am looking for some friends," Raymond told the driver.

The girl was leaning on him, pawing at his tambourine through his jacket, but he ignored her. She did not smell as if she'd been drinking, but she did not act sober either. "Let us be your friends," she offered, shrilly. She reached up to stroke his hair. He leaned away from her.

"Knock it off, Chrissy." The driver growled. "Man doesn't wanta be groped, he just wants his message. So give it to him already."

"Yeah. Sure I will. But, hey, gypsy-man, you hungry? We got some pizza here, somewhere, I think." She reached to the back window ledge, came up with a greasy white box. She opened it for him, presenting him with cheese and sausage melted over bread. He smelled the peppers and grease, and his stomach growled loudly. "Or you wanna burger? We got a burger, here, somewhere, in case you wanted a burger. Her, Jer, where did we put the burger?"

"Chrissy." The driver's voice was edged as broken glass. He glanced at Raymond in the mirror, and tried to smile. "Now be nice to the man. Give him some food and the message."

"Oh, yeah. Here." She set the greasy box in his lap and leaned back against the boy, pillowing herself on his lax body. "Lemme think, now. How did it go? It was like a poem, or something."

The pizza was unappetizing, but it was warm and it was food. Raymond took a wedge and ate it. Whoever had seasoned the tomato sauce on it had no respect for spices. He waited for the girl, who muttered and giggled to herself, then suddenly sat up straight. "I got it," she announced, and then recited,

"Butterfly sandwiches,
Crunchable things
Crisp little bodies
With flower-hued wings."

Then sagged back into the seat, laughing until she choked. The driver's face went dark with anger. He took the cigarette from his mouth, and flicked it out the window. "Damnit, Chrissy," he growled, and his voice was so ugly Raymond felt the hair on the back of neck stand up. Chrissy heard the threat, for she sat up suddenly, her face contrite.

"Eat something while I remember. I'll get it right this time, I promise. Jer, why don't you pass the bottle back? Give the gypsy-man something to drink with his pizza. And give me some time to 'member it right," she added in a confidential aside to Raymond.

"No, thank you," he said.

She took the bottle, drank from it, while streetlamps and neon crawled past the car's windows. He forced himself to stomach another piece of pizza, telling himself that no matter how insipid it was, it was food, and who knew when he would be offered food again? The driver watched him and Raymond watched him back. Chrissy leaned against him suddenly, rubbing her forehead against his shoulder. "Shit," she said miserably. "I'm losing it, I'm coming down. Jer, you got anymore stuff? No?" Her face crumpled as the driver shook his head. "Damn. This is so depressing. Lemme have another drink and maybe I can remember the poem." As she lifted the bottle again, she asked him, "Aren't you going to eat some more?"

Raymond shook his head slowly, then asked, "Earlier, there was another girl with you. Where is she?"

"Fuck, I don't know. We were supposed to give her to the fiddler—oh, damn, I wasn't supposed to say that. But I guess it's okay, now, I mean, he ate some of it anyway." Now her words were addressed to the driver, who was shaking his head angrily.

Raymond closed the box slowly. He handed it to her and she took it back, knowing he knew. A stupid way to have failed, and for one instant he thought he saw sympathy in her eyes. The driver pulled the car into an alley and the brick walls threw back at them the vibrations of the leashed engine.

"Say the poem, damn you!" the driver snarled.

Chrissy turned to Raymond.

"The Coachman has fallen to hoof and to horn.
The Raven is caught and will die before morn.
The poor Owl is buried beneath dirt and stone
Leaving the Dove, to die all alone."

Raymond didn't let his face change. After a moment, she wailed, "It's a stupid poem, I told that thing it was a stupid poem. I like mine better, Butterfly sandwiches, crunchable things, crisp little bodies with flower-hued wings, butterfly sandwiches, crunchable things, crisp little bodies . . ."

The driver swore and got out. He left his door open, and a stream of cold air flowed into the car, stinging Raymond's cheeks. He was sweating suddenly. There was no pain, not yet. Maybe there wouldn't be any. Maybe it was only this, his body ignoring him. The driver opened his door and dragged him out, leaving him against a wall between two garbage cans. Chrissy suddenly leaned from the open door. "Take his tambourine," she begged. "I really want it, it made such pretty music before," but the driver slammed her door shut, narrowly missing her.

"Bye-bye, Owl," he said, smirking at Raymond. "The poem sucks, but I think we can all appreciate the sentiment." He paused. "I understand it don't really kill you. It just makes you look dead. Course, you look dead until you really are. What a trip, huh?" He laughed, then paused to shake out another cigarette and light it. He tossed the match at Raymond. It landed on his coat sleeve and burned a small hole before it went out.

"Please, Jer, just take the tambourine," Chrissy was begging again as she leaned out the window.

"Shut up, bitch." He slapped her casually and she fell back against the seat, not even crying. Then the driver got back inside the car and it pulled away, became twin red lights that turned a corner. Raymond sat. He could still move his eyes, but it was getting harder. He looked down at his hands, lax in his lap, the fingers going white in the cold night. Then, without closing his eyes, everything became fuzzy. Then sight was gone completely and he felt as if he had fallen deep inside the black earth.

16 NOV 18:45

Cold mountain water, coming from below
Who are you to ask? Who am I to know?

"STARS OVERHEAD"

The bar was dark, and stuffy after the cold outside air. The Pig and Whistle was only four blocks from the station and had been the local cop bar for as long as Stepovich had been around. He'd heard from Ed that once the bar had tried to foster a genteel tavern/inn atmosphere, but that the owner had given it up when a bunch of the guys got together and had a new signboard made for him. The antiqued board portrayed a pig in a blue uniform tooting on a silver whistle. The sign was gone now, but so was the attempt at atmosphere. The Pig and Whistle was what it was: a cop bar.

Tonight's crowd was typical. The clientele varied from off-duty patrolmen in worn sweatshirts and jeans to detectives in jackets and ties still. What didn't vary was the way, even here, no one was ever completely relaxed. Eyes moved constantly, men shifted every time the door opened. Most of the women were cops, or office personnel from the station. There were a scattering of cop groupies, uniformly scorned by the female officers. "Like we can't get enough of each other all day," Stepovich muttered. "We got to hang around each other all night, too." He lifted his mug and drained it.

"Wha—?" Durand asked.

"Nothing," Stepovich told him.

Durand was holding a plastic sack of ice against his jaw and drinking cold beer. He still couldn't talk much. They'd moved to a table in the corner after the bartender had asked what happened to his face. "I slammed his head in the car door by accident," Stepovich had explained. "Radio squawked and he ducked to grab it just as I shut the door." The story was just weird enough to sound plausible. Something Ed had taught him a long time ago. "If you're going to tell a lie, tell a memorable one. Makes it easier to keep your story straight later." Which was great advice, coming from someone who almost never lied. Someone who would never get himself into a fix like Stepovich was in now.

Stepovich held his empty mug up, nodded back to Lois when he was sure she'd seen he needed a refill. "We should get something to eat soon," he told Durand. He could feel the beer warming his empty stomach, loosening him up.

"Uh-huh," Durand agreed. He lifted the ice pack away from his face, considered a moment, then put it back. The damn kid just kept on looking at him, like that, with those eyes. Not pushing, not demanding. Just waiting, knowing that Stepovich already knew all the questions, and knew, too, that he owed Durand some answers.

He took a breath, wondering which was getting to him faster, the beer or the puppy-eyes. "Kid. Look. This is what happened. It's all like a chain, one little thing after another, none of it really bad, but it looks bad, if you don't know what happened."

"Uh-huh."

Witty conversationalist. Stepovich took a breath. "You sure you feel okay? You maybe want to get something to eat, some soup or something? Talk later on?"

"Huh-uh."

Stepovich shifted, his belt creaking, his off-duty gun digging him, just a little, under the arm. He scratched at it, pulling the holster down a bit. "There was a knife, when we busted that gypsy. But I didn't turn it in with his other belongings. I . . . uh . . . it went down in the lining of my jacket. And . . . I had a feeling, Durand. I still do. I don't think the Gypsy we busted killed the liquor store clerk. I know you like him for Cynthia Kacmarcik's killing, but I don't think that's him either. But I do think he's a link. So I gotta find him."

"Why?"

"To talk to him."

"No." Durand shifted his ice pack, spoke with effort. "Why you think he's a link?"

Stepovich scratched his nose. "I don't know. Maybe because they're both gypsies. Mostly, I just got a feeling."

"Where's the knife now?"

Stepovich hesitated. "In a safe place." He prayed he wasn't lying. "I don't wanna, you know, well, if I can take care of this thing without it coming out that I was sloppy about booking the knife in, you know. I mean, you know how it is. It's just better if you don't give them a reason to start checking you out, you know? I do good work, Durand. This was one little screwup, I don't think I should have to pay a big price for it, you know?"

Durand lifted his beer, sipped it carefully. He set it back on the table, sighed, and dropped the sack of melting ice next to it. "I'd feel better if the lab had a look at the knife," he said carefully.

Stepovich looked at him steadily. "The liquor-store guy was shot. And I had the knife when Cynthia Kacmarcik was killed. You know that."

Durand sniffed meditatively. He lifted his big eyes to meet Stepovich's, then looked past him. "Yeah. I know that."

## SOMETIME

The candle burned down from its place on the sill.
The curtains caught fire but the house remained
Standing there still.
Turning around, saw you looking at me
With tears running down from the place where your
Eyes used to be.

"WALK THROUGH THE DOOR"

*The* nora *touches the Fair Lady on Her knee and says, "She has stopped spinning now."*

*"Oh, has she? Well, fetch her out then."*

*The* nora *goes to the door, but finds it already open, and the woman comes forth. In her hands is a length of spun yarn. She goes up to the Fair Lady, who says, "I reached my hand for one who troubled me, and you chose to put yourself in my way, so I took you, instead. Then you contrived to weave, and thought to keep me away from you that way, but your spirit is no stronger than your flesh was. You had to stop at last, Cynthia Kacmarcik, and now we have you."*

*"When I was born," she says, "My name was Rozsa. But I became ill as a babe, and would have died, so they gave me a new name and the illness could no longer find me."*

*The Fair Lady frowns, as if this disturbs Her. But the old woman says, "There is a tree of the world, and its leaves brush the moon, where King David plays the fiddle and the saints dance. You brought me here because I saw the tree, and knew who stood under it, sheltered from your hailstones, and because I stopped you when you would have cut it down. But, see, I have woven yarn from its twigs. The Dove has blinded himself, but I have taken the veils away, and soon he will see. The Raven will be saved by the love with which you cursed him, and the Coachman has his horses. As for the Owl, there is this."*

*With that she throws the yarn into the fire, where it at once begins to burn, and the smoke, grey as a storm cloud, goes out the flue and into the world of men, and yet the yarn also stays in the fireplace, always burning, never burned.*

*The Fair Lady gnashes Her teeth as the* nora *and the* liderc *pounce on the old woman and drag her away. She doesn't resist.*

# Chapter Thirteen

## WHAT THE BADGER SAID TO THE RAVEN, AND THE OWL SAID TO THE COACHMAN

### AUTUMN AFTERNOON

**How can you have lived this long**
**And not give in to rage?**
**Don't you understand that**
**We've both outlived our age?**
**There is no final curtain;**
**This is not a stage.**
**Can you read what's written**
**On this blackened page?**

"BLACKENED PAGE"

The Gypsy smelled herb tea and wondered ironically if "huh" could be some sort of magic word, because the old woman said it every time she turned a card over. She had shuffled and dealt them herself, ignoring him after he'd cut them as commanded, and then she'd laid them out on a bright red silk, patterned with designs that stirred up hints of old memories—old memories that wanted to drag him away, only now he wouldn't let them. An old woman had died to give him a chance to complete his task—not to allow him to ruminate on his past.

She quickly finished laying the cards out, her hands steady, the cards placed deliberately in a pattern the Gypsy almost recognized. Then she studied them for a long time, occasionally glancing up into the Gypsy's face as if to confirm or deny what the cards told her.

Eventually she gave a "hummph," and made a move as if to gather the deck up.

"Wait," he said.

She paused. "Yes, well?"

"Aren't you going to tell me what they mean?"

"Why? Would you believe them?"

"How did you know I was coming?"

She nodded slowly, then pulled one from beneath a small stack. It showed a man holding a globe in one hand and a staff in the other. "The Hermit," she said. "Reversed. That's you, it seems, though I wouldn't have thought it."

"Why not?"

She ignored his question. "The key is The Emperor reversed, which I knew to begin with, and the Ace of Swords crosses it. The—"

"What does it mean?" he asked, becoming annoyed.

"Mean? The Ace of Swords? Look at it."

He shrugged and did so. A single sword pointing to the sky, a halo of leaves around it, and he suddenly thought of the knife that pressed against his hip. But it certainly couldn't be anything so simple. He opened his mouth to ask again, but she said, "It's the Tower that motivates you, that drives you, although whether you work to build it or tear it down I couldn't say. But I expect you work to destroy it, for the Wheel of Fortune reversed is what has brought you to this point."

The Gypsy felt his impatience growing. "And what is this point, then, old woman?"

She held up the next card, showing an old king standing on disks with stars, holding another star, while yet another rested on his crown. "This point is gathering power, little bird. Building forces, calling up an army. Or maybe it's getting others to do your work for you. Like me, little bird, and I don't like it, though there's nothing I can do about it now."

She said, "The ten of Pentacles tells me you may get what you think you want. But whether this next card refers to you or to all of those who try to help you, I couldn't guess." He looked at the next card, in which a man lay face down with ten swords sticking out of his back, and looked away again.

"Yes," she said, her words like whips. "That's the game you're playing, that's what you're courting, fluttering in and out, cooing in everyone's ear. Think about it, since you've asked."

She sighed. "Yet, we have this for the environment, and it is hope, if nothing else." A beautiful woman drank from a cup, her eyes fixed on it as if in contemplation. "And your desire is Temperance, which gives me hope as well; it is more than I'd have thought of you.

"And you may wish for the nine of Cups, yet have the five

of Cups to regret. The outcome. Hmmph. Perhaps you'll escape."

She stopped, waiting.

The Gypsy stared at her. At last he said, "If any of this has any meaning, old woman, tell me now. I am older than you, and far more weary. I am living too many riddles to take any pleasure in hearing yet more from your lips. I don't know why I've been put on this path, but it isn't to serve your whims."

She stared back at him from behind eyes like velvet curtains, then she looked away and nodded. "Very well," she said. "Perhaps it will hinder more than help, but you have the right to know the little I can tell you.

"The Hermit reversed is someone on a path, seeking. He's looking for something. Does that make sense?"

"If I want it to," said the Gypsy.

"Yes," agreed Madam Moria. "Exactly. The Queen of Swords reversed is, huh, have you noticed that all of the women in this reading are reversed? You are either dealing with evil women, little Dove, or you have some attitudes—"

"Tell me about the Queen of Swords, old woman."

She glared at him for a moment, then said, "She is intelligent, She is perceptive, She is cruel. She reasons well. Her influence is all around you. Does that sound familiar? Have you a guess who it could be?"

"Save your irony, old woman. This card?"

"Yes. The Tower. The flash of truth or inspiration. The end of all you've believed."

"It looks worse than that."

"It will feel worse than that when it happens."

"And the card with the wheel?"

"The Wheel of Fortune reversed is just past. You have been unable to effect the course of events, and you've been forced to wait. This is passing."

"And this card, that you said meant the gathering of forces?"

"Call it the pivot point. How you will affect the events, obviously. Through the actions of others. Does that startle you?"

"Go on."

"Temperance. You wish to bring the parts together that have been sundered. But this, too, I think you know already. The outcome, though, is split. You have two choices. One is pestilence, disease, the ten of Swords. The other are these three cards, the nine of Cups for wishes coming true, the five of Cups for sorrow, the Sun for escape and protection."

"So perhaps I will die, or perhaps I will escape, but I can't win?"

"So I read it. You may read it better if you can."

"The cards you use, they seem to be of many different styles."

"I use the cards that please me, some from one deck, some from others."

"Yes, I believe this."

Her eyes flashed. "It is not for you to judge me."

He laughed suddenly. "If I don't, young woman, who will?"

She frowned. "Young woman?"

"Older perhaps than the woman who was killed trying to help me, but younger than my brothers and I."

"You are more than you seem. I think . . ." Her voice trailed off and she frowned again.

"What do you think, young woman?"

Her lips twitched. "I think you are as much a fool as the Coachman, who sees the route, but not the ending. You push us all along a path that—"

He stood up, suddenly lost in a torment of fear, hope, and anger. "Coachman? What do you know of a Coachman?"

"I know he is a drunken fool," she snapped. "I sent him away so we could have some priv—"

"You sent him away?" cried the Gypsy.

For the first time, she seemed uncertain. "He had played his part in—"

"The Queen of Swords reasons well, you say, but what if her facts are wrong? What then for her powers? What damage will she do? Perhaps *you* are the Queen of Swords reversed, woman, and your arrogance will destroy us all."

"I—"

"Perhaps the painful revelation is yours, and it is to happen now."

"I never wanted to be part—"

"Be still. Which of us *did* want to be part of it? You dare to accuse *me* of using people? Is your wit so keen that you can outguess Luci Herself? Is your Sight so great that you can see into Her heart? Are your hands so skilled that you can untangle every thread She weaves? Is your power so great that you can send Her away? What have you done, woman?"

She stared at him, puzzled and frightened. "Who are you?" she asked in a whisper.

"I? I am Csucskari the Gypsy. I am a *Taltos.* I am the one who has sworn an oath against the Fair Lady and all Her works. I am the only hope we have against Her, poor though it be. You are an arrogant fool, old woman. You see the bottom of the stream so clearly, you forget there is water above it, and you'd let us drown in your pride, then curse us for being unable to breathe. Well, if you have such keen sight, use it now, while there may yet be time. *Where is the Coachman?"*

"I don't know," she whispered after a moment. "My sister would know."

"Then ask her. Now."

She looked up at him, then looked away. She seemed to shrink into herself, then she sighed and stared down, absently, into her teacup. She stirred the leaves with one bony finger, and after a time she spoke.

## NOVEMBER SIXTEENTH, 7:20 PM

**Well, I left there running like a thousand**
**Devils were on my trail**
**Woah, lannan sidhe let me be.**

"LANNAN SIDHE"

Ed reached for the remote control, turned the TV down three clicks before answering the phone.

"Ed?" demanded a voice before he could even say hello.

He sat up on the couch, trying to place the voice. "Yes," he said guardedly.

"It's me, Tiffany Marie," she went on, and when he didn't answer right away, she added, "Say you don't know me, and I'll drag a nail down the side of that Caddy the next time I see it parked in our loading zone."

"Tiffany Marie, no one could ever forget you, or that red hair. I'm just wondering why you're calling me."

"Look, Ed, this is important. Man, I think I know how important better than anyone else," she added, almost to herself. "I can't get Stepovich, his phone just rings, and maybe it wouldn't be a good idea to get him anyway. And Randy . . . Durand doesn't answer either, so I figured I'd better call you. It's about Mike's kid."

"What?" Ed was already sticking his feet back into his shoes. All the skin on his scalp was tingling, ancient hackles standing up as his cop sense sent alarms screaming.

"His girl, whatshername, Laurie? You know her?"

"I stood godfather to her," Ed answered grimly, but Tiffany Marie was still talking.

"She's in here. At least, I'm pretty sure it's her, I only met her those two times. Anyway, she's painted up like a whore, and she's with this older guy, this gypsy-looking guy, and he's like, all over her. Christ, Ed, she can't be more than fourteen, and this guy is really moving on her, and she's acting like, well, she's not exactly pushing him away. And the guy isn't some street kid, I mean, he's a corner musician or something. Hell, he's not only too old for her, he's too old for me. Look, Ed, I don't think she's made any really big mistakes yet, and maybe if someone like you gets down here—dammit, now there's a fight. Gotta go—"

"I'm coming," said Ed and hung up the phone as he reached for his jacket. Shit. Someone was putting little Laurie out on the streets? Where the hell was Mike, what was he thinking of to let his little girl run loose at this hour of the night? He picked up his Caddy keys off the coffee table, thought briefly of calling Jenny. Decided against it. She'd just get shrill and jump into the middle of it and make it messy. Well, it wasn't going to be messy. Good thing Tiffany Marie had called him. He'd make it fast and quiet.

He stopped by the door, then turned and went back to his bedroom. In a bottom drawer was a gift box with a sap-glove in it. It had been a long-ago gag from Stepovich after Ed had done a lot of pussyfooting in an interrogation one night. "Next time, try this," the note had said.

He slipped on the black leather. It fit. "Good thing she called me," he said again to himself. "I won't kill him, like Mike would. And I won't arrest him and make a lot of paperwork and noise about it, either. Just extract the little girl, convince the guy to stay clear of her, and get her home." He flexed his hand inside the weighted glove. Sometimes it was easier not being a cop anymore.

He caught up his keys and went out the door, whistling "I'm Called Little Buttercup." The sky above him was grey, like dark smoke.

16 NOV 19:22

Ain't got time to listen,
Ain't got eyes to see.
Woah, lannan sidhe let me be.

"LANNAN SIDHE"

Three rounds of beer had come and gone. By now, he should be feeling them, should be numbed a little, should be able to let his shoulders slump against the chair back. Instead, Stepovich felt as if he were being drawn tighter and tighter, wound up like some little mechanical toy. His jaws were clenched, as if he feared too much truth would jump out of him if he relaxed. And Durand would never be able to handle the whole truth. Durand might talk wild and woolly, but when it came down to cases, he was absolutely by the book. Letter of the law. Stepovich cleared his throat, felt Durand's eyes jump back to him.

"Okay." His voice came out rusty, and he cleared his throat again. "I did some really stupid stuff. But I'm not dirty, Durand, and I didn't do anything really wrong. I mean, not wrong like morally wrong. Maybe wrong, like in ignoring standard procedure, but not wrong like ethics. You know what I mean?"

Durand nodded slowly. "Yeah, I know what you mean. I'm just not sure if I agree with it. Maybe you didn't do anything dirty, but you broke a hell of a lot of rules. And if you hadn't, your ass wouldn't be in a crack right now. And neither would mine. But I'm willing to help you out, as long as it doesn't mean breaking any more rules. You got to understand, Ste-uh-Mike, that I'm just starting out. Something like this could screw my career permanently. See, I'm not really as stupid as you think I am."

Stepovich was forced to nod, feeling both relieved that Durand could understand what he meant, and ashamed that he had always assumed his partner was too dumb to talk to.

"So. Where does all this leave us?" Durand demanded after a few moments had passed. The bag of ice was a plastic puddle in the middle of the table. He still fingered his jaw from time to time, but the worst of the swelling had gone down.

"Well." Stepovich gathered his thoughts. "It doesn't leave us with a lot. No hard information, anyway. Just feelings, and maybes, and stuff that doesn't quite add up. Here's how it looks to me. We've got a guy killed in the liquor store and the old gypsy woman dead in the hotel. You think it's the same guy, both times, you think it's that gypsy we picked up—"

"Actually, the liquor store witness—" Durand began, but Stepovich held up a hand.

"Just let me finish. Because he matched the clerk's description, and because he had a knife that might have been like the one used on the old woman."

"And he matched the description the hotel clerk gave to homicide when they asked who the room was rented to," Durand interjected, but Stepovich chose to ignore him and plow stubbornly on.

"Now I'm with you on thinking the same guy did both of them. Damned if I can really say why, it's just a feeling and it's got nothing to do with the description from the liquor store matching the description from the hotel clerk."

"If you'd listen," Durand began, but Stepovich slapped the table.

"Dammit, let me finish. Hear me out. I don't think it's our gypsy. Think about this. One killed with a gun, one killed with a knife. That's weird. Because killers choose a weapon and stick to it, because it's the weapon that makes them feel the best, most powerful, most in control. Now I know the Gypsy didn't have his knife when the old woman was killed. But it was done with a knife very similar to his, and maybe in his room. Why? Frame-up? It's not a hell of a lot to go on, Durand. I admit that. The only thread I can see hanging loose is our gypsy. Only I got no idea of how to find him."

"You done?" Durand demanded impatiently.

"Yeah. I guess." Stepovich waited for Durand to blast his fragile theories to pieces.

"Good. Because here's one more thing that doesn't fit. The witness from the liquor store has changed his story. Now he says the killer wasn't a gypsy at all, but some skinny pale dude. No one wants to believe him, so the warrant is still out for the Gypsy. They all figured someone got to the witness and made him change his story—"

"Or," Stepovich interjected, "he was lying before, for whatever reason, and now he's telling the truth. Damn. I got to talk to that gypsy. He's the key."

"That's why Ed turned you on to Madam Moria, because he thought she might have a line on other gypsies in town?"

"Yeah." Stepovich took a sip of beer. Half of it went down before he choked. He coughed, couldn't form the question, but Durand answered it anyway. Something suspiciously like a blush rose on his face.

"So," Stepovich asked heavily. "How long you and Ed been getting together and comparing notes?"

Durand spoke like the words were being dragged out.

"It's not like that, Stepovich. What's between me and Ed goes way back; it's not just this gypsy thing. See, Ed was my Dad's friend, a long time ago. Went through the academy together, I guess, then kind of lost touch. Or didn't get along. Ed's a lot like you, sort of free and easy with procedure, and my dad wasn't like that. Anyway. I'd forgotten all about him, but my mother hadn't. Mom called him when I got out of the academy, before I was even officially hired, and begged him to use his pull to get me partnered with somebody decent. Somebody he thought I'd be safe with. I guess he chose you." Then, as the anger washed over Stepovich's face, Durand added, "Look, I didn't know about it until after it happened. Pissed me off, that she thought I couldn't make it on my own. It isn't the kind of thing my dad would have liked either. My dad wasn't the kind of cop who took favors, or did them. I could have done okay on my own. I thought you knew about it and that was why you were so shitty to me, you thought you were babysitting or something."

"This is the first I ever heard about it," Stepovich began.

"I know," Durand cut in ruefully. "A couple days ago, Ed

called me up, asked how we were getting on, and I lit into him. And he said you didn't know a damn thing about it, that he figured I'd have to earn your respect on my own. So then I felt like a real jerk for all the times I'd tried to show you I was so tough and so smart I didn't need your help."

"Makes two of us," Stepovich muttered.

"So," Durand said at last. "You get anything from Madam Moria?"

Stepovich swirled the last of his beer in his glass, then drank it down. Abruptly, he held his mug up and waved it, hoping the waitress would notice they needed refills. He took a deep breath, looked up and met his partner's eyes. "You ready to hear some really weird shit?" he asked him.

## THURSDAY NIGHT

And at the end will be the place
Whence the owl has flown,
And I'll dance for you the Gypsy Dance
That you have never known.

"GYPSY DANCE"

The fight didn't have a beginning as far as Daniel was concerned. The first he knew of it, he was on his hands and knees, trying to get up, feeling bits of glass embedded in the back of his head, and knowing that a pointed-toed boot was coming, but also knowing how to avoid it. His Lorelei shrieked, and the red-haired waitress rushed in their direction with an upraised tray, and all he could think, stupidly, was that most dogs will run if you shout at them, but some will slink back later to bite you from behind. Daniel should never have walked away from him; he should have crammed his money down his throat and made him choke on it.

The boot was coming, and as he rolled onto his side and grabbed it, throwing the man off balance, his Lorelei came up out of the booth like a wildcat, throwing salt, pepper, sugar, and herself at his attacker. One of the man's wildly flailing arms caught her across the face, and sent her sprawling against another table. The redheaded waitress smacked the man once across the ear with the tray, driving him to his knees, and then dove after Lorelei, screaming, "Laurie! Stay clear of this, you'll only get hurt!"

The sight of her thrown against the tables brought Daniel staggering to his feet. His knife came into his hand and he opened it slowly, savoring the ratcheting sound and the widening of the other man's eyes. The vermin was clutching a chair, and as Daniel came toward him, he lifted it, not as a weapon but as a shield. "You wanted to know what she'd cost?" Daniel asked him softly, in a language he hadn't spoken in years. "She would cost both your life and mine, and still I wouldn't let you touch her."

The man glanced about wildly but there were few other customers at this hour of the night, and all of them were hastily retreating out the door. The waitress had gripped Lorelei by the wrist and hair, and was forcibly holding her back. Daniel saw in his attacker's eyes that he had never expected it to go this way, that he had thought he would surprise them and take the girl quickly. He was regretting his impulse, but now it was too late. And Daniel saw, too, that the man knew nothing of this kind of fight, and that made him smile.

He came forward smoothly, knife low, the even balance never leaving his body from step to step. When the man threw the chair at him, he sidestepped it as lightly as a cat. "Hey, man, I'm unarmed! I don't got a knife or nothing!" the man protested as Daniel and his knife came closer, and it made Daniel's smile wider to hear this man beg him to follow rules of honor. Even as he lowered his knife, he knew what would come next.

He was ready when the man leaped. Suddenly Daniel wasn't where the man thought he would be, but the knife's pommel found him as he passed, sending him crashing into yet another table. And Daniel followed, his fingers closing like talons on the man's throat. The man's fists were hammering at Daniel's body, but there was desperation rather than strength behind them. If that was the best he could do, Daniel could stand it for the short time it would take him to choke the man unconscious. The man's blows lost strength rapidly, and Daniel knew he was winning when his enemy's breath began to rattle and he reached up to claw hopelessly at Daniel's closing hand. With his other hand, Daniel closed his knife and slipped it into his back pocket.

"Enough. Break it up!"

The man's tongue was starting to breach his lips. His eyes were very wide, and a blood vessel had broken in one.

"I said, break it up!"

Daniel didn't realize the voice had spoken to him until he was literally lifted off his feet by the back of his jacket. There were other voices, the waitress exclaiming, "Thank God! What took you so long?" And Lorelei crying out, "Ed, if you hurt him, I'll never forgive you and I'll tell my dad."

"Let go of him, damnit!" the voice roared right in his ear, and Daniel did. He watched in a sort of wonder as the man slumped to the floor. For several long moments, the unconscious man didn't move, and then he made a wheezing noise, and then another. Daniel felt some of the tension go out of the fist gripping him, and he turned in the grasp.

Cop. He didn't need the uniform or the badge to know it. It was all in the stance and the eyes and the calm way he told Daniel, "You're coming with me." He turned and spoke more loudly to the waitress. "Cancel the ambulance, Tiffany. The one on the floor looks like he'll be able to walk in a while. And I'd just as soon not make a big fuss out of this, know what I mean?" The cop nudged the downed man with his foot. "You want I should put this one outside?"

The redhead shook her head slowly. "Nah. Leave him on the floor, Ed. When he recovers, he can get out on his own. If he's got any complaints, I don't know about them. I was in back, filling ketchup dispensers all the time."

A very slight smile cracked the big man's face. "I thought you mighta been. But you sure you want it that way? He might have a mind to be mean when he catches his breath."

Tiffany shook her head and wrinkled her nose in disgust. "S'okay, Ed. I think all his mean just ran down his leg. I don't think he'll give me any trouble."

Lorelei, who had stood quietly, suddenly twisted free of Tiffany's grip. "Let go of him," she said, taking Daniel's arm.

"He's going with me. And you're going home." The big man's voice brooked no argument.

Daniel shook his head, but didn't know what to say. Lorelei

drew herself up straight. "You can't do that! He's hurt. And besides you gotta have, uh, probable cause. You can't say disturbing the peace, because he was defending me. That other guy was trying to *buy* me!" The sudden outrage in her voice was genuine.

"Oh, golly-gee! I wonder whatever made him think you were for sale." The heavy sarcasm in Ed's voice reddened Lorelei's cheeks and shame lowered her eyes. "Look at you," he went on. "Dressed like a street slut and talking like a jailhouse lawyer. Oh, your Daddy's gonna be real proud of his little girl."

Lorelei looked up, but the sudden flash of anger in her eyes threatened to drown in brimming tears. But Daniel jerked, stung. "You will not talk to her like that," he said. He could hear the concern that underlay the policeman's words, but he could not bear to see Lorelei so downcast. "You do not understand what has gone on this night."

The policeman smiled, all teeth. "*You* will not talk to *me* like that, gypsy. You and me, we're gonna take a ride and go talk to the little girl's daddy. You wanta explain what went on tonight, you can talk to him. But I warn you, I don't think he's gonna be real reasonable about it. So you might want to think about anything else you could tell him that would make him happy. Like maybe anything you know about a dead woman named Cynthia Kacmarcik. Or one of your old gypsy buddies who's got some real interesting scars."

There was no mistaking the pattern the man traced on his face. It had to be Csucskari he referred to. Daniel simultaneously felt excitement and a heaviness inside him, as if his soul had turned to lead. His heart bid him follow Lorelei, but duty had ruled him too long. He had to go with this man, endure his questioning, no matter how he might be treated. A clever man could learn much from questions; it could not leave him farther from the Dove. He turned to Lorelei.

"It's all right," he told her. "I have to go with him. And you must go home, where you will be safe. But it will be all right. You'll see."

The man on the floor suddenly got up and made a shambling rush for the door. No one moved to stop him, nor even commented on his passage. The waitress calmly crossed the room and started to right the chairs and tables.

"But you're hurt!" Lorelei objected hopelessly. The tears spilled now, tracking lines in the smeared makeup. "Your head's bleeding! And it's all my fault. If I hadn't—"

"He'll be okay. I'll take care of him," the big man said gruffly before Daniel could. "Look, Laurie. Tiffany's going to call you a cab, and you're going to go straight home. You came a gnat's ass away from big trouble tonight. If I didn't think this creep had kept you from really getting into it, I'd bust his head right here. So you just get yourself home and safe, and stay out of trouble. Okay?"

"Oh, sure," cried Lorelei angrily. She rubbed her face, completing the ruin of her painted eyes. "Little Laurie should go home and be a good little girl. I know what will happen. I'll never see him again!" The last was a wail that cut Daniel's soul.

"You will," Daniel promised, ignoring the policeman's dark glance. "I'll have to find you to get my fiddle back, won't I?" And he nodded to where the case was still propped in the booth they had shared.

Lorelei's face lifted a little. "You promise?"

"Little sparrow, I'd sooner part with a hand than my fiddle. For one without the other is no use at all. I'll come for my fiddle." And for you, his eyes added, and he saw her hear the voice of his heart. She crossed the room and taking up the case, held it as lovingly as if it were his child.

"Get moving," the cop told him gruffly and started him on his way with a push. Daniel didn't resist. This one couldn't know it, but he was taking him closer to the Dove and the task that must be finished. And when it was finished, he would trust his fiddle to call him back.

"Ed?" It was the waitress, following them to the door. She was speaking softly. "You don't mind, I'm not going to call that cab right away. There's a few things I'd like to tell that little girl, before she goes any further. Sort of a payback to Mike, you know what I mean?"

"I don't know anybody else who could tell her better, Tiffany Marie. I'm going to take this fellow to Mike now, and I'll let him know. Hey, you need some money for the cab?"

"No. You just worry about what you've got to handle. But, uh, Ed, for what it's worth, it's true. That guy had his eyes on

Laurie. That gypsy hadn't a stood up to him, he'd a taken her. For what it's worth."

"Okay. I'll make sure Mike knows it. See ya, kid." The cop pushed the door open with one black-gloved hand, and pushed Daniel before him with the other. There was a big car at the curb, grey in the street lights. "Get into it," the old policeman told him. "You've heard of protective custody? Well, I'm going to put you in protective handcuffs." When Daniel didn't speak, but merely got into the car, the other grunted. "Don't touch nothing, and for Christ's sake, don't bleed on the upholstery."

16 NOV 19:48

Leaping in the darkness, laughing in the wind;
Look down, look down, look down, look down,
See the stars again.

"STARS OVERHEAD"

Durand slowly lifted his eyes to meet Stepovich's. "You ever do drugs?" he asked curiously.

"No, goddammit! That's not what this was about!" Stepovich's voice rose enough to turn heads at the next table.

Durand lifted his hands. "Hey, it was a joke. Guess it wasn't funny. Look, you'd been hit in the head. That was all."

"I hadn't been hit in the head when she was talking to me at her apartment."

"Yeah. Well, maybe that was just weird gypsy shit, you know? Mystical stuff, give the gull a good show, and all that."

"Maybe," Stepovich agreed grudgingly.

"Yeah. So, maybe what we oughta do is go back to Madam Moria's place. If she's there, we talk, only this time we've got a little more leverage, because we're there legitimately." Durand stressed the last word ponderously. "We'd be looking into what went on this afternoon."

"Makes sense," Stepovich said slowly. "But you can think what you like. I still think there's something to what I saw this afternoon. And to what she told me that night."

Durand shrugged. "Suit yourself. Can't hurt to keep it in mind."

"You know," said Stepovich, "there was a woman, a psychic, who got called in by Ashtabula County a few times for tough cases. County hired her to look at the scene of the crime and describe what had happened, and on a few missing persons cases."

Durand looked skeptical. "Yeah? What came of it?"

"Not a fucking thing," said Stepovich.

Durand laughed. "One for you," he said, and drained his beer.

Stepovich had just finished his and set the mug down when he saw Ed loom up behind Durand. It gave him a perverse pleasure to watch Durand jump when Ed laid a big hand on his shoulder.

Ed leaned over the table, spoke to them both. "Got something for you. Outside. In my car."

Neither one asked what it was. Ed's face was enough. They rose silently, Stepovich leaving money on the table. "The car's in back," Ed told them. "I didn't want to leave him out here under the lights. I had to cuff him. Hurry up. He looks like the type who'd do some damage left alone." Their breath made plumes in the air.

But the gypsy was sitting quietly in the front seat, ignoring the handcuffs looped through the steering wheel. Even in the dim alley light, Stepovich could see he'd been roughed up. What was Ed mixed up in now? He grabbed him by the elbow, stepped him away from the car. "He's not the right one, Ed."

"Yes, he is." Ed glanced over to where Durand was peering curiously in at the gypsy. The gypsy was staring straight ahead, ignoring them all. Light winked briefly on the key he tossed to Durand. "Uncuff him from the wheel and stick him in the back seat. But keep his hands cuffed behind him, okay?"

Durand just looked at him, eyes wide. Ed sighed. "Look, Randy, just do it, okay? I'll explain later. You won't get in trouble, I promise." As Durand moved grudgingly to obey, Ed turned back to Stepovich. "Uh, Mike. There's something I got to tell you. I'm a little afraid that you're going to overreact. So, before I start, the first thing I want you to know is that Laurie isn't hurt, and she's probably on her way home by now."

"What?" Stepovich's guts squeezed tight and cold. "What?"

"Tiffany called me down to the diner. Said there was a guy in there with Laurie, and Laurie was all tarted up. So I went down there, right away and—"

"You didn't call me?"

"There wasn't time. Anyway. When I got there, there was a fight in progress. Some guy, um, wanted Laurie, and the guy in the car there, the gypsy, he was beating the shit out of him. Woulda killed him, probably, if I hadn't broke it up."

The gypsy moved docilely from front seat to back. Durand put a hand on the gypsy's head to push it down as he entered the car. He winced and hissed in pain. But he went in willingly enough. Durand slid in after him, pushing him into the corner.

"Where's the other guy?" Stepovich felt murder building, his face reddening, the muscles in his arms and chest swelling.

"He ran for it. I'm not as young as I used to be, Mike."

"Bullshit!" Stepovich exploded.

"True." Ed's voice went harder. "I let him go. I didn't think he deserved to die for hitting on a girl dressed like a whore, even if the girl was only fifteen. Now, wait! I'm telling you true. Laurie was dressed to trick. And from what Tiffany told me, she was with the gypsy there when the other guy made her an offer. But!" Ed gripped Mike's arm hard, forced him to meet his eyes. "But the gypsy wasn't selling her, he beat the other guy to a pulp for even asking, and he even mouthed off to me when I bawled Laurie out for acting like a chippie. Listen, damnit! He's not a pimp, and I don't think he's a trick. He's some kind of street musician, and for what it's worth," Ed tightened his grip as Mike tried to shake him off a second time, "he protected her. And I don't think they did anything. He even backed me up when I told her to go home. So, before you talk to him, think where Laurie would be right now if he hadn't been around."

Both men stood silently. Stepovich could feel Ed's eyes on him as he, himself, stared at the gypsy. The gypsy stared back as if he knew every word passing between them.

"You okay?" Ed asked.

"Yeah," Stepovich said tightly. "Uncuff him. I just want to talk to him."

"You can talk to him with the cuffs on. At my place. He got hit in the back of the head with something. I figure we'll take him there, let him clean up a little, and talk to him. Where it's quiet and private."

"Uncuff him. I want to talk to him first. Right here."

"I don't think so," Ed said slowly. "I think we'll leave him cuffed and go to my place."

"Ed."

"You're not the type to hit a man when he's cuffed. And I'm not protecting just him, I'm protecting you. Two ways. From brutality charges and from beating insensible someone who might be able to tell you something about this other gypsy thing."

Stepovich strangled for a moment, cop warring with father. He reached inside himself for coldness, got a tentative grip on it. "Okay." He could wait. He'd hear it all first. And when he'd heard it all, then . . . He felt Ed's eyes on his face, forced the muscles to relax, his eyes to empty. "Okay. Your place. Let's go."

## MID-NOVEMBER, 1989

There's no whiskey in the jar
I'm so dry I need a drink
I need a place to lay my head down
I need to find some time to think.

"HIDE MY TRACK"

The horses were resting, now, content. Memories of them came back to him from a place he didn't know: Setal, who wouldn't stop moving, even in her stall; Sztrajktoro, who everyone else thought was bad-tempered, but who was only frightened; Madar, who was never really stubborn, just always had her own ideas of what she wanted to do; Nagyful, who listened so intently when he spoke. And the rest, down through the ages.

Now they were resting, as was he. The only thing left was a nagging feeling of something left undone, but it was too late now. The coach had stopped at last, and he must climb down, though he had no passenger for whom to hold the door. He regretted very little, he decided. The brandy, there at the end, had been a mistake, but he had hurt so much. Too late now, though. A feeling like a blanket was creeping over him; he felt warm, comfortable, as if the pain was over and wouldn't be back. He could rest now, and that was what he wanted. He was drifting, ready to sleep, except that he couldn't, because, off in the distance, someone was making a noise. It wasn't loud, but it was there, and it wouldn't stop. He had not been aware of it at first, but it was growing more annoying by the instant.

He was suddenly puzzled. He was dead, wasn't he? Why should there be a racket? Odd. What was it? A thump and a click-a-click, and a thump and slap. Like the tambourines the gypsies had played.

As this thought formed, he heard it louder, more insistent, more annoying. Damn those gypsies anyway. Ever since he'd met them they'd been nothing but trouble, and now they wouldn't even let him die. He tried to yell for it to stop, but his mouth didn't work. The noise stopped, however, and he saw a familiar face floating before him.

*Can't you leave me in peace?* he cried, or tried to.

*Leave you in peace? Of course not.* The other laughed. Which one was he? The Owl, yes, of course. *I am hardly going to leave you in peace, you have to drive us home when we're done.*

*But I can't. They've killed me.*

*Oh, yes, I know. And they've wrapped me in a cocoon of darkness, which I cannot leave. I cannot use my body, and yours is damaged, but I can still hear the songs of the* ritmus ordog, *can I not?*

*I see the horses,* he admitted.

*Well, there you are. Time to be up and about. I have something for my brother now, and I'll get it to him if he can find me before I die of the cold. I have a scarf the color of fire and smoke, but it may not be enough.*

*But what can I do?*

*The one who knows is dead; bring my brothers to the one who acts.*

It was all so damned confusing. He wished he had a drink. No, on the other hand, it was probably best that he didn't. *All right. Where are you, then?*

*Why, I have no idea,* said the Owl. *Tell them to listen for the tambourine.*

*Very well. But what about me?*

*Live.*

The damned gypsy seemed to be laughing now. The Coachman wondered why. Then, suddenly, he hurt too much to wonder about anything. The face vanished in a haze of bright lights and pain.

## AUTUMN NIGHT, HALF MOON RISING

For as long I remember
I've hated those red lights
And hotel rooms with plaster walls
And loud and lonely nights.

"RED LIGHTS AND NEON"

Csucskari the Gypsy hung back and let Madam Moria go up to see what the flashing lights meant. There were two police cars and an ambulance in the alley, and he had a sick feeling in the pit of his stomach. When Madam Moria returned after an interminable five minutes, the look on her lined face matched this feeling.

"Well?"

"He was in an accident. He is alive, and they are bringing him to a hospital. I don't know—"

She was interrupted by a siren. The ambulance turned around in the alley and sped away. Csucskari watched as it went by, spitting gravel, leaving a ringing in his ears. The ringing faded very slowly. Very slowly. He fancied he could hear, behind it, the ring of the zils of a tambourine. He listened, and it was still there. He looked at Madam Moria, and saw from the look on her face that she heard it, too. He started to speak, but she held a hand up and motioned him to follow. He did so, the tap-tapping of her canes blending with the rhythm still faintly thrumming in his ears.

## THURSDAY NIGHT

That old river keeps on rolling
And Old Hannah won't go down.
I can't give back what I ain't taken.
I won't give up if I ain't found.

"HIDE MY TRACK"

Timothy stared into his bathroom mirror, willing Her to him. He thought of how beautiful She had been the first time he saw Her, tried to focus his mind on how Her eyes had warmed him. He tried to see Her in the mirror, but the glass stayed cold, hard to his fingers when he pressed his hand flat against it. All it showed him was his own face, pale, his hair disheveled. Timmy hated the way he looked, so mussed and sickly. "Poor little Timmy," his mom would have said, and put him to bed and brought him a dish of warm milk spooned over soda crackers. She'd have scolded him, sadly, for getting into such a fight, and then she'd have called the police and complained about those neighborhood hooligans intimidating her son. But then his dad would have come home, and told him to get his ass out of bed and stop being such a sissy, when the hell don't you ever stand up for yourself, you little pussy.

He slapped the mirror, flat-handed, and the force of the slap rattled the medicine cabinet and started the cut on his stomach trickling blood again. He snatched a handful of Kleenex and dabbed up the trickle before it could make another mess. He shook the last six Band-aids from the box and applied them in a row over the slash, gritting his teeth and whimpering softly.

He moved slowly as he walked back to his dresser. He looked around the room. In spite of everything that had happened to him, and in spite of all the human filth around him, his room was clean. The old brown carpet was bare in places, and unraveling everywhere, but it was clean. The windows were clean, the white curtains were clean, his dresser was not only clean, but the top was clear, because everything was in its place. When you let things pile up and get messy, then you get dirty, and then you're just an animal, and he was far from being an animal. He was more than a man, so he had the cleanest room anyone could have.

He made it to the dresser and opened the second drawer, the tee shirt drawer, and looked through the carefully folded stack to find an older one. He almost wished he had one of those colored ones, black or dark blue, that wouldn't show the blood stains so much. But no, nothing looked as clean and nice as a fresh white tee shirt. He tried to put one on, but couldn't lift his arms.

He buttoned on a blue cotton-polyester shirt, and then almost cried at how much it hurt to tuck it in evenly. He went back to the mirror then, to stare, to comb his hair, to stare again, calling to Her as She had taught him. She didn't answer.

He had to show Her. He went to the dresser, moved the careful stack of tee shirts again, and took out the gun out, feeling the weight in his hand. He'd have to show Her, just like he'd showed his dad and mom. He thought once of the look on his dad's face when Timothy had said, "I'll show you who's a pussy," and pulled the trigger. But then he remembered his mom, and how she'd turned on him, how she'd screamed and run to the telephone, and started saying, "Hello, police, hello, police," and kept right on screaming it, even after he'd shot her twice. She'd turned her back on him. Just like the Lady.

No. No, She wouldn't, he'd show Her, he'd take out the old lady, and then he'd go after the Gypsy man, and She'd see, She'd be so proud. She wouldn't tease him and call him Little Timmy, She'd put Her long slender hands against his face and call him Her big, strong man, yes, and She'd kiss him with those full red lips, kiss the knife marks on his stomach, too. . . .

He stood still for a moment, thinking about that, letting it stir him, and then took his jacket from its hook in the closet. The gun felt nice in the pocket, he could hold it as he walked, pass people on the street, knowing that, if he wanted to, he could do for them but good. He shut off the lights and locked his door carefully and then walked slowly down the hallway, gun in his hidden hand as smooth and cold as mirror glass.

## NOVEMBER SIXTEENTH, 1989

Watch the storm clouds, they're telling me to run
I hear the wind say to hide;
A thousand accusations of all the things I've done,
Are after me demanding I be tried.

"LANNAN SIDHE"

He pried his eyelids open a crack. White. White sheets, white walls, white noise, all overlaid with soft shadows. Even the light that came in the small window of the door was a friendless white. And the smell. As if all the smells in the world had been killed, and their remains scrubbed up with alcohol and bleach. A fine place to die. Then they could scrub him up with alcohol and bleach. And the damn gypsies could walk home.

The Coachman let his eyes fall shut. He could feel the bandage tight around his stomach, was aware of every stitch in his thigh. No. He wasn't going to die. Dying would have been too easy; nothing had been that easy since he'd found the gypsies in the first place. Or they'd found him. Which was it? It hardly mattered. And now the Owl's words came back to him. Tekata, tekata, tekata, like a fine matched team trotting, like his own heart beating. He pulled his eyes open again. Whatever they'd given him for pain dragged at him, promising the warmth and softness of sleep. But the insistent rhythm of a tambourine pulled against it, sat him up in his bed.

The rest of the world was quiet. Someone had forgotten a television set in the corner, and its screen showed nothing as it whispered white. Its bluish light lit men sleeping or pain-drugged to stillness, shone on a few flat empty beds. The Coachman shivered as he pushed the thin blankets aside and swung his legs stiffly over the edge of the bed. The cold floor bit his bare feet. Would his clothes be in that drawer?

They weren't, and he remembered then, how they had cut them off him, the bright scissors snicking along cold against his flesh. He longed to crawl back into bed, but he forced himself to step softly down the ward until he came to a sleeping man about his height and build. No time to ask, he excused himself, for it wouldn't be long before men in ties with clipboards came, to question him, over and over and over. So far he had told no one anything, not even a name. He had pretended to be too drunk, too dazed, too much in shock to talk. Very little of it had been pretense. But morning would come soon, and with it questions he had no time to answer.

The checked flannel shirt was missing two buttons, and the jeans were too big in the waist, but they would do. He found his pocket knife, calk, hoof pick, and some change in his nightstand drawer. His boots were beneath it. The laborious task of stooping down to get them and the agony of actually pulling them on unmanned him for a time. He sat on the edge of that flat white bed, trying to breathe the pain away in deep slow breaths. He wiped the sweat from his face with the corner of the sheet. He wasn't going to get very far under his own power. The few dollars he had would buy him a short cab ride. Where? Back to his cheap room, where Daniel, perhaps, was still waiting? That might be best. Then Daniel could find Raymond. He briefly considered going back to Madam Moria's. But the thought that she might once more shut the door in his face decided him.

Getting out of the hospital was easier than he had expected. Even walking crabbed over, with one hand pressed against the bandages under his shirt, he drew little attention. The three nurses he saw were all tired and harassed. He got by them by asking for himself and being told that visiting hours were over, whereupon he sighed and went back out; none of them noticed that he'd come from the wrong direction. The area around the admissions desk looked like a bus station. A man held a bloody cloth to the side of his head while his woman chattered earnestly at the admissions nurse in a language the Coachman didn't recognize. A heavy woman sat rocking a screaming baby while three small children clustered around her. Two teenage boys sat next to a girl who stared straight ahead, eyes all pupils. The Coachman threaded his way out into the dark and cold.

The air on his face helped him push aside the confusion the pain medication made, but the chill tightened his skin. He was aware of the too-large jeans rasping against the bandage on his thigh with every step he took. The hospital was on a hill, and the surrounding neighborhood was dark. He walked two painful blocks past the hospital's parklike "quiet" zone before he felt the telltale warmth begin on his stomach. He walked another two blocks, counting each painful step, before he came to the bus-stop. It boasted a roofed enclosure, a single yellow bulb of light encased in a heavy metal cage, and a pay telephone with no handset. The Coachman sat down heavily on the cold concrete bench. The next bus, he promised himself and Raymond, no matter where it was going. He'd get on the next bus, into light and warmth, and get off when he was in some section of town that was still awake. He pressed his fist gently against his stomach wound and tried not to cough.

17 NOV 01:03

A drop, a rise, a jump, a spin;
Let the music lead you.
Keep the sunlight at your back;
There's someone there who needs you.

"GYPSY DANCE"

"I think there's a piece of glass in here. . . . What the hell did he hit you with, anyway?"

The gypsy who called himself Daniel didn't answer. Stepovich glanced back into Ed's kitchen, thinking that the scene looked like something from a bad movie. Daniel sat in one of Ed's straight-backed kitchen chairs, his hands still cuffed behind him. His dark head drooped exhaustedly forward on his chest. Blood had run down the back of his neck and stained his green shirt. If anyone walked in here, Stepovich thought, they'd think we were torturing him. But Ed's big hands handled the tweezers as if he were tying fishing flies. Durand's face showed only a mild queasiness as he held the flashlight. Twice now, Durand had raised questions about the legality of what they were doing, in frantic whispers that Daniel wasn't supposed to hear. Twice Ed had growled and shut him up.

"Dammit, kid, get a haircut," Ed muttered, and Durand tried to grin appreciatively.

The gypsy said nothing.

"For Christ's sake, uncuff him, Ed. I promise I won't touch him."

"He's been telling you the truth." Ed said it matter-of-factly, his big blunt fingers sorting through the gypsy's hair.

"I just don't . . ." For an instant, all the dizzying shock of the gypsy's tale hit him again. Laurie in that sleazy bar, a place he wouldn't even go himself. Laurie tarted up like a whore. Stepovich gripped his coffee mug with both hands, raised it, forced himself to drink from it. None of that was the gypsy's fault. But when he talked about Laurie, the way he called her Lorelei, and the quiet warmth he put into her name made Stepovich want to punch his lights out. Damnit, she couldn't be that old yet. Couldn't be. And even if she was, the gypsy wasn't what Stepovich had planned for his daughter. Some high school jock with a letterman's jacket and a beat-up old car, or some nerdy boy with thick glasses and penny loafers, even some punk with an earring and half his head shaved—those were the boys Laurie should be looking at, flirting with in the hallways at school. Not some sorrow-eyed street fiddler who knew the world from the seamy side out.

But he was the one. She'd chosen Daniel to confide in, Daniel to shelter behind when she got in over her head. She'd trusted him. And he'd been worthy of her trust. Ironically, that was what he couldn't forgive. That Daniel had been there for her, as Stepovich hadn't. Damn. Ed was watching him. Stepovich looked aside, forced the jealousy from his face. "I mean it, Ed. I'm cool. Uncuff him."

Ed glanced over at him, and gave Durand a barely perceptible nod. Durand set down the flashlight and fished the key out of his pocket.

"Gonna unlock you, kid. But I'm warning you, you make any kinda funny move, you got all three of us on top of you. Understand?" Durand was going to have to work on his style. Then again, maybe if Durand had felt better about what he was doing tonight, he'd have put more conviction into his words.

"I understand," Daniel answered in the same clear but exhausted voice he had used to answer all their questions. Or almost answer, Stepovich thought to himself as he watched the cuffs come off. Daniel maintained the same posture, only pulling his hands forward into his lap and gently massaging his wrists. No complaints. No threats of police brutality charges, no demands to know on what grounds he was being held. None of it added, not the way he had shrugged off Ed's offer of a trip to the emergency room, nor the way he had constantly asked them to clarify their questions. Hell, Daniel had asked more questions than he'd answered. He and Ed had had a fine time, questioning each other, dodging and weaving like boxers in a ring. Did Daniel know the scarred Gypsy? Well, he wasn't sure. What kind of scars were on his face? Oh? And was he a sickly old man? No? In good health, then? The gypsy he was with, did he have a tambourine? Oh, he was alone then? And on and on. Stepovich wasn't sure Ed had had the best of it. And none of it added up. Anybody could look at him and see he was related to the scarred Gypsy. It was in the cheekbones and the eyes, in the hooked nose and narrow chin. He had to know something about the man, but whatever it was, he was hiding it behind shrugs and blank stares, and "I don't understand's." But he wasn't hostile, he wasn't defiant. He was waiting for something, content to remain in their hands to see what happened next.

What happened next was that Ed said, "Got it!" and flicked a chunk of glass the size of a nickel onto the kitchen table. In the next instant he was pressing a dish towel to the back of the gypsy's head, staunching the flow of blood, so red against the black curling hair. "Oh," Durand breathed, and Stepovich understood. The sight of it dizzied Stepovich for an instant, as the sight and smell of blood did sometimes, and he found himself grinning hard to hold off the weakness.

"Boy's got enough hair," Ed muttered, and Stepovich registered that Ed had already classified him as "the kid" and "boy." Meaning that Ed had already made his personal judgment that Daniel was okay. Otherwise he'd have been "the punk" and "dickhead." "Hard to see through all this hair." Ed carefully lifted the towel away from the staunched cut as Durand craned his neck to look at it.

"Black as a raven's wing," Stepovich said softly.

Daniel's head came up slowly, as if someone were pulling it on a string. The eyes he turned on Stepovich were bird-bright and sharp, then suddenly cloaked.

Flashes: An escape from pursuit, a dream of burnt stew, an impossible coach ride, the suspect from a fifty-year-old crime come to life, an old woman dead in a hotel room, a knife that couldn't have killed.

Stepovich fixed his eyes on Daniel and cleared his throat. "Someone told me," he said, his voice still coming out hoarse, "that if I were wise, I'd let a Raven sit on my shoulder and hunt with me." Was there a flicker in those dark eyes, still fixed on his face? "And an Owl keep watch in the night for me. And a Dove tell me secrets."

Durand turned incredulous eyes to Ed. But Ed had on his "wait and see" look. After a moment, Durand gave a slow nod of agreement.

Daniel closed his eyes for a moment. He straightened slowly in the chair. Like a burden had been lifted? No. More like he had just resettled a heavy pack on his shoulders. His eyes were tired and old, but the spark of hope that kindled in them was a new, young thing. "The first thing we hunt for," he said into the unnatural silence, "is the Coachman."

## Chapter Fourteen

HOW THE GYPSY FOUND THE OWL

### THREE HOURS PAST CURFEW

I got nothing I can offer,
Like a dog without a bone.
If there's someone up there listening,
There's a poor boy out here alone.

"HIDE MY TRACK"

The cab was taking its own sweet time coming. Laurie hunched lower in the booth seat, took another sip of Coke. She was alone for the moment; Tiffany Marie had gone back to the counter to wait on an old woman and an even older man. Thank god. Laurie was already sick of her lectures. Every time she finished with a customer, she'd come back to Laurie's booth and say, "And another thing . . ." and launch into a horror story about her experiences. Laurie knew it was all bullshit. Tiffany didn't look like she knew the first thing about the street. Laurie watched her smile, making conversation with the old people as she took their order, nodding and listening like what they were saying was really important. Laurie wondered what they were doing out so late at night. They should have been at home, sleeping or reading newspapers or watching old movies.

All Tiffany Marie could talk about was how great Ed and her dad were, and what would have happened to her if they hadn't come along. Well, Laurie didn't think they were so great. For crying out loud, here she was with a whole bunch of problems, and what was her dad doing? Not worrying about her, that was for sure. Hell, he hadn't even phoned the diner to ask if she was safe. Some father. He was probably too busy picking on Daniel.

Daniel. Her heart softened at the thought of him. Dark man, shadow man, so much more real than the strutting little jerks she went to school with, with their designer holes in their designer jeans and pre-scuffed leather jackets. Daniel. He was what she wanted, what she had always wanted. He was nothing like her father, nothing like anyone else in her world. He was night and music and the mysterious kind of sex that made the bottom of her stomach drop out when she tried to imagine it.

"And another thing," Tiffany Marie said, sliding into the booth opposite her. "That guy you were with tonight, the one with the mustache. You probably got all kinda romantic ideas about him, but the truth is. . . ."

"There's my cab!" Laurie said, and slid out of the booth, clutching the fiddle to her as she went. Tiffany Marie had already given her a ten dollar bill. As she hurried out of the diner, across the sidewalk and into the cab, she toyed with the idea of not going home. Maybe Chrissy's house. No. If Chrissy still wanted to be friends after tonight, she was going to have to do some apologizing. Maybe her dad's? That might be cool. She had a key to get in, and she could wait up for him, find out what he'd done to Daniel. Shake him up a little. Shake up her mom, too, when she found out Laurie's bed was empty in the morning.

"Twelve-twenty-seven Garfield," she told the driver. He just grunted, settled his cap, and pulled away from the curb.

Laurie settled back on the seat. Cabs always stank of people and sweat and cigarettes and old perfume. She sat the fiddle case on her lap, as if it were a child, and leaned her head against its neck. It smelled like Daniel to her. She hugged it tighter. Holding it she could almost ignore the stink of the cab. Almost. It smelled like, well, not like a cab. More like the animal cages in the biology lab at school. She glanced out the window as they turned left on Cushman. After three blocks, she was sure they were going the wrong way.

"Hey, mister!" she complained, indignant that he'd try to rip her off like that. "You just went past Eucalyptus."

He made no response, only ducking his head deeper between his shoulders. Street lights and beer signs flickered past the window. He ran the light at Maple.

"Hey! I'm not some stupid little kid you can drive around for a while and then charge double. I grew up in this town, I know where I'm going."

The cabby giggled.

A stillness prickled through Laurie. For the first time she noticed how high the cabby's collar was, how low his hat was pulled, the way his sleeves hung past his wrists. In the flickering passage of light, she could see very little of him. What she could see did not seem very human.

She hugged the fiddle case. "I'd like to get out at the next light." Despite her best efforts, her voice quavered.

He glanced back at her. One eye was yellow, the other gleamed red. "Not the next light, no," he giggled. "Your light will be the light in the Lady's eyes."

## NOVEMBER SEVENTEENTH, EARLY MORNING

Walk through the door like our brother before
A lifetime remains until dawn.
The trees seem to say you'll be passing this way
In the wink of an eye you'll be gone.

"WALK THROUGH THE DOOR"

Two hundred and eight cars had gone by. Sixty-five pedestrians; two of them had noticed him, as evidenced by the pause in their footsteps before they'd walked on. From the other direction, the alley, two drunks had stumbled over him, cursing. One had started pawing at his clothing, perhaps to see if he had anything to steal, but then had changed his mind. Perhaps the scarf was protection in some way. Perhaps the scarf explained why Raymond didn't feel cold, why he hadn't died of exposure yet. He wished he knew how many hours, or perhaps days had gone by, but he had no way to measure time.

He had hoped, one hundred and seventy-three cars ago, that the scarf would lend him strength, but it hadn't; yet the fact that it had come meant that someone, somewhere, was looking out for him. It had a softness and a warmth that did not belong in this world, and there had been no one around him when he suddenly felt it, between one breath and the next, wrapped around his shoulders like a mother's arms. He didn't understand it, but as long as it kept him warm, he would not give up.

He had tried, one hundred and forty-eight cars ago, to reach the Coachman with what little strength he had, and he thought he'd succeeded. But the Coachman was dead or injured, so that might not do any good.

Two hundred and nine. Two hundred and ten. Eighteen buses, now. The buses made the big sounds like trucks, but didn't have that ratchety sound from the engine, and they had a more stately way of approaching traffic.

"Melody," someone had once told him, "is in the fingers. Rhythm is in the mind." It had sounded like nonsense at the time; to tell the truth, it still did. But in his mind he played the tambourine that rested beneath his coat. Someone might hear it, and it was something to do besides counting cars.

He shifted for a while to a complex Indian rhythm he'd learned from a tabla player he'd met in Cincinnati: Triplets within triplets, and fives within nines. He doubted he'd actually be able to play it on the tambourine, but in his mind it was a very fine thing indeed, the zils ringing out clear and precise, his imaginary fingers rolling like waves from the rim to the middle of the skin, and all the tones were warm and full and perfect.

Two hundred and eleven.

It would be a good thing if he could find the Dove—or the Raven, for that matter. Csucskari would know what to do with the scarf, and Hollo would know how to find Csucskari. (Two hundred and twelve, and one more pedestrian). It must have come to him with some purpose beyond keeping him alive. After all, what was his life worth? What was any life worth, for that matter?

Bah. Morbid thoughts. Silly. "All you think of is death, Bagoly," Hollo had told him once. "It isn't healthy. And you know why that is? It's because you never *do* anything. Everything that meets you pushes you. And you always let it happen. Push push push. This way, that way, like a stick in the river." When had he said that? It wasn't long ago, as he recalled. It was while they were searching for Csucskari. He, Raymond, had noticed the taint of the Fair Lady on their movements even then, and had tried to warn his brother, but Hollo couldn't wait. No, it was just fly this way, fly that way, looking for something to swoop down on, more for the pleasure of the swoop than because it was worth having.

They shouldn't have quarreled like that. They should never have split up. But if Daniel hadn't been so—

Now he was becoming angry, and that was as silly as being morbid. Better to play the tambourine in his mind and let the world drift, until it found a use for him. And don't forget the scarf, because, if all were truly over, it wouldn't be here.

The street was not very busy. Two hundred cars on this street probably meant a long time, and the weather had been cold, so the scarf must be doing something. Switch back to a simpler beat, so he could keep thinking. Yes, a *kajlamare.* Funny how they flowed into each other, those rhythms from cultures that had so little in common. But then, in one way or another (two hundred and thirteen), the Fair Lady was common to them all. So was the will to resist Her. Was it day or night? Had it gotten colder? Warmer? Why could he hear and smell, but not see or feel anything, save the scarf? Could he taste?

Dynamics, that's what it needed. Music without dynamics was, well, it wasn't music. He built up a nice crescendo in his mind, shaking the imaginary tambourine for all it was worth, then brought it down to a whisper.

Two hundred and fourteen. Two more pedestrians, both of them noticing him. Not leaving, either. Well, what now?

## AUTUMN NIGHT

**I'll never hear those songs again**
**But still I sometimes cry**
**When I think of how we left our world,**
**Raven, Owl, and I.**

"RAVEN, OWL, AND I"

The old woman said, "I think he's gone."

Csucskari, staring down at his brother, snorted. "I'd know if he were."

"He's cold," she said.

"Yes, I imagine he would be. I don't doubt that he's been here for hours. They found a good place to hide him."

"But how could he—?"

"Hush, old woman."

He bent down and wrestled his brother's form into a position where he was sitting up, squatted, and lifted him onto his shoulder. He was as light as air, light as a bird.

"Where are you bringing him?" she asked.

"To your home, old woman."

"But he needs—"

"A cup of tea will see him well, I think. Do you know how to make tea? Take his tambourine."

"If he's not dead—"

"Tcha! Don't you know Luci's work when you see it?"

She sighed and began shuffling back toward her home. A moment later she suddenly said, "I know Cynthia's work, though."

"Eh?"

"That scarf, around his throat. Cynthia made it."

"Indeed? I wonder how Raymond came to it."

"I've never seen it before. Except—"

Csucskari looked at her. "Yes?"

"The pattern. Does it look familiar?"

"No."

"Hmmmph. You are unobservant. The rug in my living room."

"Did Cynthia make that?"

"No, I did. But I didn't make the scarf."

"Perhaps Cynthia only made it recently."

"She's been dead since—" the old woman stopped in mid-sentence. "Yes, perhaps she did."

Csucskari matched his pace to what Madam Moria could keep up with, and said no more as he walked.

## SOMETIME

**Who can ever know your heart, who will ever tell?**
**No one will believe, my friend,**
**All that you'll receive, my friend,**
**Before she locks you in your private Hell.**

"THE FAIR LADY"

*The Fair Lady wriggles Her toes and frowns. "Well," She says, "I can hardly blame you, I suppose." The woman-child stares with eyes like twin moons at the full. The Fair Lady thinks of a Wolf howling at the moon, and has to force Herself not to shudder. "A jackal followed the trail you left and thought you were his prey, the Raven drove the jackal off so Badger wouldn't slay. The Badger brought him to the Wolf who would not eat him down. So now the Raven leads them all until the Dove be found."*

*The woman-child, left arm held tight by the* liderc, *says nothing. The Fair Lady thinks she is as frightened as She has ever seen a mortal. "But at least we have you, now, and that should be bait for both Wolf and Raven, shouldn't it?"*

*The girl clutches something tightly in her right arm. The Fair Lady notices it for the first time, and says, "What is that?" Her voice doesn't tinkle or chime, now, it snaps, and carries a shock like plunging into ice-cold water. The girl starts to cry. "What is it?" repeats the Fair Lady, but the girl is too frightened to answer.*

*Screams from the little room, and the girl stops crying. Her eyes get bigger, if that is possible, and she looks that way. The Fair Lady smiles. "An old woman," She says, "who thought to thwart me. You won't make that mistake, will you?"*

*The girl trembles and shakes her head.*

*"Good. Now, what is that you're holding?"*

*It takes a long time for her to speak, and when she does, her voice is so small it is almost lost in the crackling of the fire. But she says, "His fiddle."*

*"His?" The Fair Lady frowns. "The Raven's?" And then She smiles. "You've brought me his fiddle? You've pulled his wings and brought them to me. There may be hope for you, girl."*

*The girl sobs.*

*"Give it to me, then, and you will not be punished."*

*The girl sobs again and shakes her head.*

*"What?" cries the Fair Lady. "You think to defy me? Give me the fiddle!" There is another scream from the next room.*

*The girl sobs once more, clutches the fiddle tightly, and, again, shakes her head.*

*The Fair Lady's eyes are cold as ice, cold as snow, cold as the space between Her world and ours, cold as the heart of the* mid-wife. *She speaks to the* liderc. *"Take her away and bring her back when she's changed her mind."*

*They open the door to where the old woman is crying out from the pain of the hot coals the* nora *is pressing to the bottoms of her feet. The girl sees this and stumbles, almost falls, and her tears flow now in rivers.*

*"Well," demands the Fair Lady. "Will you give me what I want?"*

*But she shakes her head once more. The Fair Lady scowls and nods to the* liderc, *who pushes the girl into the room and closes the door.*

*The Fair Lady stares into the fire, thinking.*

17 NOV 01:48

I can't hear the fiddles when you hum,
I can't see where the raven flies,
I can't hear the rhythm for the drum,
And I can't see the forest for your eyes.

"GYPSY DANCE"

Ed set down the receiver. "No luck. Guy at the rooming house says your Coachman hasn't come back. Bitched at me about the rent being overdue, too." He flung himself down in a saggy overstuffed chair and looked up at the ceiling.

"Where else does he hang out?" Durand demanded of Daniel, who was sitting beside him on the couch. Durand balanced a mug of coffee on his knee. Daniel held his with both hands, as if to still their shaking. They looked, Stepovich thought, more like college buddies than a cop questioning a suspect. Stepovich took a sip of coffee, settled his shoulders against the door jamb again. "Bars?" Durand suggested. "Does he have a favorite? Is there a woman, a friend he'd go to? Where would he go?" Stepovich and Ed exchanged glances. Durand was pushing Daniel to answer before he'd had a chance to think.

Daniel shrugged wearily. "I don't know. I told you, I've only been here a short time. I haven't been living in his pocket."

"I saw blood in that carriage," Stepovich said suddenly. "Madam Moria didn't look hurt. Neither did the Coachman, but he might be able to take a bullet and not let it show for a while. So think about this, kid: If he was hurt, maybe bad, where would he go?"

"We could try phoning hospitals," Ed suggested. "It's tedious, but it's paid off before."

"If we have to," Stepovich shrugged. "But let's have the kid think on it, first."

Daniel was trying. The strain showed in his face. "With this Madam Moria, perhaps?" he suggested. His shoulders sagged suddenly. "I'm only guessing," he admitted wearily.

Stepovich fought back a yawn. "It's worth checking."

"Let's phone," said Durand.

Ed just looked at him. Stepovich said, "If she says he's there, we have to go get him. If she says he's not there, we still have to check. And we don't want to warn him, anyway."

"In the morning?" Ed suggested.

"Now," Stepovich and Daniel said in unison. Stepovich wondered if the gypsy kid felt the same strange urgency he did about this. Restlessness was running down his back with cold rat feet. He had that prickly feeling that something was happening, right now—something he should be in on. He caught his jacket up from the back of the chair, slung it on impatiently. Ed went to the door, jingling his keys. Durand came to his feet, stretching. Daniel rose, swayed slightly, squinting his eyes against pain or dizziness, but when Durand reached a hand to steady him, he waved it away. Tougher than he looked.

Ed drove, with Stepovich up front beside him. Daniel and

Durand were in the back. Stepovich sat sideways on the seat; he couldn't quite trust his back to the gypsy. Not yet. He'd been good to Laurie, all right. But that didn't mean he was a good guy, not completely. Durand smothered another monstrous yawn. The kid was tired.

"Tell me why we got to find this Coachman guy tonight?" Durand complained rhetorically.

But Daniel took the question seriously. "There were three of us," he said, in the voice of a tale told many times. "The Owl, the Dove, and I."

"The Raven," Stepovich said, unaware of speaking aloud.

"Yes."

Durand was sitting forward, his lantern jaw slightly ajar, and Stepovich was aware of Ed listening as only Ed could, with every pore of his body as he let the big car drift down the road.

"We were brothers, but Csucskari, the youngest, he was a Taltos. He didn't eat, and he didn't drink, and he never felt the heat or the cold, and the animals would speak to him, and trolls feared him, and he fought dragons, while we followed him.

"And the Coachman was the one who sent us here, who brought us from a tale to a place where tales are told, because that was ever the Coachman's power. Why did he send us? Why did we go? Because of the Fair Lady, who had crossed the bounds of Her world; The Fair Lady, who brings the diseases that waste the body, who brings the sickness that rots the soul. She is in this world now, having Her way here.

"Owl saw that She had left our world, and I tracked Her to this one, but it was the Coachman who brought us here, and the Coachman who can take us back, when our task is done. We each do our part—every one who conquers his fear and greed long enough to repair some of the rot does his part. But the Dove, Csucskari, is the only one who can drive Her away."

He sighed. "For that, he needs us, the Owl and I. We didn't know this, at first. Csucskari came to this world alone, and with every step he took he lost a part of himself, until at last he was wandering, alone, not knowing who or what he was or what he had to do. Years later, my brother and I tried to follow him. We found his trail in France before the Great War, and in New Orleans after it, and here and there since then, but at last, hopeless, we quarreled and went our own ways.

"Now the call has come. The Coachman was bringing us

together, but the Fair Lady struck first. I don't know what She has done to the others, but to me She sent a woman whose kiss was to be my death. And it would have been if—"

He stopped. Stepovich stared at him, waiting.

He shrugged. "But I was lucky enough to be hit on the head by the wrong man, so the right man changed his mind."

In the darkness of the car, their eyes met and locked. A dozen possible comments rattled through Stepovich's mind. He could snort and say, "Fairy tale!" He could remind him that Laurie was no woman, but only a little girl playing dress up. He could lean back and whisper that the "right" man hadn't had a chance at him yet.

But any of those would be pretense. Because he believed Daniel, fairy tale and all. This gypsy was telling the truth. Stepovich could feel Ed reading that conclusion from his own body language, and accepting it as Ed had often accepted Stepovich's other hunches. And Durand was watching them stare at each other, with no idea of what was passing between them. Just like when he'd told Durand, however long ago it was, that the Gypsy with the scarred face wasn't the man they wanted, even if he did match the description.

So to the gypsy he said nothing, and to Durand he gave only a "wait and see" nod to keep the kid steady. Durand returned it, a barely perceptible movement.

"So," Daniel continued, as if he had not paused at all, "There are three of us, my brothers and I, and there are three of you. And as the Coachman has brought us three here, he will see us all three home. And as for you . . ." Daniel paused. "I will tell you how it was, for the Owl and me. Csucskari was gone. It is hard for me to describe for you what that means. Without him," Daniel paused, struggled for a smile. "Try to weave with no warp or woof, or to paint a picture without canvas to hold the colors, to, to. . . ."

"To shoot with no target," Stepovich filled in softly.

"Yes. To live with your own purpose hidden from you. Your actions without form, no pattern of effort to what you do. We are one with our brother, a part of his tale. When he was gone, we were lost, though we traveled still with our kin over paths we knew well, and stood together upon the road, with the fires and the laughter of our *kumpania* at our backs. And there came a coach, such as we had not seen in many a year, drawn by horses such as no longer stir the dust of any road. And high on the box was the Coachman, with his fine cloak and coiled whip. And he halted his horses, and to each of us he said, "I offer a ride and I offer it but once. Whither away lies the dream of your soul?" And our bellies dreamed of rich food and potent wine, and our loins of beautiful women and the wealth of children they could bear us, and our ears were full of the music of days we had thought lost so long ago. But our hearts spoke first, and loudest, crying out, "Only put us upon the road our brother has taken and we will be content." And the Coachman's smile faded, and he said, "For good or ill, you have chosen," and the door opened to us and we entered the coach. And this place of yours is where he brought us, many and many a year ago."

Daniel paused. The Caddy was idling at a stop light. The bright headlights of a turning car washed through the interior, illuminating each of them in turn. "Suppose he comes to you?" Daniel said softly. "Suppose he says, 'I offer a ride, and I offer it but once?' What will you answer? Think well on it, while you have time."

Daniel fell silent. Stepovich watched Ed look at his hands on the wheel and flex them, perhaps seeing the small age spots, the way the tendons stood out, an old man's hands, and here he was still driving the same streets he'd driven for all his years as a cop. He'd always told Stepovich that some day he'd see the rest of the country. But was it the dream of his soul, or only the consolation of a life that, despite danger and action, had always seemed limited by his love for this stupid miserable city he'd grown up in?

He looked at Durand, who twitched and flexed and felt his untried strength hanging on him like a suit of clothes too big, perhaps wondering if and when he'd prove himself, and if he'd die young like his dad. Perhaps he felt unfinished, untried. Or maybe he wanted power; maybe he dreamed of becoming a captain, or a commander, and laying down the rules that were so important to him.

But Stepovich thought only of one moment in time, one brief instant when he could have simply said, "I'm sorry. I didn't mean to hurt you." And he could have stayed, and listened to her yell, and then held her as she cried, and then made love to her to mend their quarrel, one more time, one more effort at making it work, instead of walking out and taking the car and going to the motel, never knowing that he'd already had the last night he'd ever spend in a bed holding her while she slept, never knowing that his heart's desire would someday be to have that one moment back to do over.

The Caddy rolled on, full of silence and dreams, through streets blacker than nightmare. Slowly, one at a time, Ed rolled his shoulders and shook his head; and Durand cracked his knuckles and twitched his jaw; Stepovich wondered what they had been thinking of as each came back to himself.

"The Coachman," Stepovich prodded lightly.

"He likes his liquor," Daniel said quietly. "The good stuff when he has money, but anything the rest of the time. There are horses in his life, always, and those are the tales he tells when he drinks, of fine-blooded horses full of spirit and strength, as another man might speak of wealthy highborn women he had bedded. Look for him where there are horses—liveries, riding stables, breeding farms, race tracks. And he likes to drive. He will work as a chauffeur, or even a taxi driver if he can find nothing better. But if there is a place where he can sit high and hold the reins in his own hands, then we should look there first."

Stepovich looked at Ed, who shrugged. The Caddy rolled on quiet as the wings of an owl through the night, through the night.

## SOMETIME

I touch your hand, your brow, your lip;
Hidden by the green,
Emerging to a weeping bush
And laughing tambourine.

"GYPSY DANCE"

Even after the thing tormenting the old woman left, Laurie couldn't stop shaking. Her breath kept making a gulping, hiccuping noise in her throat. "This isn't real," she whispered aloud, and then, wailing, "This isn't real, none of this is real, please, God, tell me this isn't real."

The woman was very old, and her skin was a terrible color, as if someone had let all the blood out from under her once olive skin, and replaced it with milk. A skim milk in cold coffee color. She drew her skinny old legs and ruined feet up under her long skirts then felt about herself absentmindedly, as if looking for something. "None of this is real," she agreed in her cracked old voice. "And that's the worst part of it, you know. Real things end, somewhere, sometime."

"It'll end," Laurie whispered, unable to get enough air for real words. "It'll end when they kill us."

"I'm sorry, my dear," the old woman said slowly. "But you're so very wrong. Why, for me, it didn't even begin until I was dead." The old woman casually examined her feet. The burns on them were black places, not red, nor swollen, nor bleeding. Black, as if the coals had been held to a wooden statue or a china doll.

"If you're dead, how can they keep hurting you?" Laurie wailed. Already she was seeing it happen to her. She clutched the fiddle case as if by holding it tightly she could hold herself together as well.

"They can do almost anything to me," said the old woman. She looked around the room, a sly look creeping over her face as she did so. "Almost anything they can do to me. But they must keep me here. And while they keep me here, there is much I can do to them." Once more she looked around carefully. "Come here, child," she said.

Laurie's legs quaked under her as she crossed the room. The closer she got, the more she knew the old woman was dead. There wasn't an odor, but there was something she smelled with her skin, not her nose; when Laurie finally crouched down beside her, she knew that, while the old woman was dead, this was not her dead body. Rather it was as if the old woman was inside a mannequin, cunning as any trap. A body the Fair Lady had fashioned—one She could hurt endlessly. Laurie shivered.

The old woman looked at her shrewdly. "You've the Eye to you, then. It seldom comes to much, in one such as you, but it's a help to us here. It's probably what She didn't see about you at first, probably what drew the Raven closer to you than She'd planned. Yes, hug his fiddle tight, for it's all that stands between you and Her. Or, maybe not. Open the case, girl. Let's see what he's left in there for us."

Laurie hesitated, then set the case on her lap and unlatched each fastener. The case was lined with some deep green fabric, not felt, not velvet, not like anything Laurie had ever seen inside an instrument case. The bow was secured in its holder, and a storage box supported the neck of the fiddle and held it firmly in place. The old woman tapped the box with one arthritic finger. "In there," she whispered. "Where he keeps his odds and sods. Look in there."

Laurie lifted out the fiddle and leaned it against her shoulder. The storage box had a tiny catch on it. She worked it and then eased back the lid. Inside was a worn cube of rosin, showing infinite tracks of bow strings; white paper packets that held spare strings; smudged papers, folded up small, with musical notes on them like bird tracks; a button off a shirt; and a brush like a makeup brush. "What else, is that all? It can't be all. Look again, girl!"

"There's some lint. And a feather."

"Ah!" the old woman exclaimed with satisfaction. "Pass me that here." She took the small black feather from Laurie's shaking fingers, whetted it once, twice, thrice across the amber rosin. She smiled an old smile. "Now answer me a riddle, if you can. Why is the fiddler's music like the count's coach?"

Laurie stared at her. She'd stopped shaking. She was numb with terror now, still in the grasp of hopelessness.

The old woman smiled again, a hard smile. "You don't know, child? Why, they're both drawn forth by horses." She ran the edge of the rosined feather down the horse hair strings of the fiddle's bow. It made a breath of sound softer than a baby's whisper. "The right touch," she murmured to Laurie, "can draw them forth together." She handed the bow to Laurie and said, "Play, now."

Laurie shook her head, bewildered.

The old woman smiled and said, "No, you have Wolf's blood in you, girl. You weren't made to lie down and die; not when you have the ghost of a prayer of hope. Take the fiddle and play."

Hope? Laurie had no idea what the woman was talking about, but she was holding the fiddle, and she knew that, hope or no hope, Daniel was real, and the fiddle was his. She tucked the fiddle clumsily under her chin, feeling her tears slide down her cheeks onto the wood. She hoped it wouldn't be damaged. She lifted the bow in her right hand and, with no thought to what she was doing, drew it across the strings.

# Chapter Fifteen

## HOW THE GYPSY CALLED ALL THE ANIMALS

### AUTUMN, EARLY MORNING

**Old woman, tell me when to hold the sand**
**And when to let it spill.**
**Old woman, tell me when the sun's light**
**Will touch my window sill.**
**Old woman, tell me if it's me**
**Or those around me who are ill.**
**Old woman, promise me**
**That I will never have to kill.**

"BLACKENED PAGE"

Csucskari cradled his brother as gently as if he were holding a bird, but the solidity of him in his arms was a comfort. He studied his brother's face as he bore him through the streets. Years walked lightly on the brothers, but it had been so long since he had seen Raymond that the tracks of time were plain to Csucskari. Bagoly had begun to grow a beard, and the streetlights found red highlights in it. The depressions in his temples were accented his hair, brushed sharply back. His brows were even more full than Csucskari remembered.

*Bagoly. Bagoly*, he sang silently. *Jojjon velem, repul hazafele, O Bagoly*, come with me, fly home, he said. Csucskari walked as he sang, his eyes all but closed. Feelings he had thought banished into the cold well of his past, never to be found again save for the distant splash as a sensation brushed him, now rose like mist. It was a tingling of old power, as when a limb that has gone numb stirs back to life, all pins and needles. It came to him, and flowed from him easily and naturally into his brother, as easily as he might put his mouth to the Owl's lips and breathe his own breath into his brother's lungs. *Bagoly, Bagoly, jojjon velem*, he sang silently. From a vast distance, his brother responded.

People passed them on the street, stepping off the sidewalk to avoid his lolling burden. Later, Csucskari could not recall if they had any other reaction to him; his only thought was to get to Madam Moria's rooms, and to do whatever he must to bring his brother back.

As he maneuvered Bagoly through the narrow door of Madam Moria's building, Owl's eyelids suddenly squeezed tight, making lines in his weathered face. Slowly they opened to slits, and then sagged shut again. As he carried Bagoly up the creaking stairs, he felt a shudder move through his brother's body. And as Madam Moria unlocked her door he began to shiver.

She leaned her canes carefully beside a tall wooden coat-rack, and divested herself of her long wool coat. "I'll brew tea," she announced, as if this would probably set all the world to rights.

Csucskari looked up from his brother's face to meet her dim old eyes. "He'll be all right," he told her. She nodded once, cautiously, and walked stiffly from the room.

There was a narrow divan in one corner, upholstered in a fading red fabric, draped in a tattered afghan. There he placed his brother and dragged the afghan down to tuck around him. Owl seemed to be breathing easier. Csucskari touched the scarf around his brother's shoulders. He ran it through his fingers, feeling the fine threads snag against his callused hands as he stared at her rug. He licked his lips and considered. He felt tired. Tea would be nice, but he'd been told he ought not to eat or drink, and he knew why, now, too.

Madam Moria pushed through the curtains, preceded by a heavy tray laden with a teapot and cups. She poured one for herself, and another for Raymond. Csucskari lifted the delicate cup and held it to Raymond's mouth. The hot liquid lapped against his lips, but as yet he could not drink.

"Twenty-four," mumbled Raymond.

"What?" said Csucskari anxiously. "Twenty-four what?"

"Steps," said Raymond. "Twenty-four steps up here," and settled back more fully into the couch.

Csucskari set the cup carefully back on the tray, and turned to where Madam Moria had ensconced herself in an old bentwood rocker. "The scarf and the rug," he said without preamble. "Together, they mean what?"

Startled, she looked up from gazing at the tea in her cup. "Eh? I've no idea. And no time to consider it. I must boil more water for tea. There will be company, soon."

"Who?" He frowned.

"I don't know that either," she said irritably. "Be patient." She creaked up and went back through the tapestry.

Csucskari scowled after her. When he turned back to Owl, his eyes were open. "Well," said Csucskari gently. "You've been a far ways, it seems."

Raymond opened his mouth, then shut it. He shook his head weakly. Tears gathered in his eyes, while a smile hovered at the corners of his mouth. At last he said, "I'm coming back, brother. A few moments, is all. I'll be fine, now you've come for me."

Csucskari looked for words to say and found none. Once more he held the cup to Raymond's lips, and Raymond expended most of his gathered strength in taking one feeble sip. Madam Moria and her teakettle had just re-emerged from the kitchen when the door burst open.

## NOVEMBER SEVENTEENTH, 1989, EARLY MORNING

Drink from a deep dark pool, tell me what you taste,
Bitter mountain stream;
Flows like nectar past your lips, lying there in wait,
Falls from your hand.

"STARS OVERHEAD"

The warmth of the seeping blood inside the bandage made the night seem colder. He wished he could pull his legs up against his body and hoard what warmth was left to him, but his first effort at that had hurt too much. Better to sit still, leaning against the metal and glass that sided the bus shelter. Sit in the dark and dream. The shelter was no bigger than a good-sized box stall; but a stall at least would have had clean straw to rest on and the warm smell of horses to keep him company.

He remembered a master he had once had, so long ago that he could not remember his name, nor anymore about him than that the master'd thought he was saving money and cheating the Coachman by giving him only a room over the stable. The fool never knew that most nights he had taken his blankets down to the stalls, to sleep closer to those who loved him best.

There had been four, black as night and as soft; five if you counted the ill-tempered stud in his iron-barred stall who had sired them. Storm had been his name, as stupid a name for a stallion as the Coachman had ever heard, and it fit him no more than did his reputation for savage behavior. He had wanted a firm hand, that was all, and a man who did not flinch from his angry stamping, nor let the stable boys get away with letting his stall go dirty because they feared him. He had needed a man who would give him space and time with the tall grey mares they brought him to be serviced. Another man had owned him, but only the Coachman had mastered him. And in return, the stallion had sired the four blacks, the three fillies and the colt, who learned their lessons on his lunge line and under his gentle hands. They'd grown well, and earned the braided harness with leather tassels, and the leather-covered rope traces and the owner's finest coach, with its tall box and carved wooden back and sides, and proud, rounded lanterns.

How they'd stepped out for him, heads always high, black legs flashing in unison! As Storm was their father, so the owner called them Wind, Rain, Thunder, and Lightning. But the Coachman had had his own names for them all: Setal, Sztrajktoro, Madar, and Nagyful, and those were how he called them when he spoke to them at night. Those were the names they would come to, no matter what stood between him and them: Snakes or fires or barking dogs. Once Csucskari had wagered that they'd come to him past death itself if he called those names.

He smiled, the foolish smile of a man who is cold and without hope, bleeding in the night, and he muttered their names like a charm. His head drooped forward onto his chest.

17 NOV 02:21

**Dive into a deep dark pool, tell me what you feel,**
**The world you left behind,**
**Smooth and warm as life, the living and the dead,**
**Stars overhead.**

"STARS OVERHEAD"

"So," Durand observed as the Caddy idled at a stoplight, "If Luci is the lady you're all going to kill, and the Gypsy is this tatoesh guy that can do it, how does the Coachman fit in?"

Ed rolled his eyes at Mike. Stepovich sighed to himself. Let the guy talk himself out first; he'll tell you more that way. This was stuff he should have been teaching Durand all along.

Daniel looked thoughtful. "He is," he groped for words, but found them only in a language none of them spoke. He tried again: "like the one who plays the music that sets the other dancing. He is not a dancer, nor does he even know the steps they must pace, but nevertheless, he is the one. . . ." He lapsed once more into helpless silence, unable to explain the Coachman's role, perhaps scarcely comprehending it himself. Finally, he said, "It was the Coachman who brought us here. And when all is done, it is he who will take us back. And I feel that the Coachman should be there, to witness the doing of our task. Whether we succeed or fail, he will be the one to know of our doing, and to tell those who should know."

Ed made the lights at Woodwright and Quince, but was stopped at Central. He prodded, "Task?"

Daniel took a breath, then spoke, patiently. "To send the Fair Lady back where She belongs."

The silence that followed seemed to echo Daniel's quiet words until Durand, as if struggling with an idea, asked, "This Choo-, uh, Chuch, uh, Csucskari, this scar-faced Gypsy? The Coachman can find him for us?"

When Daniel gave a tentative nod, Durand leaned back, satisfied. "Well, as long as this Coachman can lead us to that sneaky S.O.B., then I'm happy."

The light changed and they passed under I-79 and continued on West Drewry, the boundary of the industrial area and the

Fourth Precinct. Daniel gave Durand one puzzled sideways glance, then relaxed. He leaned his wounded head carefully against the seat back, let his hands go lax on his knees. No. Not relaxed. Stepovich studied him unobtrusively. Taking rest while he could. Suddenly, Daniel's long graceful fingers tensed, his dark eyes snapped open. He sat up abruptly, cocking his head like a dog hearing a distant siren.

"What?" Stepovich demanded.

Daniel's eyes shone brighter than the passing streetlights could account for. His hands floated up as if to the signal of an unseen maestro. He began to mime the playing of a fiddle—mimed it with such uncanny precision that Stepovich could almost hear the eerie music drawn forth from the unseen strings.

Neither Durand nor Ed heard anything, judging by their expressions. Ed eased the Caddy to a stop at a red light at Pine. "Maybe that hit on the head," he muttered to Stepovich, sotto voce. Stepovich shrugged, and turned to stare ahead into the night street and the sparse cross traffic.

The light was just ready to turn, Ed was already letting the Caddy creep forward when every hair on Stepovich's body came to attention. Later it would seem to him that first his hide prickled, and then the four black horses drawing the midnight coach came out of the night and crossed their path. Sixteen hooves rose and fell in perfect cadence, high spoked wheels turned soundlessly against black asphalt.

There was no coachman on the box.

"Follow it," Stepovich whispered.

The Caddy didn't move. Stepovich glanced over at Ed, transfixed behind the wheel. "Follow it!" he bellowed, and the big car surged suddenly forward and took a hard left.

"Shit, oh shit," Durand whispered. Stepovich spared him a glance. The kid's eyes were as big as saucers. Daniel was oblivious, playing his invisible instrument faster now. He was smiling through the tears that tracked his face, leaning forward, swaying raptly to his silent music. When Stepovich turned back, the solid black of the coach was still there, but harder to see. It was visible mostly as a shape that blotted out oncoming traffic, storefronts and street signs. The coach was pulling away from them. There was a dim lantern fixed to the back of the coach, and they followed this more than the coach itself.

"Dammit, no horses are going to outpace me," Ed declared, and pushed down on the gas. The heavy car surged forward, and the coach lantern grew. Just as the black coach began to take on details, it turned out of sight. Ed cursed, and gave the Caddy more gas, and took the corner at a speed that pressed Stepovich up against the door. But the coach was moving up the hill at an impossibly smooth fast pace, turning another corner almost as soon as they sighted it. Ed spun loose gravel following it, and was barely in time to see the lantern wink around another corner as the coach turned uphill once more, on Park, passing back under I-79. Other cars went by, but none slowed down; it was as if only they could see the damn thing, which, all things considered, wasn't unlikely.

Ed floored it, sliding the big car through the turn. Daniel swayed, but never ceased playing. Suddenly, the lantern was stationary in front of them. Ed hit the brakes, throwing them all forward, to a chorus of "Jeez, Ed!" from Durand and the steady low, "Watch it, watch it, watch it!" from Stepovich as he braced against the dash.

The Caddy's tires screeched as they slid helplessly forward. All three cops braced for a collision with a coach that was suddenly not there. In front of them, the night flapped like a sheet on a laundry line, and then was still.

"Which way?" Ed demanded angrily of the empty street. But Daniel abruptly stopped playing his invisible instrument, and flung open the door of the Caddy, narrowly missing the pole of the bus-stop sign.

"Help me with him!" he commanded over his shoulder, and then was down on one knee beside a slumped figure on the bench inside the bus shelter.

Durand, Ed and Stepovich exchanged uneasy glances as the Coachman lifted his head slowly and put one hand on Daniel's shoulder. He didn't try to rise, but waited. Finally Stepovich said, "Well, nothing to be afraid of," and moved to open his door. But Durand was already sliding across the back seat and out. Ed and Stepovich watched him crouch slightly to allow the Coachman to get a good grip on his shoulder.

"How many gypsies am I supposed to fit in this Cadillac?" Ed demanded of the night, and Stepovich asked, "That an ethnic joke?" as Durand and Daniel eased the Coachman into the car.

*"Nem cigány vagyok,"* muttered the Coachman, almost too quietly for anyone to hear.

"What's that mean?" demanded Ed, turning to watch them.

"He said he's not a gypsy," said Daniel.

"He looks like shit," Ed observed congenially. "Take him to the hospital?"

"I don't think so," Daniel replied.

"No," said the Coachman, breathing out pain with the word. He drew another ragged breath and gingerly rearranged himself on the seat. "I just got out of there."

"What's wrong with him?" Durand demanded as he got in his side of the car.

The Coachman turned his head to look at Daniel as he and Durand settled into the car on either side. Whatever passed between them seemed to reassure him. He said, "I was bitten by a snake, crushed by a horse with five legs, and gored by a bull with three horns. Of course," he added, "You might see it differently."

"You been gut shot, haven't you?" said Stepovich. It was all coming together for him.

"I knew you'd see it differently," agreed the Coachman.

"Gut shot?" Durand demanded, and again Stepovich sighed, wishing he'd just let the man talk. "Earlier today, at Madam Moria's place?"

The Coachman nodded. The soft cushioning of the seat and the warmth of the Caddy's heater seemed to be reviving him.

"Who did it?" Durand demanded again.

The Coachman shrugged, an elaborately careful gesture. "One of the Fair Lady's tools. If he has a name, I don't know it. After he's been with Her a little longer, neither will he. Those She takes, She takes all from."

"Let me guess," said Durand. "This particular tool was five feet, six inches tall, one hundred and twenty to one hundred and thirty pounds, had short reddish hair, a long face, snub nose with a few freckles, blue eyes set close together, a high forehead. He seemed nervous, and he licked his lips a lot."

Now everyone was staring at Durand, who was staring at the Coachman.

The Coachman said. "Yes. Like that."

Stepovich frowned. "How the hell—?"

Durand smiled. "That's the revised description of the killer in the liquor store holdup. I mentioned that to you."

"I remember."

"I told you I wasn't as stupid as you thought I was."

"Timmy," said Stepovich suddenly.

"Huh?" said Durand.

"His name is Timmy. It must be."

The Coachman nodded. "Of course. The little boy."

"It all fits," said Stepovich. He shifted uneasily in his seat, caught Ed looking at him, but looked away. "God, this is weird," he breathed.

"You wanna explain it to me?" Ed offered quietly.

"I don't think I can," Stepovich said. "But our friend Csucskari seems to be off the hook. On one count, anyway."

"Sure," Durand agreed. "Now it's only escaping custody, and the possible murder of the old gypsy woman."

"You like him for the gypsy?" asked Stepovich, watching Durand closely.

"Huh? Of course not. But he's still wanted for it. We can't change that."

Stepovich nodded unhappily. "What next then?" he asked of no one in particular.

"I think," said Daniel carefully, "that we should find this Madam Moria, and that we should not waste time doing it."

The Coachman nodded. "Driver?" He leaned forward slightly and addressed the word to Ed as if it were a title. "You'd best do as he says. Don't spare the horses, for whatever will happen, it won't wait for any of us."

Ed nodded curtly and pulled away from the curb. The leap of the Caddy as he fed the big car gas pressed them all back in their seats, and made the Coachman smile. Stepovich marked how he held his hands in his lap, palms up, fingers lightly curled but empty, as if unseen reins rested in his hands.

## SOMETIME

I think I'll never let you go,
I think I'll never hold you.
I think I'll never loose the stars,
Forget what I have told you.

"GYPSY DANCE"

Laurie stared at the old woman, who smiled back at her. Then she looked at the fiddle and bow in her hands, but could find no words to describe how it had felt. It was as if Daniel had been there, had been taking her hands and fingers through each motion, and they'd brought forth the music together. The music. Together.

The old woman's smile widened and she said, "You've done fine, girl. Fine. You've opened a path for a summoning, and I think it happened." She looked around absently, then said, "It won't be long—"

The door burst open and an ugly bald manikin scuttled into the room, walking on its hands and feet, hissing and spitting. Laurie screamed and clutched the fiddle to her. The old gypsy woman stepped in front of her and swished her skirts at it. "Stop it! You're just wasting time and you know it."

To Laurie's shock it halted and cowered as if the old woman's skirts were burning brands. It turned its head to the side like a malicious spaniel. For the first time, Laurie noticed its flat nose and large round eyes. Where had it come from, and what was it?

The gypsy woman spoke offhandedly. "It's been done already," she informed it. "The Coachman called the horses, and the link forged of yarn and horsehair will lead them here no matter what you or your mistress do. Why waste time on us? Your mistress knows what must happen now. Go scuttle to Her call, and stop terrorizing the child."

The manikin stretched its neck up, then forward. Its head swayed from side to side as if it were a snake scenting after a mouse. Its questing tongue was fat and grey. Laurie shuddered but stood firm. Its face wrinkled suddenly, becoming even more ugly, and it beat the floor angrily with its splayed and calloused hands. As abruptly as it had come, it left, slamming the door behind it.

A great trembling washed through Laurie, bringing dizziness. The old woman was speaking to her, but she couldn't distinguish the words for the buzzing in her ears. The droning grew until it filled the whole world, but the gypsy woman kept talking. "Play!" she told Laurie, and her fierceness forced the word through her confusion. "You must play. You cannot stop."

Laurie stirred. She stared up into the woman's huge dark eyes. She realized she was sitting on the cold floor, looking up. She felt stiff, as if she had sat a long time. "I can't," she wailed. "It's gone, and he's gone—"

Old hands settled on her shoulders, and with surprising strength, drew her to her feet. "I know. It doesn't matter. Play anyway, as best you can. If you do, he'll be back."

Laurie stared. "Will he? Really?"

"He will. He must, as must we all." The old woman sighed. Her eyes went distant and knowing. "The last dance has begun, child. None, not dancers nor musicians, may pause in their pursuits, not until the last measure has been trod, the last note wrung from the strings. Then we shall see which dancers fall, who calls the next tune."

"All right," said Laurie, faintly. She lifted the fiddle, wanting only to feel herself become part of Daniel and his music again. No. That wasn't quite it. Wanting more than anything to feel the music coming once more from her fingers, from her heart. She set the fiddle to her chin and drew the bow across the strings.

And stopped.

It scraped, it sawed, it was nothing like music, it was the horrid screech of chalk on a blackboard. It made her heart ache.

"I know," said the old woman. "Cynthia knows. But you must keep playing. Play him back to you, into your arms.

Laurie took a breath, and dragged the bow once more across the strings.

## AUTUMN, EARLY MORNING

I saw the panic in Timmy Dee's eyes,
His tongue flicked out like the tongue of a beast.
I liked seeing Timmy get cut down to size,
But then someone phoned the police.

"THE GYPSY"

So much happened so quickly. Csucskari felt like a fair-goer, entranced before the puppeteer's booth. The wooden door of the apartment was flung open. Light flashed off the silver of the gun's barrel, there was the slow turn of Raymond's head, Madam Moria's gasp of surprise, the thud of the teakettle lid and splash of the boiling water as it leaped at her startled jerk. Csucskari saw them all as separate movements with a clarity he had not known in a long time. The thin man moved stiffly, and not fast. Csucskari thought about his knife, but it would take too long, and the gun looked very large, its round black mouth gaping at each of them in turn.

The gunman shut the door behind him and smiled. His tongue whipped over his lips, nervously. "Well," he said in the voice of a frightened man pretending to be brave. "You didn't expect to see me again, did you? Thought you'd killed me, didn't you? I bet you even thought She'd cast me aside, said I'd failed Her, didn't you? But I'm more special to Her than that. I'm the most important one of them all to Her." He fixed his eyes on Madam Moria as he spoke. Csucskari felt Raymond grip his arm. Only sputters of sound came from Madam Moria's pale old lips; the heavy kettle in her hands shook with the force of her trembling.

"What do you want?" Csucskari asked, and drew to himself the man's eyes and the gun's mouth.

The man stared at him, and the gun shook in a wavering circle that never left Csucskari's chest. Csucskari wondered why no fear welled up in him.

"What do I want?" repeated the man, wondering, as if the question had never occurred to him. "What do I want?" His voice cracked suddenly. "You! You're the one, aren't you? All of this is your fault! I did everything the way She told me to. It all should have worked, but you ruined it. You ruined it!" His voice scaled up to a shaky falsetto.

"I suppose I did," Csucskari replied softly. "But you're hurt, aren't you?"

"No!" he screamed. "It doesn't matter. She'll make me better."

"She'll make you worse," said Csucskari.

"No! You're lying." His knees were shaking, which made him more dangerous. "I'm going to kill you," the man said in a tone of sudden discovery. "Now I'm going to kill you, and it's going to work. My way. Not Hers. I'm going to make you dead, and I'm going to make Her like me again."

"No," said Csucskari. "You are not."

"I'm—going—to kill—all of you." He spoke in awe at his own power.

Csucskari remembered that he wasn't alone. He'd forgotten it, talking to this man. Only the two them had been there, locked into some sort of trial, but now, remembering his brother and the old woman, Csucskari was shaken, and the gunman's eyes widened, and the trembling of his hand worsened. His other hand come up to grip his wrist and steady the gun. It grew still, pointing at the center of the Gypsy's chest.

"Dirt!" shrieked Madam Moria suddenly. "You, lower than a snake's belly, fit consort for a dung beetle!"

The gun swung to her, and Csucskari knew, perhaps before the gunman did, that he was going to fire. That peculiar lucidity came over him again; he pulled his knife free as he sprang.

But it was not a knife, it was only a soft flutter of yarn in his hand, the scarf dragged up from the couch. His hand remembered the brief touch of Raymond's fingers against his; why his brother had passed him the scarf, he did not know. He must trust there was a reason. But neither knife nor scarf could be swift enough to stop the finger that tightened on the trigger. He saw the hammer fall even as he moved, even as the door was thrown open once more. The shot, the scream, and the slam of the door against the wall all happened at once.

## 17 NOV 03:32

Mr. DeCruz, how do you feel?
Why don't you just sit down so we can deal?

"BACK IN TOWN"

They were too noisy going up the stairs. Stepovich knew it suddenly, with the sickening drop of gut that hit him at the worst of times. There was a faint scent of some sort of perfume in the air, and he wanted time to remember what it was. Durand was leading the way, telling Ed about all that had transpired the last time he'd gone up those stairs. He was talking back over his shoulder, talking over Daniel and the Coachman, who were behind him. Those two were in a conversation of their own, the Coachman leaning heavily on Daniel as he helped him up the stairway. Ed was behind them, all but filling the narrow way. And Stepovich was coming last, the wrong position, for there was no way to push past them, no place for any of them to go.

"Durand!" he yelled, even as Daniel said, "Shush!" and the Coachman said, "Timmy!"

"Get outta the door!" Ed warned as Stepovich shouted, "One side!"

But Daniel had already pushed the door open. Durand drew his gun and stepped to one side as the Coachman sagged to the other. They all heard the shot, the dull whang of lead against cast iron, and the whine of the ricochet. A bullet burst from the wall in a whuff of plaster, traveling so slowly that Stepovich would later tell Ed that he saw it as it spent the last of its energy burrowing into the biceps of Durand's right arm. The kid cried out, a man's short hoarse cry, but he did not drop his gun. He brought it to level, steadying it with his good hand, and went around the corner into the room as if he'd been doing it for years. Ed and Stepovich were half a second behind him, past the Coachman, propelling Daniel into the room with the force of their rush.

For a brief yellow instant, Stepovich saw it all like a cheap Polaroid shot: The injured man on the coach reaching after someone, yes, the scarred old Gypsy, fluttering scarf in hands that were closing on, yes, it had to be little Timmy, not so little, but Timmy just the same, and Madam Moria clutching her cast-iron teakettle; the kettle now had a clean star of almost shorn iron in its side. Like a photograph, it was detail perfect but still, and he had a sense of falling into it, carrying Durand and Ed and Daniel with him.

## AUTUMN MORNING, BEFORE SUNRISE

Towards dawn I saw the ashes
Of birches long since dead
Woah, lannan sidhe let me be.
I left them clutching shadows;
Left my curse unsaid.
Woah, lannan sidhe come to me.

"LANNAN SIDHE"

The gun exploded in the small room, so loud a sound that it seemed to be a flash of light as well. Csucskari was stunned by it; his sight blurred and cleared, and in the high ringing that sang in his ears was another voice, familiar in its warmth and accent. The Coachman had returned.

"Timmy."

That was the word he had said, the word the gun tried to swallow. Csucskari struggled to make sense of it. Who was Timmy? The gunman, of course. This realization drowned out any other significance in a flood of memory so powerful Csucskari was almost swept away. He stared at the gunman, frozen in time. Voices and shadows, juxtaposed in truth and in memory, beat at his consciousness. Then and now merged and swirled. They call him Timmy Dee, and I don't know what I can do. All the grocery money's gone. Dad's gonna kill me. He cheated. I know he did. Well, all right, my friend, I will go speak with this Timmy Dee, and see if things can't be put right . . . Timmy. Little Timmy. Timmy Dee.

Csucskari felt jolted as time caught him up again. A young man—a policeman—weaseled into the room. There was blood on his sleeve, his two hands gripped a pistol, his face was calm, tension in his shoulders, his elbows relaxed. The gun went sniffing, found Timmy and held on him, and the young policeman's fingers began the steady squeeze of the trigger, oh so purposefully, oh so calmly, oh so righteously, to put an end to Little Timmy. Timmy would stagger backwards from the knife wound, hold his throat as if he could stop the torrent that laves his fingers, the red that drenches his clothes so swiftly. He'd fall to the ground, gurgling in amazement, eyes still going from Csucskari to the knife to Csucskari, no, no, from the gun to the policeman, no—

Csucskari flung the scarf like a net, keeping his grip on one corner, and for an instant, one golden instant, no one moved and the world held its breath, waiting.

Voices came, from nowhere, from everywhere, from the walls of the room and from inside his head. Raven's voice, saying, "He can lead us back," and Owl speaking behind him, saying, "Then listen to your own fiddle, brother," and Raven replying, "Then play your tambourine, brother." The Coachman was there, come back for them all as he had to, and with him a great shaggy old Wolf and a bright-eyed Badger. They all looked to him, to Csucskari, like the spokes of a wheel suddenly recognizing the hub. The burden dragged at him and for a moment the spell wavered. The young policeman should have pulled the trigger then indeed, but the music of the fiddle swept through the room like a wind of sound. Csucskari laughed aloud to be together with his brothers, for this moment, and all of them alive. He flung the scarf into the air once more, like a blessing, crying, "Well, then, Luci, we'll come to you, and see how you like it."

The scarf spun and grew larger, warp and woof becoming a fine mesh, a painted picture, a target, and then a net of glowing threads. None of them could move as the weave grew and enveloped them in a pattern that filled each mind with the textures of the fiddle's sliding high notes, and Raymond was playing the tambourine off in the distance now, shaking it like a spice box, fingers flying against the brass zils. Somewhere else, far, far away, the Coachman muttered, "Damn gypsies. I'm getting too old for their nonsense." Then they all vanished in a swirl of yarn and music.

# Chapter Sixteen

HOW THE GYPSY FOUGHT THE DEVIL

**He said, "My business is dead on the floor,**
**Though my business ain't often in bars.**
**I kill beasts when I just can't take 'em anymore;**
**Between times, I look for the stars."**

"THE GYPSY"

## SOMETIME

*The Fair Lady has been plucking a sparrow and throwing its feathers into the flames. The stench of their burning and the crying of the bird have made a pleasant harmony, but now She casts it aside and rises angrily, scowling at the smoldering yarn. Unnoticed, the sparrow hops away into the darkness. The Fair Lady turns Her head, but the music gets louder and louder, the ringing and thumping of the tambourine in the unrelenting rhythm of the* csardas *with the fiddle playing like wildfire around its edges. The Fair Lady summons the* midwife *and the* nora *and the* liderc. *The* nora *scampers wildly about on its hands and feet, its teeth chattering wildly, frantic to please Her, grimace after grimace washing over its young old face. The* liderc *sways from side to side, one arm held high like a club, threatening nothing and everything. The* midwife *has brought her knitting, and the needles rattle against each other, clattering like steel instruments in a cold tray.*

*But the music gets louder, sweeping past them like an angry broom. A piece of thread dangles down into the fireplace from above. Another follows it, and another, and see how they knit themselves together, even there in the fire? The cloth that forms is impervious to the licking flames, it only grows fuller, until it seems to be a scarf with a peculiar pattern.*

*"Soon," warns the Fair Lady. She nods, and Her chair turns to face the door. The* nora *chitters and approaches the doorway, jumping and skittering about in front of it like a gargoyle coffee table come to life. The others face the doorway as well, even the*

midwife *standing, her knitting needles poised. The cloth drapes the fire, which smolders. One pleading tendril of smoke escapes but withers as it flees. The darkness is almost total. Two doors fly open at once.*

## SOMETIME

One instant, Daniel was leaping into a tapestried and carpeted room, flinging himself to his brother's aid. Then, in mid-breath, he was falling. "Coachman! Lead us back!" he cried out, pleading. But no one answered.

He fell into darkness, and following the gun's roar he thought he had been hit, struck blind, and was falling to the floor. But there was no pain, and there was no floor, there was nothing, only the darkness and the falling. I should be frightened, he thought, but he wasn't. He'd been through too much in the last twenty-four hours, perhaps all his fear was used up. He sensed the finality of the confrontation to come. He had waited for it, lived for it for so long that the anticipation had eroded his feelings. Nothing was there but numbness and a small sense of relief in knowing it had begun; no matter how it ended, it would now, at least for a time, end.

Besides, there was the music.

For a while, the music had been part of the darkness, but now it ventured out in separate strands, fine as horsehair, glowing like frost in the moonlight. All the music he had ever drawn from his fiddle floated about him in shining strands and snatches, clinging as cobwebs, catching at him as he fell, slowing his descent, cradling him in a silver hammock of sound.

When he fell no longer, when his music had caught and stilled him, Daniel found he could stand. He walked through the emptiness on the web of his notes, clever as a spider, and each strand sounded to the slide of his feet; each strand sweet and shining in the darkness. Somewhere, the others followed him.

The music led him as it had all the years of his life. He had always felt it was not a thing he created or possessed, but an elusive *phouka* of sound that he chased, always a few notes behind the perfect song in his mind. Now it lured and guided him through the darkness, beckoning, taking him around unseen corners, up flights of tune and through corridors like familiar refrains. Twice he sensed something chill and hungry lurking in the darkness, but both times his music swirled up and concealed him.

And then he came to a place where the music faltered, where the shining web of sound became no more than a tightrope, and even that was first thick and awkward and then thin and frail beneath him. He hesitated. This was not his music, and yet it was. It puzzled him. He stooped to touch it, then followed it, smoothing it as he went, weaving it up on his way, plaiting the notes together into harmonies, and the harmonies into an old familiar ballad about three wandering brothers.

There was light growing around him, and he looked down from a great height, to where a young girl clasped a fiddle and doggedly drew a bow across its strings, torturing sound out of it. It was his own fiddle, crying out to him. Forgetting the others, he clambered down its plaintive wail, feeling himself grow more substantial with every step. His instrument seemed to sense his coming, for suddenly the notes came sweet and true, and he was there, stepping down into a room of grey stone, where Lorelei drew a single pure note from the fiddle and an old woman sat watching and nodding.

"Daniel!" she cried out at the sight him, and nearly dropped the bow, but, "Play, play," said the old woman. "Play as if your lives depend upon it. All depends on the music. Play!" The old woman drew a tortoiseshell comb through her long hair as she spoke. She shook the strands free of it, glared at them, and again ran the comb through her hair.

He stepped up behind Lorelei, positioned his arms around her. The crown of her head came just to the hollow of his throat. "Almost," he thought, "I could tuck her under my chin and play her as she plays my fiddle." Her hair smelled sweet. He set one hand on the neck of the fiddle, his fingers falling unerringly upon the strings. The other covered her hand on the bow. Her fingers relaxed. He led her into the music gently, and as he guided her, he shared with her the very days of his life and the beats of his heart. He knew he should be thinking of the Fair Lady and his brothers; his weapons would be needed. But for now he wove the music around them, cloaking them from all but this moment, sheltering them from harm.

17 NOV 03:36

The blackout hit sudden as a knife blade, and just as threatening. "Ed!" Stepovich yelled in useless warning as he threw himself down. He expected to hear the gun go off over his head, and as he fell he was watching for the muzzle flash that would let him target Timmy. It seemed to take forever for his outstretched palms to meet the floor. The instant they did, a sick dread washed through him.

Stone. Cold dank stone, almost slimy there in the crack. No thick cushioning of carpet, no hardwood floor. Stone. But the air he breathed was warm, almost stifling. Wherever he was, it wasn't where he'd been an instant ago. "Ed!" he shouted again, and thought he heard a muffled answer. Around him in the darkness, there was scrabbling and scuffling of feet against stone, the rustle of clothing, grunts as people struggled to their feet. He wasn't alone.

A flashlight beam lit up in the darkness. Durand's. The kid was thinking fast, but not fast enough. Instead of holding the flashlight out at arm's length, he was holding it right in front of him, chest-high, as he scanned the room, like a beacon to lead a bullet to his chest. He was cradling his injured arm against his belly. Another light appeared, off to the side, uneven and flickering. That would be Ed's pipe-lighter, the butane turned up high. Its ghost light was not enough to illuminate, only enough to hint at shapes in the room.

Stepovich was still on his knees, struggling up, when the flashlight hit Timmy like a spotlight. Timmy spun toward it, in evident panic, his pistol moving with him. Lights, action, camera, and Stepovich watched as Timmy's trigger finger moved.

Stepovich was still on one knee, the other foot flat on the floor, ready to rise and, in the flicker of Ed's lighter, or in the reflected beams of the flashlight, or in Stepovich's imagination, he could see Durand, and it was the look on Durand's face that did him. The kid looked down the muzzle of the pistol and grimaced. A showing of teeth, somewhere between daring death to come and get him, and a sheepish grin at how dumb he'd been. A kid's face. The injured arm was still seeping blood.

Stepovich drove down hard, pushing himself up and off, shooting toward Timmy like a sprinter off the blocks. His body was moving fast, but his mind was light years ahead of him. He could see it all as it would happened, predict it all. He already knew it was too late; the idea was to get control of the man before he fired. And this wasn't that. No.

His right hand fell heavy on Timmy's shoulder, his left gripped Timmy's wrist and gun hand and forced it up. It was supposed to go all the way up, so the gun would go off over Stepovich's shoulder; he was already braced for the blast of sound by his ear.

But the muzzle was still pointing at him when it went off. Flash and stench of powder. Blow like a rabbit punch, one that didn't stop but went right through meat and bone and whatever else was in there. Just that suddenly, there was no strength in his arms or legs. He dropped. He waited for the pain, waited, it's coming, gonna getcha, Stepovich, you dumb old cop, trying to pull a fast kid's trick like that. Ed's gonna yell at you, listen, he's starting already, screaming, and is this really how you planned to end your days, in some nightmare dungeon?

He'd thought the lights were supposed to fade when you passed out, but it was getting brighter, sourceless light coming up like stage lights, getting brighter and brighter. A cold sort of light, though, a toadstool light that made everyone look dead.

Slipped his trolley, he had, yeah, old Stepovich was sliding down the night side now. Stuff was coming out of the corners of his mind, nightmare things, and they swarmed up Durand and dragged him down. One was like a bald puppet, while the other was a hodgepodge out of some zoologist's nightmare. Durand lost his flashlight and it rolled clunkily across the uneven floor, washing them all in a cone of light. The creatures clutched Durand and held him down, and it was obscene, as if the mere touch of those hands were a rape. The bald thing sniggered and poked its long pale fingers at Durand's wound. Must hurt like hell, Stepovich thought, and wondered why Durand wasn't yelling. Maybe he's like me; too much pain and not enough air to yell.

And where the hell was Ed? Trying to get up, looked like he'd done his knee again. He'd always called it his old football injury, but Stepovich knew he'd done it trying to ride a skateboard they'd confiscated from a kid on the freeway, with all the oncoming traffic, and the goddamn drivers wouldn't turn their highbeams down, pull the sonofabitch over, hit the siren, get out of the car. Out of the car, Stepovich. Time to get moving, go talk to the Gypsy. Where was he, anyway?

He caught one glimpse of a gypsy, back in the shadows, and it wasn't the Gypsy anyway. Never a Gypsy around when you need one. Ed still had his lighter going, and he was waving it around like it would work better than garlic and crosses.

And then the time for worrying about stuff like that was gone. All the time in the world was gone. Down to a single now, the now where Timmy was standing over him, straddling him like the outlaw in a B Western, holding the pistol in both hands as he pointed it at Stepovich's face. Not in the face, he wanted to tell him, my kids don't deserve that, not a closed coffin service where you always imagine it as much worse than it could ever be. But he couldn't speak at all, could only lie there and look up at death like a car-hit dog on the freeway.

## SOMETIME

Damn all gypsies anyway, he thought, as he arrived in a place he hadn't brought them to, but would have to return them from if there were any of them left to return. He felt for the calk in his pocket, got it out, threw it into the air, and when it came down he caught the butt of the whip it was fastened to. *That to you, Luci,* he thought. *All I have to do is step outside this door, onto the road, and I'll be like a* Taltos *myself.*

He heard the sound of a gunshot, and sighed. No doubt the damned gypsies and their silly friends were getting themselves killed. Well, that was not his concern, had never been his concern. He drove the coach when he had one to drive, and now that he didn't—

Well, there was one thing he could do. It wouldn't save any of these fools from the consequences of their own actions, but if it had worked there, it would certainly work here; if any of them lived, at least they might not fall into the Nothingness.

Still weak and in pain, he slipped past impossible shapes doing improbable things to each other. He sidled along a wall until he came to the fireplace, and there, just as he'd thought, was the scarf that had brought them here. He pulled it out, not surprised that the fire hadn't damaged it. He made his way back to the door from which he'd entered. It stood wide open as if it expected guests. He leaned against what felt like cold stone. His breath came in gasps, and when a cramp hit, he thought it was all up for him, but then it passed.

He straightened, turned, and looked out the door, away from the flickering of lights and the antics of demons, to where there was nothing at all, at all, at all. And, as he did, there were two shapes there. Human shapes, of all things. Young girls, looking wild and frightened. They approached the door, and when they saw him, the fair one drew back, while the dark one raised her fingernails like talons.

"She's calling us," said the dark one. "You'd better not—"

"Oh, hush," said the Coachman. "There's nothing for you in there but death, and you know it."

The fair one turned to her friend and said, "Sue, I'm scared. Laurie—"

"That wimp's no concern of ours. This is it, the big fight. We need to help Her. We—"

"Listen to your fear, my children," said the Coachman, his voice rolling like a *cimbolon.* "Your fear is wise; trust it. It falls upon you like a wave, and in the wave are specks of pain and droplets of oblivion. The call is the call of those who've been lost at sea, whose souls float, with no anchor. Your fair mistress betrays you, even as She promised. Do you recall Her words? Think on them now, before you act."

They stared at him, there at the brink of forever, and while they did he stepped forward and slammed the door shut behind him. They cried out, but before they could touch the door, *crack! crack!* and he had put his mark on it with the calk on the end of his whip.

"It is sealed now. You cannot enter," he said. "Go home, or become Nothing." They stared at him with confusion and fear still etched on their too-young features, but, then the dark one said, "Come on, Chrissy. We can get past him. She needs us."

The fair one gave a low moan, then her eyes widened and she said, "Yes! I can hear Her!"

They charged him, scrabbling for the door, but this was outside, this was between, this was neither here nor there. It was on the road, and on the road the Coachman has the power. It gave him no pleasure to use it.

## SOMETIME

Csucskari knew where he was, for he had brought them all there. But where were the others? Beams of light flashed around him, showing glimpses of faces from his nightmares, but no sign of his friends. The servants of Luci he knew; they snuffled about in the darkness. He drew his knife, lest any come near him, and waited.

Then there came a clap of sound from one side, oddly muffled. He turned to meet it. Folk moved and muttered around him. He ventured closer, drawn by a vague glow, seeing only an old man collapsed on the floor, cupping fire in his hands. The light flickered unevenly, but he caught a glimpse of Owl, struggling to stay on his feet, and the gunman, who was pointing his gun at the floor. No, he was pointing it at the policeman, the Wolf, lying helpless before him, his left shoulder and chest already dark with blood. The hammer was going back. The gunman was smiling whitely.

There was no conscious decision. The knife was already in his hand, and Little Timmy was in front of him, just like before, and he was there, once more, with a living man before him and a glittering knife in his hand. It was like a play, each performing a well-rehearsed part, even the lights coming up brighter. Timmy must have heard his step, for he looked up just as Csucskari reached forward and put the knife in him. Timmy's eyes met his, and Csucskari felt the contact of their gaze even as he felt the shock as his knife buried itself to the hilt past Timmy's collarbone. They both cried out at once, their screams filling the room. Csucskari's hand never left the hilt. He felt Timmy become a weight on his blade. As he fell, the knife pulled free of the body. He'd done it again. Blood followed the blade. He stared at the body that thrashed mindlessly on the floor below him. This was not what he'd come here to do. He dropped the knife, covered his face, and sobbed.

Bagoly knelt beside him. He could feel the trembling of his brother's weakness. So drained, both of them. "Hollo?" he whispered, but there was no reply, and the music that should have led them to the light was elsewhere. In the end, then, She'd won, separated them and distracted them, used her poor bent tools as foils to draw them out. Fool of a Gypsy, ever thinking he could win. He reached toward Owl, knowing they'd never touch.

## SOMETIME

"I'm not hurt that bad. I'm not hurt that bad." Durand could hear himself saying it. He didn't know how long he'd been repeating it, trying to convince himself it was so. He stared up at the high ceiling that was rimmed with silver. Looked like stone roots, and huge boulders, like a stylized cave roof. He tried to keep staring at it, but the nightmare on his chest dug its fingers into his upper arm, squeezing yet more blood from the wound. It was a hallucination, Durand was sure, and he wasn't going to dignify it by watching it or trying to push it away. But if he was seeing things, then maybe he was hurt worse than he thought. He rolled his head to one side, saw Stepovich on the floor and the gunman standing over him. There wasn't enough light for the blood to be red, but the blossoming stain on Mike's shirt was still spreading. "Officer down," Durand said inanely. "Officer needs assistance." He wasn't handling this very well, he knew it. He should be doing better than this, but he wasn't sure exactly what he was supposed to be doing.

Follow the rules, even if it got him killed? Only he couldn't think what rules to follow. And these damn nightmares on his chest were so heavy, so disgustingly real. Clammy, hard-fingered hands, and really grotesque odor: Urine and sweat, and that wasn't even the bad part.

Light grew in the room, a nacreous rotten light. Ed had kindled something, part of his shirt, and was flapping it around like a flimsy weapon. The old man was grey.

Then there was the Gypsy, doing something to the gunman, but it was all happening in silence. Durand saw the knife, even saw it go in, but then one of the things began clawing at Durand's face, and chittering. He pulled away from it. None of this was real.

So he wasn't surprised when she burst from a dark corner like a dancer leaping onto a stage. Old Madam Moria, her canes gone, flourishing her iron kettle, spun in a swirl of splashing tea. She yelled something in a language Durand didn't recognize.

Probably "Begone Demons!" or something like that. Whatever the threat, she backed it with iron and water and flapping skirts, and the things on his chest cowered, and the one drew its arms in close to its bony ribs.

They flinched. That made them real.

"Real," said Durand, and the revulsion that swept him gave him strength to roll from beneath them. He rolled over cold iron of his own, his gun, dropped when they'd fallen into this place. His good hand groped for it, closed on the grips, and brought it up as he came to his knees. Two hands, he reminded himself, and hissed at the pain it cost him to steady the pistol.

Ed was advancing on the things that Madam Moria had spooked off him. As he did so, there came a shrill laugh, young and old, delightful as a girl's, evil as the devil's, and suddenly the things weren't retreating anymore. Madam Moria was gasping for breath and staggering, her curses and strength running down together like the clockwork in an old toy, until she sighed and fell over between the Gypsy and the fireplace. Ed flapped his smoldering shirt at them, but none of them seemed impressed. The two creatures that had clutched and grappled at him now clustered around Stepovich's body. There was also a woman with them, a thin old thing with stringy hair and deep lines in her face. She hissed at Ed, and slapped his smoking shirt aside with the flat of her hand. She stepped toward Ed, and in her grey hands with its filthy broken nails was what seemed to be a thin knife. She raised it.

Durand stopped them. Stopped them with his mind. Didn't think about being a hero. Just made them into silhouettes, paper things, just like on the range. Lift the gun. Squeeze, squeeze, squeeze. Bang, bang, bang. And they all fell down. Not hard, not easy. Not a particularly glorious or brave thing to do. One finger work, just like subtracting numbers on his checkbook calculator. And they all fell down.

## SOMETIME

Raymond felt himself failing; his wings unable to grasp the air. His strength, returning so slowly, was now draining away in Luci's presence. She loomed over him; he looked up.

Like looking up at Heaven and Hell. Face too perfect to describe. Eyes too hellish to bear meeting, but he had no choice. Voice smoother than honey. "Bagoly," she said pleasantly, plucking at him with his own name.

Her eyes gleamed down on him. "No," he said, gasping. "You cannot have the Dove." Where was his brother, Daniel, the Raven? He could help. He had the strength. "Leave us. Leave this world. You cannot have my brothers."

Empty words. He knew it, She knew it. Worst of all, Csucskari knew it; Raymond could feel that. Raymond's strength was gone; he couldn't even threaten her. Her cold fingers fastened to his shoulder, flung him contemptuously aside. He hurtled through the air, struck a wall and slid down it. In the flickering light, he saw the big man who held the fire rush toward Luci, but She knocked him effortlessly aside. Somewhere, sometime, he heard explosions. Now he smelt the powder, saw where Her servants sprawled and bled. But it wasn't enough. "Hollo!" he cried, and the name was black and bitter as the odor of burnt feathers. Why didn't he answer? Raymond knew that he would never find out.

He watched Luci set Her hands to Csucskari's throat. She had long, slender hands; white fingers. They would be cool as a maiden's touch. He saw them close, saw the flesh of his brother's throat bulge up between them. White against red. "Hollo!" he cried, and his hand found the strength to lift, to fall against his heart and the tambourine that rested against it. He took it into his hand, and it dropped onto his lap, jarring in a tiny death rattle.

## SOMETIME

Madam Moria lay on the floor, unable to rise without her canes, watching as Luci bent over the Dove, strangling the life out of him. The hem of Her gown, white as snow, brushed against Madam Moria. Luci was as graceful as She was evil, and Her eyes, fastened on her prey, had no thought for the old woman, or for the Wolf who lay dying on her other side. A beautiful gown, all of white, the only dark thing, the thin black belt at her waist.

And from the belt, a lock of grey hair.

Madam Moria smiled. This was not the first time she had picked a pocket, but it might well be the easiest. When she had it in her hand, she rolled over twice, and threw it into the coals of the smoldering fire.

## SOMETIME

Somewhere, in another room, a comb snagged suddenly, and a long lock of greying hair came free in an old woman's hand. Like a veil lifted from her eyes, Cynthia saw how it had blinded her, had made her a part of Luci's trap. "So!" she shrieked, and "No!" Leaping up, she lashed at the young couple who nestled like birds in the bower of sweet music they plaited together. The lock of hair struck the young man across the face. "You play for yourselves!" she shrieked at them. "That is not what the music is for. Play for the world, for life. Not safety and blindness and complacency. Play danger and vision and striving. Play evil vanquished, and survival. Play life!"

And for Laurie—

Laurie cried out as Daniel's hand tightened suddenly on hers. The sweet music stopped, and for an instant they stood frozen together, like plastic dolls atop a wedding cake. Laurie twisted her head to stare up into Daniel's face. A sudden anger was there; not at her, but at what he must do. She could almost feel him being torn apart. "There is no way!" he cried aloud. "No way to keep faith with my brothers and also with you." For a moment longer, he stood transfixed with agony. Then he shook his head, as if to clear it. "Forgive me," he said, and she wondered why. But then suddenly he wrenched fiddle and bow from her hands, and turned aside from her. He turned away from her, put his back to her, and bowed his head over his music.

His bow swept down sudden as a knife slash. Music ripped from the fiddle; it ripped the darkness and quiet of the room like a curtain being shredded. Uneasy light spilled in as the music gushed out, and suddenly Laurie could see. The chamber walls blew away like tatters in a wind of song. There was her father lying on the floor, a spreading red stain on his chest. There were other people, a motley mix of those she knew slightly and those she knew not at all nor would ever wish to. But her father was suddenly the only one she could see. She leaped to go to him, but the old gypsy woman caught her and pulled her back. "No! Stay back! It is not over, but only begun. And all, all of us lose something here." The woman's hard fingers closed tight on Laurie's shoulder and held her fast.

## SOMETIME

Stepovich wished the dying would happen faster. There was so much going on around him, so much that agonized him but he could do nothing about. He wished it were over. If he must be helpless, let him be dead as well.

The most beautiful woman he had ever seen was strangling the Gypsy. Her eyes were bright and clear, and She was laughing with a lover's joy as She choked the life out of him. The Gypsy, limp as a rag doll, was shaken in Her grip. The man was dying, and Stepovich sensed some greater Death waiting in the wings, waiting to make its entrance when the Gypsy was gone. For a moment, too, he thought he saw Laurie beyond the locked figures, thought he saw her young face horrified, stripped of all innocence. But a greyness fluttered across his vision, and he knew it for the illusion it was. He was getting so cold, but the blood wetting his chest felt so warm.

More shots. The beautiful strangler was startled; She turned to find their source. With a major effort, Stepovich scraped his head on the cold paving stones. There, at the corner of his vision, was Durand. He was walking toward them, his pistol held out in both his hands, wavering like a dowser's stick. He was firing at Her from point-blank range. The woman laughed Her wonderful laugh, and the ringing shout of it smashed against Durand and flung him like a toy.

A distraction. There was a cop inside Stepovich's head, yelling at him. She's distracted. Use the time. Protect your partner. You're going to die anyway, draw her attention to yourself, give Durand a chance. Die like a cop, you damn well lived like one, and it ruined everything you ever thought you wanted.

Stepovich wanted to lay still and die quietly. There was

nothing more he could do here. But someone, somewhere, was playing music, fiddle music. The notes plucked at him like fingers at his sleeve, scraped his nerves raw. He couldn't die. Not while that music was playing. But another man was dying nearby. One of the gypsies. The body next to him was Timmy's. Damn, who got him? Stepovich wondered for an instant. And then remembered. The knife still lay where it had fallen. It pointed at Stepovich like an accusing finger.

The knife. The goddamned knife. All this time, the same fucking knife. Cut my life to ribbons.

She was choking the Gypsy still, but he could almost feel the hands squeezing his own windpipe. He couldn't pay attention to it. All he could think of was how much he hated that knife.

It was with a curious sense of inevitability that he felt it under his hand. The touch of it was like a shot of whiskey, only in his blood instead of his stomach. Galvanizing. He closed his hand on it, then pushed down on the hand that clenched the weapon, forcing himself up from the floor and to his knees. His other arm and hand were a dangling weight that bumped against him as he moved. There was pain, too, incredible pain somewhere, but he wasn't sure it was his. He didn't have the strength to stand, but he didn't need to. His vision was going fuzzy and useless. He blinked, trying to clear it, imagined he saw Ed's grinning face behind the Lady, egging him on. Stepovich scraped forward, a crawling step, and the rasp of his shoes on the stone floor turned Her eyes to him, even as he raised the knife. Beautiful eyes. They burned into his, and froze him to stillness.

He would have fought Her if he could, but he had no strength of will—not when She looked at him. His peripheral vision tried to tell him that Ed's hands were lifting, falling on the Lady's shoulders. Ed clutched her, whispered, "Gotcha!"

In one startled instant, Her power wavered. She struck Ed aside as if he were made of straw and newspaper. Stepovich thought he heard the crack of ribs. It didn't matter. Ed had known what it would cost him, to buy Stepovich that instant. It would not be wasted.

He sheathed the knife in the beautiful woman's breast.

## SOMETIME

A scream; a woman's or a fiddle's, he could not tell. But he could pull cold air into his hot lungs, and he could lift his head. The scream again, so sweet it could only be Luci dying—sent back to where She belonged, there to wait for him, ah, not now. There was Raven, waltzing into the room as he played Her death on his fiddle strings, while Owl on the floor feebly tapped out the staggering beats of Her failing heart. Csucskari rolled his head and saw Her on the floor, thrashing with a knife, his knife, transfixing Her white gown to a red growing stain. The Wolf lay discarded, his eyes open in slits, but he seemed to feel Csucskari staring at him, because, for an instant, his eyes widened. Their gazes met, and the nods they exchanged cost them the world in pain. Then the Wolf's eyes closed tightly and he turned his head away.

It made no sense. The task had been his, and his alone. It made no sense at all. Csucskari felt something sting his eyes.

There was an old woman, and he found he knew her name. Cynthia. Cynthia Kacmarcik. She had been gripping the Wolf's cub by the shoulder, but now that it was all over, she released her. Cynthia turned her eyes to another old woman. Madam Moria. They opened their arms to one another, crossed the room like dancers treading a measure. "I found it, sister," said Madam Moria. "The lock of hair. I destroyed it."

"I know, sister," said the other. "It set me free."

They met without touching. They held each other in a gaze that would probably last forever. What passed between them not even the Gypsy could know, but at last Cynthia Kacmarcik gave a barely audible sigh and fell apart. She became bits of white bone china and a bundle of straw, a scrap of burlap and a tangle of string. For one instant the simulacrum stood, a mocking scarecrow of the soul it had held trapped. Then it tumbled to the floor, a scatter of junk. Moria spurned it with her foot as she turned aside. "It is over," she said to no one and everyone. "We must go quickly now."

The fiddle spoke a single phrase, sliding down the scale and into stillness.

As if in reply, cracks of yellow light appeared soundlessly in the walls like curtains parting. A pale blue wind whispered through them, and the freshness of it made him realize how bad the stench of the chambers had been. There was a groan, as of two worlds parting, deeper than sound.

Daniel lowered his bow. Csucskari lifted his head, fixed him with a look. Almost, almost he had been too late. But in the final count, blood had told, and the Raven had flown with his brothers. Daniel lowered the fiddle from his throat, let it ease down to his side. "Lorelei," he said, but the young woman he addressed did not turn. Step by slow step, she was advancing on the Wolf's body. Daniel lifted a hand, reached after her, but he could not touch her, not in a room lit by flickering fire and wan daylight, not where the dead lay grouped with the wounded, the demons with the men.

Luci still twitched and thrashed on Her back in an obscene dance, a parody of a woman in passion, the knife still in Her chest as She gnashed Her teeth. Blood spurted from the knife wound, then slowed as Her movements slowed, as the Owl's hesitant fingers tapped out the last beats of Her heart: *Teckadum, teckadum, teckadum.*

Hollo turned away from the young woman, back to his brother. Csucskari bled for what was dying in his eyes, but Hollo knelt down, and lifted his brother by the shoulders. Csucskari felt his strength returning. "It's over, brother," Hollo told him.

Csucskari nodded and shuddered. Gently he freed himself from his brother's grasp, managed to stand on his own. Managed to walk to Luci's body, to crouch down beside it. He put his hand to the knife. "I'll need this," he said.

"Probably," Hollo sighed.

Csucskari drew the knife from the body. He felt the last of Her life go with it. "Help our brother," he said.

"Owl can help himself," Raymond said gruffly. He heaved himself to his feet. For a long moment he and Daniel looked at one another as if they were strangers. Then he lifted his shoulders in a long, slow shrug. "In the end, you came," he said.

"Yes," said Daniel. "I did." But his eyes followed Laurie as she sank to her knees by her father, and there was a hollowness in his voice. "How many times, though, my brothers? If there is another time, another chance to escape all of this, do you think I will not take it? I don't know."

The ground gave a bare tremble beneath them.

The two policeman, young and old, were supporting one another. The young one bled from his arm, and from the bites of the Fair Lady's minions. The old one just looked very old as they gathered around the fallen Wolf.

"Laurie," said the old one gently. But she knelt by her father, gripping his good hand in both of hers.

"Laurie," he said weakly, almost inaudibly. "You can't be here. You can't be here."

The young policeman looked a fearful question at the old one, who shrugged.

The old Badger gently moved the girl, pushing her into Durand's arms. "All right," he said grimly, "Let's see what you've done to yourself." He gingerly knelt next to the Wolf and touched two fingers to the man's neck. "You'll be pleased to know that you have a pulse," he said. He moved his hand and deliberately pressed his thumb over the wound. The Wolf twitched once and his eyes closed. The girl cried out and struggled, but the young policeman held her, and spoke to her quietly.

The Gypsy put his arm around Daniel. Then he staggered and caught his balance as the whole world trembled. Cracks widened in the floor, in the walls, and the winds between the world blew through with the force of a gale, showing half a moon and half a sun.

"Gather close together," Csucskari shouted over the noise. "The Fair Lady is gone, and Her domain cannot stand without Her."

"What happens now?" asked Daniel. "Where do we go? How do we return?"

The Gypsy shrugged. "I don't know. Our task is done for this place. Of what comes after, I know nothing."

There was a sudden crack of sound that licked through the air like lightning. All, even the girl, lifted their eyes.

He was in black, but his eyes gleamed blacker. The cloak at his shoulders fluttered in the wind. His clever fingers played with the whip as a sardonic smile curved his lips.

"This way, if you please," he said, as if they had all the time in the world. "The coach awaits outside."

# Chapter Seventeen

## HOW THEY CAME BACK HOME

## ALL THE TIME IN THE WORLD

I gave you every chance to choose,
Mr. DeCruz.

"BACK IN TOWN"

*He laughs into the wind.*

*Below him the coach clatters with all the right sounds, shakes in all the right ways. There are six horses pulling the coach, in rows of four and two; four of them he has conjured from the past, uncertain he'd be able to do so again, and two are new ones: the dark trace-horse and the fair off-wheeler. The new ones are uncertain, untrained, but he has four experienced horses to guide them. Twice, no more, he has cracked the whip over their heads, and now they run, knowing the hand upon the reins is sure. The six heads are stretched forth upon their necks as they charge into the gloom of the impossible place where all is possible, while he, the Coachman, guides them along paths of memory, chance, and choice.*

*Here, a wheel dips and splashes through a small puddle of fear, but he doesn't even slow. There, stray rocks of misfortune litter the path, but he guides the horses around them with the merest touch of the reins. Above, demons of frustration taunt and threaten, but there is a calk on the end of his whip, and he drives them away.*

"So, how fast we going?" Ed knew it was a dumb question as soon as he asked it. But the wind in his face made him grin, and the simplicity of it all pleased him immensely. There were lights above them, glittering in the darkness, and a wide world stretched out around them. It was all a dream, and he knew it, just as he did when he dreamed of flapping his arms and flying through the sky. But now as then he figured, what the hell, enjoy it while you can, because he sure wasn't going to get it this good when he was awake.

"As fast as you wish, or as slow," said the Coachman, and

they exchanged a knowing grin. Damn, he liked this guy. Ed vaguely remembered he'd been feeling sad about something, but now he couldn't remember what it was. He only knew that he was traveling, as he'd always wanted to. Moving through strange lands and peoples. The night wind smelled exotic, spices and smoke and foreign flowers. The air was warm on his face.

He leaned forward into it, admiring the Coachman's fingers on the reins, the way he talked to the horses. He suspected he could do that himself, after watching for a little longer. The Coachman teased the reins, and it was just like pressing down on the gas, there was the same smooth surge of speed.

"So, where we going?" he asked the Coachman.

The Coachman glanced at him, lifted one eyebrow sardonically. "Nowhere," he said. "Everywhere." For a long time the world rocked past them, smooth as bourbon. Ed caught a glimpse of lit windows, of a woman's face peering out into the night. The houses here were low, the roofs fat and rounded. Fields rustled with some grain crop between the houses. "Everywhere," the Coachman said again. "Everywhere but home."

Home.

And the word hung there silently like a curtain dividing them. Ed had a sudden sense that the Coachman didn't really know what it meant. Not like he did. The Coachman might know the whole world, hell, he might know every world there was, but there wasn't one that he could call home. Wasn't one where he knew every single alley, and knew what it looked like, winter or summer. Wasn't a place where he remembered what the empty lots looked like before they sprouted buildings. He'd never seen a nice neighborhood go slum, and then years later get religion and go condo and become exclusive. He'd never know the wide world encapsulated in a city the way Ed did.

"Want to go with me?" the Coachman asked.

For a long moment, Ed looked at the reins. Everywhere but home. Never that sigh at the end of the day, never the grocery clerk knowing your name, the paperboy yelling hi to you on the street. Never turning to a friend and saying, "I know this great little hole-in-the-wall restaurant." Never a bar where you could stand up and call over your shoulder as you walked out, "Put it on my tab." The price tag on all the worlds was to always be a stranger.

"Naw," Ed told him. "But it's been great to be along for the ride."

*Worlds are spinning away beneath his wheels. A thousand possibilities, a million. Sometimes he thinks he knows what would be best. He thinks he could let one off here, put another there, and they would be happy. But it is not for him to decide. It is only for him to offer. He will not persuade, he will not dissuade. He offers, and he listens, as the horses run on under his hands.*

The car interior smelled like furniture polish. The seats were deep, deeper than their family car, and Durand was sunk in his so far he could barely see out the window. His mom sat beside him, holding his hand. He wished she wouldn't. He'd been hugged, patted and held beyond endurance by well-meaning people attempting to console him. What he needed was to be left alone.

Sergeant Cleary was driving slowly. Giles Durand tried to see his face in the rearview mirror, but the sergeant's hat was low over his eyes. His hands looked strange on the wheel, skinny and freckled, not like his dad's hands had looked. He'd never see his dad's hands on a steering wheel again. It was another one of those thoughts; he knew it was true, but he didn't believe it. He kept looking into the empty passenger seat, knowing that if he saw his father there, he wouldn't be surprised. Someday, he knew, it would all become real, but it hadn't yet. He tried to listen to what his mom was saying.

". . . change your mind. I know it's hard for you to understand. . . ."

*You'll understand when you're older, son.*

". . . but you have to keep believing in everything he taught you, Giles. Daddy died, but he died doing what was right. That's what we have to hold on to. That he died for what he believed in, and we have to keep on believing in it. . . ."

In the front seat, Sergeant shifted uneasily. He glanced back once at Giles, then shifted his eyes back to the road. His mother was still talking.

"That's what we have to remember. When you grow up and you're a policeman like Daddy, that's the code you'll have to live by, too. To do what's right, no matter what the cost. Your daddy believed in that, Giles. He lived for that, and he died for that, and that's what we have to remember about him. That's what everyone will remember about him, and the people he helped will always be grateful that he was that way."

"Then why weren't they there today, at the funeral?"

"What?"

The suddenness of his mother's confusion made him realize that she hadn't been talking to him at all; she'd been holding onto him while she talked aloud to herself. Maybe even saying it out loud so the sergeant would hear her say it, and would go back to the station and tell all the other cops what she had said. As soon as the boy thought that, he knew it was true. But it didn't keep him from asking the question again.

"All those people he helped by being a cop. Why weren't any of them there? It was just us and Grandma, and Uncle Ted, and all the other cops. How come all the people he helped weren't there?"

"Well, honey, it wasn't like they all knew him personally. It was what he symbolized that was important. I guess you're a little too young to understand what I mean by that . . ."

*You'll understand when you're older, son.* His dad pushing the girl's face away from his crotch, and turning away from her and Giles as he zipped his pants up. The station house locker room had smelled like dirty socks, and his dad's face had been very red. Sergeant Cleary had laughed, then. Now he didn't even smile.

". . . but it's like, he wasn't a person to them, he was a policeman. Most of them probably never even knew his name.'

"That girl did." Giles glanced up at the sergeant in the rearview mirror. He'd been there, he would know; but he didn't meet Giles's eyes. "Remember her, Sergeant Cleary?"

The Sergeant kept driving, his hands tight on the wheel, his jaw set.

Giles opened his mouth to speak, and at that moment it seemed that he could see and hear what was going to happen. She knew his name, he would say. She called him Ricky, though, not Richard like you do, but she knew his name. And Dad was helping her, really helping her to let her do that to him so she wouldn't have to go to jail, because she was really too young to have to go to jail. So if he helped her and she wasn't in jail, why wasn't she there, at the funeral today? And then his mother would turn, and ask him more questions, and Sergeant Cleary would sink lower in his seat. And in the end, after he'd told her all about it, she'd turn and coldly ask the sergeant, who would say he didn't know what the kid was talking about. Then his mom would turn and slap him, slap him so fast and hard that he never even saw her hand, would only remember hitting his head on the shiny upholstery so hard it was like a slap on the other side of his face. And then they wouldn't talk anymore, and they would never, ever talk about the ride home from the funeral and what he had said, and it would almost be like it had never happened. He wouldn't remember it, but he and his mom would never be able to forget it when they talked about his dad. So they wouldn't talk about him very much.

How could he know that?

"What girl?" said his mother sharply.

"Oh, some girl Sergeant Cleary once told me about. A girl dad had to arrest, but then he let go," said Giles.

His mom smiled indulgently. "Richard arrested someone and then let her go? Giles, I don't think policemen are allowed to do things like that. Once they arrest someone, that person has to be punished."

In the front seat, Sergeant Clearly stirred. "It depends, ma'am," he said softly. "Sometimes you give a first offender a break. Sometimes you know they don't really deserve the blot on their record, so you let them off the hook."

His mom looked puzzled for a moment, but didn't say anything else, and Giles sat back, wondering why he had the feeling that something horrible had just been averted, wondering how he could remember suddenly that Captain Cleary had sat in the front row when he graduated from the academy.

*The Coachman looks at the young man seated next to him, and finds the young man staring back at him. "What changed?" asks the policeman, and the Coachman isn't certain how to answer.*

*"You did," he says at last. "You took a different path."*

*"But I—" he doesn't complete the sentence. After a moment he says, "A better one?"*

*"I don't know," says the Coachman. "Better for whom?" Then, "Did you and your mother talk about your dad much?"*

*"Huh? Sure. All the time . . . oh."*

*The horses never tire. Nor does the Coachman. Beyond, back a forever behind them, something that wasn't real, that never should have existed, collapses in on itself. It doesn't leave a hole, for a thousand other possibilities flow in to take its place.*

*The Coachman sighs.*

*One left to ask. And the choice he must offer is bitter. This one he dreads. Never has he felt himself such a sly trickster as he does right now. He knows it is not upon him to choose what to offer. Each chooses what to offer himself. But from this, if he could, he would rein aside, would have the horses find a better path.*

*If the choice were his.*

*But it isn't.*

Each breath was painful. Stepovich couldn't understand it. The night was cool-warm, full of summer city peace, the steady slow clop of the hooves was soothing as a lullaby. Beside him, the Coachman drove silently. That was fine with him. He'd had enough noise and action lately. This peace, this was what what he wanted. It had been a long, hard day, full of stress, all blurring behind him. This quietness now, this was good.

The coach was keeping pace with a young couple strolling down the sidewalk. His arm was around her slender waist, and she leaned a dark head on his shoulder. He recognized his younger self, and his wife. No, not his wife, not then. His fiancée. How elegant it had once felt to say that word, how wealthy. He savored it.

Something struck him as slightly odd, but he couldn't quite put his finger on it. He pushed the uneasiness out of his mind when he realized he could hear them talking. He remembered the conversation, even, from so very long ago. Funny. It hadn't seemed important, back then. Hadn't seemed like a turning point.

"Honey," she said, "I wouldn't mind working. In fact, I'd love it. You could go to school full-time, then, and be done that much sooner. I think it's the only way we're ever going to get what we want. Mike, I love you. I hate to see you work all day, and then try to study all night. And you know it's making your grades suffer."

The voice of reason. Patient, encouraging. God, how he'd

wished for a cigarette, but he'd already given those up for her. No more cigarettes, or pickled eggs, and he'd quit wearing suspenders.

But he didn't want to quit being a cop.

He'd started taking the night school classes to impress her. Gonna be a lawyer, he'd told her. Lied to her, might as well admit it. He'd taken just enough law classes to find out how slippery a subject it was. Justice, that was what he wanted to learn about. And Ed could teach him more about justice in one righteous bust than any of his night school teachers. He remembered all this. This was the night when he'd told her that he was going to lay out of school, for just one semester, to catch up with himself, so when they got married in a month, he'd have time free to honeymoon with her. Only he'd known then that he was never going back, that he was telling her a lie.

He watched himself lie to her, watched her accept it. Knew he could lean down and shout the truth out, and that his younger self would have to utter it, tell her that he really wanted to be a cop, that he didn't think it was a lowlife job that kept him in permanent contact with lowlife people. He could have made that younger self explain to her just what it meant to him.

He listened to her reply.

"Well. As long as it's not forever. It just scares me so, sometimes, knowing you're out there being a target for every wacko in the city. As long as you're happy, though, I suppose it's okay. And you *will* go back to school next fall, right?"

Stepovich heard what his younger self had never heard. The lie in her voice. It wasn't okay with her. Never would be. But she had believed it was only temporary, she'd believed she was marrying a future lawyer, not a blue suit and a duty weapon.

"We believed in each other's lies," he told the Coachman.

The Coachman nodded. "Don't we all."

"I could tell her the truth," Stepovich said slowly. "I could tell her right now, and it would change everything. Maybe she wouldn't marry me."

"Maybe you'd go to school full time and become a lawyer. You had the brains for it."

"But not the stomach," Stepovich said slowly. He dragged in another painful breath. "This isn't a dream, is it?"

The Coachman turned, and looked at him for a long time.

"It's your choice," he said quietly at last. "This could be a dream. Or it could be a place where you climb back into your skin, and take a different path."

Stepovich could feel a chill seeping through his blood. He lifted a hand to his shoulder, almost remembered. Somewhere in the night, a slow finger tapped a tambourine.

"Am I dying?" he asked.

"Dying? No. Not dying, but . . . you're not dying."

"And if I were, would I get another chance?"

The Coachman shook his head slowly. "This is it. You picked this choice place, and I can offer you but one."

"What do you suggest?"

For a moment, it seemed the Coachman winced, but all he said was, "I make no suggestions. Decide."

Stepovich watched them kissing, the young cop and his fiancee. But the man thought he was kissing a cop's wife, and the woman thought she was kissing a future lawyer. They'd both be wrong. He still had a chance, right now, to step down from the coach and walk a different path, one that led away from the pains of quarrels and divorce. Maybe it would lead to no marriage at all. Maybe he'd learn to like being a lawyer. But there were no guarantees.

Then it hit like a whip: No guarantees there'd be a Laurie or a Jeffrey; that's what he was giving up, as well as everything else. That kiss they were sharing, that might be their last. He'd be sweeping away the joys with the pains. Did he want to chance that? Wiping out all those past pains, that was one thing. Giving up the picnics and family dinner in exchange for a life that might be worse, okay; but what if it meant the children never came to be?

A vague notion came to him that there was another thing he'd be undoing as well. He closed his hand on a weapon that wasn't there, groped after a deed he couldn't remember. But it had been important. And somehow it had kept Laurie safe. Funny, how foggy it was all getting. Not just his thoughts, but the night around him. Funny, how the horses plodded on, but they never passed the couple kissing under the streetlamp.

"Drive on," he finally said. "Drive on." He leaned back into his pain.

* * *

*One of the gypsies, the big one, is tapping a tambourine. He says, "So, you are taking all three of them back, then?"*

*The Coachman nods.*

*"What about the girl? Doesn't she get a choice?"*

*"No," says the Coachman. "Not yet, not here, not from me."*

*"And the old woman?"*

*"She made all of her choices long ago."*

*The big gypsy nods. He looks a bit like an owl, the way he stares. The Coachman drives on.*

*Soon he reaches a place where there is a soft glow of starlight, which is quickly joined by a half moon, waxing, and he feels sorrow. The journey is nearing its end. Only for a short time longer will he sit on this box and feel the horses talk to him through the reins. He has come many lifetimes tonight, but the journey still seems short. The thought takes him that he could turn now, and bring them all to another place—a place where this coach would remain real. Perhaps they would blink in the sunshine and thank him. Perhaps they would not. It doesn't matter; he knows he will not do it.*

*The sun is rising ahead of him, red and thick behind layers of clouds, and in the glow, the horses begin to fade and the feeling of motion to decrease. Now he sees the faint outline of walls around him, and he pulls on the reins and the horses slow. When they have stopped, they are gone, as are we all, and the reins are no more than a twist of a scarf's fabric tangled in his fingers.*

17 NOV 03:37

I spent a lifetime in Hell last year,
I'm not sure when I got back.
The plaster statues are running in place,
And some are beginning to crack.
One wears a smile, one wears a frown;
They both seem fools to me.
The game isn't over 'til one of them's lost,
You never know who it will be.

"TELLERS OF TALES"

Durand felt like he was opening his eyes, though he couldn't remember closing them. It was like a play resuming, a crowded set cluttered with furniture and people just starting to stir.

Madam Moria was already setting upright an ugly little table that had gotten tipped over. She set her ruined kettle atop it, and glared at him when she caught him staring at her. With a sigh and a wheeze, she sank back into her chair as if she'd never left it. Durand belatedly realized that he was leaning against a tapestried wall, clutching his bleeding arm.

He watched Daniel rise slowly, look around at the old woman's apartment, and bow to the Coachman, who sniffed. "Don't bow to me you, you *gypsy,* you." Daniel smiled faintly, and turned to his brothers. Raymond was leaning against Csucskari, who still held the bloody knife.

"A pleasant ride," said Raymond softly. He looked down suddenly, and, "How did he get here?" he asked the Coachman, almost accusingly.

The Coachman shrugged. "Perhaps he never left."

Durand followed his glance. Little Timmy. The one they'd killed. The bloody corpse didn't stir him at all. Only the pistol in the hand seemed real, and the only emotion it roused in Durand was anger.

Csucskari said, "We must see to the Wolf."

And the Wolf is Mike, on the floor with Ed kneeling beside him. Ed pressed a handkerchief against Mike's shoulder, while Laurie knelt beside them, clutching herself as she rocked back and forth. Durand crossed to kneel by his partner. He put his good arm around Laurie, stilled her rocking.

Durand blinked stupidly and looked around. His partner was on the floor, and his own arm was bleeding. From Ed's color, he was hurting as well, even if no blood showed. The three gypsies looked as if a bare breath of wind might blow them all away. The Coachman leaned up beside the door, whip in hand, as if none of this concerned him. "What do we do?" Durand asked them all.

Madam Moria sighed heavily. She folded a scarf very carefully and set it aside. For a long second she shut her eyes. Then she opened them, and announced, "Well, I don't have my cane, so I can't make tea." When everyone looked at her, she added, "My good kettle's ruined, too," and glared at Csucskari as if daring him to accept the blame.

Durand stirred suddenly. He walked over to her phone, a black thing crouching on a small table, and dialed.

"Officer Durand. My partner is down, and I've been injured.

We need an ambulance at thirty-four-sixteen Oak Street Upper, northeast corner of Oak and Carradine. No, no back-up needed; the situation is stable. Hurry on that ambulance though. Mike's hit bad. No, I won't stay on the damn line. Use the nine-one-one trace, for god's sake." He left the receiver off the hook. Going back to Stepovich, he took Laurie firmly by the shoulders and pushed her into Ed's arms. He knelt down, and began laying Stepovich's shirt open.

"It doesn't look good," Ed muttered, and tried to keep Laurie from looking. Durand refolded the handkerchief and pressed it once more against the wound.

Stepovich stirred and cried out; Laurie echoed him. She pulled free of Ed, but suddenly Daniel was there, catching her in his arms despite the fiddle he still held. He pulled her face into his chest and held her tightly. She grew still. Durand swayed, then sat back on the floor beside his partner. He put his fingers on the pulse in Stepovich's throat, kept them there. Ed got up and sank slowly onto the couch, one arm wrapped protectively around his ribs. "He'll live," he said. "But . . ." His voice trailed off.

Madam Moria had found her other cane. She thumped it impatiently on the carpet. "It's over then, isn't it?" she demanded.

"Over?" said Csucskari. "No. It's not over. The Fair Lady has been banished from this world, but we have tasks yet to do."

"We're together now," said Owl. "That is something."

Durand turned his head, spoke to Csucskari as he kept his fingers on Stepovich's pulse. "There's still a warrant out for you, you know."

"Yes," said Csucskari.

"Perhaps it would be best if you left."

"I don't know where to go."

"This is something new?" Raymond asked, and laughed.

"The Pennsylvania border is a good start," said Durand.

Csucskari caught Raymond's eye. "We must leave together," he said. They both looked at Daniel.

His grip on Laurie tightened. He stared back at his brother, over her head. "I could be happy."

"You've chosen already," said Csucskari. "When it mattered most. Why torture yourself?"

" 'Needs must when the Devil drives,' " Raymond began,

but the Gypsy gave a slight shake of his head. The Coachman snorted.

A tremor shook Daniel. The bow slipped from his fingers, falling to the carpet. He seemed to age before their eyes. He let go of her. She didn't seem to notice.

Daniel closed his eyes for an instant. Then he opened them and set his jaw. He gave himself a little shake.

Laurie blinked suddenly, and drew herself up. She looked around the room and Durand saw the confusion grow in her eyes. "Daniel?" she asked, puzzled.

"Daniel is gone," said the Raven.

Stepovich groaned.

Laurie spun suddenly, seemed to see anew her father on the floor. "Daddy!" she wailed, and launched herself at him.

Mike had stirred. He made a sound that might have been her name, and she flung herself to her knees on the floor beside Durand.

The Raven turned aside again.

"We have to go," the big gypsy reminded them all.

"How?" said Csucskari.

Something shining flashed through the air, struck the Coachman's chest and fell to the floor. "Get the hell out of here," Ed growled. "You been nothing but a pack of trouble anyway." The Coachman crouched slowly, rose with Ed's Cadillac keys in his hand. He jingled them in a loose fist.

"Are you sure?" he asked.

A growing wail of ambulance sirens answered him. A second siren, rising and falling, chimed in. "Get the hell out of here!" Ed snarled. "The cops are coming. And remember: Super unleaded, or she'll knock like hell on the hills."

"We'll be gone, then," said the Coachman. He opened the door. The big gypsy lifted a hand in a quick goodbye, then led the way down the stairs. The Gypsy took the Raven's arm as tenderly as if he were wounded.

"Come, brother," he said.

"I was what she made me," he said softly. "Not as my acts betrayed me."

The Gypsy tugged at him gently.

The Raven looked once more at Laurie as she bowed over her father. It was the only farewell he gave her. He straightened, squaring his shoulders. Then he stopped, and picked up his fiddle bow from where he'd dropped it. As the sirens drew nearer, he stood still, looking at the fiddle in his hands.

"Brother," cautioned the Gypsy.

Daniel stepped forward suddenly, thrust fiddle and bow at Ed. "For her," he said. "Later. When she wants it."

Moria scowled. "Are you certain?" she asked.

"See she gets a case for it." The Raven turned as abruptly as a father abandoning a child. "Let's go," he told the Coachman, and caught his brother's elbow and hurried him down the stairs.

The Coachman gave the room one elegant sweeping bow, one last sardonic smile, and followed.

# Epilogue

## THE WOLF AND THE CUB

### NOVEMBER TWENTY-FIRST, AFTERNOON

**Bells I'll fasten to your feet,**
**That you needn't be alone,**
**And I'll dance with you the Gypsy Dance**
**That you have always known.**

"GYPSY DANCE"

". . . not really surprised . . . No, it's what I'd expect her to do. . . . Because if she waited for the kid to ask her, she'd wait forever. So, what did he say? . . . Yeah, that's about what I'd expect. Well, maybe they would be smarter to wait until this whole mess got cleaned up, but smarter isn't always best, Marilyn, you tell Tiffany that for me." Stepovich listened while he thumbed through his statement again. He started to switch the phone from one ear to the other, then remembered that shoulder no longer worked. "Yeah. I know, it is quite a mess. They said they could have saved my arm if the quack who fixed my shoulder the last time hadn't bungled it. . . . Well, thanks, I appreciate that. . . . I guess I'll have to, won't I? . . . No, I don't mean to sound bitter, I'm just tired of all the damn questions about . . . sure I understand, I didn't mean you, ask whatever you want. . . . What makes it so bad is that I'm so foggy about what happened after I got hit. . . . Ed? I don't know. From what I can gather, he was under a coffee table or behind a couch or some damned thing while Durand had all the fun. . . . I was being sarcastic, Marilyn. But as I say, after I got hit, I didn't know much of anything that happened. . . . Yeah, I knew about Ed's friend Madam Moria, but . . . yeah, I'd heard that the guy who shot me was the one who did the liquor store clerk, but I don't know why he was at Moria's place. . . . Me? I told you, Ed just wanted to introduce Durand and me to Madam—Huh? Yeah, as far as I know, the killer just happened to show up while we were there. These things happen. . . . Holes? Who are you, Internal Affairs? . . . No, really. . . . *No, really.* . . . Okay, well, tell you what, Marilyn, soon as I'm feeling better, I'll buy you a cup of coffee and tell you the whole story. . . . that's right, the whole story . . . Yeah, I guess I do owe you that much, but don't blame me when you don't believe it. Hell, I was there, and I don't believe half of it. . . . Yeah, I guess that's a promise. Okay, dinner, not coffee. . . . Okay. Hey, I've got company right now, though, so I got to get off the phone. . . . huh? You bet, Marilyn. A beautiful woman." As he said this, Stepovich's visitor gave an exaggerated look around the hospital room and harrumphed. He bravely waggled his eyebrows at her. "Right . . . much better, hell, you know cops are made of unbreakable plastic. . . . How should I know, Marilyn? Maybe. I don't even know if they'll *offer* me a desk job after they read my statement. . . . Yeah, they finally got it out. It ended up lodged between two ribs . . . bounced all over hell inside me getting there, I guess, they say I'm lucky I'm even . . . Right. I will. No, really, I will, I promise. You, too. Thanks for calling. . . . Bye."

As soon as Stepovich hung up the phone, she said, "Cut the cards, three times."

He sighed and obeyed her. It was awkward, one-handed. They were peculiar cards, even for the kind of deck it was. Thick edges gone soft with age and handling, smelling like some old spicy perfume. Not even their backs matched. She shifted the piles, muttering to herself as she did so. He watched her practiced fingers lay the cards out in a careful pattern on the white hospital sheet beside him. She bent over them, her hair falling forward like a curtain. "Of course," she muttered. "I can see it."

"See what?" Stepovich asked crabbily.

Her fingernail tapped a card, two people exchanging chalices. "I see Durand asking a woman with red hair to join her fortune with his. She hesitates, but not for long."

"Actually, Tiffany Marie asked him," Stepovich pointed out. She ignored his interruption.

Her hands moved again, jabbing at the ornate cards. "This one, the Queen of Stars? She receives gifts soon, gifts due her. A kettle, perhaps, and a new cane. Perhaps a pound of good tea."

Stepovich harrumphed.

Her fingers wandered on. "An older man close to you opens new doors, or finds a new opportunity." It was a hand coming out of a cloud holding a flowering stick. Stepovich noticed that it was a single arm, then threw the thought away.

"You knew Ed got himself a part-time job. Down at the Classic Caddy. Spends all day arguing about cars with a bunch of other old farts." He coughed slightly, winced from the bruises the bullet had made inside him and the pull of the healing wounds. He took a quick breath, reached to tap a Moon card. "What's this?"

She shook her head. "One we don't wish to speak of. She is gone from here, but not so far as to give me any comfort. But there is another," she tapped a card with a guy upside down on a cross. "One who is not far behind her. This, the six of Swords, nearby? He does not travel alone." A card with ten circled stars overlay a man on a horse carrying yet another star. Her fingers stroked the two, then lifted away.

"Here," she said. "This is you. The Fool."

"Oh, thank you."

"No. Trust me. It's the right card for you. The beginning of knowledge, the beginning of a spiritual journey"—Stepovich rolled his eyes—"and someone who can walk through danger and not be harmed."

"Not be harmed?" He gestured at where his arm had been. "What do you call this, a dimple?"

"And this," she continued quickly, "the five of Cups beside it? That's disappointments, but they're past now. This is the future." It was a woman in a garden with a bird on her finger. "She's enjoying the good things in life. Alone, but getting wiser about herself."

He suddenly thought of Marilyn, then chided himself. If he wasn't careful, he could start taking this stuff seriously, and then what? Can't go out on patrol today, the cards say it isn't auspicious. But no, he wasn't going to be going out on anymore patrols. Shit. Aloud, he said skeptically, "You can tell all this from a deck of cards?"

She fixed him with a steady gaze. "The knowing is already within me. The cards are like guideposts for my Seeing." Her gaze went distant. She had aged since he had last seen her, but not in a way that was bad. Almost, he could see as she claimed to. A sadness, a regret in your past, he'd say to her, but something you've learned from.

"I have the gift, you know," she told him, in a voice gone soft with mystery. Then Laurie grinned suddenly, spoiling the effect. "Or so Madam Moria tells me."

"You should stay away from that old witch," Stepovich chided her. "Filling your head full of superstition."

"Daddy!" Laurie objected heatedly. "She does not. And she's going to take me and Jeffrey to the Farmer's Market. That's where she buys the spices to put in her teas."

"That okay with your mom?"

Laurie shrugged. "She said she'd think about it."

"I bet. Don't go telling her it was my idea."

"Don't you want to see me in the layout?" Laurie changed the subject.

"Where are you?" Stepovich asked grudgingly.

"Here." She tapped a card of a young man with a fish in his cup. "This is me. Page of Cups. It means a captivating young person, studious and drawn to the arts. And you know what this means, here, in my future?" A man with a crown on his head, holding a wand. Green was the color of his jerkin.

"I'm almost afraid to ask."

"It means like beginning an apprenticeship. Learning something." Laurie gathered up the cards carefully.

"Learning what?" Stepovich asked guardedly.

"Music lessons," she said matter of factly. "That card almost always means music lessons."

And the streetlights never waver,
And the red lights never dim,
And the neon always glitters;
And it was better me then him.

"RED LIGHTS AND NEON"

# ABOUT THE AUTHORS

STEVEN KARL ZOLTÁN BRUST was born in 1955. His hobbies include arguing and drumming. He plays psychedelic rock n' roll for Cats Laughing, twisted trad and quirky Celtic for Morrigan, and Sufi drumming for Sulliman's Silly Surfing Sufi Circus, as well as doing the occasional solo act with guitar and banjo. He supports his music habit by writing, and lives in Minneapolis, Minnesota.

For information on ordering "Another Way to Travel" by Cats Laughing (tape or CD) or "Queen of Air and Darkness" by Morrigan (tape), send a self-addressed, stamped envelope to:

SteelDragon Press
Box 7253
Minneapolis, MN 55407

MEGAN LINDHOLM lives on a small fram in rural Roy, Washington with her four children and occasionally her fisherman husband, Fred. Hobbies include cleaning up after the children and intending to have a garden. Her tastes in music include psychedelic rock n' roll, twisted trad and quirky Celtic, and Sufi drumming. She highly recommends the soundtrack from the movie that should have been made, "Another Way to Travel." Said soundtrack can be ordered from:

SteelDragon Press
Box 7253
Minneapolis, MN 55407

Oh, she also writes.